Nigel Rees was born in Liverpool in 1944. For the past twenty years he has lived in London, working as a broadcaster on television and radio. He is the author of more than twenty books.

His first novel, *The Newsmakers* (Headline 1987), received extensive critical acclaim:

'A successful blockbuster . . .' *Oxford Times*

'Revealing sidelights into the backstage world of broadcasting . . .' *Guardian*

'Rees's Midas touch hasn't deserted him . . .' *The Listener*

'All the ingredients of a best-seller' *Leicester Mercury*

Also by Nigel Rees

The Newsmakers

Talent

Nigel Rees

HEADLINE

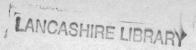
Copyright © Nigel Rees Productions Ltd 1988

First published in Great Britain in 1988
by HEADLINE BOOK PUBLISHING PLC

First published in paperback in 1989
by HEADLINE BOOK PUBLISHING PLC

All characters in this publication are fictitious
and any resemblance to real persons, living or dead,
is purely coincidental.

ISBN 0 7472 3252 0

Typeset in 10/11½ pt English Times
by Colset Private Limited, Singapore

Printed and bound in Great Britain by
Collins, Glasgow

HEADLINE BOOK PUBLISHING PLC
Headline House
79 Great Titchfield Street
London W1P 7FN

To J.M.C.
After twenty-five years

ACKNOWLEDGEMENTS

The lyrics of 'The Leaving of Liverpool' are adapted from those collected by W.M. Doerflinger in *Shantymen and Shantyboys: Songs of the Sailor and Lumberman*, New York, 1951.

Tutankhamun: The Untold Story by Thomas Hoving was published by Hamish Hamilton in 1979.

'When I am Homeward Bound . . .'

PROLOGUE

It was an indication of how far he had travelled that he now thought of the city as 'Liverpool, England' and not simply as 'the Pool'. But he had come back, an exile who had never quite been able to escape the grip of the place.

It was a city built on rock, a dark red sandstone showing through the grime. The gateway was a series of connecting railway tunnels where the sheer rock walls were black, or green with moss, and running with damp.

The train from London edged the last half mile through the chasm, briefly lit by shafts of sunlight, before pulling into the terminus. Lime Street Station with its great arched roof of glass was just about recognizable to the returning visitor.

He slowly picked up his leather bag, slipped on a pair of dark glasses, and stepped out of the first-class compartment to begin the long walk from the rear of the train to the ticket barrier. A group of people greeted friends or relatives, newly arrived, but no one waited for him. He wanted his return to be low-key. It was an attempt not to be recognized.

The attempt failed. He might have looked unapproachable in his California clothes and dark glasses, but when he climbed into a taxi, the driver knew all too well who he was.

'Look what the tide's brought in,' the familiar voice croaked, adenoidally.

'Denis! So this is what you're doing now. It'd have to be you, wouldn't it? Well, you can show me the sights.'

'Where d'you mean?'

'The Pier Head, and all that.'

'Forgotten what they look like? You've picked a high old time to come back, and no mistake.'

The homecomer noticed the dirt in the cab. The grille between driver and passenger was like those in New York cabs.

The driver swung the taxi out of the station and drove as instructed down towards the seafront where the ferries still crossed the Mersey.

'No, changed my mind,' said the passenger. 'Let's go to Mathew Street.'

'Ah, well now, I once played the Cavern, y'know.'

'Of course I *know . . .*'

'They never should've knocked it down. Knocked down too fookin' much, if y'ask me.'

It was true, the homecomer knew. The Cavern no longer stood in Mathew Street. Hadn't been there for eight years or so. Now there were just the tourist signs marking the spot, the plaque commemorating John Lennon. But he just wanted to see, breathe the air, and remember.

'Don't come back often, do you?'

Christmas and Easter, he might have said, but not even that was true any more. He admitted he'd come home for his mother's funeral, which *was* true. He might have said, I've come back to find my woman. She used to be my wife. The most important thing I ever had out of this city. But I lost her . . .

He wasn't going to, wasn't able to, explain to anybody, least of all this man, why he'd really come back.

'Oh, aye. I'd give anything to gerrout myself,' the driver went on. 'If I had a thousand pound, I'd be off.'

'Where would you go?'

'*Anywhere* to gerrout of 'ere.'

The passenger didn't know how to deal with this bleak cry. He asked to be taken to Upper Parliament Street.

'You're kidding. Want yer balls roasting or summat?'

'Why?'

4

'It's no-fookin'-go after last night, all over that way, and I'm not going . . .'

'It's still bad?'

That hot July weekend in 1981, rioting had flared up in several British cities. South Liverpool had had two nights of it. Now, on the Sunday afternoon, there was a lull.

'It'll hot up again after dark,' the driver announced confidently.

'Much damage?'

'Like the fookin' Blitz. Whole buildings down. I dunno, first the Council fookin' flattens the city, and now these lunatics 'ave to 'ave a go.'

'Drop me at the Adelphi. I'm staying there.'

'Figures.'

The taxi stopped outside the once-grand hotel.

'Any chance of a drink while you're 'ere?'

'Might be difficult, but give me your number.'

'It'd be nice to talk over old times. No hard feelings, like.'

'I know, Denis. Leave it with me.'

The homecomer checked into the hotel.

In the early evening he walked, perspiring slightly in the heat, up the hill towards the cathedral.

Thinking it was just the weather, he chided himself for bringing the wrong clothes. Then he noticed the acrid smell of burning. He heard fire engines, ambulances, police vehicles, although he couldn't see them yet. He felt unsettled, irritated at having his plans disturbed by these unusual goings-on. He had travelled back to his home city for a reason and on impulse. All this was getting in the way.

Then he saw the pall of smoke over the upper part of the city. His city. He wanted to penetrate the area in the shadow of the huge sandstone cathedral, on the graveyard side. The substantial Victorian houses in Huskisson Street, the flats in Gambier Terrace, these had been his playground twenty years before. Now what were people doing to it?

A group of police vans and patrol cars with lights flashing blocked the road. There was no chance of getting through. The police cordon was within two hundred yards of the cathedral.

Foul, black smoke funnelled up above faded white old buildings. Alarm bells rang, sirens sounded. He couldn't believe that this was happening to *his* city. They were destroying his memories, his childhood, his youth, his roots.

He began to worry about people in the area. If houses were being burned, was anyone dead? He approached the police, gave an address in one of the squares, and was let through the cordon to seek out a woman he knew. She lived close by and must surely be at risk.

Never before had he seen such devastation. What had led to all this? What kind of fate was it that had brought him back on this of all weekends?

In Upper Parliament Street a full-scale riot was in progress. There were teenage youths, white and black, with petrol bombs; looters with supermarket trollies; elderly folk carrying possessions like refugees. He did not know whether to go forward or return.

And then he saw her. At that precise moment, a sheet of flame enveloped the front of a shop and lit the sky. A spark must have ignited a broken gas main, or maybe it was a petrol bomb. The wall crumbled, hurling bricks across the wide roadway and landing in a shower of sparks and dust.

She ran forward, as if pushed by the force of the blast. Yet she appeared cool. What was she doing here?

She was clutching something to her chest, but he couldn't see what it was. A fire engine rushed to the burning shop. He noticed black and white youths running away, young, so young. Amid the terror, the woman was as beautiful as she had always been. Now he didn't know whether to let her see him or not.

In the end, he simply stood there amid the noise and the

heat, and she came towards him almost as though she had been expecting him.

He had known her, loved her, but never really possessed her. She had left him as she had left another. Two men had wanted her, two had lost her. And here she was, back home, where all three of them had started out.

Her face was flecked with black from the burning buildings. Her khaki cotton dress was marked the same way. Her mane of dark hair was still full, still seemingly untouched by time. She gave him that steady, unshakable look through those large, bright eyes. The look he knew so well. He held her and they kissed.

'What on earth have we done to deserve this?' he asked, shouting to make himself heard.

'So you've come,' she said.

He made a silent gesture.

So much had happened since they first met, almost twenty years before.

PART ONE

'It's not the leaving of Liverpool that grieves me
But, me darling, when I think of thee.'
The Leaving of Liverpool

CHAPTER 1

They really needed him in the store to serve customers during the lunch hour but Grant had pleaded to get away. It was only a short run through narrow streets before he turned into the black ravine called Mathew Street and breathed in the familiar smell of decaying fruit and vegetables from the warehouses there. Old, high, dark warehouses, and thumping down in the cellars of one of them, a heavy, metallic, amplified beat.

The queue waiting to go in the Cavern, mostly girls, inched forward. Apart from a crudely-coloured poster advertising the groups due to play at lunchtime and evening sessions, all that could be seen from the outside was a pair of stout iron doors.

Grant, wearing his suit, felt out of place among the girls. It was the wrong gear. He had to wear it in the store. If he was to sell smart clothes, he had to look smart himself, or so they told him. But he was embarrassed by the turn-ups on his trousers and by his sensible shoes. He was a little sticky after his short run, too. He felt ill at ease and totally square. The girls, office girls, shop girls, Cavernites all, looked at him once, to see what was on offer, then turned back to chatter excitedly among themselves.

He paid his shilling and followed them, shuffling down the twenty narrow stone steps into the darkness and noise, into the atmosphere of cigarette smoke and faint hint of disinfectant. A sea of young girls in suede, fishnet and leather bobbed up and down in the gloom, while the young men looked on. The beehive hairdos, black sweaters and short skirts swayed to the beat of the music, pale lipstick and white faces the only brightness. Grant found himself

11

pressed against a wall, getting hotter and hotter. He felt the dankness of the cellar and imagined the very bricks of the walls were sweating, too.

He had arrived in time for the live set. The DJ made announcements of forthcoming attractions in a droll Scouse accent. As expected, tickets for the Beatles' appearance at the beginning of August were sold out. In that summer of 1963, there was a feeling that the forthcoming gig would be their final one at the club that launched them.

Plenty of other groups waited to follow in their footsteps. This lunchtime it was the turn of the Zodiacs. Grant watched closely as the singer clasped the microphone stand and introduced the Eddie Cochrane number, 'Hallelujah, I Just Love You So'. He kicked out his legs in time with the music, but this was hard to see as the small stage was fringed with girls and yet more girls, gazing, chewing, joking, smoking, ogling.

At least in the darkness of 'the Cave' no one would be able to poke fun at Grant's suit or his square looks. No one would speak to him if he didn't want them to. He, certainly, wouldn't be speaking to anyone himself, least of all asking any of the girls to dance, or anything like that. He was simply there to observe, and to keep his shyness to himself. Watching, not doing.

The Zodiacs were good, he thought. In fact, very good, but he wasn't going to let anyone know. Everyone was on the make these days, hoping for the big time. How Grant wanted to be part of it all. He would burst with ambition if something didn't happen soon. He ought to be in a group, a lead guitarist or a vocalist, at the very least. But he wasn't sure how to achieve that ambition. He wasn't even sure he had the talent.

He'd bought the guitar. His parents, after much persuasion, had let him get at his savings. 'Hell, I'm twenty-four, you know!' he told his mother, who only noticed he'd said 'Hell', and said so.

He practised whenever he could, but progress was slow. He didn't see how he'd ever get anywhere.

'Hallelujah' – *kick* – 'I just love her so' – *kick* . . .

The Zodiacs rounded off the number. There was light applause, a few screams.

That was when he noticed her. She stood out from the other girls. Darker, more attractive, more assured. She looked a fraction older than most of the rest. They must all have been about fifteen. She was looking up at the singer of the Zodiacs, not longingly, an amused expression on her face. Grant could see only her head and shoulders. She had beautiful long, dark hair, parted in the middle, falling well below her shoulders.

He felt a charge, couldn't take his eyes off her. Who was she? *What* was she? He would never find out. He did not have the easy confidence required to chat her up. Besides, he was dressed all wrong, and his hair was a mess. Appearances counted for so much these days.

Then, as if finally to squash his chances, another young man, apparently with no such qualms, pushed past him and made straight for the girl.

'Hi, I'm Tom. Who are you?'

Carly turned to push away the arm he had already slipped round her.

'Cheeky bastard.'

'No, come on. Give us yer name.'

'Why should I?'

'All right.' Tom, undaunted, turned to the stout friend standing next to the girl he was really interested in. 'What's her name, you!'

'You heard,' said Fawn, the friend. 'Piss off, you little piece of shite.'

Tom was used to his chat-up methods provoking this kind of response and wasn't to be put off. The lull in the music enabled him at least to talk to the girl he had taken an

13

instant fancy to. Then fate smiled. The bodies squashed together under one of the Cavern arches suddenly moved forward in a mass and Tom found himself pushed towards Carly. The tide took them away from Fawn.

'You're a bit of a pushy one, aren't you?' Carly told him, unable to avoid him now, so closely were they pressed together. 'What's your name then?'

'Thomas Sheridan. My friends call me Tom.'

'You have friends?' the girl said drily. 'Get you.'

The Zodiacs struck up another number, one they'd written themselves. The whole floor started jumping up and down with the rhythm. So, in spite of herself, Carly found she was pressed against Tom in a kind of dance.

'Keep your hands to yourself,' she whispered in his ear.

'What did you say yer name was?' he shouted back.

'I didn't. But it's Carly.'

'What?' he shouted louder.

'*Carly!*'

'D'you fancy it, Carly?'

'What? Can't hear you.'

'I said, d'you fancy it?'

'Randy sod.'

'Gorra ciggy?'

'Don't smoke.'

They danced on, after a fashion. At the end, Carly said, 'I've got sawdust coming out of me knees, let's move away.'

Tom didn't mind. He liked what he'd found. And Carly, despite the coolness she felt it necessary to display towards anyone who chatted her up, could see that Tom was worth a second look. He was the type who'd never manage to wear a tie. A dark mop of hair tumbled over his forehead. His deep blue eyes were steady and determined. Carly felt uncomfortable at the way he simply gazed at her. He was pushy, confident, and good-looking. Meeting him was like being run over by a tram.

*   *   *

14

Grant observed with dismay what had happened a short distance from him. He, too, liked the look of Carly. There was a different quality to the girl, marking her off from the other little scruffs in the cellar. They were office mice, screamers and scrubbers. Carly was cool, even a touch forbidding, but so much more substantial than the rest. He liked the way she wore her hair. He liked those large eyes which had locked ever so briefly with his as she'd tried to throw off Tom.

He felt an instant dislike of Tom. Anyone with the nerve to chat up judies like that, throw himself at them, was pretty hateful in Grant's opinion. If only he had that kind of confidence . . .

He looked over at Fawn, now abandoned by Carly. How odd it was that you never saw two good-looking judies together. If there was one good-looker, her 'friend' was like the back of a bus, yet she was always dragged along. Why? He looked at Fawn again. No, he couldn't do it. A friend of his had said you should always go for the fat, ugly ones. They never said no, they couldn't afford to be choosy. But nothing stirred in him now, and anyway he didn't have the nerve to chat her up either, vulnerable though she might have been at that moment.

His clothes weren't right, that was what it was. Any girl would laugh at him. He *must* do something about the gear, as soon as he could. This irresistible fellow, Tom, had on a well-worn pair of drainies, a tartan check shirt, and a battered, zip-up leather jacket. That was all it took. Why didn't Grant dress like that?

Then he saw what Tom was doing to Carly. Kissing her gob off. As though there was some instant animal attraction between them. Why didn't that happen when *he* managed to get near a woman?

By two o'clock, Grant had had enough. He looked at his watch and wondered if he should stay to hear one more number. He saw the girl look at her watch, too, and whisper something to Tom.

Grant didn't want to see, and started to push his way through the crowd of bodies to the exit. He bought a Coke and a hot dog and fought his way up to the daylight and the air, straightened his tie, and looked at his watch a second time. Yes, he could just manage it.

His hair needed cutting. He wanted more of a Beatle cut. The place to go was Hornes where for five shillings they gave you a very nice trim. Indeed, the Beatles, individually or together, had all been there at one time or another, or so it was said. Instead, however, he went to the 'gentlemen's hairdressing salon' at Watson Prickards, a menswear shop. He was happier in a place that didn't call itself a barber.

'So it is time for the harvest, young man?' said the hairdresser, unsettlingly.

Grant couldn't fix the accent, but perhaps it was Polish.

'Well, don't cut off too much, just a trim.' He shrank from saying what he really wanted.

The Pole grunted, and set to.

Too late, Grant realized he was being shorn. Great clumps of hair fell to the floor in a circular heap around the chair. It would take weeks to grow again. Every time Grant tried to protest, the hairdresser said, 'I need to cut a little more off to balance the other side . . .'

Grant emerged eventually, itchy from the hair that had gone down his collar, hot and livid at not getting his way with the hairdresser. His scalped head embarrassed him. He hoped he wouldn't run into anyone he knew. The first attempt at improving his appearance had failed.

He went to Lord Street and looked in a number of shops where they sold jeans. He knew it was a bad thing to buy clothes when you were hot and sticky. They mightn't fit properly when you cooled down. You became even more hot and flustered dressing and undressing in a pokey cubicle.

He felt out of place, too, wearing his salesman's suit in a jeans shop. He took the first pair that caught his eye, black narrow jeans, £1.9s.6d., and struggled into them. A bit tight, but they'd do. He wrenched them off, paid the bill, and hurried two doors down to a shoe shop.

'Weren't you at the Cavern just now?'

It was the girl who'd been necking with the pushy fellow.

'Yes,' said Grant, pleased she had so much as noticed him in the gloom and crush.

'Great, wasn't it? D'you go there much?'

'When I can. I work at Hendersons, in menswear. We're not supposed to go off at lunchtime.'

'You ought to go to one of the all-nights. They're great.'

'That might be difficult.'

'Why?'

'Well, y'know, I live over the water.'

'Oh. So what happened to you then? Had a haircut? That was quick.'

'You noticed? It'll grow again.'

'You've got the shortest hair in Liverpool. Mind you don't catch cold.'

'It was a mistake.'

'Next time, you come to me. I'll do it for you.'

Grant was chuffed. 'That a promise?' He scratched the back of his neck. 'You're Carly, aren't you?'

'How d'you know?'

'I overheard.' Grant felt like adding how he loathed the pushy Tom who'd been all over her.

'Yeh.' Carly blinked as though she'd become aware her friendliness might be misinterpreted. 'So what do you want to buy? Or are you just browsing?' She looked away at one of the other girls, who smirked and went on fiddling with the shoe boxes.

'I was after some boots, actually. You know, like . . .' Grant was almost inaudible.

'Beatle boots?' Carly finished his sentence for him.

17

'Well, sort of, yes.'

'They won't go with that suit, you know. Turn-ups on your trousers, get you!'

'I know, I know. I have to wear them at Hendersons.'

'*Very* grand there, aren't they? What size d'you take?'

'About eight, eight and a half.'

'Try these then.'

Carly produced a pair of smart black boots, pointed without being winkle-pickers. They had about an inch of heel. The smell of new leather floated up out of the box.

'Come on, give us yer foot . . . what's yer name?'

'Grant.'

'Grant, then.'

Carly knelt before him and helped pull a boot on to his left foot. He looked down at the top of her head, and realized that what he was experiencing was rather enjoyable.

'It's a bit tight,' he told her. 'A size bigger?'

'You don't want 'em flapping about.'

'Don't try your patter on me. That's what *I* always say. These gents come in to buy suits. If it's too big, I say, "Don't want it too tight, sir, do we?" and if they *are* too tight, I say, "Don't want them too *loose*, sir". They always fall for it.'

Carly smiled to show she knew what he meant. 'Try standing up.'

Grant wobbled slightly and then admired the boots, sideways on, in the mirror.

'They'll do.'

'You make your mind up quick. First pair?'

'Well, sort of, yes.'

'You'll like them.'

'Yes.'

Grant looked at his watch. 'Wrap 'em up quick or I'll be late.'

When Carly handed him the parcel, her hand brushed

his. Grant desperately wanted to preserve the contact.

'You weren't wearing that at the Cavern,' he said, pointing at her smock. 'You had that silvery thing on with the bits cut out.'

'My, you take it all in, don't you? Made it meself.' She smiled, gave him a look. 'Now, don't wear them too much to start with, will you? Wear 'em in. Okay? Tarar, luv.'

Grant, more pleased than he had been for a long time, ran back to Hendersons, hid his shopping in the staff room, and returned to selling sober suits to middle-aged men who wouldn't have recognized a Cuban heel if one had stamped on them.

Tom Sheridan had no work to go back to after his lunchtime visit to the Cavern. When asked what he did, he would usually reply, 'Freelance photographer and design assistant', but no one was too sure what this meant or whether he was speaking the truth. There was more than a little Irish in Tom and he had a way of letting his tongue run away with him. Like many another in the Pool, he managed to eke out a living on the artistic fringe and in the reflected glory of the Beatles, the Mersey Sound, and the Beat Boom. He was a 22-year-old playing at the bohemian life in the area between the Anglican cathedral and the Philharmonic pub.

He had left school with one O-level, in English, and gone to art college. He was thrown out after a year but stuck with the students, cadging favours, pints and fags, as though still one of them. In a way, his was a success story, the way he'd managed to keep body and soul together with no apparent means of support.

Family or relations were never mentioned. He lived by his wits, his unshakable belief that the world owed him a living, and his undoubted charm. Nothing he did ever lasted long, nor did his girl friends. He put himself about with great success but, even when he'd split with a girl, he remained friends. He was feckless, but he was good-hearted and fun to be with.

That day, having gained admission to the Cavern by dint of a girl friend's paying, he had proceeded to lose her in the gloom and met Carly. He left with a third girl, but she soon peeled off to get back to her job in an insurance office.

So, once more, Tom was on his own, with little to do except dream for the rest of the afternoon. It was a matter of considerable amazement to him that no one had discovered his talents as a singer and guitarist when a lot of other riff-raff were doing so well. He would have to do something about it one day. But probably not until next week.

He idly wandered up the cathedral hill, taking the backstreet route, until he came to the digs in Gambier Terrace he shared with two other aimless youths, Mickey Clinch and George Evans.

Tiny Mickey greeted him with a giggle, sensing he was pleased about something. 'You look cheerful. Like a dog with two dicks. What happened?'

'Boogaroff!'

'Shafting again?' asked George, a long string of misery with a prominent Adam's apple.

'Mind your own,' snapped Tom, flopping down in a broken easy chair and reaching automatically for his guitar.

'George got a job,' Mickey announced. 'In his uncle's yard.'

'Bully for George,' said Tom.

'Yeh, it were a proper doddle,' George told him. 'I just went to see him and he gave it me.'

George looked so like a man who'd been dug out of bed to answer the phone that Tom was curious to know why he'd suddenly stirred his stumps. But he didn't pursue the matter, and moved over to pick out a melody on the hopelessly out-of-tune piano that came with the flat. It played as though it were full of moths, and several of the keys were missing.

'Play us your tune, then. Go on, play us your tune!'

Tom ignored Mickey's taunt, but later he did begin to play the song he'd written as a first step towards much-needed success.

> One, two, three
> I'm betting that you love me.
> Four, five, six
> It's something that I can fix
> Seven, eight, nine
> I'm getting off the line
> Ten, twelve, eleven
> Then we'll be in heaven . . .

Mickey and George applauded ironically.

' "Ten, twelve, eleven . . ." ' George mocked. 'You can't have that. It's terrible.'

'You'll never make it,' Mickey told him. 'Give it up while you're ahead.'

'Shurrup, lad!' Tom landed a rabbit punch on his arm. 'Go fook yerself.'

Then he started to sing the song again.

'I think I'm going for a walk,' George droned. 'It's too fookin' quiet round here. Are yer coming, Mick?'

'Okay, then.'

The two went out, slamming the door of the flat. Tom listened to their footsteps as they echoed down the stairwell. The big front door boomed and he was on his own. He put down his guitar and went to the window, looking at the vast, dark cathedral, lowering above. Then he looked beyond it and across the city, towards the river, Birkenhead and the Wirral.

The sunshine was pleasant, but you couldn't eat sun. He dreamt of success, as he did most of the time. There was only one type of success, and everyone in the city seemed to be on to it, except him. He climbed out of the window and stood among the peeling paint and the pigeon droppings on the tiny balcony. He lit a cigarette, a cheap Woodbine he'd cadged from a friend.

He thought of Carly in the Cavern. He'd done quite well with her. He'd been mad to let her slip away. But she had to be back at the shop, she'd said. He'd have to find out where she worked, then go along and date her.

He thought of kissing her properly. Of running his fingers through that luscious, dark hair. She'd got plenty in front. Not falsies, either. He wondered what she'd be like to bed. He went back to his guitar and sang the song, aimlessly, one more time. He was going to have her, that went without saying.

Grant smuggled his new jeans and boots into the house before his mother or father could catch sight of them and make a fuss. As usual, after checking out of Hendersons, he'd taken the electric railway under the Mersey to the Birkenhead suburb where he lived with his parents in a semi-detached.

Ted and May Pickering were the sort of people who worried whether they were middle class or upper working class. Whatever they were, they would have thought that a son who went to places like the Cavern was letting them down. The young chits of girls who went to such dives were no better than they ought to be. Why, there'd been two girls in the family way in their road alone that year. What with the government rocking over a 'vice' scandal that summer, it only went to show.

'That's a nice haircut,' May Pickering told him. Grant winced.

He was used to keeping his doings to himself. He just didn't let on. It only caused trouble. Remarks would be passed. How could he possibly make his parents understand the exhilaration, the sexiness, the excitement, of the music he liked to hear? Even if they did understand, they'd only be offended.

After he'd had his evening meal with them, he slunk off to his bedroom, squeezed into the new jeans and slipped on the boots, hoping his mother wouldn't come and find him in them. Then he checked them out in the mirror. He'd have to break it to his parents one day about his clothes, but not just yet. There were some things, though, he'd never tell them. Like about that girl he'd seen. They'd think she was common, being a shop girl.

'I'm a sort of shop *boy*, aren't I?'

'Hendersons is different. It's a nice shop.'

Grant knew the way the conversation would go.

He played a few of his discs, quietly, to himself, stacking up the singles on the automatic changer: 'From Me to You', the Beatles; 'Do You Want to Know a Secret', Billy J. Kramer and the Dakotas; 'Code of Love', Mike Sarne; 'Ain't That a Shame', the Four Seasons, just out that week.

Then he reverently took his guitar out of its case, played a few chords and tried to follow the sheet music he'd bought from Cranes music shop. He was quite pleased with his progress. Not too many mistakes. He'd make it yet.

Later, he read *Mersey Beat*. There were so many groups. Must be three or four hundred in Liverpool alone. The only way he was going to escape from his present lot and find the money and the sex that was hidden in the music was to join a group himself. Oh, the rows that would lead to . . .

It would have to be done, though. Otherwise, he'd bùrst. He was twenty-four, older than most, but getting nowhere. He was desperately ambitious, but couldn't see where to go.

He looked among the adverts for musicians needed to form groups or join existing ones. He spotted one likely opening, circled it in biro, and dreamt of what it might lead to. It was time he made the break from home and did what *he* really wanted to do.

Tom didn't have to track down where Carly lived after all. On Saturday night, with Mickey and George in tow, he went to the Blue Angel. He soon spotted Carly, wearing another of her own creations, a purple mini-dress with an astrological sign on it. This one revealed such a wonderful expanse of thigh that Tom, overlooking her breasts, decided he was a leg-man after all.

'Does your mother know you're out?' he announced cheerily, barging past Fawn, Carly's friend. 'It's me again.'

'I can see that,' Carly answered, giving token resistance. 'You're the bad penny, aren't you?'

'Come on, Carly, let's dance.'

Tom pulled her on to the floor. He danced well, even if he was pushy, and did everything with a winning smile.

After three numbers, they sat one out. Tom turned his back on Fawn, so he wouldn't be put off by her. He waved away Mickey and George who threatened to sit in on the chatting up.

'You're quite a little mover, aren't you?' Carly told him.

'And you.' He gave her another of those lingering looks that were both disturbing and pleasurable. This time, she tried to stare back, but after a second or two had to lower her eyelids.

'When are you going to change your clothes?'

'What's wrong with them?'

'Not very with it, that's all. Just you wait till I open my shop.'

'What shop?'

'Just an idea.'

'Oh, aye.'

Tom brightened. Here was a tart who wasn't just for fobbing you off. He wasn't used to this. He wondered about his chances of a grind, but first had to tell her about his talents as a composer, songwriter and performer.

Carly listened carefully, and didn't put him down.

'And I've written some poetry, too, you know,' he told her. 'Beat poetry. I've got this idea, to have rock and poetry together. Nobody's thought of that.'

'Haven't they really?' said Carly, in not too discouraging a way. 'How are you going to do that?'

'That's the tricky part. I'll find a way. Come on, let's dance. I like this one.'

Fawn sat glumly, toying with her shandy. Mickey and George sat ignoring her, drinking their beer. Fawn looked crossly at the two men and then away again. She didn't like to stare at what Tom and Carly were up to on the dance floor. It was as though Mickey, George and she were there to hold the coats while Tom and Carly made love.

Later on, Mickey and George became mixed up in a fight. Probably bevvied up with too much ale. Tom had to sort them out. Carly took the opportunity to slip away with Fawn. So ended Saturday night.

Tom had scarcely had a look in with Carly, but he wouldn't be letting up. He couldn't keep his thoughts off her. She was special. She made him feel aroused in a way he'd never been before. It wasn't just the whiff of sex, there was something more.

He was going to have her. And keep her.

There was hardly a queue stretching round the block for the Offbeats' auditions. In fact, that Thursday evening, after work, Grant Pickering wasn't aware of any other applicants for the vacancy of rhythm guitarist. There was talk of several musicians who *should* have turned up. However, their absence didn't mean that Grant would automatically get the job.

After leaving Hendersons, he had retrieved his guitar from the left-luggage office at Central Station and swapped his work shoes for his boots. The boots, though they didn't quite go with his suit, would have to do for costume. He took the bus out to Wavertree and found himself ringing the doorbell of a substantial semi-detached house in a quiet tree-lined road.

The door was opened, to Grant's surprise, by a would-be blonde in her early forties.

'Hello, dear. Are you Grant? Come on in.'

25

'Thank you.'

'I'm Denis's mother. Don't worry, I just open the door.'

Denis, a youngster of about eighteen, took over. 'Hi, come and meet the others.'

Grant followed Denis into the front room, much larger than the one in his home but with the standard fittings of sofas, pouffes, a twenty-one-inch TV, an elderly but monolithic radiogram, lamp standards, and *Radio Times* in a special cover. The only feature that clearly distinguished the room from any other on suburban Merseyside was a white grand piano. On it were perched the family photographs, which included a faded wedding group, presumably of Denis's parents – the groom in army uniform – and an enlarged Polyfoto of the young Denis, in a silver frame.

Over the fireplace, too, there was another distinguishing feature, a nude portrait, in oils. This wasn't the sort of thing Grant expected to see in such a setting. For a moment, he wondered if it could possibly be of Denis's mother.

Before he'd had time to think that one out, Denis was introducing Paddie who played lead guitar, Roger, the bass guitarist, and Spencer, a curious sandy-haired fellow, clearly older than the rest, who played piano.

'We need another guitarist. That's why we put the ad in,' said Denis, flicking a mop of fair hair with his hand and settling in behind his Premier drum kit, very expensive and professional-looking, ownership of which no doubt explained why he was leader of the group.

'Would you like some coffee and biscuits?' Denis's mother asked from the doorway.

'Er, no thank you, Mrs . . .'

'Call me Doreen, luv.'

'No thanks, Doreen.'

She continued to hover in the background, not the least unsettling thing about the audition.

Grant noticed that Denis used four-letter words in front of his mother, something he'd never dream of doing himself.

He detected a certain friskiness, too, between Doreen and Spencer who, it turned out, was the lodger and travelled in paints.

It also emerged that Mr Northington, Denis's father, was almost permanently away and it seemed to be assumed that Spencer kept Doreen warm when this was the case. She, for her part, clearly saw herself as patroness of the band.

Grant found all this quite entertaining, rather more so than his 'audition'. They staggered through 'Do You Love Me?' and 'Please Mr Postman', but it soon became apparent that Grant didn't have much to offer.

Doreen remained encouraging. Grant even wondered if she was after his young body, so interested in him did she seem, but he couldn't quite accept the attentions of a woman who was the mother of someone of his own age.

In due course, they moved on to beer and cigarettes, again with Doreen sitting in and speaking up for Grant.

'We've got one or two more people to see,' Denis eventually told him, after they'd jammed noisily, messily, but enjoyably for two more numbers, 'Baby It's Me' and 'They Say'.

'I'm *sure* you can find a place for Grant,' his mother said, giving the visitor a friendly look.

Overcoming his disappointment at what had been brought home to him, Grant now became decisive about his inability to play and firm over his rejection of Doreen's encouragement. 'No, please,' he protested. 'I'm not up to it. I think you can tell. I've just not had the practice. You're all much better than me.'

'We can't carry passengers,' Paddie the lead guitarist said casually. 'We've got enough of those on drums.'

'Eff off,' shouted Denis. 'The thing is, you see,' he explained to Grant, 'Stewart, the guitarist we had, he's off to university, and we've got four bookings on the strength of some gigs we did earlier in the summer. So it's a bit urgent.'

'What sort of bookings?'

'Oh, y'know, church socials, that sort of thing. But it's all such a sweat. Rehearsing, fixing, carting the amps about . . .'

· 'How d'you do that?'

'Spencer lends us his van.'

Spencer didn't appear overjoyed at this mention of his generosity.

'You ought to come along and watch,' Doreen put in, still curiously intent on preventing Grant from slipping away.

It was Doreen who first uttered the word 'manager'.

'My God, do they need somebody to keep them in order! You do, don't you, dears?'

The reaction was good-humoured, and Denis didn't seem too concerned at all the pedalling his mother was doing on Grant's behalf.

'Can I think about it?' said Grant, politely. 'You see, I really want to *play*. I'm not sure I know anything about managing.'

He had to leave soon after this, to catch the bus back to town and take the last train, the 11.20, home to Birkenhead. He felt the guitar he carried was already redundant but at least it looked as if he could establish a toe-hold with a group if he wanted.

Grant had learned one of life's lessons. A chap had to put himself in the way of things. What happened next was up to others. They'd push a chap in whatever direction fate ordained, even if it was one he'd never dreamt of till then.

CHAPTER 2

Two weeks later, the Offbeats had acquired their replacement rhythm guitarist, an apprentice gas fitter from Everton called Rod. With Grant at the wheel of Spencer's van, they set off to a social club on the outskirts of Liverpool in order to arrive by seven o'clock on Saturday night.

This gave them an hour to set up the equipment before the dance began at eight. The Offbeats were to alternate with a more middle-of-the-road dance band. But it was a gig, the first time out with the new line-up, and they would get ten quid to share between them, always assuming the club secretary paid up.

That was where Grant came in. In addition to making sure everyone arrived, driving the van, and generally making himself useful, he had to deal with Stan the Grouser. Stan was the organizer of the dance. Grant didn't warm to him at all, but if this was to be his job, he'd just have to find a way to get on with such people.

Grant still hadn't had the courage to wear his drainies publicly. Time would tell if his work suit could survive the punishment it suffered when he humped drum kits and amplifiers out of the van. The suit also underwent a certain amount of punishment from Doreen Northington, who not only assumed her presence was welcome at the gig but kept dragging Grant on to the dance floor.

'I'm very glad you've joined the boys,' she said, knowingly, holding him to her during one of the dance band's slower numbers in a way he'd never been held by a mature woman before.

'I'm not really part of the group, am I?' Grant murmured at the side of her head.

29

' 'Course you are, dear. You're just fine.'

She gave him an extra squeeze to her breasts and let him have a waft of the perfume she was so liberally sprinkled with.

'Now, Grant, be a dear and get me another snowball.' Mrs Northington fished in her purse and handed him a ten-shilling note. Grant had lost count of how many snowballs she'd drunk. He didn't like to be seen taking money from her either.

The Offbeats' second set was at ten o'clock on that late July Saturday night. It had all the younger people leaping and screaming in a manner that showed the Offbeats were already a credible act. The temperature was brought down by the other band, which drew the evening to a close.

Then Doreen Northington ruined everything by getting involved in a scrap with another woman of about her own age. Grant never found out what the real cause of it was but somebody's brooch got torn off, voices were raised, and drinks got spilled.

Grant reckoned there was something about social clubs that encouraged incidents like this and looked forward to the following Saturday's gig more eagerly. That would be at a jive-hive in Bootle. It was more for teens and twenties, which would surely make it possible for him to exclude Doreen from the Offbeats' retinue.

He looked forward to putting the first gig behind him for another reason, too. The woman with whom Doreen had tangled turned out to be the wife of Stan the Grouser. For some reason, this entitled Stan to wriggle out of paying the Offbeats for their night's work. Grant failed to change Stan's mind. There was no contract for the engagement. He vowed that that would never happen again, and only escaped the band's full fury because Doreen produced ten pounds from her handbag and handed it to Grant.

'Divide it between you,' she said.

'But how?' Grant asked.

'Even Stevens.'

'Leave me out,' said Spencer. 'I don't want anything.'

30

Doreen smiled, and touched him by way of thanks.

'So that's ten pounds divided by four,' Grant pondered, not sure what he was trying to do. 'That's two pounds ten each . . .'

'You left yourself out,' Doreen prompted. 'Divide by five.'

'Okay, that's fair,' said Denis.

That was how it was to be from then on. Grant, as 'manager', was to get a fifth of the take. It seemed to make sense, as long as Spencer played for free. Grant felt nervous, then elated, at what had happened. He had survived the ordeal, partly through his own efforts, partly by letting others sort out the mess. It was gradually revealed to him how he might proceed. He would assume an air of firmness. He would not lose his temper. He wouldn't criticize if he could help it. He would sweep people along on the tide of his will. That way, they would find him irresistible.

It might even apply to women, too, and one woman in particular.

Selling suits in Hendersons all week, Grant thought of little else but the upcoming gig at Bootle. If he wasn't to know what it was like to stand up and play rock 'n' roll before a crowd of screaming teenagers, he was at least beginning to feel a different thrill: that he was the one making it all happen. He had the power, the control.

He was going to have to exercise it, never mind how unpleasant it might be. He kept putting off the problem of what to do about Doreen. However important she'd been in securing his role in the group, Grant thought her a liability. He didn't just mean the scrap at the club. Just having her around was bad for the image.

Additionally, while she was there he wasn't going to be in complete control. That was what he wanted more than anything else. Eventually, she would have to go.

Then there was the question of Spencer. He was an

excellent pianist in a rather dated way. He was a bit too old, though, didn't fit in and, besides, pianos were a pain. They would always be out of tune in the halls the Offbeats were likely to play in. If Spencer continued to play for free, that was unsettling, too, treating the group as a charity. One day, he'd have to go, too.

Grant thought hard about these difficulties but decided the best thing for the moment was to do nothing. He had his job at Hendersons; he had his toe in the pop world; that was no bad situation for a lad to be in.

There was one thing he didn't have, though, and that was a woman. One of the perks of the pop world was supposed to be that women fell on you. But that was only if you were a performer. What fan ever threw herself at a manager?

Grant's sudden surge of confidence began to provide him with a solution.

One lunchtime he popped into the shoe shop where Carly worked. He sat down and waited till she was free.

'Hello,' she greeted him. 'Worn your boots out?'

'No, they're fine, absolutely wonderful. I'm not buying anything today. I want to ask you a favour.'

Carly looked at him, as if preparing for a long explanation.

'Have you heard of the Offbeats?'

'Could've done. Why?'

'Well, I'm sort of their . . . I mean I organize them.'

'You're their Brian Epstein?'

'Not exactly, but would you like to come to one of our gigs? They're playing Bootle on Saturday night. I could get you in for free. It's at the Jive Hall.'

'Okay,' Carly said evenly. 'Can I bring a friend?'

Grant froze. The disappointment showed on his face.

'Don't worry, chuck, it's not a fella. My friend Fawn. You can squeeze two judies in?'

Grant's relief was obvious. 'Yeh, yeh, as many as you like! No, I mean, I'll leave two tickets at the door. What's your name? I mean, Carly what?'

'Scott, like the bakeries.'

'Okay. It's a deal. Starts at eight fifteen. See you then.'

Carly laughed at Grant's pleasure.

As he was going out of the shop door, she called after him.

'What's yours?'

'What?'

'Your other name, daft.'

'Pickering, Grant Pickering.'

'Okay, then. See yer, Grant.'

She smiled, and thought what a funny name it was. But she liked what she saw of him. Busy, doing things, not too pushy, and not at all like Tom Sheridan.

Grant collected the Offbeats' money without trouble the next Saturday night and, before sharing it out, made certain the manager of the Jive Hall booked the group for a further two sessions. Then he watched the group's last set with proprietorial satisfaction.

He went over to the small table where he'd installed Carly and her fat friend Fawn. His face fell, and he had to remind himself to be cool when he saw that Tom Sheridan had turned up out of the blue. There he was, pressing his attentions on Carly.

Tom turned as he approached and remarked, 'Uh, oh, look who's here. Brian Eppy himself.'

It was wearing a bit thin, this comparison between the fledgling manager and the Beatles' rather more successful supremo. Tonight, indeed, was the night the Beatles were playing the Cavern. It hurt.

Grant made no reply but smiled inscrutably and tried to show by example that it was rude to speak while the Offbeats were playing. The dance floor was full of couples swaying and jumping to 'Please, Mr Postman'. After the final chord, they gave the group a round of applause and demanded one more number.

Grant spoke across Tom to Carly. 'They're playing well, don't you think?'

'Yeh, great,' said Carly, genuinely impressed. 'You didn't tell me they were *good*.'

'Well . . .'

Fawn was consoling herself with a cigarette. She had come dressed in drab clothes and National Health specs, as if for a folk concert. Carly, naturally, stood out in yet another of her own creations. It was a yellow mini, around which she had buckled a wide black belt.

'Where's the gear from?' Grant asked her.

'Fancy wearing it yerself?' Tom interrupted.

'Eff off, Tom.'

'I make it all meself,' said Carly confidently. 'Always have. Do you like it?'

'Yes, sure. You'll fall out of it if you're not careful! Where could I get some clothes made for the lads?'

'What's the matter with what they've got?' Tom asked, sipping his pint. 'Looks all right to me.'

'Want to put them in Beatle jackets or something?' Carly asked.

'Well, no,' said Grant, 'not exactly. It's got to be *different*, that's all.'

'I'll have to have a think. It'll cost yer.'

'I know, but it's important, isn't it?'

'You bet.'

Grant tried to prevent Tom from hearing more than he needed to and whispered in Carly's ear. He arranged to meet her the following Monday to discuss the matter further. He saw it was impossible to put any kind of hold on Carly while Tom was around, the way they were always giving each other deep looks.

Why was he in Bootle, anyway? There was no reason for him to be there, unless Carly had tipped him off. If she had, that was a real setback. They were all over each other, couldn't keep their hands to themselves.

Then, who should turn up at the last moment but Mrs Northington.

'Oh, hello, Doreen,' Grant welcomed her, reluctantly. 'You've almost missed everything.'

'Yes, I know, dear. I've been to every date so far and this is the first time I've almost missed one, isn't it?'

'You're very loyal,' said Grant, biting back his true reaction. He introduced Carly, Fawn and Tom.

'Carly's the great clothes designer round here,' he explained. 'I'd like to see her put the boys in something smarter.'

'Oh,' replied Doreen, suspiciously, 'I rather like them the way they are.'

'Of course, they look very good, yes, but . . .'

The music was so loud it was easy not to finish his sentence. He wanted to dance with Carly, just once before the evening was over, but it wasn't going to happen now, not with Tom there.

'Come on, Grant, have the last dance with me,' said Doreen.

Grant found himself doing the twist with this woman, old enough to be his mother, in the middle of a heaving mass of teenagers. He deserved a medal for devotion to duty but he decided, there and then, this was the last time. Doreen must never even be seen at another Offbeats' gig.

With reluctance, he said goodbye to Carly and Tom – who were snogging now – and went to help the lads load the equipment into Spencer's van. His Saturday night ended on a note of anti-climax. This was not how it was supposed to be. Not for the first time, Grant felt as though he'd given a party without getting off with anyone himself. He felt lonely and slightly bitter as he made the long trek home, across the water.

What was he doing anyway, living with his parents, at the age of twenty-four? There was going to have to be a revolution in his life.

*   *   *

On Monday evening, after the shops closed, he duly presented himself at El Cabala, a coffee bar in the centre of town. Earlier, Grant had popped in on Carly at the shoe shop to firm up what he insisted on calling their 'business meeting'. She arrived promptly, bearing a few sketches. Grant bought her a cup of frothy cappuccino, studied the designs and praised them highly. Carly was obviously not one to say she'd do something if she didn't intend seeing it through.

'That's marvellous,' he told her, not entirely able to visualize how the Offbeats would look in the futuristic suits she had drawn. 'What colour?'

'I thought silver.'

'Shiny silver? Like that dress you wore, with the holes in?'

'Yeh, quite. I know where I can get it in a softer material. Not too expensive.'

'And who'd make the suits? Could you?'

'No, you've got to have things done properly. You could try asking me mam. She used to be a seamstress.'

Grant was against bringing in parents and relations, even friends. They had a way of undermining his control.

'Yes, well, we'll see,' he said, making a decision by postponing it.

'Now let's talk money,' she went on with equal calculation. 'I'm not a charity, you know.'

Grant smiled and assured Carly they'd find a way, even if the payments had to be spread over a period, like on the 'never-never'.

'As long as it's not actually never, that's all right. By the road, do you want one for yerself?'

'One what?'

'A cozzie. Like the rest of the group.'

'Why me? I'm just the man in the suit, and not a flashy one either. I don't think it'd be right for me.'

'I'll have to take you in hand, me lad. Get you wearing

something a bit more trendy. We can't have you going around in that Hendersons gear all the time. It's not right at all, especially with those boots. Now they'd look great with one of *my* suits, wouldn't they?'

'We'll see,' said Grant, who seemed to be saying 'We'll see' rather a lot these days. 'Another cup of cappuccino?'

Carly nodded. When he'd ordered, she asked him another question: 'D'you really want to make a go of the pop?'

'You bet,' Grant admitted, 'but so does everyone else. Liverpool's bursting with groups, two a penny. I may be lucky. Maybe not.'

'Like me and my shop.'

'What shop?'

'A boutique, like they have in London. Trendy clothes. That's what I'd like to have.'

It appeared from Grant's unspoken lack of enthusiasm that there might only be room for one of them to have big dreams.

'I like the Offbeats,' said Carly, accommodatingly going back to his dream. 'They're real good, and just that little bit different. The cozzies'll make all the difference.'

'It's not easy, you know. There's Denis's mum hovering about all the time. She's as much the "manager" as me. And there's that Spencer, too. He's her "lodger", you know. I'm not really in charge at all.'

'Then you'll have to throw your weight about. Make sure they know who's boss.'

'But how?'

'I dunno. Make it legal. Sign a contract or something. That's what you're supposed to do, isn't it?'

Carly had a natural authority. He wished he had it, too. Perhaps he did, but it needed a person like her to bring it out.

'Yeh, yeh, I know,' he said. 'Trouble is, there's no one to give you advice in this business. But I think I know someone I could talk to.'

'Who's that?'

'Uncle Trevor. Well, he's not a real uncle, just a friend of the family. He was in showbiz once.'

'There you are. Do it, Grant. Don't hang about.'

At that moment, Tom Sheridan came into view. He was passing the coffee bar with Mickey and George. Grant tried to hide, but it was too late. They'd spotted Carly and were coming through the door.

'Ah, the two virgins,' Tom greeted them.

Grant resented the remark. It was untrue factually as far as he was concerned. As for Carly, how was he to know? Whatever the case, his agreeable tryst with Carly was about to end. He saw Carly instantly shift her attention to Tom. What *did* she see in him?

Grant tried to hide Carly's costume designs.

'Wouldn't interest you,' he told Tom.

'Oh aye, don't mind me. Right little sherper, aren't you?'

'And what's that supposed to mean?'

'Ambitious little prat. Always scheming, aren't you?'

'Now, now, fellas,' Carly soothed.

Tom was relieved to find that dumpy Fawn wasn't along with her today. She usually sat like the original immovable object when he was trying to get off with Carly. His own two sidekicks, Mickey and George, mindless and silent, were easy to throw off.

He decided on the spur of the moment that they should all go for a meal at a Chinese restaurant on Lime Street, the Eurasia. They agreed – Grant reluctantly – and started off, dawdling wherever boots and shoes or guitars and sheet music were displayed in shop windows.

As they straggled up through Clayton Square, Grant found himself talking to Mickey. He came over as an amiable soul and made clear how deeply envious he was of Grant's place in the world of pop.

'Need a roadie, or anything?'

'Yes,' answered Grant, without hesitation. To have

Mickey hump the amplifiers in and out of the van would be a great relief. 'Of course,' he added briskly, 'we wouldn't be able to pay you anything. Not at the moment, anyway.'

'Doesn't bother me,' said Mickey, with innocent enthusiasm and a giggle. 'Don't mind really.'

Grant saw they'd become separated from Tom and Carly, who'd been walking a few yards behind. He coloured slightly.

'The shits. They've scarpered.'

'Never mind,' Mickey told him. 'I still want the Chinese. Don't you, George? There'll be more to eat if there's only the three of us.'

'You're thick,' Grant told him.

Even silent George found it in him to comment, 'So he is.'

The three of them went to the Eurasia.

Tom looked continually over his shoulder lest anything interrupt his plan. Substituting a bag of chips for the promised Chinese meal, he had persuaded Carly to come and admire the view of the cathedral from the window of his flat in Gambier Terrace. He just hoped Mickey and George wouldn't return before he'd got her into bed.

'My, you're in a hurry,' she said to him, when he pushed her against the wall as soon as they were up the stairs and through the front door.

'What hurry? It's not as if you're a hole in one.'

'What's that supposed to mean?'

'Like, we didn't do it the first time we met. We've met lots of times, 'aven't we?'

'Nothing doing, chuck. I don't do that sort of thing.'

'What, never?'

'Never you mind. You're too bloody fast.'

'Okay, okay.'

He released her. She went over and looked at the cathedral tower, silhouetted against a sunset sky.

'Innit smashin'?'

Then she began to tell Tom the real reasons why he couldn't have what he wanted. She was a good Catholic. She wasn't giving herself to just anybody who asked, otherwise she'd have to spend all week at confession. She'd have to get back home to her mam before it was too late. Her father had died a few months before and she owed it to her mam, as an only child, to look after her.

'Only child, and you a good Catholic! Your mam never got a medal from the Pope, I'll be bound.'

'You shurrup. She lost one before me, and when she had me she couldn't have any more. You a Prot then?'

'Me? With a name like Sheridan? I come from a long line of Irish layabouts. I'm what they call lapsed.'

'Well, just you be careful.'

Tom looked crestfallen, a boy cheated of his prize.

He played his guitar and sang Carly his song. That was when she began to melt. He had a strong, smoky voice. And he knew how to play the guitar.

'You know how to handle that,' Carly told him. 'Where did you learn?'

'Taught meself.'

'You play even better than the Offbeats.'

'Offbeats is the right name for them. Right off. They'll never get anywhere.'

'Grant's got plans. Perhaps you ought to join them.'

'No fear. I don't want to play for any group. Certainly not with that prat in charge. I'm a soloist. A singer-songwriter.'

'Oh, so that's what you are? I was wondering. You're world famous, too, I expect?'

Tom threw down his guitar and made a lunge at her. He wasn't going to be put off by any girlish coyness.

'Here, you're not *really* a virgin, are you? What kept you so long?'

Carly didn't reply, but her look told Tom he was right.

'Not frightened are you?'

'Frightened of what? You're getting a bit ahead of yourself, aren't you?'

'Come here,' he said, pulling her by the hair towards him, so that his face was in line with hers. He planted a surprise kiss on her lips, as if to silence her. Talk would get in the way.

He started touching her breasts through the skimpy dress. Carly didn't resist. He pulled up the dress, slipped his hands under her bra, then moved them down to her stomach. Then to the inside of her thighs.

Carly sighed, then tried to be sensible.

'Tom, you're going too fast . . .' But it sounded more like encouragement than a plea to stop. 'We hardly know each other. It's too soon . . .'

'Oh, come on,' Tom breathed huskily, already in a world of his own where only one thing was important. He hoped against hope they wouldn't be interrupted. If Mickey and George came back now, he'd kill them.

He knew that she was ready, that she would let him. What had made her give way at last, and to *him*? Her long fingers grazed the sides of his legs. Then rhythmically and firmly she stroked him through his jeans. It had been bound to happen, from their first meeting.

He took her to the narrow bed, gently undressing her. Carly experienced no pain, nor any of the awful things that were supposed to happen first time. She even came. So this was what people talked about . . .

After, they lay, not talking, she stroking his hair. Then she spoke.

'Just as well I'm not going to get pregnant,' she murmured.

'Even Catholics get pregnant.'

'Not at this time. I *know*.'

'I thought you were a good girl, and here you are working all that out.'

'Quiet.' She pressed her lips on his to silence him.

Tom knew it could hardly be better next time, but wasn't

going to say so. He felt ludicrously triumphant. She was a wonderful girl.

'How old are you?' he asked.

'Would you settle for nineteen?'

'Whatever you say.'

Then Tom noticed the tears. 'For heaven's sake, what is there to cry about? I thought you liked it.'

'It was lovely, Tom. I'm just happy, that's all.'

'Women!' Tom mocked. But he wasn't really the heartless seducer he liked to think. Despite the cocky manner, he was quite soft underneath.

After they'd cleaned up and Carly had dressed, Tom insisted on walking her home. He even went in and met her mother, Ruby Scott, who would never have guessed what he'd just been doing to her daughter. She took an instant liking to him. Well, it was hard not to. He was charming, good-looking, and fun.

The only way to dislike him was to be his rival.

Grant arrived unannounced at Old Trevor's in Waterloo, knowing that his 'uncle' was bound to be home. The suburb, ten miles to the north, slumbered on a warm Saturday afternoon. A few couples were walking themselves or the dog on the shore. The great river swept out amid vast sandbanks to the Irish Sea. A ship, seldom larger than a coaster, would occasionally sail down the channel, a mile or two out. Beyond the bay, the hills of North Wales sat mistily in the summer sun.

Grant rang the doorbell of the large Victorian house facing out to sea and now converted into flats. He patiently waited, bending in order to stretch the still-new jeans. After a minute, Old Trevor's shape slowly came into focus on the other side of the frosted glass.

'Oh, it's you, lad. Come on in, then.'

Grant stepped into the gloom. There was a smell of stale tea leaves in the small flat. Beyond the entrance hall, in the

42

lounge, a television fitfully erupted with the cheering from a crowd at some sporting event. Old Trevor slowly pushed back the curtains to allow sunlight to stab into the room. Then he switched off the TV.

'Take a seat, Grant. Like some tea?'

Grant settled into an armchair amid the old man's clutter.

'No, don't bother, thanks, I'm all right.'

'How's your mum? And your dad? All right, are they?'

'Yes,'

'So what've you been doing?'

It was hard to believe, sitting there, that Trevor had money. There was no sign of it. Grant had always been told by his parents that Trevor wasn't short of a bob or two, but they'd never explained where he'd got it from. It couldn't just have been because he hadn't married.

Grant told him about the Offbeats. He knew Trevor would listen sympathetically in a way real relatives never would. The old man's watery eyes brightened and he let out a lively 'Well!' and 'You never!' from time to time.

It was hard to know what kept the man alive. Was he fifty or sixty? He just seemed old and finished. Always had done. He was always in and out of hospital. In Liverpool, *everybody* was either in hospital themselves or going to visit somebody who was. Trevor coughed over the cigarettes he was smoking more or less continuously; that, presumably, didn't help.

'No, I won't, thanks,' Grant said, when the packet of Senior Service was offered.

The hand that wasn't nicotined frequently rubbed and smoothed the jowls on Trevor's face. He listened intently, took a drag on the latest cigarette, and spoke.

'I envy you, lad. I never had the chance. Me health kept me back. But you're young enough. Is there something you wanted?'

'You used to work at the Empire, didn't you?' Grant had never been sure exactly what job Trevor had done at

43

Liverpool's largest theatre. He might just have done the accounts, but he'd had a connection with show business and that was all that mattered.

'Yes, I did. It's a while ago now. So you're getting into the business yourself then, with this group? Is that it?'

'Hope so. God knows whether we'll ever make any money out of it. I'd love to perform, myself. But you just kind of know, don't you, what you can do, and what you can't?'

'Maybe.'

'But there's no rules. Who's to teach you?'

'Nobody can. You have to make your own mistakes, that's the only way. Put things in writing, I do know that. Treat your acts like human beings. Children, maybe, but humans. That's all there is to know. All you *can* know.'

'Tell me, how do you get rid of people?'

'What kind of people?'

'People that are in the way. Interfering.'

'Tell them to their face what the problem is.'

'I see.'

'There's another thing,' Old Trevor told him, fussily smoothing out a crease in his scuffed brown jacket. 'Don't put all your eggs in one basket. You need more than one string to your bow. If you're going to manage, then manage more than one act. Then if your talent turns out to be no good, or falls out with you, you're not left high and dry.'

Grant let this sink in. They talked on quietly in the semi-shaded room. It didn't really matter what was said. Grant was seeking the encouragement he'd get from no one else, certainly not from his own father. In Trevor, he had someone to take him seriously, who'd be prepared to dream a while with him.

At five o'clock Grant had to go and prepare for the evening's gig. Old Trevor wedged the front door open with the mat and walked to the gate with him.

'Have you ever thought, lad, what lies out that way?' He pointed out to sea with his cigarette hand.

'Well, first there's Anglesey. Then the Irish Sea, then Dublin and Ireland.'

'And then?'

'Then there's the Atlantic and America, I suppose.'

'That's it. Just imagine what the Mersey was like fifty or sixty years ago. Full to bursting with ships, many of them going to America. First it was the slave trade, then cotton. This was a great port, a third of all British exports going through it. And now? Dying.'

'I'd love to go to America one day, I really would.'

'You will, lad, if you want to. If you *really* want to, you can do anything.' Old Trevor laid a friendly hand on his shoulder. 'And if you ever need any help, or any money, you won't have to ask twice.'

'Thanks.'

'Let me know how you get on.'

'Yes, I will. And thanks again.'

That night, Grant tackled the problem of Doreen Northington, but not head on as Trevor had advised. Instead, he spoke to Denis about his mother.

'You'll have to tell her. I can't. She can't keep coming to our gigs, though. It doesn't make sense. Doesn't look right.'

'She'll like *that*, Grant, she really will. She's always backed us. If it wasn't for her, you wouldn't be with us, either.'

'I know that. I'm not thick. But she's in the way. She's holding us back, Denis. She's holding you back. Not right for the image. Can't you tell her that?'

'Okay,' sighed Denis, adenoidally. 'I'll do your dirty work for you, if you insist.'

'Thanks. I think it's better if you do it.'

Grant gave Spencer the elbow more directly. He had to do it without losing the group the use of the van.

'I've been thinking,' he said casually, not looking Spencer

in the eye. 'About the future of the Offbeats, I mean.'

'Oh, yes,' Spencer replied. 'I'm always suspicious of a man who says he's been thinking.'

'You see, it's like this . . .' Their eyes did meet now, but that was accidental. Grant began again: 'We really are most grateful to you for the use of the van. I don't know where we'd be without it. I just wanted to say thank you.'

'Oh,' Spencer smiled, surprised, 'is that all? You're welcome to keep using it, as long as you like. Or as long as I'm still lodging with Doreen, and I mean that.'

Now, Grant looked him straight in the eye. 'Most kind, Spencer, most kind. So that's a deal then?'

Having cleared that hurdle, he could deal with the other one. 'Trouble is, and I hope you don't mind, we've decided on a new line-up. Took a vote on it, really. I'm afraid pianos are a bit old hat. It's just guitar and drums now in groups, as I expect you've noticed. Different sound. So, as I say, we won't be needing you from now on.'

Spencer wasn't too bothered. He was older than the other Offbeats. Had a job. He'd only gone along with it because he could play the piano, had the van, and because Doreen pushed him into it. Grant didn't explain that he didn't fit in with the image of the group. Too old, not lively enough, certainly not sexy.

Grant spread the news that Spencer had chosen to give it all up of his own accord, and he never found out that the tale of the rest of the group 'taking a vote on it' was a fabrication.

Later, when Doreen had been told her fate, too, she muttered to Spencer that Grant behaved as if he owned the group. She got it into her head that Grant wasn't the only one behind the shake-up. She'd seen enough of that Carly girl to imagine she'd had a hand in putting Grant up to it. He would never have behaved so ungratefully on his own, surely?

*　　*　　*

The following week, the slimmed-down Offbeats appeared for the first time in their new silver suits. Grant was thrilled by the improvement in the group's appearance. But he was reluctant to wear the suit that Carly's mother had already run up for the departing Spencer: Grant thought the flashy jackets were all right for 'the boys', as he'd taken to calling them, but not for him.

'You wear it,' he told Carly. 'It'll fit you, you'll look fabulous. Not me.'

'Don't you like it, then?' Carly asked him, faking despondency.

'I love the cozzies, I just don't think they're right for me. I have to trust my own judgement. I'm not a fool when it comes to clothes. I know something about them, you know.'

'Square! Still . . .'

'Still, nothing. But thanks a million, Carly. The boys look tremendous, and it's all due to you.'

He clutched her arm and kissed her.

My, she thought, he's coming on. He was the complete opposite of Tom Sheridan when it came to confidence, but she liked him. In a different way, she liked him almost as much as Tom. But Tom was the first person in her affections.

Carly altered the suit so that she could squeeze into it. Tom took a photograph of her and sold it to the *Echo*. The newspaper described her, ambitiously, as a 'designer and model' rather than 'shoe shop assistant'. It also recorded her desire to open her own boutique. The dream, once expressed in print, somehow became more attainable.

Grant was none too pleased with Tom for making use of Carly to make money for himself.

'Why shouldn't he?' Carly asked. 'I think it was smashing of Tom. He was only trying to help. Help the group, I mean.'

'Fat chance. The Offbeats didn't even get a mention.'

'That was the *Echo*'s fault. You know what they're like.

You mustn't be so against Tom. He's not always wrong, you know.'

'Okay, I'm sorry.'

'That's better.'

'You really like Tom, don't you?'

Carly looked away and didn't answer. Grant wondered just how far they'd gone together. Were they lovers? He might burst with envy if he thought any more about it.

'You really mean it about the boutique, don't you?' he said.

'You bet. And, know what? I've just seen the fabbest place for it. The old craft shop in Paradise Street. The one that closed.'

'Paradise Street? What'll the rent be? Then you've got the wages and the staff to think about, and where will you get the gear? Are you going to make it yourself.'

'Hold on, hold on. If you can play Mr Showbiz, why can't I? I don't know anything about running a shop but I'll do what you're doing, learn as I go along.'

'I wish I were as confident as you, Carly. What are you going to call it?'

' "Paradise". Stands to reason, don't it?'

Grant's eyebrows rose. 'You're amazing! I bet you do it, too.'

His own business was far from secure. The Offbeats weren't happy with the way things were going. He was getting them a good flow of bookings, but they'd had no publicity. Above all, and most depressingly, they were not getting auditions, let alone a recording contract.

'What are you going to do about it?' Denis asked impatiently. He looked all too reminiscent of Doreen, Grant noticed.

'That is the most difficult thing in the world to get, Denis, you must know that. We'll have to cut a demo. Get it done locally. Perhaps Beaver Radio . . .'

'What's wrong with NEMS?'

'We're not going there, that's Epstein's camp.'

'Do you think we're good enough?' asked Roger the bass guitarist, in a rare burst of humility.

' 'Course you are,' Grant told him, 'good as anybody. But that's not what the business is about. It's to do with luck and knowing the right people. If our demo landed on the right desk at the right moment, then we'd be okay. But where d'you buy that kind of luck? I'll see what I can do, though. You keep on practising. You've got a tape recorder, so use that to start with.'

'Spencer's got a Grundig . . .' Denis hesitated. He'd begun to get the message that he wasn't to mention Spencer any more. Spencer was a non-person. But, if he had the only tape recorder there was, then, as with the van, he might still have his uses . . .

'I don't care whose recorder it is,' Grant said, 'just get it. And rehearse, rehearse. Trouble is, because we've all got jobs there's not enough time. Especially if you and Rod are ever going to write any songs. You need to have your own material. Have you started yet?'

'No.'

'Well, there you are then.'

'You know that Tom Sheridan? He writes songs.'

'Maybe he does.' Grant didn't say what he really felt about Tom. 'We can manage without him, though.'

'Please yourself.'

At other times, Denis would come right out with it and accuse Grant of taking his cut without earning it. After all, he didn't have to get up on the stage and actually perform.

Grant would then try to put on the right personality to deal with the problem. His inclination was to hit back and accuse Denis of being sloppy and less than professional in the group's presentation. But if he could, he would accept any blame that was going and not spoil for a fight. So they never actually came to blows.

*　　*　　*

Tom Sheridan didn't calculate or exercise control over himself the way Grant did. On the whole, he let life take its course and was happy to wait for opportunities to arise of their own accord. But without consciously manipulating other people, he was quite capable of getting the results he wanted.

Just now, he had two ideas he wanted to push forward. His flat-mates, Mickey and George, had now been enrolled as the Offbeats' unofficial, unpaid roadies. Tom had it in mind to drive them out of the flat near the cathedral so that he and Carly could live together. It was extremely doubtful whether either of them would fall for this and, indeed, when Tom tried, they stayed put.

Tom sensed that Grant, of all people, was the key to his ambitions. Not only might Grant, in some way, take Mickey and George off his hands, he might also help with the second idea.

So Tom persuaded Carly to ask Grant to come for a meal in Gambier Terrace. There would be five to feed, of course, if he couldn't get rid of Mickey and George.

Grant was puzzled by this sudden about-turn in Tom's attitude. What lay behind it? But he told Carly he'd come.

In the event there were only the three of them. Carly made Lancashire hot-pot, but so original was it that neither Grant nor Tom recognized it as such. They had canned beer to go with it. Carly drank tap water. She was not a drinker.

Grant sat huddled away from Tom, hardly bearing to look him in the face. Carly sat between them, smoothing the way.

'Have you heard my song?' Tom asked eventually, putting on the charm.

'No, I don't think I have,' Grant told him.

'You must be the only person on Merseyside who hasn't,' said Carly.

'Shut your face, woman.'

He sang it.

'That's okay,' Grant told him, charitably. 'Have you written any more?'

'Reams. And poetry.'

'Poetry?'

'Yes, that's what I want to talk to you about.'

'I don't know anything about poetry.'

'You see, Grant, I've got this idea I'd like you to chew over, you being an organizer and all. Have you heard of the poetry and jazz concerts at the university?'

'Never been to one.'

'I've got a better idea, see. How about *rock* and poetry?'

'How d'you mean?'

'Mix the two together.'

'You mean, spout Shakespeare in the middle of a rock 'n' roll gig?'

'Not Shakespeare, more modern. There's a lot of good poets in the city just now. Not arty-farty stuff, y'know. It'd go very well with the music. Beat music, beat poetry.'

'Could kill a gig stone dead.' Grant thought it was a terrible idea, especially coming from Tom. 'Is that what you're after, seeing as you write poetry, to be involved yourself?'

Tom pretended he wasn't very important but, yes, he had that in mind.

'Perhaps a group of poets, one short poem each?' Grant tossed the idea about. He was being accommodating to Tom in spite of himself. 'You wouldn't expect to be paid, would you?'

'Well,' Tom began. 'Not at first perhaps, but in time . . . God, you're a hard one, Pickering. ''Picky Pickering'' we'll call you.'

Carly smiled, intrigued by the way the two men were irritating each other.

Grant opened a second can of beer, knowing there was no avoiding dealing with Tom's proposition. He was also very sensitive to Carly's presence. He didn't want to appear stubborn and unhelpful in front of her. He sensed her wanting him to help Tom. She had been so good about designing the Offbeats' costumes, she was so supportive of all he was trying to do, he couldn't disappoint her.

'Let me think about it,' Grant conceded. 'I'm not sure how it'd go. I don't know how commercial it would be. I'll have to put it to the boys. They mightn't want to have anything to do with it.'

'It doesn't have to be the Offbeats,' Tom said. 'Any group'd do.'

'I'm afraid I don't manage any other groups. Not at the moment, anyway.'

Carly gave him a warm look, but not too warm. She could tell Grant fancied her, but she was Tom's girl and didn't want to encourage the other fella.

'Tell you what,' she said, half-teasingly, 'when you've got that all fixed, you can give a pop and poetry concert at the opening of my shop.'

'Oh, not you and your ruddy shop,' Tom said. It was clear from the expression on Grant's face that they were united on this one.

'Speak for yourself.'

Carly made a lunge at Tom and pushed him off his chair and on to the mattress lying next to it on the floor. Tom pulled her on top of him and shot his hands right up her skirt. Grant had to look on, amused, forbearing. But the way Carly acquiesced said it all. They were lovers all right. In any case, Grant thought, there must be some relationship between them for Tom to be able to persuade Carly to cook this meal for the three of them.

Why were women so easily manipulated by sponges like Tom?

'Walk you home, Carly?' Grant volunteered provocatively when it was getting late. He'd said it to annoy Tom, and it did.

'No need for that,' Tom said. 'I can look after her.'

'Ta, luv,' Carly said to Grant. Then to Tom: 'I'd better

go, actually. I'm tired. We'll do the washing up first, though. You can both give me a hand.'

'Then I'll see you home,' said Tom.

'We'll both see you home,' Grant seized this opportunity, triumphantly.

That was how it was. The two admirers walked her back between them to the little terraced house in Lily Street.

Tom went on about how Liverpool had many series of street names. There were streets named after characters from Dickens (Pickwick, Dombey, Dorrit), there were Old Testament streets (Moses, Isaac, Jacob, David). Just round here it was flowers: Rose, Orchid, Daffodil, Lily.

At No. 23, the three went in. Carly's mother was watching the telly on her own and she brightened when she saw her daughter home safe. She decided she liked both Tom and Grant in their different ways. She wasn't sure, but she thought they might both be interested in Carly. They chatted for a few minutes, then Tom and Grant left together, bidding Carly a chaste goodnight.

As they walked away from Lily Street, Grant could see that he'd been caught in a trap. In order to keep a hold on Carly, he was going to have to organize Tom's rock 'n' poetry show for him.

'All right, Tom,' he said. 'I'll take it on. I'll be in touch.'

Tom was rather pleased with his night's work.

CHAPTER 3

The autumn of 1963 was when 'Beatlemania' seized Britain and the world. Liverpool was news again after slumbering for decades as a place where nothing happened except dock strikes. Now it had given birth to a phenomenon that was already being taken up elsewhere, leaving a vacuum in the city itself. True, there were journalists and broadcasters enough descending on the place to poke about and expose the roots of the phenomenon, but already there was a feeling that it was all over as far as Liverpool itself was concerned.

In October, the Offbeats played the Cavern for the first time. Grant had lobbied the management with tapes, photos and letters for a go at the lunchtime slot. It went well. There was a groundswell of support for the group. Loyal fans who'd been alerted to the Cavern appearance by announcements made at other gigs made their way to the cellar that Thursday lunchtime.

The Offbeats looked stunning in Carly's suits. The occasion was a success and Grant allowed himself a little self-congratulation at the thought that four months before, when he and Carly and Tom had first been together in the Cavern, none of it could have happened.

But still no record company showed interest in the Offbeats.

The next date they played, two nights later, was at the University Union on Brownlow Hill. Grant still wasn't sure about the wisdom of this, but he'd succumbed to Carly's unspoken pressure. If Tom wanted to try his rock-poetry evening, students were more likely to be a receptive audience than stompers at a church hall social.

Denis, Roger, Paddie and Rod had bridled at the idea. They didn't fancy playing before a crowd of snotty-nosed students. They were suspicious of Tom Sheridan and his sudden claim to be a poet when, to them, he seemed a con-man.

'Well, I don't know anything about poetry, either,' Grant found himself telling Denis, 'but that's what Tom calls it. He says you should just think of it as the words to a song, without the music.'

'Where did he learn to write poetry, then?'

'School, I suppose. But they've got something, these beat poets. It's not like *poetry* at all. Quite funny some of it.'

'Sounds to me like Tom's cashing in.'

'You could well be right. But everybody's doing it now, even John Lennon.'

'It *must* be all right, then.'

'Look, all we can lose is an evening of our lives. The money's cast-iron, I've made sure of that, even if no students turn up.'

'Well, okay then, but I don't like it . . .'

The evening went surprisingly well. In between the Offbeats' sets, Tom and two other 'beat poets' took it in turn to read their pieces. Tom had seen that the more obviously humorous poems would go down best when read aloud to an audience. But among his own, he included a serious poem about a woman called 'Lorelei'. He was working on a cycle of them, so he said. Not even Carly was aware they were really about her.

Grant stood at the back of the hall, observing reactions to the event, not regretting having fallen for Tom's idea, but doubting whether there was much of a future in it. It was significant that the most successful moment, when the Offbeats weren't playing, was when Tom took up a guitar to which he had attached a mouth organ harness and launched into a take-off of Bob Dylan. It brought the house down. Tom only wished his 'poetry' had done the same.

Afterwards, as the Offbeats played their final set, Tom went to pull Carly on to the dance floor, only to find her sitting with Grant. He was incensed to see that Grant had an arm draped proprietorially round her shoulders. Tom, encouraged by a series of poet's pints, though now spilling more than he drank, attempted to separate Grant from Carly. She resisted and tried to stay with the more sober of her two suitors. Grant, not wishing to create a disturbance on foreign territory, tried to usher the conflict out of the hall and into the corridor.

This incensed Tom the more. Drunkenly, he made to pull Carly away from Grant. He only succeeded in landing a blow in Carly's face. Mickey and George pulled him back. Even Tom could tell he'd gone too far. He retreated, mumbling refusals to apologize.

Grant held Carly's hand, but said nothing. He could see how things were moving his way.

'You see to Tom,' he told Mickey, quietly. 'Take him home. I'll look after Carly.'

Grant only had to wait. Tom was cutting his own throat. Three nights after the row, and no word out of him, Carly went to his flat unannounced. She knew he, or somebody, was in because a light was on. Yet when she rang the bell no one came to the door. There was a murmur from within, then a guffaw.

'Come on, Tom. It's me. Why don't you open?'

There was a very long pause. Then Tom opened the door, stark naked.

'Just in time to join us for a threesome, eh?'

He pushed the door as far open as it would go and gestured with his thumb towards the mattress on the floor. Lizzo, a scrubber from the College of Art, was clutching a sheet to herself and trying to look seductive.

'Oh, Tom, you shite!' screamed Carly, and ran down the stairs.

57

Grant took over. If there was a price to pay, it was that he had to support Carly's dream of opening her 'Paradise' boutique.

'What are you going to sell?'

'Oh, mod fashions. Women's mostly. And accessories, of course. Sweaters, shifts, scarves, hats, jewellery, and bric-à-brac.'

'That all?'

'If there's room, I'll have a men's section, too. You can run that. Not that it'll be like menswear at Hendersons, of course.'

'Aren't you being a bit ambitious? You're only nineteen. You've no experience of running anything.'

'Listen to him! You've no experience of running groups and you're not doing so badly.'

'And then there's your suppliers . . .'

'I know where I can get the stuff. I've done my homework.'

'And you need money. For stock. Where's that coming from?'

'You'll help me find it.'

'Oh, I will, will I?'

'If you were setting up a business,' she went on, 'where would you find the money?'

'Go to a bank?'

'Wouldn't look at me. Have you got any rich relations? I know I've not.'

'Hold on . . .' It was obvious. 'I haven't got any rich relations, certainly none I'd dare ask or want to have involved, but I have got an uncle who isn't a real uncle, if you see what I mean. Lives in Waterloo.'

'Who's that?'

'He's called Trevor. *Old* Trevor, I've always called him. Lives on his own. I saw him the other week. He said if I ever needed help . . .'

'Looks like I'd better meet your Old Trevor.'

* * *

The audition with Decca came out of the blue. Grant had written to all the record companies in London, sending tapes of the Offbeats. His clumsily-typed notes failed to impress, as did the tapes (if they had even been listened to) and he hadn't received a single acknowledgement.

The lunchtime gig at the Cavern had not gone totally unnoticed, however, and one day a message was relayed to Grant at Hendersons. (He'd had to put Denis's home phone number on the letters. Decca rang there.) Mrs Northington rang Grant's mother with the news and even Mrs Pickering had realized it was probably important enough for her to try and get in touch with Grant at the store.

'So whaddya think?' Grant grinned at Denis later.

'Fucking fantastic! Decca, too. 'Spose they still kick themselves for turning down the Beatles!'

'They'd better not turn *us* down . . .'

For reasons best known to Decca, the audition was to take place on a Saturday afternoon in early November. This was bad news on two fronts. Grant would have to miss a day's work at Hendersons and the group would have to cancel a Saturday night gig. But they had to do it. The audition meant everything.

They left Liverpool at six in the morning. It was dark and raining. Aboard the van, with Grant at the wheel, were the four Offbeats (dressed in black scruff, as silver suits were deemed unnecessary for a sound audition). Then there was Carly, accompanied by the inevitable Fawn ('to provide ballast', Denis suggested), and Mickey and George, duffle-coated against the November chill, to hump the equipment. It was a squeeze with all the equipment on board, but it was an adventure.

Carly had taken a day off, unpaid, from the shoe shop. She really needed to work on her plans for the boutique, but a trip to London was not to be missed. Grant tried to get the day off from Hendersons but without success. He'd just have to plead sickness when he went back on Monday.

It was the first time Grant had ever driven to London. Finding the Decca studios in Wimbledon proved difficult. They were due to start at one o'clock, but it was one fifteen before they even reached the gates.

Grant hated being late for anything, but for this, he could hardly forgive himself. Surely he'd allowed himself enough time for the two-hundred-mile journey?

The man at the gate didn't seem the slightest bit put out by the late arrival. As everyone was always late, they hadn't planned to start till two in any case.

The Offbeats duly rattled off their four best numbers, 'Do You Love Me', 'Please, Mr Postman', 'Baby It's Me' and 'They Say'. They were all recorded with the minimum of fuss. The Offbeats felt they'd given it all they'd got. But, on listening to the playback, there was slight disappointment that the infectious spirit so apparent in live performances somehow hadn't registered on the tape.

The A and R man, a sober-suited, quietly-spoken person called Tony Preston, was soothing and supportive. Grant took it as a good omen when Preston asked what the lads were doing over the weekend. Were they staying in London?

'Well, no, we planned on going home. We hadn't thought . . .'

'If you stay, there's a party you can come to tonight.'

'Thanks very much,' said Denis, eyes brightening at the prospect.

'It's in Chelsea. Just some friends, you know. They'd be amused to meet some real Liverpudlians.'

'Any judies?' asked Rod.

'Millions of them,' Preston assured him. 'See you later, I hope.'

Grant studied the map and gave instructions to those who wanted to wander off and explore. Carly was desperate to look round the boutiques before they all closed.

Eventually, around nine o'clock, everyone managed to converge on a large townhouse in Chelsea where lights burned in all the rooms. Paddie and Roger were already carrying several skinfuls of beer. The others, more sober, slightly apprehensive, hesitantly rang the doorbell.

A girl in gold leather trousers, her face deep in make-up, opened the door.

'Tony Preston told us to come,' Grant said, straightening his tie. 'We're the Offbeats.'

The girl nodded, took a drag on her cigar, but said nothing. They trooped in, the Offbeats, Fawn, Mickey and George, and Grant holding Carly's hand. They soon felt eyes turn on them. They were certainly a band of scruffs compared with the people already at the party.

'I'm not sure I'm going to like this,' Grant muttered to Carly.

'Yes, you will,' Carly replied and gave him an encouraging squeeze.

They perched uneasily on the sofas or in the high-backed leather chairs and looked like fish out of water. Eventually, Tony Preston himself materialized with a woman who might have been his wife and attempted to introduce the Liverpudlians to the other guests.

One woman with breasts bursting out of a short, polka-dot dress, and a large beehive hairdo, decided to patronize Grant.

'Tony says you're from Liverpoo'. Where *is* Liverpoo' exactly?'

Grant was lost for words.

'I suppose you know the Beatles?' she went on.

Grant hesitated. 'Well . . .'

'Tell her you do,' Carly hissed.

'Well, sort of, yes.'

'Ronnie, in the office, met someone who was *at school* with a Beatle. Isn't that *simply amazing*!'

'Yes, well, a lot of whackers claim to have been.'

Grant felt Carly dig him in the ribs.

'But you haven't got the accent,' the woman pressed on. 'Do you *really* come from Liverpoo'?'

'Oh, aye, not everybody has one, you see. Not everyone down here talks like Tommy Steele. Actually, I had the operation at an early age. Took it out with me tonsils.'

'How frightfully amusing!' the girl shrieked, and moved on.

'Phew,' said Grant. 'I think I'd rather be somewhere else. How about you, Carly?'

Rod, the bass guitarist, took a different view and had decided that, when in Rome, he might as well. Accordingly, he was trying his rough, untamed Northern charm on a succession of dolly-birds, treating them to his version of Liverpudlian wit. But, amused though they might be, the dolly-birds visibly shrank from his scruffy appearance. If the Beatles came from Liverpool, at least they looked *clean* . . .

Never one to be choosy when the odds were against him, Rod reverted to his more usual technique, perfected at countless teenage parties back home. After a perfunctory dance in the middle of the floor, he steered the inevitable and all-too-available Fawn away from the party and into a bedroom upstairs.

Noticing this, Grant told Carly, 'We'll never get them all back home now.'

'Don't fret, luv,' she told him. 'They can look after themselves.'

'I hope those two will be okay,' Grant remarked, gesturing to where Mickey and George were being chatted up, unknowingly, by a Guards officer in an Old Etonian tie.

'Well, how do you like London, then?' It was Tony Preston.

'Oh, fine,' Grant said.

'It's great,' added Carly.

'And what's your role in all this?' Preston asked her. 'Are you the girl friend?'

'No, she's not,' Grant shot back, a little too briskly. 'Carly's a designer. She did the boys' suits. She's going to open Liverpool's first boutique, too.'

'I'm also a fan,' Carly laughed.

'Well, they've certainly got something,' Preston let on. 'I hope we'll be able to do something with them. There's one or two things I need to discuss with you. I'm not sure about the name. Offbeats is a bit, well, "off", wouldn't you say?'

Carly could sense Grant revving himself up to flatten anyone who suggested any such tinkering. She laid a restraining hand on his arm. He noticed, and stopped.

'Well, yeh, maybe,' was all he said.

'I'll be in touch, Grant. I don't have the final say, of course. It has to go before the committee.'

'Of course,' said Grant.

'Still, thanks for coming all this way. When do you go back?'

'Tonight, I think.'

'Oh, surely not? Stay and enjoy the fun.'

'He's right,' Carly said, when Preston had gone. 'You're in no state to drive. You'll fall asleep.'

'Okay,' Grant agreed. Then, not looking her in the eye, he asked, 'Why don't we tell the others to sleep in the van. Or in the park if they want to. We'll find a *proper* bed . . .'

Carly wasn't happy that he'd finally made his move. She'd been wondering when it would come, but somehow she didn't want it. As though, with Grant, sex wasn't the important thing.

He took her firmly by the hand. They went round to find the others. Grant gave Denis the key to the van. 'For Christ's sake, don't let anyone swipe the equipment. We'll leave at eleven tomorrow.'

Then they went upstairs and after going into a couple of bedrooms occupied by heaving couples, they found the one where Rod was in the midst of straddling Fawn. She lay on the bed where guests had left their coats.

'Sorry to interrupt,' Grant whispered. 'Keep on shagging. We're not leaving till the morning. Be at the van before eleven, or we'll leave you behind.'

'Oh, aye,' Rod gasped, and went back to his pursuit of a climax with the quivering mass beneath him.

Carly and Grant checked into the Regent Palace Hotel, just off Piccadilly, with only her make-up bag to show for luggage. At the reception desk, she knew what she had to do. She unobtrusively moved one of her rings on to the wedding finger of her left hand and wore it like a badge. Grant noticed the receptionist glance down to check. He inscribed 'Mr and Mrs Preston' in the register and added a false address. A deposit on the room was demanded and he paid it.

The couple stared at the floor as a porter travelled up in the lift with them, carrying their 'baggage'.

'Up for the weekend?' he asked.

'Yes,' Grant murmured inaudibly.

'Come far then, 'ave you?'

'Liverpool.'

'Ah, like the Beatles, eh?'

Grant moaned quietly to himself. 'Oh, aye.'

He tipped the porter half a crown, and felt overwhelmed by the experience. He had managed to bring it all off.

Carly looked around the room. It was the first time she had been in a proper hotel. She looked at the notepaper and the leaflets, even at the Bible by the bed.

Grant was staring at the room-service menu, wondering about the cost. Then he confidently rang down and ordered chicken cooked in some French way, with chips, and a bottle of champagne.

Well, thought Carly, this was certainly different to the way Tom treated her. His wallet had moths in it.

'Oh, no, love . . . not for me,' she said when Grant tried to fill her glass with champagne.

'You must have some,' he told her. 'We've got to behave as though we've got the contract. That's the way to make it happen!'

She sipped some, liked it, and had some more.

They cuddled up together on the bed; the champagne helped them both.

'That Tony seemed all right, didn't he?' Carly said. In her vocabulary, 'all right' was high praise. 'I mean, he wouldn't have invited us if he thought we were rotten, would he?'

'I don't know, I really don't. It went pretty well this afternoon.'

'You're a cheerful one. So what happens if Decca don't take you on?'

'We'll just have to keep on trying. I'm in danger of losing my job at Hendersons, skiving off like this. I can't stand it anyway. So we'll *have* to make it. I've got to get fixed up in Liverpool, organize myself, get away from home.'

'I know . . .' Carly said quietly. 'You're very ambitious, aren't you?'

'So are you, with your shop and all.'

'There's not much else to be in Liverpool, is there?'

'Ha!' Then suddenly he said: 'I want to sleep with you, Carly.'

'I know.'

'I'm not very good at this sort of thing . . .'

It would have been a clever ploy, if it had been intended as such.

'I'm sure you're lovely, Grant. It's not the first time, right?'

'No. You neither?'

'No.'

'How old were you when you first . . .?'

'I'm not telling you.' She certainly wasn't going to reveal how recently it had happened and with whom. He'd hate it. She turned the question back on him instead.

'How old were you?'

'Seventeen, sixteen, I don't know. It was at a party. Upstairs, the usual thing.'

'Did you enjoy it?'

'You bet. Fantastic.'

'Not everyone likes it first time.'

'Didn't you?'

'Actually I did. I thought I was lucky.'

'So you *do* sleep with people?'

'What a cruddy thing to say! Of course I do. You're a funny one, Grant. You scheme to get me off to a hotel with you for the night, and you're not even sure I'll let you do it!'

It was an odd way to go about it, indeed, but, with a little help from the champagne, Carly had already decided she would sleep with him. She wanted to show what she thought of him. He was rather a lonely figure, doing a difficult job. She appreciated what he did. And she liked him. He wasn't glamorous like Tom, but he was nice.

She was also rather hoping, now that Tom had eased her so successfully into the world of free love, that Grant would give her just as good a time.

He methodically went round the room putting out unnecessary lights. Then he started fiddling with the thingy he'd kept in his wallet for just such an occasion as this. He'd sent off by post to Brighton for a supply, to save him having to ask for one at the chemist. Carly quietly accepted this and said nothing. She might have been a good Catholic, but she wasn't stupid.

They began to undress one another. Carly turned out the bedside light and waited for Grant to get started. She could just about make him out by the glow from a red neon light outside the window.

'You've got a young body, haven't you?' she commented, tracing the outline of his shoulders with her fingers. 'Boyish.'

Taking his cue, he licked his right forefinger and felt the outline of Carly's large, soft breasts. He felt the nipples stir. She sighed.

He had to remember not to rush his love-making. After the first time, the girl at the party had wondered if he *cared* at all about the person he was making love to. She'd even wondered if he wouldn't have been happier making love to a *man*. That had been very shaming. He hadn't been able to make the excuse that it was his first time, because he hadn't wanted to admit that. Afterwards, though, he had read such books as were available and discovered all about foreplay and about increasing 'feminine fervour', as the medical author put it.

Now he was in danger of going to the other extreme: going on and on, taking too long over it.

In the end, he came, and she did not. He clung immobile on top of her for several minutes, sweating now, until their breathing returned to normal. Grant pulled away from Carly, hoping the thingy hadn't broken. He wasn't sure whether it had or not.

She wasn't going to let on how much better Tom had been as a lover. Brought her off first time he had, much more urgent, much more passionate.

Next morning, Grant and Carly slipped out of the Regent Palace without paying the remainder of the bill. They were both grinning as they linked up with the Offbeats back in Chelsea.

Remarkably, everyone was there and, apart from Fawn, who was refusing to speak to Rod in the daylight, they were all in good humour, though most were hung over and a few were stiff from sleeping with their bodies pressed up against the equipment in the van.

Grant drove them back to Liverpool. Back to reality, too.

He was greeted by long faces in the menswear department at Hendersons on the Monday. His boss told him to report straight to the chief personnel officer on the top floor. She was a smart woman in her early fifties, but disfigured by cigarette ash. She didn't look at him until he was sitting across the desk from her.

'Well, Mr Pickering.' It was just like being at school again. 'I thought you were supposed to be working with us on Saturday?'

'Yes, but I didn't feel . . .' He was going to add 'well' but clearly matters had gone beyond that stage. They must know he hadn't been ill.

'It seems you took a trip to London. Or so a little bird tells us.'

'There may have been a misunderstanding . . .' He faltered.

'It's not only that, you know.'

Grant reddened. He promised himself, at that moment, that he was never going to be employed by anyone else, ever again, if it put him in situations like this.

'You're not too highly thought of in menswear.'

'I thought my commission spoke for itself.'

'That's not everything,' the personnel woman said. 'They say your mind's not on the job. You're dreaming, and you're always nipping off. Where do you go? The Cavern, is it, or one of those places?'

Grant agreed that it was.

She told him he was being given his cards, with four weeks' pay. He'd have to leave immediately. Today. Make his farewells and depart.

Grant should have known this would happen but felt he'd been punched in the stomach. He walked all the way down the stone stairs rather than take a lift to the basement. It helped fill in time and allowed his burning cheeks to cool. He watched the other assistants confidently going about their business that Monday morning. Well, sod the lot of them, for the boring, stuck-up crew they were.

He made his apologies to the boss of menswear who surprised him by smiling back.

'I'm sorry, too, Grant. But you'll be happier at something else. You're not really cut out for this.'

Grant felt close to tears, as often when people were kind.

'You'll do all right,' his boss went on. 'I know you will. How's that music of yours coming along? Make any money out of that?'

'Not yet, no.'

'I expect you will. Come back when you're famous.'

He shook Grant warmly by the hand, and gave him the biggest wink he was capable of.

Grant wandered out into the street, shaken. He couldn't face going home just yet to break the news to his parents. He popped into the shoe shop to see Carly. She knew instantly that something was up.

'What is it, luv?'

'I've been sacked.'

'Because you skived off?'

'Yes . . . mostly.'

'What'll you do?'

'I'm going to get me that flat in town. I've got four weeks' wages, that'll do it. Even if it's the size of a shoebox.'

'Great!'

Grant could tell that Carly was waiting to tell him something, too.

'I've got a letter to show you.' Carly went to fetch it from her bag, round the back of the shop. She came back unfolding it. 'It's from Old Trevor. He's agreed.'

'Let's see.'

'It was good of him to decide so quickly, wasn't it? He even sent the cheque.'

Grant swallowed. He might be in need of Old Trevor's financial support himself now, but it was too late.

'You did a good selling job on him.'

'And you, Grant. You helped. Don't look so glum.'

Grant couldn't help it. 'Sorry, but, you know . . .'

'Look, chuck, if the worst comes to the worst, you can come and help me with the shop. You won't starve.'

'I know, but that's not the point. I want to do what I want to do, and –'

'The chance is there, anyway. If you want to take it.' Carly had to remember to keep her voice down. She didn't like to say too much about her plans for Paradise when she was in the shoe shop.

'You'll be able to get enough gear to open the shop, with that cheque?' Grant asked.

'Oh, yeh. I want to see if I can open early December. Before Christmas, any road.'

Grant could see how excited she was. It was a shame her success coincided with his defeat.

There was nothing for it but to make show business his job. Unfortunately, Grant didn't yet have anyone to manage apart from the Offbeats, and twenty per cent of their income wasn't going to buy him a Rolls-Royce. Nevertheless, he quickly found himself a bedsit and pretended it was his office. The telephone was a shared, coin-operated one on the landing outside the door.

Ted and May Pickering didn't approve. What was he doing leaving home when he didn't even have a job? But though Grant could feel the chill of reality whipping into him that November of 1963, he was equally thrilled to be free. He didn't know what was going to happen to him, but the days were bright and exciting, the air full of promise. There was a tingle of expectation such as he'd never felt before.

Carly refused to live with him. She wasn't going to leave her mother, and that was final. Yet 23 Lily Street was only half a mile away and Carly was always popping over to spend time with him, cook on the tiny stove, or make still-awkward love on the rickety, single bed.

Then came a further blow. Grant's mother redirected a letter from Tony Preston at Decca. His eyes shot down the few short paragraphs, hoping to find the words he wanted to see, but they weren't there.

He reread the letter slowly. Decca was 'very impressed' with the Offbeats. The selection committee 'spoke highly' of their audition. They would be put on a 'list of recommended artistes'.

What the hell was that supposed to mean? Without an offer to record or sign a contract, Decca were merely keeping their options open, covering themselves so they could say they hadn't actually turned down the Offbeats. The group was 'not quite right for us at the moment'. That could mean everything or nothing, probably the latter.

Grant was very angry. Losing his temper was not something he'd done often in his adult life. Only once or twice had his anger been so great as to take him over. He crumpled up the letter in the palm of his hand and threw it at the wall.

Eventually he calmed down. A few days later, after he'd broken the news to the others, Grant retrieved the crumpled letter, smoothed it out, and put it in a file. It might make an interesting memento one day.

CHAPTER 4

At the beginning of December, the Beatles returned to Liverpool in triumph, not to play the Cavern, because that was finished now for them, but to record a TV show at the Empire and appear on *Juke Box Jury*. Grant could hardly bear to think about it. Those four and Epstein were coining it. If Eppy wasn't careful, he'd suck every last drop of luck out of Liverpool. There'd be nothing left for the hundreds and thousands of dreamers, dabblers and no-hopers who remained.

Grant didn't want to watch the Beatles' TV appearances that day, let alone think of trying to get tickets for them. He had no TV in his bedsit, anyway. If he wanted to see something very much, say the new *That Was The Week That Was* late on a Saturday, Carly's mam's set was always available. But on 7 December 1963, he wasn't even going to be in Liverpool. For the first time he was going to miss a gig and let the Offbeats look after themselves.

On that day, Grant and Carly went by train to Manchester. Margaret, Carly's cousin, was getting married to her boyfriend, Gerald, in Salford, and Carly wanted company. Her mother didn't feel up to going and told her to take Grant. 'He could do with a trip. Take him out of himself. He's not looking well.'

Carly knew also that her time would soon cease to be her own. Paradise was opening in seven days, provided the shop-fitters had finished, and that would be totally absorbing.

The wedding was a cosy, family affair. Every piece of mutton was dressed as lamb and there was a distinct smell of shampoo in the air. Carly had put on another of her self-designed numbers, Grant his suit for the hundredth time. Mancunians were a race apart, of course very different from Liverpudlians, but Grant liked them. There was a sit-down meal at a hotel near the church. Prawn cocktail, chicken, fruit salad. They were soon relaxed after a glass or two of sticky Cyprus sherry. There was a small band for the guests to dance to – sax, guitar, piano and drums.

And vocalist. Grant and Carly paid no attention to him at first. In his dinner jacket, he was singing ballads of the type popular in the fifties – 'High Hopes', 'Too Young', all very Light Programme and old-fashioned. He gave no hint of being aware of the storm the Beatles had been creating for the past year or so.

Yet he could certainly sing. Grant found himself listening and watching with close attention. The other guests were much too busy chattering, smoking and getting woozy to do the same. Carly was admiring the tuxedo. She always thought men looked good in evening dress. It was hard for them not to look smart in it. Like brides in white: even the ugliest woman bloomed radiantly when the uniform was worn.

'He's got a good voice, hasn't he?' she whispered to Grant, and he was glad to have his view confirmed. 'I wonder who he is? You ought to sign him up.'

'What would I do with him?'

'Change him. Get him to sing with the Offbeats. They need someone.'

'You reckon?'

'Yes. Go on. Have a word with him.'

The singer finished his set and finally won the attention of the guests with a sentimental rendering of 'You Are My Heart's Desire' sung directly to the bride, while her new husband fidgeted at her side.

Grant took his opportunity.

'I didn't catch your name.'

'Michael Armstrong.'

'You do a lot of this?'

'What I can. And the odd club.'

'Full time?'

'Hell, no. It doesn't pay much. I work in a warehouse.'

Grant caught sight of the cut and calloused hands, which were all too plain when you were right up close to him.

'Got an agent?' Grant asked.

'God no! I just do what the fellas tell me to.' He indicated the four musicians who were now putting away their instruments. Then he laughed, a full-throated laugh that seemed at odds with the smooth, crooning tone he had been producing. Grant noticed he smoked and drank. Maybe he was blessed with a voice that could take punishment and yet was always there when needed.

'Are you on the phone, Michael?'

'No.'

'Well, look . . .'

On the train home, heavy rain flicked against the dirty windows. Carly gave her opinion. 'He's a touch old-fashioned, I agree. All those Sinatra ballads, Jimmy Young type of thing. If only he'd sing more up-to-date material, he'd be really good.'

'He's willing to try.'

'He is? Well, there you are then.'

'And change his name. I talked to him. You can't sing and be called Michael Armstrong.'

'How'd he feel about that?'

'He didn't mind when I asked him.'

'So you did?'

'Yes. I'm going to see what I can do for him. Manage him.'

'Great. You won't regret it.'

'No. He can sing in key, and he's a damn sight sexier than the Offbeats. Just think what he could do with a tighter pair of pants.'

Carly was delighted by Grant's enthusiasm. Never mind if she would be overstretched from now on by the shop. She'd do all she could to help. 'He's certainly kind of nice. Attractive. I wonder how the boys'll take to him?'

'I'm not looking forward to it. It may help that he's not from Liverpool. All that could count against people when the Beatles thing dies out. But he's a find, isn't he? The Pool's getting fished dry. After Epstein's had his pick, and the London agents have been on their fishing trips, there's not much left. But they won't know about Michael. I'm going to see how to sign him up.'

Carly loved Grant's big talk. He was getting into his stride.

'Will you help me, Carly?' he asked. 'Give him a going-over? I think he could be really big, and I value your opinion.'

'Okay, Eppy . . .'

When they reached Central Station, Grant walked her all the way up to Lily Street in the rain. On the doorstep, he kissed her but didn't go in. Then he went back to his bedsit where he lay awake for several hours, planning the future, too excited to sleep.

Denis had to be dealt with. It was still in a way 'his' group.

'I've got an idea,' Grant told him, bluntly. 'How about getting a singer?'

'For the Offbeats?'

'Yes.'

'Like who, for Christ's sake? What's wrong with me?'

'You're great, but drummers can't sing.'

'What about Dave Clark?'

'A freak. Not even sure he plays his own drums. Somebody may do it for him. That's the rumour anyway.'

'What about Roger, Paddie?'

'Neither's outstanding.'

'Thanks a lot, mate. Don't tell me, you've got someone in mind.'

So Grant told Denis about Michael Armstrong. He had the quality. He just needed to be nudged towards more up-to-date material. If it didn't work, it didn't work, but they had to do *something* to give the Offbeats a new lease of life. The vague promises made after the Decca audition were obviously leading nowhere. They must find new talent. Michael Armstrong could be it.

Denis didn't take to the idea. He knew the move would mark the end of his own ambitions to head a group that would make the big time. How was it that Grant had got into this position of control? His mother had had a soft spot for Grant from the moment he turned up to do that crappy audition. Then he had engineered her removal. Now look what was happening.

One evening Michael was brought over from Salford and tried out on a few of the numbers which the Offbeats usually sang themselves. He was good and the Offbeats' initial resentment at having him imposed on them began to melt in the heat of music-making.

'You're quite a little rocker, aren't you?' Grant told him.

At Grant's specific request, Denis's mother had been allowed back in to watch and listen. Grant astutely realized that Michael was likely to appeal to her, too. She gave her stamp of approval. The fact that an older woman appreciated Michael's act was a bonus. 'We've got to be different,' was how Grant explained it. 'We've got to appeal to more than just kids. Michael can appeal to all ages. All we've got to do is find the right songs for him.'

Carly gave up her job selling shoes two days before opening Paradise. The shop-fitters were putting last-minute touches to the racks and changing cubicles. They weren't terribly sure what she meant when she told them, 'I want it to look like . . . Paradise!'

'Yes, but what colour were you thinkin' of, miss?'

'You know, all the colours of the rainbow.'

They did their best. Carly was more concerned to see that her stock arrived on time. There was to be no skirt longer than a mini and the two hundred she'd ordered to her own designs from the factory in Warrington hadn't materialized yet.

'And a boutique without minis would be like a pub with no beer.'

Eventually, they did arrive and Grant had a wonderful time helping her unpack them, imagining what would one day get wrapped inside the skirts.

There was a small consignment of PVC caps and raincoats, sent from London. Carly had to restrain herself from trying on each one. The only real disappointment was that she couldn't manage to sell the complete package – so no boots or shoes. Too expensive, and best sold by a specialist shop.

Grant tentatively helped her put out the stock for the menswear section. He'd known nothing like this at Hendersons: narrow leather ties and waistcoats, black polo-neck sweaters, high-collared shirts, narrow pants.

He was worried that Carly had taken on too much.

'It'll be *all right*, Grant. Don't be such a fusser. The worst that can happen is I can go bankrupt, but we'll have had a lot of laughs along the way.'

'Your confidence puts me to shame.'

Grant was puzzled by Carly's choice of Fawn as one of her assistants. 'She's such a lump. She'll put people off. Bad for your image. Not exactly my idea of Paradise.'

'Oh, you and your image. You're always on about that. Rather Fawn than some fashion piece who'd make my customers feel inferior, that they could never look good in mod clothes.'

Then there was the question of the guest list for the launch party on the Friday night. There wasn't much room in the shop and only fifty friends and potential spenders had been invited.

'You don't want them spilling wine and cheese all over your stock,' said Grant. 'Why did you invite so many?'

That wasn't the problem, though, when the day arrived. For Grant, the party was marred by Tom Sheridan's presence. He could see how Carly's eyes lit up the moment Tom walked in and started touching her. Him and his easy charm, his jokes, and his sexy ways.

'Why did you invite him, of all people?' he asked her, when he could get her on her own.

'I didn't. He invited himself. Gate-crashed, but what else do you expect? I haven't set eyes on him since, well, since you know what, but now he's here, he's here.'

'I've a good mind to kick him out.'

'No, Grant, please. He's been very nice and said he was sorry.'

'Huh.'

'And, anyway, if it hadn't been for him getting that picture of me in the *Echo*, all this might never have happened. It was a great help. Let bygones be bygones.'

Next morning, Paradise opened officially for custom and although many of the young people who strayed through the door were 'only browsing, thank you', Carly sold enough to give her high hopes for the future. She was going to keep on working hard, and playing hard, too.

Tom Sheridan was one of the first customers, though where he'd found the money to pay for his polka-dot shirt, Carly couldn't think.

'Say,' he said, 'you need more publicity. I'll do you a leaflet, that's what. I'll paint a picture of all these goddesses wearing fashions in Paradise. I'll even write you a pome to go with it.'

'That'd be great. Thanks.'

Carly caught that look in his eye once more. Never mind if she never heard of the leaflet again, she was sure Tom would be in and out of the shop on any excuse from now on – just at the time when Grant was preoccupied with his business affairs elsewhere.

* * *

On a cold Saturday in January, the dancers at the Apollo Social Club in Dingle were privileged, though they weren't aware of it, to hear the first public performance by Johnny Todd and the Offbeats.

'Who the fuck's Johnny Todd?' Tom Sheridan asked Carly when he heard about the newcomer.

'Grant's new discovery,' she replied. 'His real name's Michael Armstrong. Comes from Manchester.'

'Not Scouse, eh? That's a bit of cheek, calling himself Johnny Todd.'

'It was Grant's idea.'

'He should be fucking shot.'

There was something to be said for Tom's view. 'Johnny Todd' was a name Grant had taken from an old Liverpool sea shanty, 'Johnny the Sailor Boy'. The tune had recently been adapted as the theme for *Z Cars* on TV. But 'Johnny Todd' sounded like a good name, Grant thought, and there was to be no arguing.

'Now you leave Grant alone,' Carly said. 'He's doing a great job for the Offbeats.'

'And a great job for you, too, so I've heard.'

Carly blushed and looked away. 'Gerroff, Tom. He's very nice. Treats me a good deal properer than you ever did.'

'He's only using you. Getting you to do the cozzies, and all. He'll suck you dry and spit you out, you'll see.'

'Look who's talking.'

'We'll see who's right, Carly. I'll still be waiting when that stuck-up twat's got bored with you.'

'Rubbish. You'll still be waiting, sure. Waiting and waiting. What are you up to anyway? You're not exactly doing well for yerself, are yer?'

'I hear he got you the money for your shop, and all.'

'No, he didn't. It was his Uncle Trevor did that. Not the same at all. Grant's a good deal more help to me than you've ever been.'

'But I'm doing you a leaflet, aren't I?' Tom stalked off with another oath. It was back to the way things used to be. Carly hated this awkwardness between them. She still fancied Tom, but she wasn't going to let him rubbish Grant the way he always did and interfere with the help they gave each other's businesses.

Grant knew he'd made the right decision when his white hope said to him after playing another gig: 'I like the name. Never call me Mike again, will you?'

'Of course not, *Johnny*,' Grant grinned. 'I'm glad you like it. How about Maureen, though? Will she mind?'

'She likes it, too.'

Grant wasn't sure that Johnny was telling the truth. He could see that a wife who'd married 'Michael Armstrong' mightn't take to waking up with 'Johnny Todd' in her bed. But there wasn't much Grant could or wanted to do about it – except to make sure Maureen was kept out of the way. She was given strict instructions never to be around when her husband appeared in public, nor to draw attention to the fact she was married to him. Wives were 'bad for the image', according to Grant. This was hard on Maureen, particularly as in those early months of 1964 she learned she was expecting their first child.

Johnny made reassuring noises but he had already seized on his new status as a rock 'n' roll singer to obtain sex elsewhere. The job Grant and Carly had done on Johnny was highly successful in producing a willing reaction in female fans. His hair had been allowed to grow longer and tumble wildly about his ears. His earthy quality was emphasized by his new costume. Carly found him someone who could make a leather suit, out of which he would appear to burst without actually doing it any damage. His hairy chest was allowed to hint itself at the top of his open-necked shirt. His boots had substantial heels which gave him that extra stature he needed, as well as knocking his knees forward to emphasize his powerful thighs and legs.

People who had been entertained by Johnny at cosy dances, weddings and barmitzvahs in Manchester a few months before would hardly have recognized him now. Johnny enjoyed the difference. Women had never thrown themselves at 'Michael Armstrong', but they were all eager to get into Johnny Todd's trousers. Faithful Mickey and George now had new tasks: protecting Johnny from screaming fans, and standing guard outside the door while the 'star' took his pleasure inside.

Johnny soon had it down to a fine art. Excited to bursting point by an evening's gyrations and pelvic thrusts, he would be pouring sweat to the point that his leathers had to be peeled off. A slow and laborious process this, so he kept them on until he went home. He could just about work down the stiff zipper at the front.

On one occasion, he found himself faced with pubescent twins after Mickey had said they couldn't possibly be split up. They were dressed in identical short skirts and little white boots. They had identical blonde haircuts and urchin faces. Johnny shook them by the hand, rather formally, and then casually picked one and kissed her while the sister looked on.

'What are you called?' he asked.

'I'm Thelma. That's Rosemary.'

'Well, Thelma . . .'

He didn't have to wait long. Her hand glided down his damp shirtfront to the big clasp on his belt, then on to the tight leather of his trousers.

That was Johnny's cue. He awkwardly unzipped. Thelma was despatched in a minute and Rosemary lifted on in her place, while the sister watched. It was an excellent trick and after he had kissed the grateful, giggling girls goodbye, it wasn't long before they spread word of their joint conquest.

Grant was in two minds about Johnny's sexual activities.

He felt envious of the certain pull Johnny so obviously exerted over an audience. He felt, too, that it was a tawdry, unsatisfactory way of carrying on. He was aroused and repulsed by it, equally. It would be a pity if it got out of hand. How would it be if he got a girl into trouble? Or if his wife cut up rough?

For Johnny, the sex was almost reward enough for his night's work, though he wasn't going to tell Grant that, of course. Johnny had natural intelligence rather than intellect. He could sense what was going on, when he was being manipulated, and also when it was in his interests to go along with that. His verbal skills were no match for his physical ones. He didn't have arguments with Grant over money so much as inarticulate sessions in which he attempted to get a better deal for himself without actually saying what he was after. His chief weapon was persistence.

'But you know, Johnny,' Grant would explain patiently, as if to a child, 'everybody's cut went down when you joined us. Even mine! It's a six-way cut now, rather than five.'

'Yes, I see that,' Johnny drawled, 'but I'm just not too happy about it . . .'

Being 'not too happy about it' became a catchphrase.

'You've got to be happy,' Grant told him. 'Leave it with me. But don't forget, we do provide you with transport. And there's your leathers. They cost a fortune. It all adds up, you know.'

Grant didn't explain that the van was still on loan from Spencer. The group was using it on sufferance. He didn't explain, either, that the leathers weren't actually paid for and wouldn't be unless the manufacturers sent in the heavy mob.

One Sunday afternoon in February, Grant and Carly took time off from worrying over money and their two businesses. They did so in the best way they knew, by making love. Afterwards, they lay clutching each other tightly in the narrow bed at Grant's flat. His love-making was improving, though Carly still had to tell him to relax. He was always so tense, and not nearly as sure as Tom.

Unaware of the comparison, Grant nestled against her warm breasts and smelt the naked skin, untainted with perfume. Life was wonderful, for a moment or two, around love-making. Then, as the effect wore off, Grant felt his customary niggle of nervousness return.

'Johnny's been on at me about money again.'

'So, what's new?' asked Carly.

'I've got to do something about money soon,' Grant went on. 'Unlike you, unlike everyone else in this racket – if you leave aside Mickey and George – I don't have a job. I'm skint. I've got to get more money if I'm to make a go of this.'

'Why not ask your Uncle Trevor?'

'You got in first. We've been through that. I can't keep begging off him.'

'Tell you what, I could almost pay back the money he lent me. We've made enough at Paradise since Christmas.'

'You mean that?'

'Why not? I don't like borrowing money, any road. If I paid it back, he'd let you have it.'

Grant swallowed his pride and paid another visit to Old Trevor. The old man said yes, Grant could take over the money from Carly. He had no one else to spend it on. Grant accepted gratefully, promising it would be repaid a thousandfold when success struck.

'I tell you what,' he said, 'can I pay it back when I have my first really big hit . . . on the stage. I don't know what it'll be, but you'd like that, wouldn't you?'

'That's all right by me, lad. I suppose it's only a matter of time before you'll go away. Leave town.'

'What?' Grant was surprised at the old man's suggestion. It was true, but he hadn't admitted it even to himself.

'It's odd, isn't it?' he mused. 'People say coming from Liverpool's important, but they have to leave to be successful.'

'That's right. As long as you're Scouse to start with, that's the main thing. Bit of iron in you, bit of edge, bit of soppiness too. That's what it means.'

'I hope so.' Grant smiled. 'Not so sure about the soppiness.'

Old Trevor asked him what name Grant would give his outfit when it was properly established.

'I've no idea. I haven't thought.'

'Something with "Star" in it,' the old man suggested, his eyes brightening at the thought. 'That'll raise people's hopes. My dad used to work for Cunard White Star, you know, in the steamship days. Funny that, Liverpool once known for boats, now for beat.'

The right name fell into Grant's head, ready-made. 'How about "Starfinders"? That's what I'd be doing, wouldn't I? Finding stars of the future.'

'That sounds just proper, lad. Starfinders it is. But you'll have to live up to it. And you'd better start soon . . .'

CHAPTER 5

'Hey, Carl-o, coming to see me on Saturday?'

It was Tom Sheridan who had pushed his way into Carly's tiny office at the back of Paradise. She was trying to sort out her accounts, her face getting longer and longer.

'Why, what's happening on Saturday?'

'I've got a gig in Wavertree.'

'What sort of gig?'

'With a band called Sauce. I'm going to be their singer.'

'That's great, Tom. I'll tell Grant.'

Tom pulled a face. 'No need. Why not come on your own? He'll be too busy to bother with a small, insignificant show like ours. Eh?'

Carly began to plod through a bundle of invoices and receipts.

'I can't really talk, Tom. I've got to get this done. The books are in a terrible mess.'

'Making lots of money?'

'No. That's the trouble. I don't know why it is. I thought we were. I've just paid back my first loan. Perhaps I shouldn't have.'

'There's usually someone in here whenever I go past. And it's always packed on Saturdays.'

'Yes, but a hell of a lot of them just try on clothes and never buy them.'

'But you must sell some.'

'Yes, we do, but we don't seem to make much money.'

'Maybe your prices are too low.'

'But that's what I want. I don't want to charge ridiculous prices to kids.'

Tom started playing with a paper clip he picked off her

desk. He straightened it out, then bent it into a new shape.

'So you won't be able to come then?'

'Where, luv?'

'To hear me sing.'

'Oh, sorry, I'd really like to, Tom. I'm real glad you've got fixed up, but . . .'

'Okay, some other time then. By the way, that geezer Pickering's not the only bloke in town, y'know.'

Carly turned to him, smiled, and put her hand on his. Tom saw the tears and put his arm round her.

'Am I forgiven, then?'

'For what?' Carly sniffed into a handkerchief.

'Being a bad boy. You know.'

' 'Course you are. There's nothing to forgive.'

'Well, I hope you can sort out everything. The shop, I mean. You're a brave kid, taking it on. Amazing, in fact.'

'Thanks, Tom, and good luck Saturday. It's about time you had a few breaks.'

Having a name for Grant's company helped when it came to drawing up a contract with Johnny Todd. This followed hard on what for them amounted to a raised-voice quarrel.

Johnny had thought there would be nothing wrong in slipping back to being 'Michael Armstrong' when asked to sing at another couple of weddings in Manchester. It was reassuring to him to know that his rocking with the Offbeats hadn't interfered with his ability to sing old-fashioned ballads, or ruined his voice.

Grant took a different view when word of Johnny's double life dribbled over from Manchester.

'We've got to get this sorted out, in writing,' he said. 'We can't have you running off on your own.'

'Well, I'd not be very happy if –'

'I don't give a shit whether you're happy when it comes to this one. What you're doing is just not on. Quite illegal.'

Grant was bluffing. There was nothing in writing about

such matters. Still, he sensed that if you stated firmly that something was *so*, people even less informed about the law than you would be inclined to believe it.

Johnny said nothing. It was slightly pathetic, Grant thought, to see the great heart-throb humbled by these mundane considerations. He heard himself giving a little speech of the kind he would rather have avoided. 'Let's face it, Johnny, you don't do too badly out of us. I know the money's not great, but we do look after you and there's everything to look forward to. The fringe benefits are pretty good, by all accounts . . .'

Johnny gave a shy grin. 'Oh, sure.' Grant didn't have to threaten to tell Maureen.

'We've got to get all this sorted out,' Grant repeated. 'Down on paper.'

Johnny meekly agreed.

It was quickly done. Grant committed himself to using his 'best efforts' to promote Johnny Todd under what was grandly described as an 'exclusive management agreement'. Grant was now formally a manager.

The audience was bewildered. The kind of music played by Sauce was not what they had been expecting at all. Tom Sheridan failed to make an impression with his singing. Just because he and the line-up of Sauce liked the blues didn't mean the audience at the Wavertree social club would. They'd expected pop music; this stuff was incomprehensible.

The fact that what Tom and the band played was good made no difference. It was hard to dance to and, worse, lacked familiarity. Tom's first proper gig as a singer failed almost before it began. On reflection, he was glad that Carly hadn't managed to be there. He had no wish for her to witness his humiliation. The trouble was, given the flop, no other girl was going to look at him either.

What Tom and Sauce lacked was a person who could

knock them into shape, get them to smarten up their dress and presentation, sharpen up their choice of material, add a little discipline. Yet what would a group vaguely believing in anarchy do with a manager like Grant Pickering? They represented two widely different approaches to entertainment. For the moment, it did not look as if they would ever get together.

Grant felt it was time to eat humble pie and approach Decca again. He waited until he had received a batch of notepaper with 'Starfinders' emblazoned on the top. The notepaper had been delayed until a telephone was installed. Then he was ready and set. Rather grandly, he was able to give his address as 'Huskisson Chambers'. In fact, he had only a third of a chamber to live in and run his agency from.

Next, Grant obtained a tape of Johnny Todd from an amateur recordist who'd been allowed to record one of his performances. It wasn't a professional job. With only one Reslo ribbon microphone at his disposal, the recordist had had to favour Johnny. The Offbeats stayed firmly in the background. That, however, reflected their status in those days.

The best thing about the recording was that it was of a live performance. The fans' screams could be heard, and so could the husky rawness of Johnny at his best. Grant carefully packed the five-inch spool of Scotch recording tape, worried that a speed of 3¾ inches per second would be wrong for Decca. But it would have to do.

A week went by, and then the phone rang in Grant's office. It was the first call he'd received and it startled him.

'Can I speak to Mr Pickering? It's Tony Preston of Decca.'

Grant wondered whether to pretend to be an assistant and do the 'putting you through now' routine, but he was so eager to hear what Preston was calling about that he simply said, 'Speaking.'

'Thank you for letting me hear Johnny Todd.'

'The tape was all right then? You were able to play it?'

'Yes, but what does he look like? You didn't send us a photo.'

'Oh, sorry, must have got lost in the post.' Starfinders hadn't yet been able to afford photographs of Johnny.

'When can I see him?'

'He'll come to see you, I'm sure.'

'No. Just tell me when he's next appearing and I'll pop up and see him.'

Grant was very much alone in those days. Starfinders was him. He had no secretary, no one to talk to. Carly was supportive, of course, but she had her own business to worry about now. And everyone else seemed to be in some way against him – the Offbeats, the people who booked them for gigs, even Johnny Todd up to a point. They weren't exactly *for* him, anyway. He had to dig into himself to find those resources of courage and confidence to get him through.

If anything carried Grant forward, it was a feeling that somehow the world owed him, if not a living, then success. It was difficult to say where the feeling came from. His parents hadn't an ounce of show business in them. They knew nothing of management. They couldn't begin to imagine how he earned even what little money he did earn.

He had entered a new world, and God's gift to him was a conviction that if there were prizes to be won, he was going to win one. He convinced himself that the Offbeats' rivals were even worse than they were, with no talent at all.

Then he would think of the Beatles. Weren't they genuinely talented? Grant had to admit they were a little. But chiefly they'd had luck. He believed in luck. That was the first step to acquiring it.

Telling Carly about the Decca interest, he held her tight, to absorb some of the confidence she gave so readily.

'You're doing all right,' she told him, touching one of his clenched fists with a single finger to make him relax. It was a gesture she was to repeat many times during the weeks to come, symbolic of her faith in him and her devotion.

'Fugginell,' he exclaimed, 'I'd never've got mixed up in all this if I'd known what it was like.'

'You wish you were still selling suits?' Carly looked at him, pointedly. 'Some people would give their eyes to be doing what you're doing, y'know.'

'I know.'

He asked Carly to be with him the day the man from Decca came up to Liverpool.

Grant had leant on one of his contacts to insert Johnny Todd and the Offbeats into a Big Beat Session at the Tower Ballroom, New Brighton, so that Tony Preston could hear them. They wouldn't get paid, but that wasn't the point, as he patiently explained to them. Mickey and George were told to pick up Johnny from his warehouse in Manchester and deliver him safely to the seaside resort over the Mersey from Liverpool. Grant and Carly would meet Preston at Lime Street and escort him there.

When the day arrived, Grant had to pick up Carly from Lily Street. He was met at the door by Mrs Scott.

'She'll be down in a mo, luv. Just changing.' Grant sat in the parlour, eyeing the china huntsman and shepherdess on the mantelpiece and looking at his watch every half-minute. Carly's mam chatted to him amiably but he didn't take in much of what she said.

Eventually, cutting it fine, Carly appeared wearing a bold black and white check frock. Over it she wore a shiny black PVC raincoat with a matching cap, like a helmet. She had on her white boots, too.

'Well, March winds won't blow you away. Come on!'

They half walked, half ran down the hill all the way to Lime Street. They had no car to offer Tony Preston, so they improvised. He'd like to walk down to the Pier Head, wouldn't he? See a bit of the city on the way . . .

'Yes, I'd love to.'

They took him down past the Royal Court Theatre and the Playhouse, across Williamson Square, then turned left.

'That's NEMS where somebody called Epstein used to work,' Grant commented. They crossed the road and walked up to the Cavern entrance where already a queue of beehive hairdos was awaiting the evening session.

With brisk March winds whisking their own hair about, they finally boarded the ferry for New Brighton. Slowly they steamed past the docks and the low-lying shore, then over to the other side. Tony Preston seemed delighted. 'I've heard so much about all this,' he said. 'I'm really glad to see it.'

At the Tower Ballroom, the Offbeats were all present and correct; Johnny Todd, however, hadn't turned up. He was due on at nine thirty and there was less than an hour to go. A well-established group called the Undertakers was playing. Grant kept talking so that Preston wouldn't be able to hear and sign them up instead.

Breathlessly, just after nine, when Grant had almost given up hope, Mickey and George arrived with Johnny in a minicab. They'd been involved in an accident on the East Lancashire Road.

'The van's a write-off, I'm afraid,' Mickey told Grant. 'Not our fault, you know.'

'Of course not,' Grant sighed, bleakly foreseeing endless fuss with Spencer over insurance. 'But still, you got here. Tony, I'd like you to meet Johnny Todd.'

'Pleased to meet you, Mr Preston,' said Johnny with a boyish grin. He wiped his hand on the seat of his pants before extending it.

'Looking forward to hearing you, Johnny,' said Preston primly, shaking his hand.

'So am I,' added Johnny, with an attempt at humour. ' 'Scuse me, I've got to get my kecks on.'

'His trousers,' Grant explained. 'A very important part of his act.' They laughed, and the tension eased for a moment.

There wasn't enough time in a guest spot for Johnny to get the audience quite in the palm of his hand, as he was capable of, but Preston appeared to like what he saw. As Johnny worked his way through his best numbers, Preston turned and whispered to Grant, 'He certainly seems to wear his, er, equipment on his sleeve.'

Grant laughed loudly.

Carly stood on one side, worrying over her own business problems. She hadn't really been able to spare the time this evening, but when Grant asked, she felt she had to respond.

Next morning, Grant was down at the Adelphi having breakfast with Tony Preston – grapefruit segments, a 'full house' of fried things, including the pink delicacy called Ulster Fry, black puddings, lashings of eggs and fried potatoes. Preston wolfed it down, as if on a visit from another planet. And in a sense he was.

Over the toast and marmalade he finally got round to telling Grant what he felt about the previous evening's entertainment.

'I like Johnny. You've got a good property there, no doubt about it. But something needs to be done about the group.'

Grant's heart sank at the prospect of more wrangling with Denis. 'Such as?'

'Change of name. "Offbeats" is awful, frankly. Makes them sound out of tune.'

'Yes, yes, of course, I'll change it. No trouble.'

'So what'll it be?'

' "Johnny Todd and the Troglodytes" sort of thing, you mean?'

'Yes. You can't have Troggs, though. You've been beaten to it.'

' "Johnny Todd and the Travellers, Tourists, Teds . . ."

I tell you, ''Johnny Todd and the Knee-Tremblers'' would be kind of descriptive.'

'Maybe, but I don't think the world of pop's quite ready for that just yet. The other day, you know, I had an audition tape from a group calling themselves The Erection. I ask you! But ''Teds'' isn't too bad. Let's think about that. Then there's the question of material. What we've got to do is find him his own song.'

'Oh, I agree, absolutely,' said Grant, hardly able to contain himself. It wasn't being said in so many words, but a deal was in the making.

A few months later, in early August 1964, a song was found. 'You've Got What It Takes' was an ideal mix of ballad and rock; it might have been written with Johnny in mind.

The Starfinders van once more set off for London. Not Spencer's van, which had been sold off as scrap metal after the crash. This time Starfinders had had to hire one.

The chief number recorded was 'You've Got What It Takes' (coupled with the B side, 'Never'), during which Preston quietly told Grant that the disc would be released under the name of 'Johnny Todd and the Modds'.

'But they're not mods, they're rockers,' Grant objected.

'I know,' said Preston. 'But if you spell it M-o-d-d-s, that's a nice twist, and you get to please *two* audiences.'

Grant couldn't face having to tell Denis, so he decided to postpone telling anyone until it was too late for them to object.

He was learning.

Tom Sheridan picked up on the grapevine that Grant had pulled off a coup. Could it be that Grant had something after all? If he could realize the potential of a minor talent like Johnny Todd, what could he do for a major talent like Tom Sheridan?

Tom invited himself in for a talk. By now, Grant had rented proper office accommodation in Whitechapel. Two rooms, one for himself, the other for a shorthand-typist called Janice whom Carly had persuaded him to take on. Tom shuffled in. Grant told him to sit down and make himself comfortable. There was a table between them.

Tom didn't waste time. 'I want you to take me on.'

'On my books? You must be joking!'

'No, I'm not. I need someone to help me, and you're obviously the person. First, there's the poetry. I see a great future in that. Readings and so on. And there's my songs.'

Grant choked. He didn't want Tom anywhere near him – or Carly. And the man's arrogance was unbelievable. Grant held on tight to his anger, then abruptly told Tom to get the hell out. Tom had no marketable talent, he wasn't going to waste time on him.

Tom said nothing, for once, but bolted from the office.

Grant sat at his desk smoothing his fingernails, tense and preoccupied, unable to get on with anything else.

Ten minutes later, Tom reappeared with Carly. He had gone straight to Paradise and pulled her out to plead his case.

'Carly? What the hell –?'

'Grant, look, I'm sorry, I know I shouldn't be here at all, but you really should think about taking Tom on. He's got talent, bags of it. And it won't do you any harm. If it doesn't work, it doesn't work.'

'Carly, I wish you wouldn't get involved in these things.'

'I didn't have much choice.'

Grant knew he didn't have much choice either.

'All right then,' he said finally, 'sit down, both of you. I tell you what.' He stood, not looking Tom in the eye. 'There's a way of doing things I've just heard about. We can sign an agreement. It would be exclusive. Whatever you earn from performing or writing is handled by me, and me alone. I take twenty-five per cent in your case. But if at the end of a year you haven't earned more than a certain amount, say five hundred pounds, that's a tenner a week, so not too difficult, the agreement is broken and we can split.'

Tom didn't like the sound of the twenty-five per cent, but otherwise it seemed a fair deal. Actually, he'd have accepted on any terms.

'I'll do what I can,' Tom said piously. 'And behave. I promise.'

Carly moved over and kissed Grant. 'Now I really must get back.'

'Don't I get a kiss?' asked Tom. 'Thanks, Carly, you're an angel.'

'Good,' said Grant, walking to the door. 'All we need is a song for you to record.'

'I've got a song,' Tom said confidently.

Grant put him down: '*Another* song was what I had in mind.'

Johnny was used to being ribbed by his workmates about his singing. His job at the Co-op warehouse in Manchester was to gather together a list of items required by a particular store and get them ready for putting on the lorry.

It paid reasonably, it was indoors, but it was a long way from the bright lights of show business which Johnny had glimpsed since Grant Pickering went to work on him.

'What kind of songs is it you sing, boyo?' asked Taff, wheezing on a Woodbine.

'Nothing you'd know about. Have you ever heard "Boney Moroni"?'

'Who's he?'

'It's a song, fatso. It goes like this.'

Johnny stood up in the middle of the canteen and sang it unaccompanied, just as he would on a Saturday night, with all the leg movements and the pelvic thrusts. The canteen ladies looked up from cutting rounds of sandwiches. Their eyes widened.

Cyril the foreman narrowed his eyes and concentrated on

the racing form in the *Mirror*. He didn't like to see his men show off.

At the end, there was a round of applause.

'So when's your next record coming out?' one of the women asked cheerily.

'I don't know about that,' said Johnny with fetching modesty. He scratched his crutch and begged another cup of tea, which they gave him free.

Then it was back to stacking. Stacking. Stacking. Singing was the only escape from the drudgery. He might have looked forward to going home to Maureen of an evening, but now she was in an advanced state of pregnancy things weren't the same between them. Certainly not the sex.

Singing and the women it enabled him to pull were all that he had. He saw his working life stretching ahead of him for ever, day after day of stacking. He dreamed of escape but it didn't seem likely. Where he came from, people simply didn't escape.

Or perhaps they could nowadays . . .

Grant started to badger Johnny about doing lunchtime sessions at the Cavern. But to do them would mean his taking a whole day off work. The Modds could slip away from their jobs in Liverpool, just about, but he had to travel over from Manchester. So it was impossible. Grant made his displeasure clear. It was holding back Johnny's development as an artiste.

Johnny saw the crunch coming. He would have to decide one way or the other: give up his job in the warehouse, or give up all hope of making it as a singer.

In the end, it wasn't such a hard decision. The release date for 'You've Got What It Takes' by Johnny Todd and the Modds was set for mid-September. In the meantime, publicity and marketing men set about Johnny. He was bought a new set of leathers. He was told to make no mention of his real name, and certainly not that he had a wife. Then, with Grant's agreement, he and the Modds were told to make no mention of Liverpool either. They were simply a 'Northern group'. No need to drag Liverpool into it. Johnny took unpaid leave from his job for the launch of his disc, and Cyril the foreman told him through clenched teeth that his job would still be there if he failed at 'this pop thing'.

The Modds made their own arrangements for getting days off work. They weren't going to miss any of this, even though there was an undercurrent of resentment at the way they'd been relegated to the status of backing group. They were equally resentful of the ridiculous name Decca had stuck on them. It was only a matter of time before the resentment would boil over.

As the day drew near for the record's release, Johnny discovered that he'd given up his job only to spend days on end doing nothing at home with Maureen, who got on his nerves with her pregnancy. The publicity machine didn't appear to be delivering. Nothing seemed to happen at all. Then Brian Matthew played the record on the Light Programme's *Saturday Club*. Also, so someone said, it was very popular on Radio Caroline, the pirate station.

Johnny took to going into record shops and hanging about, even asking to listen to the record in one of the small booths provided. But no one recognized him. There was nothing to recognize yet.

Then, three weeks after the release (during which Starfinders was paying Johnny an 'advance' equivalent to what he would have earned at the warehouse, and running up its first overdraft in the process) he was in a record shop in Deansgate, Manchester. His heart leapt when he saw a girl of sixteen or seventeen clutching *his* record, with four shillings and ninepence in her hand, making for the till.

Johnny was childishly delighted at this and wanted to tell the girl who he was and thank her. Instead, he ran out of the shop, leapt into the air, and rang up Grant to tell him.

'Thank God, you rang. When are you going to get a telephone?'

'When I've earned some money.'

'Yes, yes, now listen. This is the biggy. They want you to appear on *Thank Your Lucky Stars*. They record it in Birmingham a week tomorrow, then they show it the following Saturday.'

Johnny made a whooping noise. 'You bet!'

He went straight home to tell Maureen. She was glad for Johnny, though she knew it would only take him further away from home.

Johnny would never forget his first TV recording: 17 October 1964. Throughout the day they spent at Aston, Grant noticed something about his budding star. He was without nerves. It couldn't be said that he was 'cool' or had 'nerves of steel'. He was much too sweaty and earthy for that, but he had a natural calm at the centre of his being. It was as if he were absolutely confident he'd be accepted on his own terms.

Jim Dale was introducing the programme and billed Johnny as a 'fabulous new discovery' whom he was 'sure you viewers are going to enjoy'. The audience, mostly girls, yelped and squealed to order, as though more than willing to help the new man on his way.

During rehearsal Johnny had kept looking up to see his face on a monitor. For the recording, the director had to tell the floor manager to turn it away so he couldn't see it. At the playback afterwards, Johnny sat stupefied by his own image, glistening with sweat, on the black and white screen. He wasn't disappointed with what he saw and heard.

The Modds were. They were hardly visible at all in the gloom behind Johnny. Even during the instrumental break, when they might have expected to be featured, the director was too busy pushing his cameras round tricky bits of scenery. Denis Northington was so put out he vowed he wouldn't even bother to watch when it was broadcast.

They drove back to Liverpool in the hired van with not a

word spoken. Johnny just sat there, bathed in elation, so high he could have travelled home without the van to carry him.

'That'll sell some records, won't it?' he asked Grant, when they dropped him off in Salford.

'I hope so, Johnny, I certainly hope so. Then all we have to do is wait for the money. I'm afraid it'll be a long time.'

Johnny wasn't bothered about that right now. He was so excited he hardly slept a wink all week.

The day before the *Lucky Stars* broadcast, Janice put her head round Grant's door and told him there was someone to see him. 'She says you know 'er.'

'Who is it then?' Grant dropped his voice, annoyed at being put on the spot like this by an unannounced caller and by his secretary.

'She says she's called Fawn Flack.'

'Okay, show her in.'

If there was one woman Grant had no wish to see in his office, it was lumpy Fawn. It was bad enough seeing her at Paradise where she worked for Carly. Perhaps she was bringing a message?

She came in looking like an unmade bed, as always. Folksy, drab and dreary.

'What can I do for you, Fawn?'

'Carly told me I should speak to you.'

'What about? The shop?'

'No. I want to be a folk singer. I want you to manage me.'

Grant couldn't believe it. Was this what you had to put up with if you had a business called Starfinders? A stream of no-hopers wanting to get on your books?

'But you've never sung in your life!'

'Yes, I have. It's just you've never heard me.'

'You're right, Fawn. What makes you think you've got anything to offer?'

'I *know* I have. I've been practising for zillions of years.'

Grant laughed at Fawn's innocence and yet was struck by the nerve she had, simply coming to make her proposal.

'You can't just announce you've got talent. You've got to prove it.'

'I'm willing to, given the chance.'

Grant felt trapped. He didn't want to have to bother about Fawn. First it had been Tom Sheridan, and now her, sitting there, practising her obnoxious form of arm-twisting. He looked at the matted hair, the National Health specs, the drab dress, the scuffed shoes. She was a baggage; never in a thousand years would she be able to make herself presentable.

'Why've you suddenly come here, Fawn?'

'Well, Tom Sheridan said you were going to make him a star, so I thought you could do the same for me.'

'Oh, he did, did he? It doesn't work like that, Fawn. Nothing doing, I'm afraid. I'm busy. I've got work to do.'

Fawn wondered what on earth Carly saw in him.

'Well, I'll show you. You wait and see,' she said. 'When I'm a famous star, you'll have to come and grovel. You'll miss all that ten per cent –'

'Twenty-five, actually.'

Fawn picked herself up and rushed out of Grant's office, tears pricking her eyes.

'Janice,' Grant called out, 'for God's sake bring me a cup of coffee. I need a stimulant.'

'Okay, luv,' came the voice through the door.

Five minutes later Janice waddled in bearing his coffee in the Union Jack mug with 'Be British' on the side.

'What was the matter with *her*?' Janice asked perkily.

'She's just mad. Crazy, that's all. Fat lump.'

'In the club, more like.'

Grant's head shot up. 'You really think so? She's so fat, it's hard to tell.'

'Oh, it's obvious. It's the angle it sticks out at. Me mam had six after me, so I should know.'

102

'Fawn, eh? Well, well, well.' Then Grant remembered how Rod the guitarist had been having it off with Fawn at that party in Chelsea. Had she thrown herself at someone else now?

Janice pulled a face. 'You don't 'alf know some peculiar people, if you don't mind my saying so, Mr Pickering.'

'Thank you, Janice.' Grant made to drain the coffee down in one gulp, and burned his tongue.

That night, Grant had it out with Carly.

'Fawn said you put her up to it.'

'Of course I did. Why not? It's part of your job to see people, isn't it? Just like I have to. No skin off your nose.'

'Well, I wish you wouldn't bloody well do it. I've got better ways of spending my time than thinking up reasons to tell deadbeats I don't want them. Or having to deal with them because they're up the spout.'

'Up the spout? Fawn? You're kidding!'

'She's *your* friend. Don't you know? Janice thought it was obvious from the bump on the front of her.'

'She hasn't told me. Bloody 'ell!'

'Well, it's her problem if it *is* true. What does she expect us to do? Fix an abortion with that woman in Anfield? Fork out a hundred quid? We're not a bloody charity, y'know.'

'Christ, you're bloody hard, Grant Pickering. It's not Fawn's fault if she's pregnant. We've got to help her. That's what friends are for.'

'She's no friend of mine. You're her chum.'

'Your friend's friend is *your* friend. So there.'

Grant felt walled in. He started pacing up and down, rejecting Carly's small affectionate touches; they interfered with the argument.

'I tell you, I'll get out of this place, just as soon as Johnny's record takes off,' he announced suddenly, confirming Carly's worst fears. 'There's no future for anybody. This godforsaken place drags you down.'

Carly told him flatly: 'Well, you'll have to go on your own. I can't leave Mam, or the shop. And the way you're behaving, I'm not sure I'd want to go with you.'

Grant slumped down on the couch beside her.

'Am I as bad as that?' he asked, shamefaced, putting on the little boy act he knew usually pulled Carly over to his side.

'Yes, you bleeding well are.'

'Oh Carly.' He put his arm round her shoulders, but she didn't respond. 'I've wanted to get away from here since I was born. Nothing ever happens. The Mersey Sound's a flash in the pan, anyone can see that. It's all controlled from London, anyway. You have to go down there to make the records, make it happen. There's never been anything here, really.'

All the time Grant was talking, Carly found she was thinking about Tom. She couldn't help it. She was hankering after him again.

Sensing her distraction, Grant went on, 'I *need* you, Carly. Can't you see that? You help me all the time. I mean it. You give me the courage to do the difficult things I have to do. You've got good judgement, a good eye, everything.'

He was saying all the right things. But what he said didn't change a thing for Carly. It only made a break harder.

'Let's not talk about it till it happens,' she told him softly, and swung round so she could rest her head in his lap.

Grant couldn't think of anything else to say.

Tom Sheridan was holding court in his flat in Gambier Terrace. Mickey Clinch and George Evans were still his flat-mates and purveyors of tit-bits about Grant Pickering. Tom was ever eager to hear these, if annoyed at their content.

'I don't know what he sees in that Johnny Todd.' Tom

104

began the familiar refrain. 'Singing cardboard, if ever I heard it.'

'Give over,' said the normally monosyllabic George. 'Let him alone. He's all right.'

'Not getting anywhere with that disc though, is he? I reckon Grant's got it wrong. Johnny's not a rocker, you see. He's not Liddypool either. And it's all at the expense of those Offbeats. Calling them "The Modds", I *ask* you! Fucking embarrassing. I'd never dare show me face in public with a name like that. They were a good group when they started and now they're just support for old squeaky pants.'

Mickey Clinch had heard it all before and responded by giggling, like a small woodland creature who wished no harm to anybody. 'You're jealous,' he told Tom, 'because Grant hasn't got you any work yet.'

'You're bloody well right. Not a thing. It's my belief he signed me up so nobody could get at me. Now he's just going to let me rot.'

'He's thinking of moving to London, you know, if Johnny's record does well.'

'Where did you hear that?' Tom asked, his mind working busily at the news.

'From Denis or Roger, I dunno. One of them.'

'Well, I bet if he does go he won't take any of us with him. Just Johnny.'

'Mmm.' Mickey hadn't thought of that and wondered how he'd feel at losing his link with the pop world, however menial the job.

'Doesn't bother me,' said George, unshakable as always.

Tom wondered, if Grant did go south, whether Carly would go with him. He had an idea she would not. So, it would be no bad thing if Grant and Johnny did pack their bags. He brightened at the thought, picked up his guitar and began to strum. Mickey and George both got to their feet and made for the door.

Tom didn't care. As he played on his own he was suddenly seized with an idea. If Johnny Todd were to record *his* song, that would make up for any failure on Tom's part to make his mark as a performer. He must lobby Grant about it. First, though, he'd have to write the music down and he didn't know how. Make a tape recording instead? He'd have to find someone with a machine he could cadge.

CHAPTER 6

Johnny Todd had to go back to work in the Co-op warehouse. It was humiliating, but there it was. Cyril the foreman actually said, 'I told you so', and gave him the hardest, most energetic loading jobs to do, almost as a punishment for having had ideas above his station. Johnny's workmates, who had all either seen or heard about his appearance on *Thank Your Lucky Stars*, were less inclined to crow. Even if 'You've Got What It Takes' had only reached No. 25 in the charts, that was still something. He'd had his taste of fame. A damn sight more than they would ever have, unless they won the pools.

Johnny bore up well. He tried not to lose face while loading up the canned goods cartons. He sang quite often as he worked. It made him sound as though he were contented. In fact, it was fatherhood that had put him in such unexpected good humour. Maureen had given birth to a son, David, the very week it looked as though Johnny might enter the Top Twenty. She'd had a tough time with the birth, but now she was recovering relations might improve between them. They might be able to live a normal life together if Johnny was free of fame and the distractions in skirts and boots that came with it.

Grant, equally disappointed by the setback to his ambitions, hadn't wanted to send Johnny back to the warehouse. He knew it would be a terrible come-down for him, but the record royalties would be insignificant, and they hadn't arrived yet anyway. Starfinders was still operating on a shoestring.

Soon, however, Decca said they were keen for Johnny to make a follow-up. Grant was pleasantly surprised by this,

107

barely able to fathom the way the record world operated. It appeared that as long as you fell short of complete failure, they could still be interested in you.

There was one slight change, insisted on by the record company.

'I want to drop the "Modds" part,' Tony Preston told Grant on the phone from London. 'Never was entirely happy with it.'

'Do you mean drop the name or the personnel as well?'

'No, just the name.'

Grant felt like pointing out it had been Preston's choice in the first place, but bit his tongue. 'Yes, great, I agree, Tony.'

'I think I've got a new number for Johnny. It's "One Night Stand" by Rupert and Green, two up-and-coming young lads.'

' "One Night Stand", eh?' Grant laughed. 'Sounds like the story of his life. And the B side?'

'Doesn't really matter,' said Preston. 'The boys'll run up a little something.'

'Any chance of me getting in on this carve-up?' Grant asked as sweetly as he could.

Preston didn't seem to mind. The B side wasn't important, though should the A side be a hit, the composer of the B side stood to earn an equal amount in sales revenue, even if no one ever played the B side.

'You see, I've got this other client,' Grant told Preston. 'Tom Sheridan. Bit of a poet, singer-songwriter. He's come up with a song he's been working on with Denis of the Modds.'

'Is that the Tom Sheridan who was mixed up with the Beatles?'

'No, that was Tony Sheridan. If you could see your way to putting Tom's song on the B side, sung by Johnny, of course, that would help me smooth over the disappearance of the Modds from the billing.'

'I see. Always like to be of help, Grant. You'd better let me hear the song, soon as you can.'

'I could play it down the phone.'

'Okay, give it a whirl.'

'Hold on, then. It'll take me a second to warm up the machine.'

> *One, two, three*
> *I'm betting that you love me . . .*

The words of the song crackled down the telephone to London. Tom had recorded it himself. His voice was good and he put over the lyrics well. However, if it hadn't been for Carly pushing Grant to spend the money on a tape recorder for the office, Tom wouldn't have been able to have this unusual form of audition. Tom had used Carly as his go-between and had given her the tape to give to Grant. If it had worked once, it could work again. She willingly fell in with his plan.

'One Night Stand' (Rupert/Green) coupled with 'One Two Three' (which Tom had finally finished with Denis's help) proved that Decca's faith in Johnny Todd was not misplaced. It reached No. 5 in February 1965.

Johnny was able to give up the warehouse job once and for all. Grant felt vindicated, too, and Denis and Tom were compensated for their various professional disappointments by the prospect of royalties on the 'unplayed' B side.

The high point came when Johnny and the now unnamed band dashed down to London to appear one Friday night on *Ready Steady Go!* Associated-Rediffusion's TV studio was on the corner of Kingsway and the Aldwych, in a vast building that once housed the Air Ministry. Studio 9 wasn't very large and by the time the live programme went out at just gone six o'clock, it was bursting with excited fans deployed between the cameras. They had been chosen for their dancing ability and their taste in mod fashions. There was also a small audience of non-dancers in a kind of cattle pen. The presenters were Cathy McGowan and Keith Fordyce.

Johnny remained his usual calm self amid the crush of fans. It was a calmness mingled with a daze at being up, at last, in the big city. Ten days before, he'd been lugging cartons in a warehouse in Manchester. Appearing on the bill were two other (more obviously) Liverpool groups: Billy J. Kramer and the Dakotas, and the Merseybeats. Then there were Sounds Incorporated, Madeline Bell, and the Rolling Stones. Grant wasn't sure about the Stones, they seemed a bit . . . wild. He preferred the more controlled sound that came from the North.

Brian Epstein judged the Mod Fashion Competition. Grant kept out of his way. They might have quite a bit in common, but Grant shrank from an encounter.

Johnny sang his song well, walking slowly forward through the mods in his leathers. The words to 'One Night Stand' were being mouthed by those already familiar with the number. Then it was all over. Johnny and the band were packed away and sent back home in the van, Mickey at the wheel.

Grant stayed on over the weekend. No Carly to hold his hand, or make love to. He was trying to decide what it would be like in the capital on his own, without her.

In the end, he concluded it wasn't the moment to move. He wanted to go, it made financial sense; but he was beginning to rely on a decision-maker within himself. If something felt right, he found himself free to act on it. If it didn't, something inside him prevented action. He began to say, 'I don't take decisions, decisions take me', though that didn't do him justice. He was blessed with an ability to tell when the time was ripe for change. It wasn't ripe just yet.

Carly was glad when he told her. It meant she wouldn't have to make a decision, wouldn't have to agonize over whether to chuck in the shop, leave her mother, and go with him. Somehow, she doubted she'd have the nerve.

In the meantime, she encouraged him to sign up more local talent. After all, his stable was tiny. Apart from Johnny and the backing group, all he had was Tom Sheridan. Tom was now much happier riding on the back of a hit, though success as a performer still eluded him. The group, formerly the Modds, formerly the Offbeats, grudgingly became reconciled to backing Johnny Todd.

Carly accompanied Grant on several star-finding trips. At a dance in Wrexham, they came across a band made up of Welsh lads, called Bedrock. Grant was now able to drop impressive-sounding remarks about *'RSG!'* and *'Lucky Stars'* and what Brian Epstein had said when they last met. He signed them up. On going backstage after the show, he was impressed when Gareth Jones, the leader of the group, produced an eight-inch length of rubber tubing from the front of his jeans.

'Doesn't do any harm and gives them something to think about,' Gareth laughed. Grant felt this showed an agreeably realistic view of the business.

Carly, on the other hand, was worried about the name 'Bedrock', even if it was an apt summary of the group's main interest in life. They agreed to change the name to 'The Wreckers'. This was to prove prophetic.

Grant next signed a comedian called Rex Room, a fair-haired, good-looking man, an insurance salesman by day, who had a winning way with a joke. In his early thirties, and thus ten years older than Grant, he was as Liverpool as they come. Many top comedians had been born in the city and Grant considered it no bad thing to broaden the base of his agency. Rex could act as compere should Starfinders ever get involved in packaged pop shows on the road.

Carly found, however, that she didn't warm to Rex offstage. There was something off-putting about him, a hard edge that frightened her. But she didn't allow this to influence her advice to Grant. 'He's good,' she said. 'The real thing. You've got to sign him.'

Grant didn't really need persuading. He, too, was slightly ill at ease with Rex, but thought the deal would turn out all right, especially if Carly was behind it. Her judgement was good, or always had been until now.

This modest expansion of Starfinders took time and effort. It took money, too, and there was still little of that coming in. Grant began to feel the burden of this responsibility. He had all these people dependent on him, ranging from Johnny Todd, on the edge of the big time, right down to Mickey and George, the loyal dogsbodies. They were now getting paid for their trouble, but it was quite a job finding enough to keep them busy. They had taken to hanging around the office waiting for errands to run. When it came to making the real decisions, Grant was still very much on his own, and the strain began to tell.

He became irritable and fractious, short-tempered and abrupt in dealing with people who stood in his way. The only possible restraint on this development came from Carly. He would listen to her when she told him a few home truths or relayed grumbles from down the line. She bossed him into relaxing and not being too hard on people. When he didn't respond, she wondered why she bothered. But then she knew he needed her. He was, in his way, demanding. Not physically demanding like Tom, but when he asked for help, she had to give it.

Grant wondered how he could involve her more deeply in Starfinders. It wasn't right using her as part-time, unpaid, unofficial help. She had Paradise to run, as well. That was her baby. She wasn't going to give that up, and Grant knew it wouldn't work if he saw her all day as well as every evening. They already tended to row over petty matters. Working together would only increase that tendency. He consciously began to do things more on his own and not to rely on Carly so much. He didn't like to feel she was indespensable, even if she was. He didn't want to acknowledge that he had been taken over.

Carly recognized the woman and could tell she wasn't going to buy anything in Paradise. She was too old for the stock they carried. She glanced quickly through the miniskirts and blouses, and then moved over to the new boot and shoe display. Carly winked at Fawn and indicated that she would look after the customer herself.

'Can I help you?'

'Yes, dear, I'm looking for a pair of black slip-ons.'

The more boxes Carly brought out from the back of the store, the vaguer the woman's requirements became. Now it was, 'Well, just let me see that same one in blue', then 'grey', then 'white'. From there it was on to, 'I wouldn't really mind a buckle' and 'I don't mind the high heels, really . . .'

Carly politely went along with the woman's demands. It took a lot to make her speak out, although the spikiness of her language and her pronounced Liverpool accent often made her seem more forthright than she actually was.

Finally, the woman said: 'I know you, don't I?' She levelled a not-too-pleasant stare at Carly, who knelt before her, putting the unwanted shoes back in their tissue paper and boxes.

'You're Denis's mother,' Carly replied.

'Yes. We've met before. You were with that Grant Pickering.'

Carly looked at her, wondering what was coming. 'Yes.'

'I thought so. You know, I was the first person to put that group together, the Offbeats, or what used to be the Offbeats. I did it for Denis, really.'

'I know,' Carly answered matter-of-factly.

'And you still see that Grant Pickering?'

'Yes.'

'He's a clever little worker, don't you think? A year ago,

113

our Denis's group was doing very nicely until we let Grant Pickering into the house. That was a mistake. Soon behaved as if he owned us. Now look what he's done. The Offbeats aren't the Offbeats any more. They just play in the background while Johnny Todd hogs the limelight. We're not happy with it, I can tell you.'

Carly went on putting away the rejected shoes. 'I don't know why you're telling me all this, Mrs Northington, it's got nothing to do with me. If you want to pick a quarrel with Grant, you'd best go see him. But if you want my opinion, I think you're wrong. Grant has to do what he has to. It was Decca made the changes, any road.'

Mrs Northington wasn't listening. 'He's a manipulator, that's the word. Came from nowhere and pushes people about. I hear he cheats over money, too. Doesn't give the boys their share.'

Carly looked at her blankly, refusing to be provoked.

Fawn came over to the rescue. 'Is everything all right, madam?' she asked pointedly, with a sideways glance at Carly.

'Yes, thank you,' said Denis's mum. 'I don't seem to be able to find what I want.' Turning to Carly, she brightened momentarily and said, 'Thank you, dear.' Carly walked her to the door.

'You ought to tell Grant if you're upset,' she told the older woman. 'He'll explain everything.'

'It wouldn't do any good, the damage is done. But I'd steer clear of him if I were you, dear. He'll come to no good if he carries on like that.'

'I'm sure you're wrong.'

'What do you know, dear? A little chit like you.'

'But this is my shop!' Carly blushed. 'How *dare* you come in here and talk like that! Who the hell d'you think you are?'

Mrs Northington said no more and strode out, glad to have it off her chest.

'Hot flushes, if you ask me,' Fawn concluded.

'Bloody nutter. Got a bee in her bonnet.'

Carly succeeded in shrugging the incident off, but it left a nasty taste. It was inevitable in Grant's world, that there would be these rivalries and jealousies, disappointments and accusations of treachery. Grant didn't make it any easier for the people he overran by covering up his own doubts and inhibitions with a brusque manner. He could bulldoze people with considerable lack of grace. Carly could see that. He bulldozed her quite a lot of the time.

Yet she was sad when people spoke of him in any way critically. She felt they didn't see what a difficult task he had. Egos were bound to get bruised where the stakes were so high, where luck and chance played such a part, where judgement of a person's performance was like dismissal of his whole character, his worth as a human being.

Carly would tell Grant what Mrs Northington had said, warn him, if he didn't know already, of the resentment he was capable of stirring up. She didn't like to. It spoiled her relationship with him. Yet she began to wonder how close she could ever get to a man who behaved, or was just seen by others to behave, like that. If Mrs Northington had intended to sow seeds of doubt in Carly's feelings, she'd made a very good job of it.

Johnny Todd, always the focus of Grant's growing empire, rode high and was thoroughly enjoying himself. No doubts troubled his straightforward mind. Even if his success were not to last, he'd be able to look back on the present time with happiness. He'd be able to say, at least, that he'd done it, once. Besides, whatever might follow, at the moment his life was so much better than it had been before.

On the strength of the hit record, he was touring. A Leeds-based promoter called Alan Greenlee had done a deal with Starfinders to incorporate Johnny Todd in a package that was doing one-night stands in the Midlands and North. Johnny and his backing group weren't being paid very much, they were number three on the bill, but Grant saw that the exposure and the experience would do them good. It would keep them busy, too, and out of his hair. He had also managed to get Rex Room, his comedian, on to the bill as compere.

Grant dispatched Mickey Clinch to act as Johnny's minder. Mickey said he was chuffed at the opportunity and eagerly did all the things Grant told him to do, in addition to what Johnny asked him to do. He made sure that masses of shiny black and white photos of the singer, all apparently autographed by the man himself, were handed out, free of charge, to girls in the audience. He also tipped off some of the fans that Johnny would not be leaving by the stage door after the show but through a 'secret' door on the other side of the theatre. This ensured that Johnny was mobbed, and was seen to be mobbed by a photographer from the local paper.

Johnny went along with all this, quite content. It was better than working in a warehouse. It was also a good deal more fun than hanging about a tiny council flat in Salford with Maureen and a screaming baby. His sexual needs were heightened by the fervour whipped up around him and satisfied in an intriguing manner.

No longer was it possible for Johnny to pleasure one or two fans in his dressing room after the show, as he'd done when playing halls around Liverpool. Backstage security was more organized at these larger venues and Alan Greenlee, the promoter, didn't take kindly to such goings-on.

So Johnny evolved a system whereby, relaxing in a bar at the hotel where they were overnighting after a show, he would point out to Mickey any talent he fancied. Mickey would go over and the girl would be chatted up, by proxy. Did she know that Johnny Todd was over by the bar? He would very much like to meet her. He'd sent Mickey over, personally, to say so . . .

It seldom failed, this third-party seduction, and, at first, Mickey saw nothing demeaning in the activity. It was all part of the job and sometimes he might benefit himself. If there was a spare bit of skirt, he'd be right in there. He found he hardly needed to chat up the girls. Just being part of the pop world was enough to turn them on. Never mind that he was just a tour manager. He was glamorous and fanciable in their eyes because of his closeness to Johnny Todd.

Relieved of the cares of the chase, Johnny was able to concentrate on refining his love-making technique. He consciously plodded through a variety of positions – on tables, bean-bags, stairs; half in bed, half out; with ice cubes, leather belts, honey or wine; with any number of pickles and relishes. 'It's kink night tonight, folks,' he would chuckle. It was as though he had been given a new train set to play with and the only question was, would he grow tired of it? Whatever the answer, it was certainly more fun than sex with Maureen. He was beginning to live out his fantasies, including some he didn't even know he had.

Grant had a fright when it was pointed out to him that he was running an entertainment agency and needed to be licensed by the local authority. He had been ignorant of this requirement. There were no *Teach Yourself* books about being a manager or agent.

The matter was quickly put right. Then his new accountant, Denzil Brooke, suggested that Starfinders be incorporated. It would put the business on a more secure footing, able to cope with any surge in income that might be about to occur. Starfinders Ltd it became. It sounded grand, but it gave Grant more than a twinge of anxiety. Would he really be able to deliver? Would he even be able to justify the promise in the name?

'Are you getting enough to eat, dear?' That was what bothered his mother when Grant finally dragged himself back home to the Wirral on a long postponed visit to his parents. Mrs Pickering had spent the afternoon getting all the things he liked for tea – scones, shortbread, Eccles cake – but he hardly touched them.

'Of course, I am. Don't be daft.' The question didn't accord with his new-found status. Nothing in Grant's background had fitted him for the career he now found himself pursuing. It wasn't surprising if his parents doubted there was any substance to it. He'd have to show them. But he wasn't sure what he'd have to do to convince them he was truly successful.

What he wasn't telling his mother now was that he didn't feel like eating any of her tea. As soon as he'd come through his parents' front door, he'd begun to feel queasy. It had happened before. When he went home he felt ill – one reason why he didn't do it that often.

'Have you got a girl friend?' His mother plodded through her usual list of questions.

Grant didn't want to get onto that subject at all.

'Yes, I have,' he admitted, as finally as he could.

'What's she called?'

There was no avoiding it. 'Carly.'

'Protestant or Catholic?'

'I believe she's a Catholic, Mum. What the hell does that matter? You're just prejudiced.'

'Please, no "hells" in our house. I'm not prejudiced. I'm just saying RCs can cause *difficulties*.' She didn't elaborate. 'She got a job?'

'Yes. If you must know, she's in the fashion business.'

'You mean she's a shop girl.'

'No, she isn't. She owns the shop.'

'Oh. What's it called, then?'

'Paradise.'

'Where's that?'

'In Paradise Street.'

Any more of this and he'd have to leave. Knowing his

mother, she'd go along and take a look. Grant twisted inside and longed to be free of the cloying atmosphere. Could he really have come from this?

May Pickering changed the subject. 'I don't like that Johnny Todd. He's all sensuous, with those lips. I know what that means. I think it's disgusting.'

Grant couldn't help laughing. It was useless trying to counter his mother's bigotry.

'Mum, I don't care what you think of him. He's not meant to appeal to people like you. He's not Alma Cogan or Dickie Valentine. He's doing all right.'

If Grant's mother had seen Johnny Todd when he was still plain Michael Armstrong and singing at weddings a year or so earlier, she'd probably have liked him. He was tuneful and straight. Still could be. Grant must remember not to lose sight of that quality in Johnny. One day it might have to be resurrected, to broaden his appeal. Tommy Steele was always on about being an 'all-round entertainer'. Johnny was never likely to be that, but he had more to offer than he was giving at the moment.

Grant's father, Ted, said nothing during all of this, but sat quietly, puffing and re-lighting his pipe. It had long been a habit of Grant's to count the number of times his father struck a match within a fixed period. Once he had counted sixteen in an hour. His father only took one puff before putting the pipe down on the ashtray. No wonder it went out.

Grant started inching towards the door. He kissed his mother goodbye and she held him briefly as though they'd never meet again. He struggled free.

Ted Pickering followed his son into the hall and walked down the short garden path with him, still fiddling with his pipe.

'Well, it sounds as if you're doing well. Fine opportunity.'

Grant expected him to launch into a golf club speech at any moment, though actually his father had never been near a golf club in his life.

'You'll be meeting all sorts of different types in this show business,' he announced. 'Some funny types, too, I imagine. Men and women.' Grant wasn't sure what his father was driving at. 'Some of them won't have the same standards as your mother and me.' What *was* he on about? 'Take my advice, keep out of the way of those *bad apples*.'

Grant agreed airily and said he surely would. On the bus to Birkenhead he chewed over his father's coded speech. Did his parents know more about him and Carly than they were letting on? Had someone been on to them about his business methods?

Then he thought about the 'bad apples' his father had warned him against. He couldn't have been hinting at homos and queers, could he?

It just showed how wrong people could be, even about their own sons. Grant couldn't wait to get back to Carly again, to be able to drive his father's niggles from his mind. The question was, though, would Carly be in the mood to respond?

With Mickey off on tour, pandering to the needs of Johnny Todd, and George running slow errands for Starfinders Ltd, the flat opposite the cathedral was solely occupied for much of the time by Tom Sheridan. He felt himself to be in a no-man's land between failure and success. The royalties from the B side recording of his song hadn't yet arrived. Grant Pickering hadn't responded to his suggestion of more rock-poetry concerts, nor was he keen for Tom to attempt any more blues concerts with Sauce, because the band was not part of Starfinders. It was hard for Tom to call himself a singer/songwriter when he didn't perform either function in public.

He was trying to write a follow-up song. He played his guitar for hours on end with no one to listen to him except the old couple in the flat above (who would rather not have had to). He fantasized much about Carly, but saw no chance of reclaiming her from Grant. In fact, he was too idle to try.

When he was desperate for a woman, he'd take whoever he could find. There was always Mandy from the College of Art, ready to experiment in bed, never mind how complicated the position. There was Penelope, a pretty secretary at the university, who actually believed him when he said it wouldn't go down unless she slept with him. And there was Jane, the usherette from the Jacey Cinema in Clayton Square, who wore dark sweaters and a ponytail, having seen too many French films. But too often she was on ice-cream duty when he wanted her.

That evening, he went out to look for someone new, as accommodating as these, but chanced instead to bump into Fawn Flack. As they were in Hope Street, he asked her on the spur of the moment to have a drink with him in Ye Cracke.

He hadn't bargained for having to listen to her woes: how she'd tried to get Grant to be her agent; how he'd laughed and sent her away; how the rumour had got about that she was pregnant whereas she was merely overweight.

Tom listened to Fawn's tale and gave her a hug. 'You've had a bad time.'

'Yes, I have. But you're all right, aren't you? Grant took you on.'

'Hasn't made any difference. Doesn't get me work. And at least you've got your job in the shop.'

'I suppose so.'

She mightn't look very appetizing, with her mascara streaked with tears, but she was female, and if there was one thing Tom liked, it was a woman. He was glad to hear her slagging off Grant. It was all grist to Tom's mill.

'And worst of all,' Fawn announced, taking a swig of stout, 'Grant's tried to get Carly to sack me.'

'He *hasn't*!' Tom exclaimed. 'The shit! He can't do that.'

'Well, he has.'

'What would he do that for? Did Carly tell you?'

'He told her I wasn't the right person to work in a fashion shop. But she doesn't listen to him. She's a mate.'

'Trouble in Paradise, eh? I hear it's a bit dicky on the money side.'

'I wouldn't know. There's lots of customers, but we're supposed to be not charging enough. I don't say anything, though. I take me money and run.'

'Poor old Carly. She deserves a lucky break.'

'That's what she says about you.'

'Does she now? You talk about me, do you?'

'Sure. All the dirt. She really fancies you, though.'

'Sensible girl. That what she says?'

'Not in words, but I can tell.'

Tom was pleased, and started to pay more attention to Fawn herself. He even told her he'd like to hear her sing.

'Okay, then,' she said, brightening. 'Your place or mine?'

'What's your place?'

'In Sefton Park. I live with my uncle and aunt.'

'My place, then.'

'You've got a guitar?'

' 'Course I've got a guitar, you daft biddy.'

Tom ushered Fawn out of Ye Cracke, happily indifferent to whether anyone saw him leaving with a joke like Fawn.

'Of course, I usually accompany myself on the *piano*,' Fawn said when they reached the flat, 'but I can manage with a guitar.'

She played and sang Dylan's 'Blowin' in the Wind' and threatened to work her way through the folk repertoire.

'You can certainly sing,' Tom told her, sincerely. To his surprise, out of that pudding came a pure, sweet voice. There was no doubt Fawn had talent. How typical of Grant not to have seen that. On the other hand, talent wasn't worth a halfpenny if you couldn't sell it, and with her forbidding

122

looks and unfortunate manner, Fawn was certainly going to have a job doing that.

Tom sang her his song, which she knew from the Johnny Todd record, and then the song he was working on now. 'And there's me pomes. D'you want to see them?'

Fawn leafed through the old school exercise book which contained far from fair copies of Tom's scribblings. She gave them the attention they'd never have got from a man.

'Hey, these are great, they're about Carly, aren't they?' She searched his face for confirmation.

'You mean, you know who "Lorelei" is?'

'Well, isn't it her?'

'I'm not telling.'

'D'you fancy her a lot?'

'You could say that. But just now she's beyond my reach. Grant's got her. But they won't last for ever. He'll go away, and she'll come back to me. It's just a question of time.'

'You're a cocky bugger, aren't you?'

'Yes, I know.' He grinned.

Fawn took off her glasses, reducing her vision to nil, and wiped the lenses on the hem of her dress.

'I suppose I know what she sees in him,' Fawn told Tom. 'He's quite attractive, you know, but it's more *him* she's interested in. Some girls are like that. Interested in men who *do* things, who boss people around. That's why she's always doing things for him. But she also organizes him, helps him a lot. It's just she's nicer with it.'

She carefully put her glasses back on.

'It's rather a waste really because she's so talented herself. She may not be brilliant at running the shop, but she's very handy with a pair of scissors. She cooks, she's capable. Make someone a lovely wife.'

'Not Grant, I hope,' Tom said flatly. 'But he can have her, if he wants. She plays hot and cold with me. Half the time she puts up a fence so I can't get at her, the other half she's making come-on gestures.'

As an afterthought, he added, 'Why don't you keep your glasses off. You look better that way.'

'Shove away, Tom. You won't make me. I'm not just anybody's, you know.'

'How old are you?' he asked.

'What's that got to do with anything?'

'Go on, how old are you?'

'Nineteen.'

'Same as Carly.'

'Yes, we were in the same class at school. And you?'

'Twenty-two.'

Tom made his move quickly and put a hand on Fawn's substantial thigh. 'You've a very good voice, you know,' he told her.

Naturally, she melted. Flattery would get him anywhere.

'The old magic at work, eh, Tom?'

Tom removed her glasses, flicked out the light, and they made love on the rug in front of the window. The cathedral, as always, loomed silently against the dark sky through the uncurtained window.

It was a relief when Fawn announced she must be going. Tom made a mug of tea for himself, munched a ginger biscuit from the packet by the sink. He picked up his guitar and completed the lyrics of a song he'd been stuck over. His thoughts, as always, centred on Carly. The title of the song was 'Tantalizing'. Fawn would never know her part in the composition. Carly would find out eventually. It was not a song that, once heard, would easily be forgotten.

CHAPTER 7

At the end of the first week of Johnny Todd's tour with the 'Startime' package there was no sign of any money from the promoter, Alan Greenlee. This meant that Grant, who was firm on these matters, wouldn't write any cheques for Johnny Todd or for Rex Room. A phone call to Greenlee's office in Leeds only elicited the response that the money was in the post.

By the middle of the second week, not only was Johnny getting fractious with Grant, Grant was getting furious with Greenlee.

'Why are you messing me about like this?' Grant demanded over the phone. 'The contract quite clearly states how the money should be paid. There's no excuse for any delay.'

'Believe me, Grant, it's coming,' Greenlee replied, maddeningly and lamely. Grant felt he was being treated like a schoolboy by the older man. He felt his blood starting to pulse. The amount of money owing wasn't all that important. It was the principle. Even if only a tenner was at stake, Grant all but got a hard-on bringing home what was due.

Alan Greenlee had, unwisely it now turned out, done a foolish thing in the early days of making the deal with Starfinders. He had given Grant his home number in Leeds, 'Just in case there's ever an emergency'.

Grant began to ring the number each evening, never mind how late it was.

Greenlee would wriggle, plead that the money was 'genuinely on its way, I give you my word'. Or it was a case of there being 'a little slowness on the part of the bank'. Then it was the fault of the venues: 'They've been slow giving *me* the money, very sorry about that . . .'

Grant's manner got progressively harder and blunter, but still nothing arrived through the post.

By the third week, with the end of the tour in sight, Grant was wondering if they'd ever see the money. Would he have to send a solicitor's letter? He didn't want to do this; it might cost more to collect the debt than the debt itself.

He was saved by Rex Room. Rex was a tough nut from one of the hardest districts of Liverpool. He might come over as a lovable, warm-hearted fellow on stage, but off it, as was the case with many comedians, he had a streak of steel which would have surprised his audiences if they'd ever glimpsed it.

Like Johnny Todd, Rex hadn't been paid a penny for the tour so far. On the coach taking them to the next venue, which happened to be Carlisle, Rex was sitting next to the singer and bent his ear.

'Grant paid you yet?' he asked.

'No. Has he paid you?'

'No. I rang him from the digs this morning. Reversed the charges. He said Greenlee was dragging his feet. Well, I think it's a fucking, bleeding disgrace.'

'So do I,' Johnny replied, but with little anger in his voice.

'What are you going to do about it?'

'What can I do, Rex? Refuse to go on?'

'It might come to that. We could all refuse to go on. Especially if it was just before the show. Greenlee would soon come running with the cash then.'

'I'm not sure I could do that.' Johnny was a comfortable fellow, reluctant to rock the boat or disappoint his fans.

'Why not? I'm not doing this tour for the good of me health. Neither are you, I imagine.'

'Well, I'm not going to spoil the show, and that's final.'

The comedian saw he wasn't getting anywhere with

Johnny. He turned to Mickey Clinch. Mickey didn't have much to do on the tour, but he was the nearest thing there was to Grant's representative.

He knew that Johnny and Rex hadn't been getting their money. He himself was paid by Grant, in cash, and simply didn't think about asking for his next hand-out until he'd used up the last one. 'You've spoken to the boss?'

'Yes,' said Rex. 'He always says he's leaning on Greenlee and he'll let us know when he gets it, but that's chicken talk. We could end up with nothing for all the shows we're doing, bloody good shows, too. I think we ought to get hold of Greenlee and lean on him ourselves. That's the only way we'll get our money.'

'He doesn't show his face much.'

'Well, next time he does, we'll have to push it in for him.'

'Okay, let's do that,' Mickey giggled, in the odd way that he had, and stretched out on the back seat of the coach to have some kip.

After Carlisle, they doubled back to Barnsley. There were only two more dates to play and then the tour would wrap. Rex soon gathered the information that none of the artistes in the package had been paid, whoever their agents were. In the light of this, it was surely tempting providence when Greenlee himself turned up that night to watch the show, Barnsley not being far from his base.

'Great show, chaps,' he enthused from dressing room to dressing room between the five and eight o'clock performances on the Saturday night. He was nattily dressed as ever, but as it was a Saturday he was wearing a sports jacket, a fudge-coloured tie, and suede shoes. He was quietly spoken, hair well cut, manicured fingernails, a neat well-trimmed moustache. He wrote notes on a small pad with a silver propelling pencil. He spoke with a light, almond-coloured Yorkshire accent, and might have been a schoolmaster on his day off rather than a show promoter.

Greenlee suspected nothing when he reached the dressing room that Rex shared with two musicians. Mickey Clinch entered behind him, shut the door, and locked it.

Rex suddenly stood up and turned to the promoter. 'Well, Mr Greenlee, this is indeed a pleasure.' Till then, Rex had appeared to be staring at himself in the mirror with the bulbs round it (not all of them working). In fact, he'd been studying Greenlee. He slipped his thumbs into his waistcoat pockets as though about to launch into a routine.

'Did you hear the one about the impresario who didn't pay his acts?'

For a second, Greenlee seemed to be searching his memory to see if he could recollect the joke. Then he broke into a nervous half-smile.

'Now, Rex, it'll be all right. I've spoken to your agent about it. It's been a very good tour. Everybody's very pleased. And there's absolutely no problem.'

'I've heard that before,' said Rex sourly, looking for support from the two musicians. They turned away, not wanting to be involved. 'I want, we all want, the money due to us. *Now.*'

'It's just not possible, Rex. It doesn't work like that.' He tried another watery smile.

'Right,' said Rex, moving towards him, 'then there'll be no eight o'clock tonight.'

'You can't do that!'

'Oh, yes, we can. I've already got Johnny Todd's agreement,' he lied. 'He's as pissed off as everyone.'

'No, he isn't. I just spoke to him.'

'So, how're you going to pay?'

Greenlee looked towards the door and saw Mickey standing in the way.

Rex gave a jerk with his head. Mickey checked that the door was locked.

'Now, look,' said Greenlee, 'you're making a mistake . . .'

Rex moved closer. Their faces almost touched. The comedian began to jab the promoter with his finger.

'You're the one who's making the mistake. We want our money, and this'll do for a start.'

He deftly slipped his hand into the promoter's jacket and flicked out a large leather wallet.

'How dare you!'

'I said, this'll do for a start.' Rex began counting out the large white five-pound notes. 'Silly to carry such a lot about, eh?'

'Give me that back! I'll make sure you never work again!'

'No threat, coming from you. Shurrup. Now then, what are you going to do about the rest of the money? Eh?'

Greenlee tried a rush for the door. Mickey, still blocking the exit, seized him by the arms and pinned them behind his back.

The comedian, smiling now, aimed a low punch at Greenlee's stomach. Greenlee doubled up, gashing his face on the side of the hard, stone washbasin as he fell. A smear of blood spread across his face from his nose.

Rex threw Greenlee a towel and told him to clean himself up. 'Right, chum. Now we'll go to the manager. You'll get him to hand over your share of the first-house takings. Right? You'll give it to us, all of it, and that'll be the first part of the money due to Starfinders. You'll then give us a cheque for the remainder. We will then do the eight o'clock as though nothing had happened. God help you if there's anything wrong with the cheque. Understand?'

Greenlee mumbled, still holding the towel to his nose.

'Oh, here's your wallet,' Rex went on. 'Now take us to the manager. You don't have to tell him what's happened. We'll keep your little secret. Let's go.'

The two musicians sat, appalled but half-admiring, as Rex pushed Greenlee out of the dressing room.

Outside the door stood Greenlee's assistant, Desmond. Greenlee gave him a look as if to say, 'Where were you when I needed you?'

As they passed Johnny Todd's dressing room, the door was open and he was just coming out. He beamed at Greenlee, unaware of what was being done in his name.

The performance that night was one of the best of the whole tour. Rex had never been funnier, and he even managed to make the giggling girls listen to his act while they waited to wet their knickers over Johnny Todd.

Alan Greenlee looked on, unsmiling. However, he didn't hold what had happened against Rex. He quite understood how the comedian felt. No, he suspected the hand of Grant Pickering. Pickering must have put Rex up to it. Greenlee wouldn't forgive him that.

Next morning, on the Sunday, Mickey cadged a lift from Leeds to Liverpool, bearing the cheque Rex had extracted from Greenlee, together with several hundred pounds in cash, all casually stuffed in a canvas bag. With it was a painstakingly written note from Rex detailing the transaction. He had been pretty pissed off to discover how much more Johnny Todd was getting paid, but wasn't going to say anything about it just now.

Grant was having Sunday lunch with Carly and her mam at Lily Street when Mickey tracked him down.

'What's this?' he asked. He hadn't been expecting Mickey. 'Anything the matter?'

'Nah, something right,' Mickey answered with a grin. 'We sorted out Greenlee, least Rex did. This is the money we were owed.' He opened the canvas bag.

'Christ! What made him cough up all of a sudden?'

'Rex persuaded him.'

'How?'

'Leant on him.'

'What's that mean, for heaven's sake?'

'Banged his nose on a washbasin. That was a mistake, but least he paid up.'

Grant felt a flutter of butterflies in his stomach.

Carly's mam butted in. 'You been fighting again, Mickey?'

'No, I haven't.'

'But you say the man was roughed up? That's wrong, Mickey.'

'Yes, Mickey, she's right,' said Grant. 'I know we were owed the money, but –'

'Well, we've got it now, haven't we?'

'Yes, but you can't go around thumping people. Where's Rex? I'll have to have it out with him.'

'I dunno. Could've come home by now.'

'But not with you?'

'No.'

Carly sat through this, hugging herself nervously. She seemed very interested in the goldfish silently gawping in her mam's aquarium. What sort of world was Grant in, where this kind of thing went on?

There was a long silence while Grant flicked Rex's accounting note between his fingers and sucked his lips audibly.

'Bloody 'ell', were his last words on the subject, for the moment.

'Mickey, have you eaten?' Mrs Scott was asking. 'There's some pudding left if you're hungry.'

'Great, Mrs Scott, thanks.'

The cloud lifted, but only a little, while Grant brooded on what had been done in his name. Although he was glad to have the money, he didn't like having the initiative snatched from him. Rex shouldn't have done it. Heaven only knew what the consequences would be. Still, when word got round about what had happened in Barnsley, it was less likely that anyone would ever try to mess with Starfinders again.

'Well, I suppose it's all right,' he said. 'Greenlee's a slippery bugger. If he'd got away with it this time, he'd have kept on doing it.'

'But it's wrong, what Rex did,' Carly spoke up at last.

It was unfair to blame Grant for what he hadn't done himself, but it had been done in his name and she didn't like that, felt as uncomfortable as if he had done the deed. It wasn't enough to say that it was the sort of thing that went on in show business.

'Keep out of this, Carly, it's nothing to do with you.'

'Oh, yes, it has. I know a thing or two about bad debts. I run a shop, in case you'd forgotten.'

'Yeh, and if you hadn't been so soft, it wouldn't be in the mess it's in.'

Carly blushed deeply, but she wasn't going to cry, however angry she felt. She snatched up the *News of the World* and pretended to read it. Mickey, having polished off the pudding, sat on the narrow arm of the sofa and, as if wishing to be friendly, looked at the paper with her. Carly wished he'd go away, but continued pretending to read. All she could hear was Grant talking to her mother.

Grant really liked Mrs Scott. She was the mother he'd never had; he was the son she'd never had. She had all the motherly virtues. She made him feel good, was encouraging, a sympathetic listener. She was practical and cooked well, just like Carly. But the daughter resented their getting on well together. It was nice, in one way, but it might not be good in the long run. It was as though the relationship wasn't just between Grant and Carly, but with her mother, too.

'It's always nice to see someone doing well.' They had moved on from the Greenlee business, and Mrs Scott was flattering Grant now. 'It makes me glad to see how you've come on, how you're doing great things.'

'So, I'm forgiven, then?'

'For what?'

'All that just now. What Mickey came to say, about the money.'

'Rubbish. You've got to do what you have to. I bet there's plenty of sharks in your line of business. You have to deal with them as best you can. I'll leave the worrying to others.' Here she winked at Grant and nodded in the direction of her daughter.

Carly hid further behind the newspaper. How awful it was when people knew you well, knew what you were thinking.

Grant grinned. He had wanted to broach the subject of his leaving Liverpool, moving South, a question which had begun to reassert itself. He felt so cut off from the record companies, the radio and television, in Liverpool.

Should he try buttering up Mrs Scott, so that she'd allow Carly to go with him to London? He felt sure she'd be in favour, but it was hopeless putting the question while Carly was around. She always said she had to stay with her mother. Grant decided to wait. He'd have to play them off against each other.

Eventually, after cups of tea all round, Mickey wandered off, having hardly spoken since delivering his first piece of news. Carly and Grant only had a moment or two on their own together before Grant 'made tracks', as he put it, back to his bedsit. There was a distance between the two and they parted uncomfortably.

As he walked home in the evening light, Grant was annoyed at the weather for being so warm and pleasant. It failed to take account of his mood. Then he met Tom Sheridan.

'Is she at home then?' asked Tom.

'Who are you talking about?'

'Carly, stupid. Thought I might call.'

'You do what you bleeding well like, chum.'

Grant walked on, frowning, and Tom was left wondering

whether there'd been a row. If so, he ought to step it round to Lily Street right away.

The tour organized by Alan Greenlee had ended with all the artistes paid what they were owed. Grant made no move in Greenlee's direction, either to smooth over what had happened or to rub it in. Johnny sailed blithely on, untouched by the whole episode, as was his way. Rex Room went back to doing single nights around the Northern clubs, while word of his small debt-collecting achievement quickly spread.

Johnny had nothing in prospect now so Grant asked him to come over to Liverpool so they could talk about the future. Johnny arrived by train from Manchester trying to look anonymous. It was a mild April evening but he wore dark glasses and his raincoat was buttoned up to the chin.

'Afraid of being recognized?' Grant teased him.

'Why do you say that?'

'Oh, nothing.'

They sat in the Philly from opening time to nine o'clock, Johnny still wearing his shades, Grant fascinated as ever by the frosted glass and the Victorian splendour of the 'Philharmonic Dining Rooms', as they were more properly called.

Of the small stable of talent Grant had put together, Johnny was the client he was happiest dealing with. He had discovered him, named him, moulded him. There were no hurt feelings as there were with Denis and the former Offbeats. Nor any hint of trouble, as there was with Rex. Nor any actual trouble with marijuana and sloppy gigs as there was with the Wreckers.

Grant liked Johnny and he was proud of what they had managed to achieve between them in a short time. There was a comradeship between them. They had fought with each other hardly at all, they had already experienced much. Grant projected himself through Johnny, the performer he was never now going to be. It was also a fact that Johnny's musical talent was the kind Grant understood. It was like the difference between the Beatles and the Rolling Stones. Grant could understand the Beatles' appeal and appreciated their music. He could see why the Stones appealed to others, but he didn't enjoy them himself. As for the Wreckers, the same applied. He had high hopes for their future, but their brand of rock was too extreme for his taste. He would take his percentage and keep his true feelings to himself.

'I'm trying to find a new song for you, Johnny. Tom Sheridan's come up with quite a good B side, called "Tantalizing". Good title, eh? Decca are still looking for the A. They do want another disc out of you, even if they're still not talking LPs, or contracts, or anything.'

Johnny looked as unconcerned as ever.

'Oh, for God's sake,' Grant suddenly exploded. 'Take those shades off. I promise I won't recognize you!'

The singer did as he was told, put them in his pocket and smiled his big smile.

'How's Maureen?' Grant asked ritually, but could see at once that the inquiry didn't please his client.

'Okay. How's Carly?'

'Bit moody, but then women always are, aren't they? Up and down. Now me, I'm basically all right, most of the time. But them, once they're down, they're so far down.'

'Are you going to do the decent thing? Perhaps that's what she's after?'

'I'd like to. But that's a long way off.'

'Keep out of it, that's my advice.'

'Things not good with Maureen?'

'It's finished, to be frank.'

Was this why Johnny had been so willing to come over for a chat?

'It finished when we had our kid, really – least I felt it had. Then when I got home from the tour, *phfft*. I could tell she didn't want me around any more. She'd got used to being on her own with the kid and slagging me off to her friends.'

'Um.' Grant bought another round. Was this going to be the cue for a joint move out of the North? He had never felt very much for Maureen. She was a 'negative', that was how he would have put it. She did nothing for Johnny's career, in no way added to his allure, probably believed that Grant was manipulating him. It was odd how, if you just waited, problems sorted themselves out.

'What d'you say to moving South?' Grant asked.

'Everybody?'

'Well, you and me.'

'They're so la-di-bloody-dah down there. I mightn't feel at home.'

'It's up to you, Johnny. I tell you what, though. We'll both be going there soon. It's bound to happen. I can feel it, can't you?'

'But what would I do without Maureen and the folks? Sit in a flat in London, playing with myself?'

'Well, there's women in London, you know. You could have a nice time.'

Johnny brightened.

'Just think about it,' Grant said, tapping him on the knee. 'You've got to, we've all got to see there's a world beyond here. There's no knowing where we can end up. I think you could be a big, big star.'

'I don't believe you, Grant, but thanks all the same.'

'No, I'm serious. I'm not just saying that to make you happy. You've got to make the jump. What's the alternative? Back to the warehouse?'

'Get on with you.'

'Well?'

Without making any hard and fast decision, the two men

deepened the bond between them that evening. They both understood a little more about each other. They were heading towards the same destination.

Grant walked Johnny back to Central Station to catch the Manchester train and almost felt sorry when he had to wave goodbye. He looked at his watch, saw it was only just gone ten o'clock and decided to make a late call on Carly. He caught the bus, hopped off before it reached the stop, and briskly walked round to the terrace house. As he turned into Lily Street, he stopped, looked, and then walked away again.

He had seen a couple in each other's arms, necking, on the doorstep of No. 23. He knew instantly that it was Carly and Tom. So Tom had oiled his way in there again and was providing Carly with a shoulder to cry on.

Grant couldn't bear to have it out with them, there and then. He walked home by himself, brooding and angry.

Next evening, Grant was back at Carly's to tell her of his plan, to ask her to come with him to London, to move Paradise down there; even to ask her to marry him, if that was what it would take.

She wasn't at home. Mrs Scott opened the door wearing a pinny under her going-out coat. She looked uncomfortable when she saw Grant standing on the step.

'Can I come in?'

'I don't know, son, I really don't,' Mrs Scott said, answering some other question. Then, 'Yes, of course, luv. Would you be wanting some tea?'

'No. Thanks all the same.'

Mrs Scott seemed even more distraught than Grant; it didn't take much digging to find out why.

'Carly saw Tom last night?' he ventured.

'My, you've got big ears then. I'm not saying anything.'

'What's going on between them?'

'I don't know, Grant. I don't like to interfere. For a long

time I haven't had to, you and Carly seemed so nicely set. She seemed to have given up Tom. Least, she never mentioned him except to say how rude he'd been, and such like. Then, well, last night . . . well, I won't say. I didn't know where to put myself. Had to go to bed early.'

'I saw them by the door. I was coming to see her.'

'Did you, then? I don't like to say it, she's always been a very good girl, and seemed so right with you, but she stopped out last night. Never done it before. I don't know what's going on.'

Grant changed his mind and had a cup of tea, after all. If Tom had lured Carly back, was it that Grant had been neglectful? Well, he had his work to do. He'd had to talk to Johnny last night. It might not have seemed like work, only boozing, but that was showbusiness.

Mrs Scott was tying herself in knots in order not to seem to be siding with Grant. Carly must be allowed to choose her own men friends. Of course, she preferred Grant, a much sounder type. Tom was better looking, but there was nothing to him. Carly would do better for herself if she stuck with Grant.

'She's annoyed with me about something,' Grant suggested.

'She thinks you've gone all hard, because of your job. She hated all that business of the man being beaten up for the money. She was sick at the thought of it. But then, she's not been happy for some time. The shop's a big worry for her. Such a thing to do at her age. I'm sorry, luv, but there it is.'

Grant took one of the biscuits he was offered straight from the packet.

'Is she with him tonight?'

'I don't know, Grant. I don't know anything. But I expect so.'

In time they were both reduced to silence. Eventually Grant did something he'd not done before. He kissed Mrs Scott goodnight.

'I'm sorry, luv,' she said. She was almost crying. She watched Grant go down the street and gave him a small wave as he turned the corner and disappeared from sight.

Carly was tight-lipped when Grant went to see her at Paradise next morning.

'We can't discuss it now,' she said softly, but firmly.

'After work, then. We must talk.'

'It won't do any good.'

'Please, Carly.'

When they met and walked along the street together, things were hardly any better. Grant took her arm, but there was no affection coming back.

'What is it, Carly?'

'I can't explain.'

'Well, I must have done something wrong for you to be like this.'

'Not really,' she said.

'It's that business about the money, is that it?'

'No, of course not,' she insisted. 'I know that wasn't your fault.'

'Is it what I said about your shop? I really didn't mean it. Just came out.'

'No, Grant, don't go on so.'

'And Tom was waiting there, wasn't he, just waiting for this to happen?'

'Don't go *on*, Grant.'

A moment or two later, it was all over. He couldn't believe it was happening. He had stopped walking to try and make her talk sense, to get her to express her feelings, and she had simply kept on going, wind in her hair, down towards the Pier Head.

That was how they parted. He looked after her until she disappeared, a small dot, turning a corner and finally moving out of sight. He felt foolish standing there in his raincoat with tears stealing into his eyes.

Oh, women! How much easier life would be without them.

But it helped make up his mind. Next day he was talking with Decca about Johnny's next record and quietly announced that, as from next month, he would, of course, be working out of an office in London.

'Good,' said Tony Preston, 'and about time too.'

'And Johnny Todd'll be in London with me. He's leaving his wife, you know.'

'I didn't even know he was married,' said Preston.

CHAPTER 8

'I don't want to hurt you, Mam,' Carly announced abruptly two days after her last meeting with Grant.

'You're leaving then?'

'Yes.'

'Grant's taking you to London?'

'No. I'd never do that, Mam. You know I won't leave you.'

'Sounds as if you are, though.'

'No. It's Tom. I'm going to . . . live with him, in the flat.'

Mrs Scott wasn't going to be caught disapproving, and restricted herself to the practicalities. 'But there'll be no room. You'll be falling over Mickey and the other fellow all the time.'

'Mickey's going to London with Grant, as part of the business. George is moving out.'

'Ah well . . . This is all very sudden, isn't it?'

'I'll not be far away, Mam. I'll still see you, just as regular.'

'Oh, fiddlesticks to that. What I mean is, you've chosen the wrong man! Grant's the one for you. Tom's a nobody, any fool could see that.'

'He's not as bad as you think, Mam. It would never have worked out with Grant. He lives for his work. He's got no room for me.'

'Have it your own way, Carly. I'll still be here when you've had enough of him.'

Carly cried, her mother cried, and they both held each other until it was time for Carly to go.

Living with Carly put Tom in a very good mood indeed. It was like winning the pools. The flat was kept tidy, he worked solidly every day writing songs and poetry. They made love several times a night. Carly cooked him proper meals. He behaved himself. He no longer needed to go out and get drunk.

Carly found making love with Tom so much more exciting than with Grant. She started to come more freely. Tom was selfish as a lover, up to a point, and yet he was straightforward. With Grant she'd always had to tease him out of his shell, always had to find the key to what would make him happy in bed.

Tom had carefree gusto. As a result, she completely forgot her earlier worries about him. He had redeemed himself and now she could only think of her time with Grant as having been claustrophobic, unhappy, devoted to pandering to his ego.

But Grant hadn't disappeared from their lives for good. It was more complicated than that. Ties still bound them. Ironically, the further apart they grew as friends, and the further away Grant was in physical distance, the stronger were the links that bound them together.

Grant was pretty sick when he heard that Carly had moved in with Tom, something she had always resisted doing with him. What had come over her? Was it just to spite Grant, or what? Although there was nothing he could do about it, Carly's action rankled.

Tom's song 'Tantalizing' was recorded by Johnny as the B side of his next single. The A side came, as before, from Rupert and Green. It was called 'The World Goes Round'. Grant would pick up his share of Tom's royalties after they had made their way to Starfinders from the record company and the music publishers and the Performing Right Society. This might irk Tom, but it meant Grant could say he was doing something for Tom in a professional sense, as he was obliged to do.

What neither had quite bargained for was the stroke of fate that led Decca to make a change of plan at the last moment. They felt, on hearing Johnny's recordings, that

'Tantalizing' was the stronger of the two numbers. More to the point, it would make a better title track for Johnny's first LP which they were now at last talking about.

Grant was torn two ways: wanting to put down the man who had stolen Carly from him, but equally excited at the prospect of telling him he'd written the A side of a potential hit. Grant did in fact care about his clients. It was just that he didn't actually *like* this one.

There was no stopping Grant when he reached London. At first he was slightly bewildered. Everyone else seemed so at home, so on top of things, and he didn't even know his way about. He borrowed more money from Old Trevor in order to buy a short lease on an office. He took on a new secretary called Jan Ferry, and Mickey came South to act as general dogsbody. The office had fitted carpets and giant black-and-white shots of his clients lined the entrance hall.

Grant was visibly high on the atmosphere that began to surround his enterprise. The atmosphere of London in that spring of 1965 gave him a tingle of excitement too. But he was nervous as well. He worried whether he had taken the right step, worried that he would run out of money before he'd got properly started. The money from records took a long time to reach his pocket, and he was only on a percentage of his artistes' earnings, after all. They had to earn a great deal before he had anything to show for it.

At first he took a small flat for himself in Dean Street, not far from Starfinders' Soho office. He was impressed to find that a stripper called Busty lived on the floor below. Two tarts noisily plied their trade on the floor above him. If he couldn't bear to listen to the creaking of bedsprings above him, he simply put on his record player very loud.

He was drawn to the boutiques springing up in and around Carnaby Street. The men's shops with names like His Clothes and Adonis had an atmosphere utterly different to what he'd been used to, selling sober suits to businessmen at

Hendersons. They were brightly lit and loud with music. He was amazed by the campness of the male assistants, who poked around his inside leg measurement and squeezed his shoulders, making remarks like 'You've some good muscles there . . .'

The girls' shops, he noticed, made Carly's Paradise seem tame by comparison.

Looking at the floral ties and brightly-coloured shirts, he decided he was born to be square. He settled on a cream-coloured suit, plain shirt, and a wide, dark kipper tie. The suit became his uniform for the rest of the sixties and, indeed, beyond.

Although Grant had groomed his appearance to his reasonable satisfaction, he knew he must do much better for his star. Johnny's leathers were beginning to look dated. There had been mutterings from the record company that Johnny's image was wrong for the kind of songs he was recording. They were not so much straight rock numbers now as broader pop. Grant took Johnny off to a showbiz tailor in Carnaby Street and they agonized long and hard over the choice of suits, settling mostly for ones with flared trousers and wide lapels.

'If you can't get the cut right, Bernie,' Grant said to the tailor, 'we'll have to give him some sort of contraption, like a cricketer's box or a jock strap.'

Bernie, very seriously, said, 'Yes, just give the word, that's quite usual these days.'

Johnny laughed.

Then Grant had to make a deal with the tailor. He didn't get much of one. Bernie would knock a few shillings off the price if Johnny gave him a signed photo to put in the window with those of other stars he served. Grant didn't feel he'd handled this very well. He could have done with Carly to give advice on the clothes and the deal. But that was all over now.

One Saturday he was passing an Elliot's shop and saw a

queue of girls stretching out of the door, waiting to buy their kinky boots. It caught Grant on the raw and only reminded him of what he had lost. He brooded for the rest of the day. Only when he gained admission to the Adlib Club with Johnny did he manage to throw off the mood. They got down to the serious business of finding female company.

'Two tykes on the razzle,' Johnny whispered to him.

'You said it, Johnny, you said it. Now, see those two dolly-birds over there? Go tell them you're Johnny Todd, the singing sensation, and see how you get on.'

'No, they won't have heard of me. You do it for me. That's what you're for, isn't it?'

'No, it's bloody well not. Oh, hell, come on, we'll do it together.'

Tom took to spending much of each day in Carly's small office, round the back of Paradise. For him, it was a change from long days strumming his guitar at the flat or attempting to write more songs and poems. For her, it was pleasing to have him around, so full was he of good humour and charm. It did no harm to business, either, except when he paid more interest than he should to girls passing in and out of the changing cubicles.

But it wasn't an ideal arrangement because he prevented her from getting on with her work. And when they started popping off to Tom's flat during the day for a bout of love-making, with Fawn left minding the store, it didn't bode well for the business.

'So what?' Tom would ritually answer when Carly raised the matter. 'What d'you want all the money for, any road?'

'It's all right for you, you've got money coming in.'

'Hasn't arrived yet.'

'It will, though. The shop's not making much, you know, and if you keep draggin' me off, it'll get worse.'

'I don't understand you. You make all the money you

need. If you want money for its own sake, you should've stuck with Grant.'

'Oh, Tom, don't say that.'

Tom brushed his hand through his tousled hair and then held Carly close to him. It was their way out of every disagreement. The physical way. If Tom disclaimed ambition, for money or fame, he was not, of course, being totally honest with himself, merely providing protection against failure. Quietly, he tried to prod his career forward. When he heard that 'Tantalizing' had been chosen as the A side of Johnny Todd's new single, he set about trying to capitalize on the fact.

'I rang that Tony Preston today,' he told Carly.

'The Decca man. What for?'

'To see if he'd come and hear me sing.'

'But that's Grant's job. He's your agent.'

'Grant'll never do anything for me. He wouldn't lift a phone to help if I was hanging by me fingers from a window ledge. No, I'm going to have to do it myself, until I can free myself of Star-fucking-finders.'

'You'll never do that. Your songs'll always make money, and Grant will always handle them.'

'Whose side are you on, for Christ's sake? I can still make the break as a performer without him. That's why I rang Preston. He came up here to hear Johnny Todd, so why not me?'

'And is he going to?'

'Well, not at the moment.'

'He turned you down?'

'Well, actually I didn't get to speak to him, only some grotty secretary. She said he'd ring me back.'

'But he hasn't?'

'No.'

'Poor Tom. If Grant had rung him for you, he'd have listened.'

'That's not the point.'

Which was a pity because Tom had begun to sing again with Sauce, playing to small gigs attended by real blues enthusiasts. If Tony Preston had answered Tom's call, he might have been genuinely impressed.

Carly went with Fawn to watch Tom perform. It was an odd experience, seeing someone she loved and had made love to singing his heart out up there, making love to all the women in the audience. She tried not to worry about it. He was hers. She looked away, and examined what the other girls there were wearing. If only they would all pay a visit to Paradise, she would sort them out. It would help sort out the business, too.

She overheard two blues fans talking about Tom.

'He's not the real thing, that's for sure.'

'Well, he's not from the Deep South, and he's not coloured, if that's what you mean.'

'No, he's too young. Not suffered enough. To sing the blues properly, you've got to have been through it.'

Carly thought to herself, 'I wonder if Tom will *ever* go through it?' Being half successful and maybe a quarter famous wouldn't rate very highly on any scale of suffering.

Grant was the most surprised of all when Johnny Todd's record reached No. 1 in June 1965. He hadn't had to bribe any disc jockeys to play it on the radio or fix the charts by buying up stocks at certain record shops. 'Tantalizing' had reached the top because people liked it.

Another countrywide tour had to be arranged, this time with Johnny at the very top of the bill. Grant set it up with one of the big London promoters. There was to be no more working with Alan Greenlee. Rex Room was again the compere and the rest of the bill was filled out with acts from other managements.

Johnny was mobbed everywhere he went. Mickey was in charge of looking after him and organizing mad dashes about the country in pursuit of publicity. Between shows in

Bolton they rushed to Manchester for an appearance on *Top of the Pops*, which the BBC broadcast from a TV studio in a converted chapel.

The dash meant there was no time for Johnny to visit Maureen and their son in Salford. Grant had already asked a showbiz lawyer to put together a separation deal. The actual divorce would take a good deal longer to arrange.

Johnny was written up in the papers as the lastest pop heart-throb. He was photographed in nightclubs with various models, or 'girls' as they had been described previously. At one point, Grant himself was featured in a newspaper interview. He was dubbed the 'new Brian Epstein'. Grant had tried unsuccessfully to play down his Liverpool origins. 'After all, Johnny Todd's not from Liverpool,' he said. 'Anyway, tomorrow he'll belong to the world . . .'

'Crap,' exclaimed Tom when Carly showed him the piece. 'It's gone to his head. Mind you, they're all mad in London.'

Carly took another look at the article and said, diplomatic as ever, 'The journalist probably made it up, they always do. You can't blame Grant.'

'And what about the poor guy who actually wrote "Tantalizing"! Not a bloody mention. I *am* one of his clients, after all.'

'Quit slagging him off, Tom. Or I'll put a ban on any mention of him.'

'Good idea.'

Carly was worried that the honeymoon period with Tom would end now that his song had got to No. 1, that somehow it would come between them. Indeed, Tom did start throwing his money around. He wanted to go out and show off rather than stay at home with Carly. He increasingly held court in the Philly or the Blue Angel. Carly tagged along but didn't much like it. She was quietly impatient when Tom went into his routine, usually for the benefit of a young girl, rather younger than herself.

'You know "Tantalizing"? The Johnny Todd song?'

'What of it?'

'Well, d'you know who wrote it?'

'Didn't *he*?'

It always went like that. Songwriters had little to show for their trouble, except for the royalty statement at the end of the year. Carly hoped that Tom would get over it eventually and come back to her, in spirit, just as he had been in their first few wonderful months together.

It wasn't long before she began to suspect that he was seeing other women during the day, when she was busy in the shop and he had time on his hands. There was always someone who would be impressed by his talk and by his success in the pop world, whether it was obvious success or not. Carly shrank from asking him directly about these other women; in a way she simply didn't want to know.

She couldn't make up her mind whether she missed Grant or not. As soon as he'd gone, she realized life wouldn't be the same. She also began to sense that whatever man she was with always ended up more important than she was. She was Grant's or Tom's girl friend, no one ever saw them as her boy friends. With Grant, she had made a major contribution to the success of Starfinders. She had been with Grant when he talent-spotted Johnny Todd. But she had nothing to show for it now. Tom admitted that 'Tantalizing' had been inspired by her. But where was her reward in that?

Worse, though, was her feeling that she'd been left behind. Had she been right to ditch Grant? Was it really so that she could stay with her mother? Or was it so that she could be with Tom? Did her mother even mind whether she stayed at home or not? It was two years now since Carly's father died. Feelings changed. Why should she restrict herself?

She brooded over these questions, and yet she also had a kind of commitment to Liverpool itself. The circus might have moved on. They all laughed at what Allen Ginsberg said, that the city had become the 'centre of the consciousness of the human universe', but it was all they had to hold on to. Liverpool was already beginning to live off its recent past as a cradle of pop music just as it had for so long lived off its past as a great port.

No, Carly wasn't going to leave it. She was going to stay on with the others, in the wake of the tornado, and try to live her life as best she could. All the people who had used the city to fuel their talents and careers, and then moved on, could do what they liked, but she wasn't going to join them.

And yet, she and Tom in Liverpool were like Grant down South in one respect. They felt they had missed out on something. Carly, because she thought she had achieved little for herself, only through her men; Tom, because he wasn't recognized for what he'd done; and Grant, outwardly successful, felt he'd let slip the one thing he really needed to make sense of it all.

He would have to win her back.

PART TWO

Fare thee well to Princes' Landing Stage,
River Mersey fare thee well.
I am off to Califor-ni-a,
A place I know right well.

The Leaving of Liverpool

CHAPTER 9

There had been a house on the site since the twelfth century. Now there was the Jacobean mansion with nineteenth-century renovations, together with the farm which had existed since the eighteenth century. In addition, there were two hundred acres of land, not to mention a medium-sized lake with a boat hut, and a small river no more than eight feet wide.

The last Sunday of June 1968, the first of the real summer, there was a light haze over the fields at dawn. Then the birds began singing lustily, heralding what promised to be a long and gorgeous day. There was buzzing and scratching in the hedgerows, and on the finely razored lawn two black labradors, Hansel and Gretel, leapt and barked as the temperature rose.

Otherwise, it was quiet. Only the distant roar of planes taking off from London Airport twenty miles away caused any distraction. It was peaceful, an idyll such as might have been enjoyed at Quornford House in Berkshire any time during the past several centuries. The only sign of modern times was a yellow E-type Jaguar parked on the gravel drive by the front door. And the sound of rock music which suddenly burst through stained-glass windows in the Great Hall round about lunchtime.

The music ceased as abruptly as it had begun and Grant Pickering appeared at the garden door. Hansel and Gretel raced towards him and he patted their heads, while they wiped their muzzles on his hands. He wore a pair of blue flared jeans and a psychedelic T-shirt bearing the Starfinders logo. He was stockier than he had been back in the Liverpool days. Too much good living, too much wine.

Now, he walked contentedly about his estate in a pair of flip-flops, throwing a much-chewed rubber ball for the labradors to catch.

His hair was much longer than it had been when he first came South and he now wore a pair of granny specs, small round lenses in wire frames, such as John Lennon had made fashionable with last year's *Sergeant Pepper*. Grant actually needed them, but he'd probably have worn them anyway. There was a gold bracelet on his left wrist and a thin gold chain round his neck. On it was written a woman's name, though few could decipher it.

Alerted by the dogs' barking, Mrs Pugh, the housekeeper, came out to ask what Mr Pickering would be doing for lunch.

'I don't know, Dot, I'm not fussy. It rather depends on the visitor.'

Mrs Pugh made no comment.

'Is she up yet?' Grant asked.

'Don't ask me, dear.'

'She's awful in the morning. Some women are like that.'

'I'll take your word for it.'

'Really dreadful, and she's always late, never ready on time. She'll be late for her own funeral. Takes *days* fiddling with her hair. Pathological.'

Mrs Pugh felt like asking why, if the girl in question had so many drawbacks, Grant had brought her down to Quornford for the weekend. But that would be a silly question. Her employer had his pick, now that he was such a big noise in the pop world. They were queueing up for him.

She settled for saying, 'Dear, dear.'

'So we'll have lunch round about teatime, I expect.' Grant laughed loudly and went over to a door in the old stables and wheeled out sunchairs and lilos. It was a standing observation among cronies who'd been invited there that Grant had everything at Quornford, the house, the grounds, the lake, but he didn't have a swimming pool.

What was the point of a Hollywood life style if it didn't include a swimming pool?

Grant stripped off the T-shirt, put on his shades, and sat in the sun leafing through the Sunday papers and colour supplements. At times he would laugh to himself over a picture, occasionally murmur an expletive, but on the whole he seemed pleased whenever he came across a mention of one of his ever-growing stable of talent.

In the *News of the World* there was tittle-tattle about Johnny Todd's latest girlfriend. Grant knew it was untrue. Merely some 'model' or 'actress' using Johnny to get publicity. Whether there had really been any change in the girl Johnny was carrying on with would be revealed later when the singer came over from his own country house, sixteen miles away.

In the *Sunday Mirror* was a piece about Quentin Saint, the talented young pianist/singer/composer whom Grant had discovered. He had been set to work writing songs for himself and others; he'd had a minor chart success, but there was no hurry, he would turn up trumps one day.

It was in the *Sunday Express* that an item really caught Grant's attention. He first of all pulled the outstretched newspaper towards him, then folded it carefully so he could read the short caption a second time. There was a pin-up, an attractive blonde in a Monroe pose with one arm held aloft at an angle, the hand on the back of her head. She had a laughing face, a wide-lipped smile, and she was called Suzie Paul. It said she was an actress and a singer, but then so was every girl whose picture was in the *Sunday Express*. Usually, they were just chorus, or had appeared a couple of times on TV.

There was something about this girl, though. An openness, a kind of yearning appeal, as if she was asking to be looked after. And despite the pose, she had unmistakable class. Grant responded to that and slipped a tiny notepad out of the back pocket of his jeans. He scribbled a message to himself which he would probably have difficulty in deciphering next day: 'Suzie Paul – agent?' Then he forgot about her.

He had company now. Slowly ambling across the lawn towards him, conscious of her grace, was a tall, slender, black girl in a miniskirt, top, and little else. No shoes. She moved like a gazelle, or a fawn, or some even more exotic creature.

Grant folded the paper and put it among the rest. 'I thought you'd never get up,' he said.

The girl knelt on the sunbed at his side and stroked the back of his hand. 'You weren't there when I woke.'

'Can't stay in bed all day. Had any breakfast?'

'Orange juice, that's all.'

'Look at the papers?'

'I'd rather sit by the pool.'

'There is no pool,' Grant said with a touch of mock exasperation. 'But there bloody soon will be if we have any more complaints! You'll have to sit by me instead.'

Halo gave one of her odd little smiles and unpacked her limbs. She stretched out ravishingly on the sunbed, her leopard-skin miniskirt just skimming the tops of her legs.

Grant looked down at the body he had enjoyed the previous night. What a pity she was always finding difficulties, always putting on an act, because physically she was a knock-out. It was hard to tell whether she was truly mysterious or truly thick. Or was she on drugs?

Whatever his other vices, and he was adding to them daily, Grant never touched drugs. He didn't see the point, life was good enough as it was. Everyone else in the business seemed to be on them though, or acted as if they were. They made people moody, unpredictable, maddening. How was Grant supposed to know whether people's behaviour had been brought on by a spot of mainlining behind the sofa or whether they were really like that?

Halo was a dancer, incomparably graceful, wonderfully

proportioned, even if her tits were the size of raisins. Grant would have preferred a proper ballerina, or so he had thought for some time, because such women seemed to convey effortless, uncomplicated sexuality, although a touch hermetically sealed. Halo didn't have quite that class. She had been to ballet school, so she said, but she was too tall. Or, as Grant suspected, too difficult.

She was on the make in a very open way. She would sleep with anyone who might advance her career. Grant was now an important person, glamorous in himself and by association. Anyone who controlled the destinies of Johnny Todd, Quentin Saint, the Wreckers, the Whiter Shades, Pacific Sunrise, and Effie Dunne was no fool and worth keeping in with. Grant was not her agent or manager, yet, but that was something Halo was working on in the only way known to her. Even if she had to work long nights on her back, or, given Grant's current preference, her front, she would achieve it.

Like so many of the women who had passed through Grant's bed since he came South three years earlier, Halo didn't feel she really knew him. Nor was she getting to know him. He always kept too much back.

'I've never been to Liverpool,' she began.

He cut her off: 'Nah, they wouldn't let you in.'

She lay for a moment with her eyes still closed while the sun burned down on her black face, then continued, 'What's it like?'

Grant wondered where this question had come from. He never mentioned Liverpool these days. The place no longer had any meaning in his world. He was keen to forget he'd ever come from there. But Halo must have read something about him which made the connection.

'It's a great place to get out of,' he said. 'I'm glad I lived there once, though. At least I don't have any funny ideas about it. But the best part is the road out.'

'Did you know the Beatles?'

Grant sighed inwardly. 'Oh, sure, sure. Great guys, great guys. Pity they've gone all peculiar and psychedelic now, but there you are. There's no knocking them, though.'

He took off his granny specs. 'Of course, they're up the creek since Eppy topped himself. Not that he was much help to them when they really took off.'

Halo turned on her side, so that she could study Grant as he talked to her. 'Yes, what happened to Brian Epstein?'

'How should I know? He was queer and Jewish and couldn't cope. Will that do?'

'At least he wasn't black.' Halo laughed at her own joke. 'Oh, you're a hard man, Grant,' she said, gripping the calf of his left leg. 'Feel those muscles!' Then, after a pause: 'So you'll not be committing suicide yourself?'

'No bloody fear! The last thing I'd do.' Grant chuckled. 'I'd be too scared. And I just can't imagine life ever getting so bad that I'd feel like doing it. Okay, I get pretty het up at times, but there are compensations.'

Grant, for the thousandth time, cast a proprietorial eye over his estate, and saw that it was good.

For lunch, Halo had a few pieces of lettuce, while Grant had a hamburger which Mrs Pugh made using a special machine he had brought back from the States. He had a neat bourbon to accompany it and was going to pour another when Halo poked her fingernail into his flabby stomach and whispered, 'Fatty!'

They wrestled with each other, both shrieking with laughter, until in time the shrieks and child's play subsided. Halo wondered if they'd end up screwing there and then on the sunbed; the fooling about had made her feel randy. Instead, Grant briskly pulled her up and took her for the obligatory walk down the long garden terrace, through a small wood, and into the fields beyond.

The light summer breeze combined with the sun was perfect. Grant took Halo down to the lake.

'I must get all these reeds seen to one day,' he said.

'Or build a swimming pool.'

'Steady, girl, steady.' They ambled down to the old boathouse. Grant managed to get the door open. Part of the roof had fallen in and a rowing boat lay full of water, blocking the slipway. Through the doors facing on to the lake there was an enchanting scene across the water and back up to the house.

Maybe it had something to do with coming from Liverpool, but even if he couldn't live near a proper river, Grant liked to be where there was water, of a kind.

He knew what he would do next, almost as though he had planned the walk to lead up to it. There was a fallen tree near the boathouse, felled by lightning. The grass had grown up round it like a skirt and it was clear that it had lain that way for several years, though the bark was reasonably intact.

Grant motioned to Halo that she should lie back along the trunk. Then he pushed up her skirt and discovered, as expected, that she was wearing nothing underneath. He closed his eyes and thought, as ever, of a woman far away. In his mind, he was making love to Carly.

Afterwards, they lay rigid on the tree trunk for several minutes, both breathing hard and fast. Then Grant became aware of a voice calling far away and gradually came back from where he'd been in his mind. It wasn't a voice now but a cat-call.

'I think Johnny Todd's arrived,' Halo said with difficulty from under him.

Grant turned on top of her and looked and said, 'God, you're right. Trust him to turn up now.'

He lifted himself off her, then dragged Halo, weak at the knees, back up the hill to the house. Johnny sat, leaning out of his Rolls, still laughing at what he had seen.

Sitting with him was his girl of the moment. Virna Jones was bright as a button. Her copper-coloured hair was cropped short in a Vidal Sassoon five-point cut. Grant wasn't sure what she did. He thought Johnny might have met her at some TV date. Now she seemed to hang around with Johnny full time. In spite of all the temptations that came his way, he appeared to have been quite faithful to Virna for six or seven months now. Grant thought that when Johnny's divorce finally came through, they might well marry.

'Frightening the fucking ducks?' Johnny said in his still broad Northern tones, and banged his hand on the window sill of the Rolls with glee.

'Shurrup, you peeping Tom,' said Grant in mock embarrassment.

'Serve you right if a bee had stung you on the bum!'

Halo was quite unfazed.

Virna opened the door on her side of the Rolls and hopped out on to the gravel. She walked over to Grant and gave him a kiss, touched Halo on the arm and winked at her. Then she went back to Johnny, who had opened his door now and was sitting, kitted out as if for golf, half in the car but with his feet on the ground.

'Bloody trespassers,' said Grant. 'I mean, if you can't have a hump in your own back yard, what is the country coming to?'

'It's because he's from the North, you know,' Johnny said to Virna. Then he turned to Halo. 'People always do it in their clothes in the North.'

'If they do it in the open, I'm not surprised,' she snapped back.

'They always have the lights out, too,' Grant added.

He waved them round to the main lawn and poured them drinks from the portable cabinet.

'Been reading about you,' he mentioned to Johnny, touching the pile of newspapers with his toe.

'Where, where?'

Grant was amused how eager Johnny still was, even now, to read about himself in the papers.

'*News of the Screws*, in the middle somewhere.'

Johnny took time to find the piece alleging the identity of his new girl friend.

He read slowly, then said, 'Silly bitch! I've never even met her.'

'Let's see,' said Virna.

'Well, what are we going to do, then?' Grant asked. It took great restraint for him not to be doing anything. He had a housekeeper, an odd-job man, two gardeners, a chauffeur/butler, as well as several groundsmen to keep Quornford in order. He could delegate jobs as though born to it, which was just as well. He wasn't even thirty yet and he was said to be on his way to his first million. He didn't have to lift a finger if he didn't want to, but it was against his nature to stand around; he always had to be doing something or organizing other people into doing things. If Johnny and Virna didn't come up with an idea soon, he'd have them dead-heading roses or weeding.

Johnny, on the other hand, had long since mastered the art of doing nothing most of the day. He only had to work about one day in seven, and golf was now his main interest in life. Grant tried to keep this quiet. Golf was all very well for Bing Crosby, but it didn't quite suit Johnny's image. At least, not according to the life plan that Grant had drawn up for him.

'You'll stay for dinner, you two?' Grant asked.

'Yeh, sure,' they answered in unison. Grant rang a bell and told Mrs Pugh.

In the end, they couldn't think of anything to do that they could all agree on. So, to Grant's dismay, the four of them sat idly all afternoon in the sun, looking at the scenery, pouring endless drinks and making small talk. They mostly rubbished other people in the business, or speculated on their sexual preferences.

Every so often, Mrs Pugh would come to the garden door and tell Grant he was needed on the telephone. He would lope inside, ostensibly cursing the interruption, but actually glad to have something to do.

At dusk Grant made the decision that they would eat in the open air. If there was one thing he had acquired a taste for since he'd come up in the world it was dining *al fresco*. It was the most beautiful thing to do. As the sun went down, they sat on the terrace, drinking Mouton-Rothschild '64 and greedily devouring the lamb stuffed with mushrooms that Mrs Pugh had prepared.

When Johnny came to put some redcurrant jelly with the lamb, he inspected the jar expertly and told Halo, very seriously, how it was exactly the same stuff they sold at the Co-op when he'd worked there, except the label was different.

'This stuff costs five times as much,' he added, 'but Grant's worth a bob or two, as you probably know.'

'You never!' Halo joshed him. 'I'd no idea.' She was only pecking at the feast, preserving her shape for dancing.

Grant pushed his nose into the wine and held it up to the sun sinking behind the trees. They lingered out of doors in the warm evening, as happy as they were able to be.

Around nine thirty, Grant was called away again to the telephone. He put on a show of being irritated by the interruption but when he came back to the table his mood had genuinely changed. He sat silently absorbed by what he had heard, until at ten o'clock Johnny and Virna left to find livelier company. Halo was despatched back to London in the Bentley with Webb, Grant's chauffeur, at the wheel. Grant excused himself on the grounds that he'd had some bad news and wanted to be alone to think about it. Halo was clearly annoyed at this curt dismissal, barely giving Grant a farewell kiss. She didn't take kindly to being reminded that she was little more than Grant's plaything.

Grant headed straight for his den where there was a record player, a piano, and where the walls were lined with gold and silver discs that his clients had given him for safekeeping, or because the trophies meant more to him than to them.

He sat alone in his special chair and brooded over the news he had just received. It was sad news, but it gave him hope. His house and the grounds, his style of life, were the rewards of his skill and hard work, but they lacked the human touch, just as he lacked a woman's love.

Now, a stroke of fate had given him the chance to achieve what most he wanted.

CHAPTER 10

Carly and Tom were still more or less together after three years. They were seen to be a couple, almost man and wife, though living together in Tom's flat hadn't lasted longer than the first couple of years. After the initial togetherness, Tom had begun to revert to his old ways, apparently unchanged by the peculiar form of success he had enjoyed as the writer of two songs recorded by Johnny Todd and the royalties that had at last come in from them.

He'd had some success as a performer, but still only locally. He sang with groups, but never on a regular basis; he occasionally appeared as a solo performer; he wrote many more songs than were ever performed; he had written nothing substantial, like a musical for instance.

He was still writing poetry, but had yet to have any of it published except in the most minor of magazines. A particular humiliation had come his way in March 1967 when a book called *The Liverpool Scene* was published, celebrating the work of the Liverpool poets. He was not one of them. He had, however, been invited to the launching party held, inevitably, at the Cavern.

He could hardly bring himself to go there since it had been renovated. They had destroyed the old, sweaty atmosphere and replaced it with plastic fittings. There were rooms marked 'cavemen' and 'cavewomen'. As for the bunch of journalists, freeloaders and pseuds the publishers had brought from London for the day by train, he could barely disguise his contempt for them. He dragged Carly along with him, telling her that Paradise was quite capable of looking after itself for a few hours, and they both stuffed themselves with canapés and lukewarm champagne until they felt sick. This brought matters between them to a head.

'God, how I hate those journos. Hacks!'

Tom had pulled Carly into a corner and was slagging off the day-trippers. 'Like bloody missionaries come to see how we're getting on.'

'No need to be bitter, Tom. You've not done too badly. Just because you're not in the book, it's not the end of the world.'

'No, but it's just bloody typical. I hate our lives being run by these toffee-nosed prats from London, treating us like a load of provincials. Well, we're not provincials, we're Northerners, or Liverpudlians, or whatever. Grant Pickering's just the same.'

Carly had been waiting for that. Grant's name always came up when Tom felt like whingeing.

'He sold out going to London and taking up with middle-of-the-road wankers like Quentin Saint. And he turned Johnny Todd into more of a middle-of-the-roader than he was in the first place.'

'Rubbish, Tom, you don't know what you're talking about. When Grant and I first heard Johnny he was the poor man's Frank Sinatra. The rock stuff was just a stage he went through.'

'Doesn't matter. It still means he's middle-of-the-road, and it's all Grant's fault.'

'You always say that.'

'Well, what's he ever done for me?'

'Oh, not that one again.'

'Well, I'm supposed to be one of his clients. He's very good at taking his percentage, for which he never lifts a finger, but when did he last get me anything?'

Tom was trapped in what to him was an impossible position. He was still under the exclusive contract with Starfinders that Grant, under pressure from Carly, had offered him three years before. All his earnings had to pass through Grant's company and the only way he could get out of the arrangement was for his earnings to fall below a certain level. But the royalties from his songs were unlikely, in the foreseeable future, to fall below the stated level.

Tom felt the contract was an example of Grant's sharp practice. He had forgotten how desperately he had leant on Grant to be put on Starfinders' books.

'Seems to me Grant's very useful to you,' Carly responded provocatively.

'What the hell d'you mean by that?'

'He's a useful peg on which to hang your failure, isn't he?'

'*What?*'

'It's true. You're always on about him. Never stop. I don't know where you'd be without him to moan about.'

Tom was angry. All the more so as he knew Carly was right.

'Shut your big gob,' he said. 'At least you get a good fuck from me. You're like a little spaniel, the way you dote on him, always speak up for him. If that's all I'm going to hear, I just don't need you.'

He stomped off, leaving Carly standing in the gloom of the place where she'd first met him. Her eyes brimmed with tears; she refused comfort from Fawn Flack, who hung around her as ever, waiting to pick up the pieces, still hoping for any kind of luck herself.

Tom left the Cavern with a girl called Lindsay on his arm. She was a reporter from the *Echo*.

The row in itself wasn't justification for their splitting up, it was the culmination of months of discontent with each other, discontent fuelled by Tom's lack of progress, by too much closeness, now no longer made any easier by the energetic sex they still enjoyed.

In later years, one of the poets in the book was to tell Tom that three other relationships or marriages had crashed on the occasion of the *Liverpool Scene* party, which might have been some compensation if he'd known it at the time.

As it was, Carly went back to her mother's house in Lily Street. It wasn't the end of her relationship with Tom. He came and made it up soon enough, but they didn't go back to living together.

Tom decided, not for the first time, that he must do something and quit moaning. He was in the ludicrous position of not wanting to work at all, because Grant stood to gain a share of the proceeds. He sat at home drinking, smoking, getting scruffier and scruffier, experiencing the spiritual degradation of being out of work with little of the actual discomfort. He knew he had to break out of it.

It was impossible to shake Grant Pickering's complacency, not least because he was two hundred miles away and usually facing in the opposite direction. But Tom would have a try. Small beer he might be in Starfinders' terms, but he would somehow exert his independence. He had already cheated by not putting all his gigs through the agency as he was supposed to do. Now came another opportunity. At first, Tom was suspicious when word reached him in December 1967 that two researchers and a producer were coming over to Liverpool from Granada Television in Manchester. They were looking for 'young, dynamic members of the Liverpool scene' to take part in a new programme that would go out in the Granada region only.

The team arrived and plied the local youth with drinks at the Philly. They had already co-opted a couple of Liverpool journalists who were noted for maintaining their Scouse roots while contributing to national newspapers and magazines. There was a girl designer, some would-be models, the odd published poet, and Tom and Carly.

Tom was the vaguely familiar singer and songwriter who somehow contrived to get himself written about in the papers from time to time. Carly was the girl who had opened Liverpool's 'first boutique', but of whom not very much had been heard recently. Paradise was suffering from increased competition. Other boutiques and the larger stores had moved in on her patch.

It all seemed a touch confused but the producer in the cashmere sweater explained that the idea was to have a well-known person up from London, a politician, entertainer, or whoever, and get him to answer questions from the young audience. The guest would sit in a special chair on a podium while the audience clustered round and put him or her 'on the spot', which was a possible title for the show. A pop group would be thrown in for good measure and 'happenings' were promised.

Tom and Carly put on their act of being charming, fluent and with-it for the researchers and were duly invited to take part in the first programme broadcast live from Manchester at 10.30 on a Wednesday night. It had finally been decided to call the show *The Hot Seat*.

The first guest, in that opening week of 1968, was Sir Edgar King, a doughty Conservative ex-minister, now in opposition. He had to answer a series of cheeky questions from the young audience but he put up a predictably good show. The Who had been brought in to supply the musical break and chattered among themselves until it was time to play. Then the youngsters sprang to life and danced. Carly, having been put up to it by the producer, pulled Sir Edgar on to his feet and did something approaching the Twist with him.

Tom's teeth were on edge during the whole proceedings. He considered the show patronizing to the young, to the North, and to the viewers. After the musical break, he took out his feelings on the wily old politician, who ducked and weaved like a veteran under Tom's provocation. It wasn't clear whether Tom had taken in too much from the hospitality trolley before the show, but he behaved as though he had.

A row developed about whether the Conservatives had done anything for the North-west when they'd been in power. Sir Edgar attempted to rattle off the statistics he'd brought along but Tom belaboured him with abuse and wouldn't let him get a word in. With one deft movement he pinched Sir Edgar's notes and threw them away. It was riveting stuff, or puerile and embarrassing, depending on the viewers' point of view.

But Tom was never a very good judge of when he was going too far and, as on so many occasions in the past, he ended up getting physical. He started jabbing Sir Edgar with his finger.

'What have the Tories ever done for Liverpool, eh?' he kept asking.

The other youngsters heckled and cat-called until, just as the final credits were about to roll, Tom, with uncanny timing (which made people wonder whether he'd been put up to it) aimed a punch at the now bewildered and eager-to-be-away politician.

After the final credit had faded from the screen, Sir Edgar was rapidly smothered in apologies by the smooth-talking producer in the cashmere sweater and bundled off to the Midland Hotel.

'Great, great, Tom,' the producer bounced up to the Liverpudlian. 'Wonderful television. Can you come back next week?'

'And do the same again, you mean?'

'Well, no, we've got Godfrey Winn coming. But you were great, really great. The switchboard's jammed.'

Carly was in two minds over what Tom had done. She could see that Sir Edgar was an irritating, pompous fellow whose methods needed to be rumbled, but she hated it when Tom started using his fists. It was all very well him being physical with her, but did he have to get physical with *everybody*?

They travelled back to Liverpool in the mini-van laid on by Granada. Carly went to spend the night at Tom's flat and he finally calmed down. He was certain in his own mind that he hadn't made a fool of himself, or done anything amiss.

There it would have ended, except that next morning's papers picked up the story in their Northern editions. Then because a national politician was involved, the London evening papers printed the news, too. In this way, the incident came to Grant Pickering's attention. Tom had been appearing on television without telling him, in breach of their agreement.

'Oh, it was nothing,' Tom replied, when confronted by Grant over the phone, 'just a local show, you know. I was hardly even "appearing", just a member of the audience.'

'How much did they pay you?'

'Does it matter? Ten guineas or something. I signed a bit of paper, the way you always do, but it's not like a fee.'

'If you signed a piece of paper, it was a contract, Tom, and it should have come through this organization.'

'You fucking money-grubber, we're talking about a couple of quid. I'll send it to you, in stamps, if you must be so petty.'

'We'd better have a talk about it soon,' Grant snapped back, and carefully replaced the receiver.

Tom considered this as merely another example of Grant's megalomania. A few bob kept back by Tom was of no importance to anybody. Grant hadn't even got him the engagement.

Carly, when she found out, was surprised that Grant was making a fuss, but wondered if there was more to it. Was Grant looking for an excuse to dump Tom?

'One thing, luv,' she said to Tom, 'if Grant says he's entitled to it, then he is. He's big on contracts. He spent ages swotting up the law before he left here. That's his job, anyway, reading the small print.'

'He's mad, then. He's still out to get me because of you and me. He'll never let up until he gets you back. But I know you won't go. I'm dead sure of that. You'll never go back to him, will you?'

Carly said nothing, appalled by his arrogant assumption.

'God,' he went on, 'I curse the day I went and bloody begged for him to take me on.'

'You'll have to get out of the agreement then.'

'Easier said than done. He won't want to lose his share of the royalties from my songs, will he?'

'I suppose not. But why don't you go and have a talk with him, *sensibly*, Tom? I hate this rowing that's been going on ever since you first met him.'

'Okay, luv. I'll see what I can do.'

When they did have a chat, Grant was all charm. He'd got Tom to travel to London to see him – 'I'll pay your train fare, of course' (which made Tom wince) – and then behaved as though it were a small matter, a terrible mis-understanding, and he didn't want anything to come between them.

Tom was momentarily taken aback by this ploy. He'd arrived at Starfinders with such a head of steam that he'd been ready to knock Grant's block off.

'I don't care what you say, Grant. That contract you got me to sign was a fix. It's not fair and I bet it wouldn't stand up in court.'

Grant, sitting on the other side of his desk, smiled at the confidence of the amateur lawyer.

'I demand to be let out of it!' Tom shouted. 'What use is this contract to either of us?'

'Ah, well . . .' Grant sighed calculatedly. He started to play with some worry beads his secretary had brought back for him from Greece. 'I tell you what,' he said after a moment's thought. He suddenly got up out of his executive chair and walked slowly round to Tom's side of the desk. 'I don't want to be difficult. Life's too short, isn't it, for this kind of wrangle?'

'The prick,' Tom thought to himself.

'If you really want to be free of Starfinders, we'll let you go. How about that? All song royalties, I'm afraid, are sacred. They've got to come through the company. In fact, if they didn't, you might never see them at all. But if you want to handle everything else yourself, or even go to another agent . . .'

'Well, yes, there is somebody, actually,' Tom bluffed.

'Then I'll let you go, with no bad feelings on either side, I trust.'

Tom was thrown by Grant's sudden capitulation. They even shook hands and had a drink from the ormolu cabinet, while Grant asked inevitably how Carly was, how Carly's mother was, and all the folks back home.

As Tom left the building, Tom noticed that *his* picture wasn't up there in the corridor outside Grant's office among the rest of his 'stars'. But he travelled North from Euston convinced he had triumphed. He had escaped from the trap and his career would be glorious from now on. He was relieved of a terrible burden.

Grant, of course, was thinking exactly the same.

Tom started to chase after work and after other agents on his own account. Curiously, all the agents seemed reluctant to take him on. Couldn't recognize talent if it stared them in the face, he concluded. And he found next to no work of his own. So, little had changed in his life, except that he no longer had Grant as a focus of discontent.

Mrs Scott, Carly's mother, always so bright and warm in the past, began to age visibly. She had bravely tried to hide her disappointment over Carly's choice of Tom over Grant. There was nothing she could do about it now. She tried to modify her view that Tom was a good-for-nothing, unworthy of her daughter's care and affection. As for the incident involving Tom and the politician, she learned about it with resignation, as though she wouldn't be surprised now whatever Tom got up to. He'd end up in gaol, the way he carried on. She was unhappy that Carly was always linked

173

with Tom in people's minds, but there was the small compensation that Carly had stopped living with him, and was back home where she belonged.

Mrs Scott wondered, of course, whether Carly would ever marry. She saw no sign of it. Having decided against Grant and established a way of carrying on with Tom, it was difficult to see how she would ever be in a position to. It made her mother sad, but Mrs Scott resigned herself to the disappointment. She would never live to see Carly go up the aisle of the Church of St Mary Immaculate and St Peter. She would never have grandchildren.

She snuffled into a small cotton handkerchief whenever these thoughts occurred to her. She was a great one for reviewing to herself her happiness and unhappiness, and these days she had plenty of time for it. Carly did most of the cooking, and very good she was at it, too; the house was so tiny it wasn't hard to keep spick-and-span; all Mrs Scott had to amuse herself with, apart from her own thoughts, were the telly and the papers.

She took to clipping out any mention of Grant or his clients and putting the cuttings in envelopes. She soon had half a dozen of these and was oddly proud of them.

On that Sunday afternoon in June 1968, Mrs Scott had read the *News of the World* as usual but when she tried to use the scissors to cut out the story about Johnny Todd's alleged girl friend, she couldn't manage it. She couldn't really be bothered, didn't seem to have the strength in her fingers.

Carly was sitting at the table with a sewing machine, making clothes. The house was hot and stuffy, but they had no garden to sit in.

Her mother said something to her. Carly thought she was talking in her sleep at first, but then she repeated it. 'I must speak to Grant,' she croaked a little hoarsely.

'What do you want to do that for?' Carly asked, surprised by the sudden mention of a name that was almost taboo in their house.

'I must speak to Grant,' Mrs Scott repeated.

'Oh, Mam, why?' She continued working the second-hand Singer, stopping only to shift her long hair when it fell in front of her eyes, hooking it back behind her ears.

From five to seven, she listened to two hours of *Pick of the Pops* on Radio 1. Her mother was used to the tinny sound of Carly's transistor and appeared not to mind listening to it now. Her expression didn't change, even when a Johnny Todd record was played. Carly looked over to see whether her mother realized.

It was only then that she understood, with a terrible jolt, that her mother was dead.

Carly let out a small scream, which sounded strange because there was no one to hear it. It was like laughing in her sleep.

She stood up quickly from her work, spilling it on the floor, and went over to where her mother sat. Carly didn't like to touch her in case the body fell forward out of the chair into the empty fireplace.

She didn't know what to do. They weren't on the phone. Carly had always felt the lack, but never complained, except half-jokingly. She picked up her purse and the front-door key from next to the china huntsman and shepherdess and ran down the street to the coin-box on the corner. She rang Tom and was relieved to find him at home.

'Me Mam's dead,' she blurted out. 'Come and help me, Tom.'

Tom said he'd be right over. The moment he reached Lily Street, Carly let go her pent-up tears. She found herself incapable of doing anything. Tom held her to him, cajoled her, did everything, in fact, the dead woman had doubted he could do.

'We'd better carry her upstairs,' he said. 'To her bed. Put a sheet over.'

Carly sobbed again. Tom soothed her until she went and helped lift up her mother. Between them they carried the small body up the narrow stairs and laid it on the bed. All Carly could think of was how her mother would have preferred Grant to be carrying her.

Yes, Grant. That was why she had asked for him. She had known she was dying.

'Have you any spare silver?' Carly asked Tom. 'I'll have to ring me Aunty Joan.'

'Ring Father Kenny, too. He'll be over like a shot. He'll tell you what to do.'

'But it's Sunday . . .'

In the end Father Kenny did arrive, smelling faintly of whisky, said a prayer over the body, blessed Carly and Tom, and said he'd be in touch about the funeral and the Mass.

When he'd gone, Carly mentioned to Tom about her mother's last request to speak to Grant.

Tom made no comment at first, but then asked 'Had we better ring him, d'you think? Tell him, like?'

Carly was pleased. 'I've no idea what his number is, or where he'll be.'

'In his bleeding country house, I expect. Mickey'll know.'

Suddenly, the matter of telling Grant took on much greater urgency than it really warranted. But Carly saw it as a way of getting out of the house. She suggested she go to Tom's.

'You mean, spend the night?'

'Use your phone.'

Eventually, they got through to Grant at Quornford. He had to be dragged away from his dinner.

Tom told him the news. There was a silence on the line.

'I'm sorry,' Grant muttered, edgily. 'Is Carly with you?'

'Yeh, here she is.'

'Hello, Grant,' she said. His heart went out to her as he heard the sad, small voice.

'I'm sorry, luv,' he said. 'I really am. I always liked your mam.'

'She was asking after you. It was the last thing she said.'

'What was?'

'She wanted to speak to you, and then she just died.'

Grant felt a lump in his throat, felt foolish standing there two hundred miles away from the woman he should have been putting his arms round.

'When's the funeral?' he stammered. 'I'll come at once.'

'Heck, I dunno, we'll have to let you know. Don't come yet, there's no need.'

'Okay, luv. Let me know when you've made all the arrangements.'

'I will. 'Bye.'

Grant put the phone down, wiped his eyes, and went back to the dinner table, to Johnny, Virna and Halo.

Grant didn't get it quite right. When he heard that the funeral was to be on the Wednesday morning, he went out and bought a new black suit at Aquascutum in Regent Street. He chose a lightweight one as it was still hot. Then he set off on the journey North with Webb at the wheel of the Bentley.

It was mostly motorway now and Grant settled back in the Bentley with a briefcase full of letters and contracts to catch up on. At Liverpool, he checked into the Adelphi Hotel, and felt like a fish out of water.

He felt isolated, with no one around to do his bidding. In the street, no one appeared to recognize him. It was as if he had never had anything to do with the place. He thought of going to see his parents, of whom he had been neglectful. They did not appreciate his success. They might not approve of his reason for coming North at this time.

He tried visiting some of his old haunts in the city but felt conspicuous in his posh clothes. He couldn't sit in clubs and pubs on his own dressed like that.

There was nothing for it but to go and call on Carly at Lily Street. The Bentley drew up a door or two short. Net curtains were pulled back at more than one house. Immediately, a bunch of youths rushed up and started to lay their fingers on the car's paintwork. When Grant stepped out, they asked him, 'Eh, mister, you famous?'

'No, I'm not,' said Grant, flatly, and went to ring the bell of No. 23, indicating to Webb that he should shake off the kids and wait at the end of the street.

Carly opened the door. He might have changed, put on weight; she had not. She was her old, desirable self, even if her eyes were pink with crying.

'Oh, hell,' she said, wiping hands on her pinny. 'Come in.'

'Don't I get a kiss?'

' 'Course you do. There.'

He looked steadily at her, and saw what he'd been missing. Such a frail thing in her sadness, and yet substantial, too. He took her by the hand and squeezed it.

'I'm sorry about your mam.'

'That's all right. Thanks for coming.'

'Always had a soft spot for your mam, you know that. And when you said she'd been asking for me . . .'

'Yeh, I feel real guilty about that. But how could I have done anything? We still don't have a phone.'

'I wonder what she wanted.'

'I 'spect she'd read about Johnny in the paper and just wanted to see you. She never forgave you for leaving, you know.'

'Oh.'

'Well, there was nothing to forgive, I suppose. But she'd like to have seen more of you.'

'Rather than Tom?'

Carly gave Grant a look, but said nothing.

'Are you still together, then?'

'Oh, yeh, in a manner of speaking.' The words trailed away. 'He'll be round soon, I 'spect. I was getting ready for the party. The wake, isn't that what you call it? Someone said I needed a bottle of sherry and some nuts, but I thought I'd better make some sarnies and a cake.'

'Let me buy some.'

'Tom's getting something special in the morning.'

'Tipsy cake?'

'No, wet nellies.'

'Wet nellies!' Grant exploded with laughter. He hadn't heard wet nellies mentioned since he'd gone South, not in relation to food, anyway, and he found irresistibly funny the idea of mourners at a funeral sinking their teeth into those soggy cakes made from yesterday's leftovers.

Carly laughed, too. She hadn't thought it was funny until now.

'Better than fly cemeteries, anyway,' Grant added when he'd caught his breath.

'Grant!' Carly shrieked. 'That's no way to talk of Eccles cakes, especially at a funeral.'

They laughed some more until, gently, they came to a stop. They wiped the tears from their eyes, then felt the silence.

'She's not still here, is she?' Grant asked, in a soft voice, embarrassed at the prospect.

'Don't be so daft. They took her over to the funeral parlour.'

'Of course.'

'So how are you, then? Still got the big house?'

'You must come and visit.'

'Are you happy, Grant?'

'Why, shouldn't I be?'

'Want a cup of tea?'

Grant knew then that he'd been right to come up for the funeral. It was going to be to his advantage, as though Mrs Scott was still angling to get him and Carly back together. By asking to see him before she died, she had made sure of that.

Now that he had set eyes on Carly once more, Grant knew exactly what he had lost to Tom. He also knew that nothing must stand in his way. Now there would be no one and nothing to tie her down to Liverpool. He would have to organize his forces, play every card, not let slip any opportunity. Whatever would have to be done, he would do.

Next morning, Grant told Webb to drop him off at the end of the road. He didn't want to arrive at the tiny terrace house in the Bentley again. The handful of mourners set off for a simple Requiem Mass at the Church of St Mary Immaculate and St Peter. There were only two cars following the hearse. Grant went in the second one with some relatives he'd never seen before, coughing and wheezing as though they were next in line themselves. Carly and Tom were in the first with Aunty Joan and Uncle Don.

Grant sat bolt upright throughout the Mass. It was double-dutch to him. He was self-conscious, too, about his expensive new suit, and the silver buckles on his shoes. He began to sweat slightly. The warm weather continued. What was the sun doing shining on a funeral?

Mrs Scott's last port of call was Anfield Cemetery. Her coffin was lowered into the grave. Carly threw a handful of earth on top of it followed by a single red rose. Tom held her when she started to cry. Grant tactfully kept back.

Afterwards, at 23 Lily Street, Father Kenny took charge of the sherry bottle and Tom passed round the wet nellies and Eccles cakes. Carly had to tell him off for not offering the specially made egg-and-cress sandwiches first.

Mrs Scott's brother turned to Grant and said, 'Another page turned in the book of life, eh, son?'

Then the conversation turned friendly and soon laughter was heard, just as if the old woman had been there herself. Father Kenny, going to the heart of things, introduced the topic of Grant for general discussion. 'And now, me boy,' he said, purring in his soft Irish accent, 'have you made your first million yet? For if ye have, there's a use it could be put to down at the church. All contributions gratefully, and so on.'

Grant involuntarily wiped a hand across his face. He expected to be teased about his new-found wealth, but when it came he was no better prepared to deal with it.

'You're behind the times, Father,' Tom spoke up, saving Grant from having to answer. 'He's on to his second million now. Aren't you, Grant?'

'Well, I have to admit, things aren't going too badly, but I'm not really a millionaire, or anything near it.'

He smiled deprecatingly, with a glance to Carly for help. She just smiled back, with a hint of 'What do you expect?' in her look.

This small terrace house in Liverpool was a long way from his estate at Quornford. It had only taken a few short years. It was hard, sitting here, to believe it had happened at all, or that he was the same person who spanned both places, except that, in a way, he felt it was perfectly natural, hardly remarkable, that he had done it.

To change the subject, he raised his glass: 'Here's to Ruby. May she rest in peace.'

The others murmured agreement, briefly sober again.

Grant did not want to linger long at the wake. He felt he was in danger of starring at another person's funeral. Nor did he want to be left alone, finally, when the other guests departed, in the company of Tom and Carly. So he made an early departure.

He kissed Carly warmly and gave her a hug full of longing. He begged for them to keep in touch. He thought of asking her there and then to get in the car and come away with him. But the moment wasn't ripe. The words stopped in his mouth. He would do it soon, though.

After shaking hands with Tom, and then with everyone else, Grant walked to the end of the street where the enormous black Bentley stood waiting for him, the engine quietly running.

After he'd gone, Carly learnt that he had taken care of all the expenses of the funeral and had put down a deposit on Mrs Scott's gravestone.

Within a week, it transpired he had arranged with the

Post Office for a telephone to be installed at 23 Lily Street. In addition, he was going to pay all the bills.

Carly suspected he was also behind the wonderfully warm note she received from Johnny Todd, expressing his sorrow at her loss. Johnny said he was aware how much he owed to Carly for his start in show business and how he would never forget those early days in Liverpool. He said he'd heard that Carly was the inspiration for 'Tantalizing' and how he would love to sing it to her in person one day. Finally, he told her how he knew her mother collected newspaper cuttings about him. Maybe the enclosed signed portrait, though too late for her mother to enjoy, would be something Carly would accept.

Carly was immensely touched by all this. Even if Grant was behind it, upstaging Tom in the way he knew best, she wasn't suspicious of his motives, nor was she going to reject the kindness of the gestures. They reminded her of what Grant had to offer and fortified her for the very different life that lay ahead.

On his way back to London, Grant turned off the motorway and went to see the Wreckers playing on stage at a cinema in the centre of Birmingham. He didn't announce his visit to anyone in advance but bought a ticket from a tout at a grossly inflated price and slipped into the Circle, conspicuous in his black funeral suit among the sea of denim and leather.

He was appalled by what he saw. The supporting act, not from his agency, wasn't fit to be seen on a stage anywhere, let alone act as the warm-up for one of his clients. Fortunately, the audience didn't appear to mind. They chattered restlessly among themselves and kept climbing in and out of their seats to head for the lavatories. It took Grant, fundamentally square as he was, some time to realize that this was not because of the amount of Coke they were drinking, but in order to partake of the various forms of soft drugs that were on offer.

His spirits were not raised when the Wreckers ambled on to the stage more than forty-five minutes late. They were a shambles. They had no presentation to speak of. Only fitfully did the music spark into life and hint at what they were capable of. As for Gareth Trigger, the lead guitarist and singer, he was obviously stoned out of his mind. If he wasn't, he deserved to be put down.

Grant worked his way backstage after the performance, his ears flattened by the noise. He located George Evans who seemed unperturbed by the boss's unannounced arrival. Grant chewed him up about the lack of discipline in the performance. George barely registered the criticism. He was quite clearly stoned himself.

'And he's supposed to be the minder!' Grant thought to himself.

He didn't bother to speak to Gareth or the others in the group, but climbed into the Bentley. Through the window, he told George, 'They're a bloody disgrace, and so are you. I've never seen anything like it.'

'What's the matter?' George asked mournfully. 'The kids loved it, didn't they? We're sold out for three performances. What more do you want?'

'I don't know, George. I don't understand it, that's all. I don't like selling people crap, even if they want to buy it. You must know that.'

George made no response. Making an impression on him at the moment was like trying to telephone Australia.

Grant wanted to be away. 'Oh, incidentally, I've been to the Pool. Carly's mother just died.'

'I'm sorry,' said George. 'Did you see Tom?'

'Yes, of course I saw Tom.'

'How does he feel about it?'

'About what?'

'Well, I mean, there'll be no stopping her now.'

'What *are* you talking about?'

'Carly, of course. If her mam's dead, she'll leave, won't

she? She'll sell the shop, then she'll be after you.'

Grant paused, unsure how to respond.

'You think that?'

'Yeh. See, she doesn't get on with Tom like she used to do. They're just together 'cos they're together, nothing holding them to it.'

Grant blinked. 'George,' he said, 'I don't think you're as stoned as you like to make out.'

CHAPTER 11

Carly's first view of Quornford was a month and a half later. Grant had had to make a trip to New York on contractual business for the Wreckers whose records, despite the lacklustre live performance he'd seen them give in Birmingham, had started to take off in the States. As soon as he came back he gave further thought to luring Carly South, first to visit him and then re-enter his life permanently.

As he saw it, the main obstacle was her attachment to Tom. And then there was her attachment to Liverpool, though surely that was lessened now her mother was dead.

What was in Grant's favour? He could only think of his wealth and style of living. When Carly saw what he had achieved at Quornford, that might win her over.

But he needed her love desperately. He was bored with women like Halo, the gold-diggers, the one-night stands. The chase was getting more tedious as he grew older. And, if he was to marry, was there anyone in the world who would bear his children better than Carly?

Grant knew that a head-on assault, even in her current vulnerable state, was likely to produce an opposite reaction to the one he wanted. So his first move was to enlist the services of Jan Ferry, his personal assistant, in helping to secure his private life. He had made it plain to Jan, from the moment he engaged her, that even if she didn't like the term Girl Friday, that was exactly what she was expected to be. She was to be Grant's leg-man, representative and ambassador.

He had also made one thing clear to himself. Jan was out of bounds. She was married to a doctor, right outside show business, and happily so. She was attractive enough not to be an embarrassment if she had to accompany Grant to a function, but not enough to distract him in the office, or to have him actively lusting after her.

Her rewards were tangible. It wasn't just a case of changing her job description from secretary to personal assistant. Grant encouraged Jan to work actively as an agent. She quickly learned the ropes. When Effie Dunne, the singer, was asked to make a commercial, Jan cleverly negotiated a fee of £2,000 and also an unusual method of payment. Half was in cash, half came in the form of a mink coat for Effie. Jan's commission on the deal was a white Mini-Austin for herself.

Such sweeteners helped smooth the way when Grant drew her into plans which were certainly not covered by her job description.

'You know I went to a funeral in Liverpool recently?' he asked. Jan nodded. 'Mother of an old girl friend of mine, Carly Scott. Nice old thing. Thought I ought to go. Well, I want you to see if she and her bloke can spend a weekend at Quornford. A trip would do them good. Arrange a car to bring them down, or get Webb to go for them. Okay?'

'Who's the bloke?' Jan asked.

'Tom Sheridan. You know, he wrote "Tantalizing" for Johnny. We still have his songs, but I got rid of him when he started fiddling about on his own. I took him on for old times' sake, always the worst reason, and for several other reasons. Anyway, he bums around Liverpool these days. He'll probably never leave there.'

'Will he want to come?'

'I don't know, but he'd prevent Carly from coming if I didn't invite him. So, you see, it's a bit of a duty invite.'

'I'll fix it,' said Jan, unaware quite what sort of plot she was getting involved in. 'When do you want it?'

'See about the weekend after next, the Bank Holiday. Come down Friday evening, back on the Monday. She'll have to abandon her shop on the Saturday.'

'What shop?'

'A boutique called Paradise. On its last legs, I think, so no great hardship there.'

Grant didn't add that he'd done some research and found that Paradise was considerably in the red. He had the money waiting to bail Carly out, and also to provide her with future financial security.

Jan noticed how Grant's voice trailed away, longingly, and wondered what it was all about.

They accepted. Tom actually approved the idea of taking a chauffeur-driven car ride off Grant. In any case, getting to Quornford by any other means was impossible without taking days over it. Carly was pleased that Grant had invited Tom. The three of them could maybe patch things up.

They arrived at Quornford about eleven in the evening. It was a beautiful, warm, starlit night at the end of August. Not a cloud in the sky. They saw the lights burning in the big house, but no one hurried out to greet them when the car crunched up the gravel drive.

They stood for a moment in the delicious, clear night air. Carly looked up at the sky, so still, so quiet, so black. The driver picked up her small plastic-looking suitcase and Tom's holdall.

They moved towards the steps. Carly was wearing a yellow maxiskirt and a pair of white cowboy boots. Tom had on his regulation 'poet's gear', an extremely crumpled corduroy suit and pointed suede shoes, all in black.

There was the bark of a labrador. It was Gretel scuffling and snuffling at the door. It was opened by Grant, a glass of whisky in his hand, looking every inch the country gentleman.

'Hey, good to see you both,' he enthused, giving Carly a hug and shaking Tom by the hand. 'Come along. Have you eaten?'

'No, we're starving,' said Carly. 'A cuppa on the motorway and that was it. We didn't want to be any later.'

'Mrs Pugh'll lay on anything you want. Come on in.'

Grant showed them up to a room containing a large four-poster bed. The room itself would easily have accommodated the entire ground floor of 23 Lily Street. Tom involuntarily started exclaiming a succession of 'bloody 'ells', 'wows', and 'that's fantastic, Grant'. Then their host led them down to the kitchen where Mrs Pugh made a tray of salads and quiche lorraine, which Tom insisted on pronouncing 'queech lorrany'.

After they'd eaten, Grant led them into his den.

Nothing had been said about anyone else being invited for the weekend, so Carly and Tom were taken by surprise to find a third guest waiting for them.

'This is Halo,' Grant gestured as they went towards the long sofas, big enough to drown in.

'Oh, hi,' she said from her place on the floor, where she'd been sorting through LPs, looking for music to play.

Carly wondered how much of a 'friend' of Grant's Halo really was. Trust him to go for something exotic. Tom's eyes were out on stalks. Grant was doing all right, wasn't he? Tom decided he was going to enjoy himself. He was going to take whatever hospitality Grant offered him.

Carly was thrilled by the house and was as determined as Tom to enjoy her visit. It was all very much as she had imagined, but slightly intimidating, too. She'd have to think before making up her mind about it.

Towards midnight, Tom was dropping off to sleep on the sofa.

'It's the journey, you know,' Carly said affectionately, closing his mouth to stop him from snoring.

Grant thought it was the half-bottle of whisky he'd put away, but didn't like to point it out. 'Well,' he said, 'nothing to do tomorrow. Lie in as long as you like.'

Carly glanced at Halo, who caught her look. Carly turned back to Grant, embarrassed.

'It's a lovely home,' she said awkwardly.

'There's lots more you haven't seen yet.'

Halo said nothing, curious about these specimens that Grant had raked up out of his past. Curious to know, too, why she had been invited back after being so brusquely disposed of the previous time.

Eventually, they went to bed, Carly half carrying Tom up the long staircase, Grant leading Halo by the hand and switching off the lights intently, as though the war was still on.

Halo was out of her clothes and on to the bed before Grant had removed his watch. He stripped off and, unusually for him, left his clothes where they'd fallen on the thick pile carpet. She spoke quietly and noncommittally: 'They're nice people.'

'They are, aren't they?'

She wasn't to know that Grant couldn't bear the thought of being under the same roof as Carly while she was in bed with another man.

Swiftly, Grant killed the bedside lights and took Halo. It was better than the last time he had made love to her, but Grant was still selfish in his love-making. She moaned sufficiently for him to think he was doing well. He came as if he, for one, was satisfied and, after a perfunctory cuddle, rolled over and went to sleep. Halo was left lying on her back, listening to the silence of the country night.

In another room, Carly lay on her back, too. Tom, even with half a bottle of whisky inside him, was still capable of making love.

Two days at Quornford worked on her just as Grant had planned they should. She was entranced by the house and the farm, the fields and the lake. It was more than she had ever dreamed of. And Grant, starting from almost nothing, had acquired it all himself. She tried to express how wonderful she thought it was but only heard herself uttering trite phrases, that caused Halo to look scornful.

On the Saturday, both couples lazed in bed until lunchtime. In the afternoon, the two men watched as Halo and Carly went riding in the paddock. Halo was a natural with a horse and selected a hunter as black and sleek as herself. Carly had never ridden before but patiently and sensibly responded to instruction from the stable hand.

While they trotted and cantered in the paddock, Grant leant on the white railings with Tom. 'I don't know anything about horses,' he announced, 'but I know what I like.'

'You don't ride yourself, then?'

'Oh no. They came with the house. Cost the earth to run, but I decided to keep them. They're lovely beasts.'

'So's she.'

'Halo, you mean?'

'Yes, you're a lucky bugger. Where'd you find her?'

'She's a dancer. Very physical and all. What she can do with that thing between her legs, you wouldn't believe.'

Tom hadn't heard this sort of talk from Grant before and wondered what prompted it now. He certainly wasn't prepared for what came next.

'She fancies you, you know.'

'What? How do you know?'

'She said so. Took one look at you and decided she wanted to get inside your jeans.'

'You're kidding.'

'No. Scout's honour. You're well in there, mate.'

It wasn't true. Halo had expressed no such feelings, but Grant knew that dropping the thought into Tom's mind would produce the desired result. Halo would play along with it.

Around teatime, Grant knew that it had worked. Tom and Halo had wordlessly slipped away, leaving Grant with Carly. He took her on a tour of the house, showing her the many rooms and what needed to be done in them. She was full of ideas and Grant encouraged her to think that she would be the one to carry out any improvements. As was intended, his showing off of the domestic joys he could provide made Carly realize how she could never have any of them from Tom. He had no interest in that side of things. He'd be as happy sitting on an orange box, or sleeping on the floor.

Grant gently drew her attention to Tom and Halo's absence.

'Tom and Halo seem to be hitting it off, don't they?'

'How d'you mean?' Carly stopped and suddenly saw what had happened. 'Where are they?'

'Best not to know, I expect. They'll be back in due course.'

'The shit! Just wait till I get him on his own.'

Grant laughed. 'Don't be upset. At least it means we can be together for a moment . . .'

Tom faced no obstacle when he indicated to Halo that he wanted to be alone with her. Though Grant might have been pulling the strings, he genuinely fancied the dancer and she, for her part, had taken a shine to him.

They made it together in the small wood, in a clearing that let in the warm August sun between the trees.

'You're a darn sight better fuck than Grant, that's all I can say,' Halo confided as soon as they'd finished.

'You don't have to tell me, if you don't want to,' Tom said, all ears.

'No, it's true. He's a lousy lay. The things you have to do in this business.'

'Huh.' Tom smiled. Carly had never once commented on Grant's skills, or lack of them, between the sheets. Tom had rather assumed, but it was interesting, what Halo now said.

'Carly won't be too pleased, if she finds out, will she?'

Tom said he didn't care. She knew him well enough now not to mind when he strayed.

'Very convenient arrangement you've got there,' said Halo. 'Ready to do it again?'

* * *

Johnny Todd came over with Virna for Sunday lunch. Carly took an immediate liking to Virna, thinking she recognized a soul-mate as soon as she set eyes on her. She was pleased that Johnny had apparently found someone sensible who made him happy, and spent so long looking at him and thinking of all the changes he'd undergone since she'd first seen him singing at the wedding in Manchester that even Johnny noticed.

'Hey, Carly, haven't you seen a star before?' he chuckled.

'I'll call you Mike Armstrong again, if you're not careful.'

Johnny laughed. Halo asked who Mike Armstrong was, and Carly explained.

Johnny was polite but distant with Tom. He could sense slight hostility from the man who had written his first No. 1, but couldn't begin to work out what it was. 'Gonna write me some more?' he asked, relying on being affable and kindly, as always.

'Oh, sure, sure. One of these days.'

'Hey, that's a great title! Need the best we can get,' Johnny announced presidentially and patted the hair tidily about his ears. Then he played with the gold medallion that showed at the top of his open-necked golfing shirt.

Grant kept one ear on the prattle but his mind was on how to get Carly on her own again.

Virna was saying to Tom, 'And what's Liverpool really like?' Grant noticed the slight irritation in Tom's face before he plunged into a ritual recital of the city's virtues.

'Fine city . . . great people . . . not like the rest of the North, or Lancashire . . . like an island, really . . . you must pay us a visit sometime.'

'Oh, I'd love to,' said Virna in the equivocal way of visiting royalty. 'Johnny's told me so much about it.'

'Not that he knows much,' said Tom cheekily. 'He's from Manchester, you see, or some such place. Not Liverpool at all, a different planet.'

'Oh.' Virna felt put in her place, but she liked Tom. He

had a sparkle, a hint of promise in his eyes. In fact, he had some of Johnny's raunchiness. She turned to Carly. 'Johnny told me you've just lost your mum, you poor thing.'

'Yes, Johnny wrote me such a lovely letter. That was very sweet of him. It's not really hit me yet,' she added. 'Not like when my dad died. I cried for weeks.'

'Oh, luv,' said Virna, touching her arm. 'Grant said what a lovely person your mother was.'

So Grant has been talking about me to Johnny and Virna, thought Carly. *Grant said, Grant said*.

'Well, she had more than a soft spot for Grant.' She lowered her voice so Tom wouldn't hear. 'She wanted me to marry him.'

'Why didn't you, then?'

Carly wondered how much Virna knew about what had happened between Grant and her. 'Oh, you know . . .'

'It's never too late,' said Virna. Carly looked from her to Johnny – he was fingering his gold bracelet now – and back to Virna, wondering how much of a gold-digger she was.

Grant couldn't hear what Carly and Virna were talking about. He ran an occasional hand down Halo's arm to show he hadn't entirely forgotten her. He wished she would take Tom into the bushes again.

In the end, Grant stopped dithering and asked Carly to come with him, he had something to show her. So matter-of-fact was his move that the others saw nothing in it. Tom flirted with Halo while Virna looked on enviously. Johnny sang snatches of song to himself, as he always did.

Grant took Carly down the steps from the back lawn to a large greenhouse out of sight of the mansion. Grant always liked the hothouse smell, he couldn't explain why, except it held memories of his childhood. His father had kept a small greenhouse. These days, since coming South, he had neglected home shamefully but, as he saw it, with good reason.

It was a warm, vegetable, humid smell that was simply, imprecisely, nostalgic.

He opened the glass door, ushered Carly in, and closed it.

'Aren't these beautiful?' he said. Carly leant forward to look more closely at the orchids, humming to herself with pleasure. It was like being in a warm, fragrant bath. She looked at each in turn.

'Look at the label on that one,' he said softly.

She felt for the label and turned it over.

It said, 'Carly'. She smiled.

Grant sat on a tub and gestured her to do likewise, next to him.

'I've a confession to make,' he told her.

Carly's eyes widened, expectantly.

'I only asked you down here with Tom so that . . . well, I knew you were unlikely to come on your own.'

Carly waited.

'The thing is, I want you to stay, Carly. I'm not very good at saying what I mean, when it comes to . . . well, you know. But, the thing is, I really do miss you. Have missed you, ever since we . . . There's no reason now for you to stay in Liverpool with your mam gone. And Tom's . . . well, I can't say what Tom means to you, but you can do better than that.'

Carly gave an appearance of not listening to the bits she didn't wish to hear.

'There's nothing to keep you in Liverpool,' Grant repeated. 'Everybody has to leave at sometime if they're going to do anything with their lives. When are you going to make the break? You could always open a shop in London if you really wanted to. I'd set you up. But really all I want is . . .'

Carly listened quietly, touching the plants, smelling them, bending the stems the better to see inside.

'Go on,' she said, not giving the response Grant was expecting. 'Go on and say what you have to say.'

194

'I want you to come here, and be with me.'

'Live with you, you mean?'

'Yes. I need you very much. And look, I've got this for you.'

He produced a box from his jacket pocket, wrapped in tissue paper. It contained a diamond ring.

'Oh, Grant, you shouldn't . . .'

She slipped it on; it fitted perfectly.

'Is this a proposal then?'

'Not in as many words . . . but yes, I want you. I don't care if we marry or not. I just want you.'

She kissed him very gently. She was accepting what he had to offer, not frightened of the very different world she was choosing to enter by doing so.

'But what about Tom?' she suddenly asked, raising those large eyes to stare questioningly at Grant. 'I can't just leave him. It would look awful.'

'Look awful, to whom? What does it matter how it looks? You only stuck with Tom because there was no one else. You know very well how unreliable he is, how undependable.'

It was harsh of Grant to say these things, but Carly knew they were true, in a way.

'You did love me before we broke off, didn't you?' Grant asked, plaintively.

' 'Course I did, luv. I still do. I just didn't like what was happening to you. Because you were going away.'

'And all this doesn't worry you now?' He gestured beyond the greenhouse to the estate.

'I love it, but I wouldn't want to sit around here all the time, if you were up in London.'

Grant knew what he must say. 'Then we'll have to find you something to do. Real work. Keep you occupied. Re-open Paradise in Chelsea.'

'I don't know about that.' Carly lowered her eyes. 'I'm not sure I'm really much good at running a shop.'

'I think you are. You've got to believe in yourself more.'

'But we're way into the red at Paradise.'

'Never mind. I'll take care of that.'

He embraced her gently. 'So, you will stay?'

'Tom'll be mad at me.'

'No, he won't. At first, maybe. But he'll soon find some-one else. You know what he's like, he doesn't have much difficulty in picking up people. Besides, you'll have to tell him sooner or later. I'll help you.'

'No, don't do that. I'll talk to him. This is sudden for me, too. I expected it, though.'

'I've been lonely. I've needed you. And I've missed you.'

Tom should have seen what was going on, what was likely to happen, but he'd been absorbed by Halo, and now it was too late. He tried to make Carly change her mind.

After she'd left Grant in the greenhouse with a squeeze of the fingers, she had gone out, her heart beating heavily, her mind clouded by the heat and the heavy perfume of the plants, to look for Tom and break it to him as swiftly and as gently as she could. She pulled him up from his chair, away from Halo, and took him by the hand over into the small wood where he had been before with the black girl.

'What is this?' he gasped, as she pulled him up a steep slope. 'What were you doing with Grant?'

'Tom, I'm not coming back with you.'

'What?'

'I'm not –'

'You what?' Tom stopped and pulled his hand away from hers and faced her.

'Grant's asked me to stay.'

'Stay tomorrow night?'

'No, stay, *stay*. Full stop. And I've said yes. I'm sorry, Tom, but you can see why, can't you?'

'You've fallen for it, haven't you, Carly? All this . . . so bleeding, fucking obvious. You're a pushover.'

'No, I'm not. Of course, it's nice here, and it's a home. You've never been interested in that, and if Grant's got money, well, thank God. I can't spend the rest of my life living from hand to mouth.'

'Why not? What's wrong with it? All he wants you for is decoration. So you can sit around and be Lady Muck of the Manor. God, he's a shit!'

'No, Tom, it's not like that. I've thought about it.'

'But you don't love Grant any more. You told me so.'

'That's what I told you, because I didn't *then*. But some things don't die. You and I could never really be cosy together. You're too restless.'

'It's his money you're after.'

'No, Tom, no!'

She tore herself away from him and ran back down from the wood to where the others were sitting, aware that something momentous was taking place. When she reached the sun terrace, she sat down by Grant's deckchair. Tom ran up a second or two later.

'You're a right fucker, Grant Pickering, and no mistake.'

'All's fair . . .' said Grant quietly. 'Carly agreed to it, so you can't complain, can you?'

'I'll get even with you. Even if you're the richest fucking ponce in the music business.'

'I'll wait for you to do that,' Grant replied with a half-smile. 'Now, I expect you'll want to be getting back to Liverpool. I'll get Webb to run you –'

'No. I'm not accepting any more of your ruddy hospitality. I'll find my own way.' He stormed off into the house to pick up his holdall.

A few minutes later, he was to be seen strutting off down the drive, as though he were going to walk all the way back to Liverpool. The others sat silently while the electricity continued to crackle.

Halo fumed, and started playing with the gold watch on her long black arm. 'Well, I'd better get my things, too,' she said. 'I don't expect I'll be needed any more.' She went into the house and Grant followed her.

'I'm sorry,' he said, 'I've been a rat. Carly and I have known each other for a long time, and it's only just been sorted out.'

'You're a shit, Grant, the way you use people. How do I get to London from this God-forsaken place?'

'Webb'll drive you. I'm sorry, but I expect you were only in this for what you could get, so . . .'

He didn't finish, but turned from her, cutting her out of his life with a ruthlessness she found stomach-churning. He went back to the garden.

It was a defeat she wouldn't forget. She wasn't going to let Grant off the hook that easily.

Johnny Todd and Virna had observed the spectacular shake-out with a mixture of embarrassment and amusement, but hadn't said a word. Now, Johnny was telling Grant and Carly, 'It's only right, all this, you two were always meant for each other. You'll be okay.'

Grant gripped his hand. Virna kissed Carly.

'I tell you what,' said Johnny. 'We'll go now, pick up Tom and put him on a train. He won't mind me helping him.'

'Would you?' said Grant. 'That'd be great, thanks.'

They went away in the Rolls and duly found Tom. Webb took Halo back to London in the Bentley.

Grant and Carly were finally on their own together.

The sun was now low in the trees and it was getting late for sitting out in the open. He reached for her hand and squeezed it.

'We've so much to decide,' he said. 'Will you want to sell your house?'

'There's nothing to sell. It's council.'

'And Paradise? We'll have to get you out of that.'

'Please, Grant, it can wait. This has been so sudden. I

just want to be with you, until all these people are out of our way, out of our hair.'

'It's only a matter of time now. Only a matter of time.'

There was peace once more at Quornford. Grant had achieved what he wanted. Carly was starting a new life.

That evening they dined alone, saying little. Carly sat on an old, gnarled wooden chair. Grant, quiet, dark and rock-like, was only visible to her through the warm glow of candlelight.

For once, she drank wine. Sancerre, cold but comforting. It helped her come to terms with her new position. She told herself it was sometimes necessary to behave as Grant had done. It might appear a cold, calculating thing to do, but Carly felt flattered. It was gratifying to have men fighting over you.

That night they made love in Grant's four-poster. She told him how strong he was, what a wonderful body he had, how she'd ached for him, how she'd often dreamed of him when being made love to by Tom. Like the night before, in fact. How she loved him, dearly, more than anyone else in the world.

It was the best love they had ever made together. Grant had come on a lot. She didn't want to know how he'd done it. As the sighs lessened afterwards, and the two of them regained their breath, Carly's last thought before falling into the deepest of slumbers was that she had never felt so much like having a man's child as she did then. This surely must be the occasion. She would conceive, of that she had no doubt.

The thought made her very, very happy as the dark walls of sleep closed firmly, but gently, around her.

CHAPTER 12

Percy Hodge, as he had been born, on the wrong side of Wimbledon, didn't just have a funny name. As a boy, he had looked funny. His puppy fat was ridiculous. The flesh on his thighs would spread out on the school bench, itching to break out of his shorts. His initial and surname were accordingly combined into the nickname 'Podge'.

His saving grace was an ability to play the piano. He learned his scales and went in for music exams, getting as far as Grade V. Finally, he broke free of the restrictive grasp of his music teacher, a humourless spinster called Miss Draper, who was so strict her pupils were often reduced to tears. Her idea of popular music was allowing Podge to play a duet version of 'Teddy Bears' Picnic'. Podge knew otherwise: there was a popular music, unknown to Miss Draper, unknown to his parents, unknown especially to the BBC.

In those late 'fifties, he would tune his battery-operated Bush portable to pick up Radio Luxembourg. The signal came and went, whistled and buzzed, yet Luxembourg was the promised land. It provided a popular music, brash, commercial, American. Podge knew that he must learn to play it. One day he might even make his living from it, however unlikely the fat schoolboy might seem as future Hit Parade material.

He studied music theory, he learned how to play by ear. Some ungainly kids earned the respect of their fellows by being funny. Podge impressed them with his ability to play whatever tune they asked for. It was his only plus. He was no good at his other school work, hopeless at anything athletic. He didn't know where he stood sexually. Half the

201

time when his schoolmates boasted of their sexual experiences, he couldn't understand the words they used. He managed to find boys with whom to fumble sexually, but it wasn't totally clear whether or not he was interested in them as substitutes for girls. Girls were a totally unapproachable and unavailable breed.

On leaving school, Podge scratched a living as a pub pianist in south-west London, and then found work as a rehearsal pianist for stage and TV shows. He became a familiar figure, his cherubic bulk seated at a (usually broken-down) piano, playing his heart out and providing much-appreciated confidence to singers of both sexes.

They relied on his ability and expertise, and they adored him in their way. He gave them strength, and so adept was he that if they made a mistake he could turn it to their advantage. They missed him acutely when, for the shows proper, they had to sing with full-blown, inflexible orchestras.

Grant discovered Podge in 1965, soon after he arrived in London from Liverpool. Podge was playing at a TV rehearsal for one of Grant's female clients, the singer Effie Dunne. He was instantly taken by the fat man beaming over the piano, the music pouring from him.

'Write music yourself?' Grant inquired.

'There's no demand for that. I'm here to play other people's stuff.'

'But have you ever written anything?'

'Nothing much, the odd song. I'm no good with the words.'

'I'd like to hear an "odd" song.'

'You're mad.'

From such unpromising beginnings, a professional relationship was built up. Grant had no real reason for thinking that Percy Hodge had anything to offer in the song-writing line, but his instinctive reaction was to see something that all other producers and performers had missed. To them,

Podge was merely a useful chap to have about the place. To Grant, he had the makings of a showbusiness personality. A chubby pianist could be turned into a successful act. After all, if Russ Conway and Winifred Attwell could do it, simply playing and smiling, why not Percy Hodge?

Grant took him on to Starfinders' books. Podge could keep playing at rehearsals, and Grant certainly wouldn't touch a penny of those pitiful fees. But Podge could double his income on one simple condition. He had to write one song every week.

Podge, with the facility he had, never failed. Once a week, usually late on Friday afternoon, he would turn up at Grant's office (in which a small grand piano had by then been installed) and thump out his latest composition. Grant didn't know that Percy sometimes made it up as he went along and found considerable difficulty in remembering the song when he tried to write it down afterwards.

Podge could sing as well as he could play, with a wonderful feeling for pop rhythms. He'd been a closet rocker all the time he'd been playing middle-of-the-road material for rehearsals and auditions. His voice didn't have the hard edge a rocker was supposed to have, but even that was no handicap. His high tenor, capable of nimbly leaping to falsetto when required, was both novel and appealing.

Podge's first record was a jolly little nonsense song. It was one of his improvisations because, once again, he hadn't bothered to write down his weekly number for Grant. He called it 'The Rhubarb Song'. This was based on the belief that actors say 'rhubarb-rhubarb' when trying to re-create the noise of a crowd. The chorus was inane and could well have won the Eurovision Contest had it been entered:

> *I said,*
> > *Rhubarb-rhubarb, rhubarb-rhubarb,*
> *You said,*
> > *Rhubarb-rhubarb, rhubarb-rhubarb . . .*

The record was played repeatedly by Tony Blackburn in the early days of Radio 1, and became a surprise and dotty instant hit, reaching No. 15. Podge had to sing it on *Top of the Pops* and was kitted out in a 'rhubarb suit' for the occasion.

The record was put out under the name 'Quentin Saint', because Grant had been reading a newspaper story that mentioned San Quentin prison.

Quentin next appeared as guest on a number of TV shows, including some hosted by stars he'd been accompanying at rehearsal only a few months before. He became a popular figure, camp without being outrageously effeminate, in the honourable tradition of a number of long-lasting British entertainers.

Grant pressed him to dust down the substantial catalogue of songs he'd written during their association. An LP was made up of the sillier songs and sold quite well. Then Grant gave Quentin his head. He told him to write and play rock, though where the humour stopped and the rock began was blurred.

The only problem was that Quentin was still, basically, a lonely, fat, overgrown schoolboy. He had no friends of either sex, as far as Grant could tell. He lived in squalid digs with only a piano to keep him company. He wasn't interested in money. Grant was aware of this and continued to pay him only sixty pounds a week, 'as an advance on royalties', just as he had done when there were no royalties in prospect. It could be argued that this was a hard bargain. Grant would have countered that it was a fair one. He had paid Quentin a weekly salary, pocket money really, before he was famous. More by default than anything else, that was how the matter rested.

Quentin was happy enough, not at all worried by the deal. But what would happen if somebody opened his eyes to the fact that Grant and the Starfinders organization had been taking him for a gigantic ride? He was a potential time bomb.

* * *

Grant was a new man now he'd won back Carly. He briskly helped sever her contacts with Liverpool. Paradise was closed, the stock sold off, the debts settled. She moved out of Lily Street and into Grant's London flat in Montagu Square. He took her everywhere, introducing her to London life. They became members of fashionable clubs, danced and played hard into the small hours every night, and only went to Quornford to flop about at weekends.

Carly found plenty to occupy herself during the day, spending Grant's money on clothes at Biba and Granny Takes A Trip, buying records, devoting long hours to choosing fabrics and materials for refurnishing Quornford. It was a whirl and she loved it. Grant was jubilant at the way he had finally won her. The future looked extremely bright for both of them.

However, two months after Carly moved in, they had to part for a while. Grant was due to go to Australia for two weeks to be with Quentin Saint at the beginning of his first overseas tour, though Mickey Clinch would once again be the Starfinders' representative who really held the artiste's hand during the trip. Quentin's records were very popular down under and Grant thought a short tour backed by local musicians would be an excellent introduction to the business of touring. It would also be a way of getting Podge to hone up his act away from the bright lights at home.

Grant wanted to see for himself what opportunities were open to his clients in Australia – he had never been there before. He understood that Aussies made excellent audiences because they knew what British artistes were on about and were fairly desperate to see in the flesh acts they'd only heard on record or seen on TV.

'Can I come, too?' asked Carly.

'Okay, why not? But it's an awful long way, luv. You'd only be tagging along behind. You might get bored.'

'But I like tagging along behind! I used to help you with your work, remember?'

'Indeed you did.'

So Grant started including Carly in the arrangements for the trip. Although he didn't say so, having her with him was a way of insuring she didn't drift back to Tom again.

But then, a week before departure, it was Carly who provided the reason for her not going.

'Grant,' she told him when they were having a rare night at home, 'I've got something to tell you.'

'What is it?' he said, reaching for her and seeing how bright her eyes were, 'What's happened?'

'I thought it must be true. I've been to the doctor. I'm pregnant.'

'That's wonderful!'

'It was that first time at Quornford, I'm sure of it.'

Grant hugged her. 'Are you sure you still want to come to Sydney?'

'I s'pose not . . .'

'I'll take you on another trip when I get back.'

'What d'you mean?'

'Fancy a honeymoon?'

'You mean get married? When?'

'As soon as we can. We'll have a big, big wedding at Quornford. We'll invite everybody.'

'Oh, can't we have a quiet one? Just our friends?'

'No, we'll put on a show! Why not? Let everybody know! That's what I'd like anyway . . .'

While Grant was away, Jan Ferry was given the task of making all the arrangements for a wedding in the New Year. Carly took to Jan and they worked happily together. They arranged for a centrally-heated marquee to go up on the lawn and for a stage to be erected so that Starfinder clients could perform. Every one of them was to be invited, as well as press, radio and TV. A coach would be provided for friends and relatives to come down from Liverpool.

Carly agreed with Jan and Jan agreed with Carly that

there was absolutely no way they could leave Tom Sheridan off the guest list. Whether he would turn up was another matter.

Grant left them to it and set off for Australia with Quentin Saint in mid November. The tour was due to end in January, and if necessary they'd cut it short, Grant said. No one would be allowed to miss the wedding of the year.

When Grant and Quentin had recovered from their jet lag, they fell to publicizing the Australian tour. They did the rounds of TV and radio stations and the newspaper offices, Quentin being outrageously camp but winning many friends.

He was not the only British act down under in that Australian spring. There was also a dazzling blond singer called Suzie Paul.

The name meant nothing to Grant or Quentin until they met her at a barbecue hosted by Peter Lazarus, the Australian impresario who was presenting Quentin's tour in association with Grant. It was held on a mild November Sunday, two days before the first Sydney concert. A car was sent for Grant and Quentin at their hotel. They were driven a few miles out of Sydney until they reached Palm Beach, a headland resort jutting out into the Pacific. Hundreds of yachts and boats were bobbing about in the Pittwater River. Sunday morning surfers were at play in the blue shining waters. 'It's a little taste of paradise!' exclaimed Quentin.

Peter Lazarus and his wife Barbie lived in a sprawling mansion high up on the headland. To welcome the Brits, a Union Jack fluttered from the flagpole. As guests arrived, steak and sausages spluttered on the barbecue by the pool. Barbie was making her special potatoes in an oven indoors. The potatoes had been sliced in half, then sprinkled with salt. After a long time in the oven at high temperature, the salted side of the potatoes blistered up deliciously.

She supervised the catering wearing fashion clothes, styled hair and copious make-up. Grant noted this interesting combination of the upfront and the outback. Running around the guests were the Lazarus children, Justine, Viv and Di, hotly pursued by an Alsatian.

More than a dozen guests were already there, none of whom Grant thought he knew. But then his eyes were irresistibly drawn to one woman. She stood there, almost as if lit up by her own personal sun. She was blond, very blond, and she had a face that simply shone.

Grant was faintly embarrassed by the way he found himself gawking at her. He'd just won Carly back, was about to marry her, and now his eye was roving again.

'Jesus, Pete, what is *that* you've got over there?'

'Don't you recognize her?' Lazarus replied. 'She's over from England, too. Singer called Suzie Paul. I thought she was a household name in the old country.'

'Well, I don't think so. Suzie Paul? Someone's kidding you, but she seems sort of familiar.'

'Her manager told me she was the coming thing. Mind you, he is her husband.'

'Which one's he?'

'Next to her. Dapper bloke with the moustache. Used to be in forces entertainment, I think. She's doing cabaret dates. Nice, isn't she? Are you sure you've never heard of her?'

Grant began to think perhaps he had. Then it came to him. Hadn't he seen her picture in the paper and wondered if she had an agent? He'd never discovered the answer.

'I'll introduce you.'

Lazarus took Grant by the elbow and led him in the direction of the striking blonde. It might have been her day off, but you wouldn't have thought it. Grant thought she must have been up since dawn applying all that mascara and fixing her incredible mass of curly blond hair. She wore diamond earrings, and about the only gesture she'd made to the location was to wear a tan safari suit.

'Excuse I, Suzie, here's someone who's followed you all the way from England. I dunno why he couldn't have met you there.'

Suzie Paul looked a little grandly at Grant, clearly not recognizing him either.

'Grant Pickering,' Lazarus pointed at him. 'You know, Starfinders and all that. Suzie Paul.'

'Oh yes,' she said, turning on a devastating smile and revealing rows of immaculate pearly-white teeth. 'Isn't Johnny Todd with you?'

'Yes, he is, and Quentin Saint. That's why I'm here.'

'You came with Quentin? He's doing concert dates, I gather.'

'Yes. Starts the day after tomorrow.'

'I think he's *adorable*. You must introduce me.'

'Sure. I've a feeling I've seen your picture in the papers.'

'It's possible.'

Grant wondered why he'd never set eyes on her before. Not on TV, nowhere, and yet she apparently had enough going for her to get work in Australia.

'You're doing cabaret? Where can I see you?'

Suzie shrugged. 'Wherever you like. Just ask my husband.' She gestured to a tweedy, un-showbiz-looking Englishman who stood talking in another group.

Husband. Grant began to take in the information now that it was being presented to him for a second time. Another singer married to her manager. There were so many of them. Attractive songstresses had a way of marrying grizzled monsters who dressed them up and projected them and took all the proceeds. It was a form of slavery that Grant thought ought to be abolished.

They prattled on about this and that – Australian audiences, how talented Quentin was, where the tours were taking them. Grant found it an odd sensation and a new one. Here he was, engaged to be married to Carly, a father-to-be, suddenly confronted with a woman he fancied terribly – indeed, had fancied even before he met her in the flesh, before he'd heard her perform, fancied from a black and white photo in the newspaper.

There could be nothing between them, and yet they continued to talk as if there might be. They went through the ritual moves. Peter Lazarus sensed he was unwanted and slipped off to greet a newly-arrived couple with a cheery 'G'day'.

Suzie wanted to know why Grant was going back to London as soon as Quentin started his tour.

'Oh, business, business,' Grant explained airily. 'And another thing. Rather more personal.'

'What's that?'

'Getting married.'

'Welcome to the club.' At this Suzie paid much more attention to him. Grant sensed the change in her attitude. If he was getting married, he wasn't seen as a predator. Or perhaps she was one of those women who were more interested in husbands, their own or other people's.

'Who to?' she asked. 'Would I know her?'

'I doubt it,' he said. 'Childhood sweetheart from Merseyside, in a manner of speaking. Well, not really childhood, but longtime. It's quite sudden, actually.'

'You don't mean . . .?' asked Suzie boldly. 'If it's babies, you're welcome to them.'

'You're not supposed to ask about things like that.' To soften the blow, he added: 'You'll have to come to the wedding. Everybody's going to be there. We're determined to enjoy ourselves and have a great big party.'

'You'd better tell my husband. He's the one in charge of dates. I leave all that to him. Alan!' She called him over and he came with obvious speed and willingness.

For a fraction of a second, Grant hesitated before plunging his hand into the other man's, as Suzie introduced them. 'Alan, this is the famous Grant Pickering. This is my husband, Alan Greenlee.'

Grant's hand froze in the other man's clasp, but Greenlee held it firmly in place while his eyes betrayed more than a hint of enjoyment at Grant's discomfort.

'I've always wanted to meet you, Grant Pickering, after all this time.'

'So you know each other?' Suzie asked.

'Sort of,' mumbled Grant.

'Oh yes,' continued Greenlee, still holding Grant's hand. 'Mr Pickering and I have worked together before, though oddly and regrettably we've never met till now. Mr Pickering usually prefers his staff to deal with humble persons such as myself.'

Grant finally managed to retrieve his hand. 'So this is what you're doing down here?' Grant nodded gently towards Suzie.

'Yes, not so many of the package tours around Barnsley,' Greenlee said meaningfully. 'Well, not these days. My company went bust.'

'I'm not surprised.'

'So I moved to London. Happily, I met Suzie. Now I'm concentrating on developing her career. It's going very well, I'm glad to say.'

'I'm sure it is,' Grant said, trying to remove any irony from his tone. 'I'm sure she'll go a long way with you behind her. At least she won't have any problems getting paid.'

Suzie looked at her husband, perplexed. He, giving nothing away, looked steadily at Grant and laughed mirthlessly.

'Mr Pickering would like to see one of my cabarets,' she said.

'I'm sure we could arrange that for him,' Greenlee said, his gaze never leaving Grant. 'Tomorrow she's doing a television, for the ABC. You could come along to that.'

'I'd like to,' Grant smiled, and accepted a topping up of

211

Hunter River Burgundy. He wished that Greenlee would disappear into a hole in the ground. How odd people were. What was a girl like Suzie doing married to a shit like Greenlee? It was too unpleasant to think about.

Relief was soon at hand. Quentin Saint bounced up to them, looking as outrageous as ever: dark glasses three times too large, an orange T-shirt, pink tracksuit pants, and gold-encrusted tennis shoes.

'Podge, this is Alan Greenlee and his wife, Suzie Paul.'

'Hi, everyone!'

'As you can see,' Grant soberly advised Suzie, 'he's just come back from church.'

'God, I feel awful,' Quentin moaned. 'Give me a drink.'

Barbie Lazarus squeezed another glass of red wine out of a coolabah flask and handed it to him.

'Thanks, love,' he said, draining it in one go.

'Podge, these are people you really ought to get to know. Mr Greenlee is an old, old friend of mine from touring days up North. He's not only married to this lovely lady, he also manages her.'

'Hello, darling,' Quentin smiled broadly at the woman. 'You sing, too?'

'Try to.'

'And pleased to meet you, Alan.' Quentin shook the agent warmly by the hand.

'Pleasure's mine,' said Greenlee. 'I've long been a fan.'

Grant was beginning to feel the effects of all the wine and itched to get away from Greenlee.

'Aren't you hungry, Suzie?' He drew her over to the barbecue, leaving Quentin and Greenlee happily in each other's company.

Peter Lazarus was spooning large slices of sizzling steak on to plates, while Barbie popped on her baked potatoes, and guests helped themselves to lashings of coleslaw and nut salad from large wooden bowls.

Grant and Suzie sat down at one of the long trestle tables on the lawn while the sun warmed them.

'This is the life, isn't it?' Grant exclaimed exuberantly. 'I wonder what it would be like to live here.'

'Lovely,' Suzie smiled cautiously. 'I think you could have a wonderful time. Everyone seems to have two cars, two houses, a yacht. And the sunshine. It's rather how I imagine California to be.'

'I'm sure the Aussies would agree with you there.'

'The trouble is, it isn't England, is it?'

'That's it. You can be a big fish in a small pond, but you'd always feel the real action was in Europe or America.'

'I reckon,' Suzie confided, 'that if I stayed here, I could have my own TV show in a year, but it would hardly be worth having if it was so easy to get!'

Grant was struck by Suzie's confidence.

'I expect you're right.' It was what he always said when he wanted to keep his own views to himself.

He glanced over to where Quentin and Greenlee were still chatting.

'Those two are hitting it off, aren't they?' Suzie remarked. 'You'd better be careful. Alan'll run off with Quentin.'

'Oh really?' Grant was noncommittal. 'Let him try.'

'Tell me,' Suzie lowered her voice and murmured confidentially, 'is Quentin, you know, *funny*?'

'Don't ask me. I'm only his manager,' Grant said, as though to an inquisitive journalist. 'His private life's his own affair.' Then, realizing he sounded pompous, he added, 'I don't mean that. People are expected to be either one way or the other, but either way they're expected to be *something*. But a hell of a lot of people aren't AC or DC. If you ask me, he's NSLTSO.'

'What's that?'

'No Sex Life To Speak Of. It's a more common condition than anyone ever lets on.'

Suzie looked again to where the plump pop star chatted animatedly, hands fluttering, with her husband.

The next day, while Quentin went off to rehearse his first concert at the auditorium next to Sydney Cricket Ground, Grant ordered up the limo to take him out to the ABC studios. The atmosphere there was rather like the BBC back home, institutional, almost military.

Alan Greenlee greeted him warmly and introduced him to the ABC producer and director who were about to record Suzie's songs for slotting into a magazine programme called *Sunburst*. Grant's reputation had at least preceded him here, and everyone knew about his 'legendary' role as the discoverer of Johnny Todd and Quentin Saint. They asked, did he want to watch from the control gallery or the studio floor?

'Can I sit in the studio? I won't get in the way.' Grant saw it as an opportunity to avoid Greenlee.

'Come through, then,' said the producer, ushering him into the small studio. 'Suzie's gone to make-up. She had a problem with her hair.'

Grant found himself a seat well away from the cameras. He would be able to see Suzie herself and her image on a large colour monitor. She emerged at last, her luscious blond curls immaculately arranged down to her shoulders. A shining turquoise gown fitted snugly over her ample curves.

She walked on to the small set. It was all in black with four or five white round tables with chairs upended on them, like a nightclub waiting for the floor to be swept. Tucked away in a corner were a pianist, drummer and bass player.

Suzie took her position on the first of a series of white cross marks on the floor. She would progress from one to the other during the song, enabling the cameras to focus on her, and the director's carefully-plotted shots to frame her artistically through the hooped chairbacks.

She peered out of the bright pool of light in which she stood, shaded her eyes and looked in Grant's direction. She visibly brightened when she made him out, mouthed a soundless 'Hello', and trilled her fingers in a tiny wave.

'Thirty seconds, we're on the clock,' the floor manager called out. At twenty seconds, he matter-of-factly spoke the 'ident' which would go on the tape: 'Sunburst inserts/Suzie Paul/TSL 481.' The clock on the screen ticked up almost to zero, then faded into black. At the start of the music, up came the picture of Suzie in long-shot.

At first, Grant didn't realize what she was singing. He was too taken by her visual image. Striking though she was in the flesh, she was enhanced immeasurably by the camera. Grant noticed that, although there were other cameras and cameramen in the studio, the director had chosen to shoot the whole song entirely on one camera.

It began to snake and glide softly and sensuously around Suzie as she sang. The effect was mesmerizing.

My funny Valentine
Sweet comic Valentine . . .

The choice of song was an obvious one. But why not? Recording single numbers like this, you had to make an instant impression on the viewer and the old Rodgers and Hart standard was ideal for the purpose. It was corny, but it got Grant just *there*. He felt a lump in his throat and tried to work out why. Was it the song? Was it the performance? Was it because he was actually there while it was being sung?

Was he foolish himself? Did every other man in the room feel the same way? It was as though Suzie was singing just for him.

Then the mood was broken. The director demanded a second take. The camera had wobbled or gone out of focus and Suzie would have to repeat the magic all over again.

215

Grant couldn't face it and asked to go up to the gallery. He looked steadily at Suzie and mouthed one word: 'Marvellous.'

He was taken up the iron staircase and shown into the viewing room where Alan Greenlee was hunched over a TV set, waiting for his wife to reappear.

'Why does that always happen?' Greenlee frowned. 'She sings her heart out and they chuck it because of a tiny detail no one would notice. That's the trouble with recording. Because you can do it again, you do. If it was live, it wouldn't happen.'

'She was great, Alan, great. She'll be just as good second time, I know she will. She's got it. And you've got yourself a wonderful little property there.'

'I know,' Greenlee shot back, smugly but suspiciously.

After a few minutes' delay, Suzie once more launched into 'My Funny Valentine' and again performed it perfectly. Grant was speechless with admiration. It was not just that he was immensely taken with the young woman, as a woman, he had also been reminded of his own failure as a performer. Oh, to be able to give pleasure like that. He felt humble and dazed.

That night, just before Quentin's concert, Grant put a call through to Carly in London.

'How's everything?'

'Fine, fine,' she told him, delightedly. 'We're getting ready for you. You'll be back Thursday?'

'Well, that's what I'm ringing about, really. I may have to stay another day or two to make sure Quentin's all right. He's very nervous, you know.'

'Oh, Grant, do you have to? I miss you. You said you'd be back this week. I *hate* it without you here.'

'I know, I know, but since I *am* here, I have to look after Quentin.'

'I thought Mickey was there to do that.'

Grant barely realized he wasn't giving the real reason for the delay in his journey home, but he changed the subject.

'By the way, there's a couple more people I'd like to invite to the wedding. Have you got a bit of paper? It's a Mr and Mrs Alan Greenlee. L-E-E.'

'Sounds familiar.'

'Well, if you've got a very long memory you'll remember a famous occasion when Rex Room socked someone who hadn't paid him.'

'Only too well.'

'Well, that was Greenlee.'

'You want *him* to come to our wedding?'

'We've kissed and made up.'

'All right, if you say so.'

Grant gave her the address to send the invitation to, reading off the engraved business card that Greenlee had given him.

'Love you madly,' Grant said, 'and that friend of yours who's always with you.'

Carly didn't grasp what he meant at first.

'Oh, *him* . . .'

'Him? What makes you sure it's going to be a him?'

'I just know it is,' said Carly. 'With your genes, being forceful and all that, he just couldn't be a girl.'

Grant laughed over the thousands of miles. She could well be right.

Alan Greenlee and Suzie Paul joined Grant for the opening concert of Quentin's tour. A storm greeted the occasion. It thundered, it flashed with lightning, but the auditorium could withstand all that, and the young Sydney audience, wet and bedraggled though they were at the start of the concert, turned up in force and gave Quentin a huge welcome.

Grant, sitting in a box at the back, was happy with what he saw. He was slightly puzzled, too. Why were these young people going quite so wild over this chubby freak called

Quentin Saint? There was no doubt his magic worked, however. His music was happily accessible, impossible to resist, even if his personal appeal was hard to analyse.

Quentin tore tirelessly into number after number, starting with his novelty songs and working up to a climax of rock hits by himself and others. The audience was soon out of its seats, dancing in the aisles and right up to the front of the stage.

Suzie Paul was the subject of frequent, surreptitious glances from Grant. It wasn't quite her sort of music, he didn't think, but she seemed unable to keep still, swaying and tapping the rhythms. Her husband hardly stirred at all, but sat staring at Quentin, enjoying what he heard but giving little hint of it.

Finally Quentin tore into 'The Rhubarb Song' and the whole audience erupted. It wasn't hard to remember the words, but Grant was still amazed that a crowd of a thousand or two on this side of the world could be intimately familiar with a song written and recorded on the other.

Peter Lazarus, secure in the knowledge that the tour was certain to make everyone a lot of money, guided the Pommy visitors backstage. They entered Quentin's dressing room bearing buckets of iced champagne. Quentin already had his top off and his tubby, white, hairless body glistened with the sweat of two hours' physical activity. He was high on adrenalin.

'Good on yer, maestro,' Grant said to him in a passable Australian accent.

Suzie kissed him and, Grant noticed, so did Alan. The champagne corks popped and a party started which was to last until dawn, adjourning around midnight to Quentin's suite at the hotel.

While Greenlee sat with Quentin, Grant spent most of the time sprawled next to Suzie.

'You were brilliant this afternoon,' he told her. 'If I had to choose between you singing "My Funny Valentine" and

''The Rhubarb Song'' from you-know-who, it's not in my best interests to say it, but you'd get my vote!'

'You're sweet, Grant. Thanks.'

The party went on. From time to time, the hotel management would send up a polite request that noise be kept down as other guests were trying to sleep. No one took any notice.

Grant was tired and drank more than he usually did. He told Suzie he was staying on a day or two longer, without intimating that she was the chief reason.

Eventually, in an indiscreet moment, he asked, 'When are you going to let me manage you?'

'What *are* you saying? It's hardly very likely, is it?'

Grant noticed Greenlee was still deep in conversation with Quentin, who shrieked with excitement.

'Perhaps your old man'll swap? I'll take you in return for Quentin.'

'You'd get the worst of it then. Love at first sight over there, eh?'

'Could be. Think about it. I'll get what I want, if I *really* want to. You'll see.'

'Okay, *pushy*. I'll leave the details to you.'

Unfazed, Grant then said he would leave the party. He had just decided he'd be going home earlier than expected.

'I thought you were staying on?' Suzie said.

'I don't stay where there's no point in staying,' Grant replied.

Accordingly, he flew home, surprising Carly.

CHAPTER 13

On a freezing Saturday in mid January 1969, Father Kenny was prevailed upon to journey South to celebrate Grant and Carly's Nuptial Mass. If Carly wanted to be true to her faith, Grant wasn't going to get in her way. The Mass was celebrated before a few close relatives and friends from both sides. Carly, parentless now, was given away by her Uncle Don. Grant's parents, frostily making their first visit to Quornford, attended the service with a marked lack of enthusiasm.

Father Kenny made a graceful address, recalling Carly's mother. With the hint of a nod at Carly's growing waistline, he pointed out that any child of the marriage would be brought up as a Roman Catholic.

Almost the entire lawn at Quornford had been covered with a pink and green striped marquee. At one end was a concert platform. Grant and Carly stood at the entrance and shook hands with the five hundred guests who were photographed individually as they came in.

Everyone was there, including the Liverpool contingent who had been coached in as though for an away match at Wembley. Tom Sheridan had decided to let bygones be bygones and was his more charming self. He spent most of the time in the company of Fawn Flack who had done herself up in all her finery and seemed quite a different person. But she was no nearer stardom as a singer and since the closing down of Paradise hadn't had a job.

'Well, rather you than me, mate,' Tom said to Grant. 'But look after her, won't you?'

Grant, smiling through gritted teeth, said he surely would, and wasn't it time for them to bury the hatchet.

'Hatchet, what hatchet?'

Grant broke off talking to Tom when he spotted the Greenlees bobbing towards him in the line-up. He introduced Alan and Suzie to Carly. The new wife gave away nothing when Grant said, 'This is Alan Greenlee. You've often heard me talk of him.'

'Pleased to meet you,' said Alan. 'I hope you'll both be very happy. As happy as we are, in fact.'

Suzie was exceptionally gracious towards Carly. 'You look absolutely gorgeous. Grant's a very lucky man.'

Carly wasn't sure what to make of Suzie. She was dressed from head to toe in white silk and satin herself.

'My,' Carly whispered out of the side of her mouth to Grant, when they moved on. 'Whose wedding is this?'

'What?' he asked, not catching what she said.

'Never mind.'

Tom couldn't believe his eyes when he first set eyes on Suzie. Whatever their own differences, he and Grant had a way of being turned on by the same women.

Out of the corner of his eye, Grant was aware of Tom buzzing around Suzie and trying to detach her from her husband. Oh, that man, he was maddening. Grant wasn't to know that Suzie was deftly cutting Tom down to size with every word she spoke to him.

Carly was accepting every compliment that was paid her. It was not the day for analysing them, she was entitled to swallow them whole. In fact, every compliment was fully justified. Her eyes had never been wider, her smile never more achingly inviting. Her wedding dress shone and glistened. It was all a very long way from the frail little number she had run up herself and worn that day at the Cavern five and a half years before when Grant had first set eyes on her.

The guests tucked into huge banks of food and drank themselves into the ground on the finest champagnes. Then Father Kenny proposed Carly's health in a touching and amusing little speech which demonstrated that, in his case, the church's gain had been show business's loss.

Johnny Todd, as Grant's closest male friend, was best man but Rex Room had been enrolled to act as compere of the entertainment that followed. He did a turn which could well have earned him his subsequent booking at the Palladium. It probably did, as the Palladium manager was, of course, among the invitees. Rex had spent most of the reception up to this point giving Alan Greenlee a wide berth, deeply suspicious as he was of Grant's claim that the past was buried.

Grant made a short speech, straight, no jokes, and when he said that he loved Carly, there were one or two surprised at the naked expression of sentiment.

Then the entertainment really began. While Carly and Grant sat in special seats, like royalty at a command performance, a succession of star names from Starfinders took the stage. Rex explained that, in olden days, they used to celebrate marriages with an 'Epithalamium'.

'And, if I'm honest, I'm a touch epithalamium myself just now,' he added.

Quentin Saint, fresh from his Australian triumphs, bounced on next and, having been quietly dissuaded from singing 'The Rhubarb Song', sang a more suitable song he had written specially for the occasion.

The climax came when Johnny Todd took the stage and made a short speech.

'I owe everything to you, Grant and Carly. You know that, but not everyone does. And I mean it, because although the world knows what Grant has done, not everybody knows that, but for Carly, he'd never have set eyes on me. It was at a wedding, too, in Manchester that they first came across a runt called Michael Armstrong. They invented this fella called Johnny Todd. They clothed me. And they've fed me, too. God bless you both. I love you and I hope you'll be eternally happy together.'

The sixteen-piece band, made up of top session

musicians, took the cue and started to play opening notes which everybody recognized. Then Johnny began to sing words that everybody in the marquee knew by heart, though only a few knew they had been inspired by Carly.

> *It's*
> *Tantalizing . . .*
> *Realizing*
> *How surprising*
> *You can be . . .*

Grant took Carly's hand and squeezed it hard. He glimpsed a jewel-like tear roll down her cheek. He felt a lump in his own throat. That song! It was a very public statement of her allure. The way Johnny sang it now made it a hymn.

Tom Sheridan could hardly bear it. He choked. His words were being used to celebrate a match between the woman he'd lost and the man he despised.

It was bitterly cold outside the marquee, but Tom had to slip out and get away. He stood shivering on the frosty grass and lit a cigarette, while his words floated out to haunt him. He looked away from Quornford and out over the rolling green countryside, dusted with snow.

Inside himself, he boiled with resentment. Such a beautiful place, yet somehow it was spoiled by Grant's owning it. *Everything* was spoiled by being owned by Grant.

> *It's*
> *Tantalizing . . .*
> *Realizing*
> *How surprising*
> *You can be . . .*

Grant took over everything in the end. You, your woman, your work, your life. Tom had to move further away to escape his own song.

Eventually, he went down to the lake where large sheets of ice were floating. Ducks fluffed themselves up against the cold. Tom resolved he'd not allow himself to be humiliated like this ever again.

He did not know precisely what he'd do about it, but in a while, his hands blue with cold, he stalked back to the marquee and rejoined the wedding party.

Carly spent much of the honeymoon sitting in a deckchair facing out to sea, worrying lest the West Indies sun would have some effect on the child growing ever bigger within her. She loved to sit and look at the white sands running down to the dazzling blue waters of Antigua. It was blissful, but she would have been just as happy on a rainy day at Quornford, or even back in Lily Street. She itched to be busy with her hands, making food, making clothes. She didn't like being idle, and she was impatient to have her child.

Grant didn't have that impediment to his perpetual, restless activity. He spent as much time as he could phoning London, keeping track of his ever-growing empire. Even if it was a honeymoon, the world had to keep on turning, and Grant was not the person to let it do so of its own accord.

Carly was saintly in the face of this. She sat for hour after hour reading stacks of paperbacks and magazines. In *Time*, she discovered a newly-minted word which she brandished that night at dinner.

'You're a *workaholic*, Grant, did you know that?'

'No, I'm not. I enjoy my work. You're only addicted to work if you don't enjoy it.'

'That's not what it says in the article. It's when you can't stop.'

'The thing is, and nobody ever seems to understand this, when you're in show business, your business is what everyone else turns to for pleasure. So there's no difference between work and play.'

'Well, you'll drop dead if you're not careful, and I'd rather you didn't, if you don't mind. You're far too precious to me. I don't fancy being the merry widow just yet, thank you.'

'Okay, okay.' And Carly saw Grant float off into reverie, which was the only other state he ever entered. He was either working or dreaming about work.

What Grant was not dreaming about at this moment was Suzie Paul. He had told himself firmly that his feelings for her were all too complicated and he mustn't waste valuable time dreaming pointless dreams.

As honeymoons go, theirs was a happy one. The fact that Carly and Grant had been living together, on and off, for so long meant they didn't have to spend much time discovering who they were. They did notice a difference, however, now that they were actually man and wife, and they both genuinely liked it. They felt safer, more committed, less prone to stray. They also both felt relieved that the chase was over.

On the third or fourth day, Grant absented himself from the telephone a while and belatedly began trying to get the pasty colour of his body to match the facial tan he'd acquired before Christmas in Australia. As he lay next to Carly, who now spent most of her time, cautiously, under the sun umbrella, he read a bulky script he'd smuggled out in his luggage.

'What have you got there?' Carly asked.

'Well, it could be what I'm looking for.'

'And what's that?'

'A musical. I've been wanting to break into that scene. This could be the one.'

'What's it about?'

Grant took a deep breath. 'It's not your typical musical. I mean it's not *South Pacific* exactly. In fact, it's about as far from that as you can get.'

'Like *Hair*?'

'No, not a rock musical. It's the *theme* that's different. I think it might work.'

'What's it called?'

'The working title is *Acts of Folly*, but I'm not sure that's grabby enough. The music's by Arthur Friedmann. He's a Yank who did a lot of good shows with Brandon Pope, who's dead now. The book and lyrics are by a bloke called Barclay White. I haven't heard any of the music yet. They were going to send me a tape, but it hadn't arrived when we left. Friedmann's got such a good track record, it shouldn't be a problem.'

Grant began to tell Carly the story and the background to it. 'It helps, of course, that the Lord Chamberlain's been abolished because, as I say, it's not exactly *The Sound of Music*. He'd have wanted to censor half the show. Barclay says it's based on a real case, but he's changed the details a lot. Evidently there was a politician, a Liberal MP, in the twenties called Sir Leo Money. He was caught with his hand up a girl's skirt on a bench in Hyde Park and charged with offending public decency, or some such. There was a big court case and he got off, a triumph for British justice, etcetera. Then, five years later, they got him again, this time on a train. He was found guilty, so everyone thought he must have been guilty the first time, too.'

'No, it doesn't sound like Rodgers and Hammerstein at all!' Carly's reaction was what Grant had feared. He knew her judgement had been sound in the past, but he slightly resented her flair and didn't want to defer to her on everything.

'That's the bare bones of it,' he went on. 'What Barclay White has done is swap it all round. He's amalgamated the bit in Hyde Park with the "Kiss in the Car" case. Do you remember that, about ten years ago? A couple were accused of having it off in a car in Paddington. They denied it, the woman's good name was at stake, and so on, and after a terrific tussle they got off. Barclay's put it back a few years to the Suez crisis, and the MP's now a Tory one, so it all links up.'

'I expect a lot'll depend on the music,' said Carly, more encouragingly. 'But it sounds a bit depressing.'

'No, not really, because in the show the man's really innocent all along. Anyway, courtroom dramas never fail and this time the twist is, it's all set to music. Then there's these marvellous parts for women, the MP's wife who has to stick by him through thick and thin, the two girls he gets mixed up with.'

'You've got no one at Starfinders who's done a musical.'

'I know, I know. Johnny's desperate to do one, of course, but there's certainly nothing in it for him. But the women present all sorts of possibilities.'

'Who are you thinking of?'

'I don't know yet.'

'Perhaps the same singer could play all three women?'

'Now that's an idea. The three aspects of womanhood as they relate to the MP. You're a genius, Carly, and I love you.'

'She'd have to be a very good actress to be able to carry it off, though.'

'Such singers do exist.'

'Do they?'

Dinner was over now and through the open walls of the restaurant Carly could see much activity. A steel band called the Harmonites was unloading and arranging its drums on a small floodlit patch under the palm trees. In time, they struck up with Bach's 'Air on a G String' and Suppé's overture 'Light Cavalry' before moving on to popular melodies, all slightly disguised by the instrumentation. The effect was rather like listening to music underwater.

Grant was tickled pink by the performance and applauded loudly at the end of each number. It took him until the Harmonites were well into one of the numbers before he recognized it. The oil drums were booming out 'Tantalizing'. Surely it was just a coincidence? He determined to buy the LP the Harmonites were selling of their work, to have as a curiosity, and as a memento of the honeymoon.

Carly smiled. It was getting a bit beyond a joke, the way this song was always being played as though it was their signature tune. At least it provided a distraction from Grant's current enthusiasm for *Acts of Folly*. That sounded a decidedly rum project to her. Perhaps Grant was right, though. You never could tell. The show might just be the breakthrough the British musical theatre had been waiting for.

Tom Sheridan brooded long over Grant and Carly's marriage. He failed to understand how she could so easily have thrown away her former life. He could only think that the loss of her mother had made her vulnerable to the kind of lures that Grant put before her. But Tom wasn't going to blame her, or hate her, for what she had done. His spirit was too generous for that.

He became more unsettled about living in Liverpool. For the first time, he began seriously to think of leaving and going to London. Perhaps he would find there the success that had so far eluded him.

His first, tentative, steps in a southerly direction were not encouraging, however, perhaps because his motives were concerned with wreaking some form of revenge on Grant, though Tom was barely aware of this.

His first move was to ring Jan Ferry at Starfinders.

'Hi, Jan, I need your help.'

'Oh, yes, dear.' Jan had soon acquired the harsh cosiness of the female agent.

'Could you do me a favour? I know how you fixed for me and Carly to visit Pickering that time, in the country.'

'Yes, dear.'

'Well, can you tell me where to get in touch with that Halo woman who was there? I don't even know her proper name.'

'Nor do I, dear. She's just Halo to everybody, you know, like a model. But, yes, I think I can help you. If she was one of our clients I couldn't give you her number, but as she's not . . .'

Jan wasn't to know how intimate Tom and Halo had been at Quornford, or why Tom wanted to get in touch with her now. She gave him the number.

Tom soon grew weary of dialling it. There was never any answer, whatever time of day he rang. He wasn't even sure why he wanted to speak to Halo anyway. It was a vague feeling that if he had slept with her once, he could do so again. And they could both air their grievances over Grant.

He wasn't going to give up, though, and as a last resort he decided to ring her very late at night. Never mind what situation he might blunder into. He kept on ringing, later and later and later.

'Oh, yes,' she answered finally, 'of course, I remember you, Tom Sheridan. But, hold on, I've only just come in the door.' It was half past midnight.

'You've been working?' asked Tom. 'What are you doing?'

'Yes, I've been working, but perhaps I won't tell you at what.'

All kinds of thoughts ran through Tom's mind. He even wondered if she was on the game, but didn't say so.

'Are you dancing in a show or something?'

'I'm in a show, but not exactly what you'd call dancing.'

'Go on, Halo, tell me.'

Halo continued to be elusive. 'How about you? What are you doing up there in Liverpool?'

'What I usually do. Bumming about. A few gigs.'

'Did you go to the wedding?'

'Carly's? Yes, I did.'

'I wasn't invited, of course.'

'Hmm. Well, I hated it. We both lost out over that one, didn't we?'

'He's a shit, that Grant,' Halo affirmed. 'But he's not the only one I've met.'

'So, what are you doing? Come on, you can tell me.'

'No, you tell me, first, what I can do for you.'

'I just wanted to see you again, that's all. We may have things to talk about together, even things to do . . .'

The following weekend, Tom took the train to London, quite excited at the prospect of seeing Halo once more. She was working very hard, she'd said, and gave him an address, telling him she wouldn't be free till after midnight.

Tom wandered about London, feeling very much the outsider. He filled in time by going to a cinema. Then he decided to go to the address Halo had given him, just in case she came back early.

He felt quite the foolish provincial when he arrived. The address he'd been given was Brewer Street, Soho. It was not a block of flats, as he'd imagined, but Raymond's Revuebar. A look at the colour photographs on display outside confirmed that Halo was now taking part, twice nightly, in the International Striptease Festival '69.

Tom quickly recovered and decided to join the Japanese and Scandinavian businessmen who were paying their five guineas each to see the show. He found a table in the small plush theatre where he hoped he wouldn't be spotted. He ordered the cheapest drink he could find and sat back to enjoy the succession of striptease acts, interspersed with a conjuror and even a juvenile *corps de ballet*.

The ninety-minute show consisted chiefly of short tableaux in which a girl – or sometimes two or three – would gradually strip while miming various forms of sexual excitement to records. The themes were vague – pirates, cowgirls. The odd whip was thrown in among the pubic hair. They were slick, well-produced performances and went about as far as they could go without actually doing it. And, as Tom found, they were quite capable of arousing the spectator.

Halo's turn took the form of her writhing about in various skimpy pieces of leather and boots which gradually parted company with her body. She was now sporting a fashionably immense Afro haircut. Tom was confused in his response. He wanted to enjoy the knowledge that, unlike other men in the theatre, he'd actually had sex with this woman. But he found her act curiously uninvolving, perhaps for that very reason. He didn't like the idea of sharing her with the fantasies of other men.

'So, now you know what I'm doing,' she purred at Tom when he'd beaten his way backstage. 'I've got a twelve-month contract. Same act every night for a year. Mr Raymond's very kind. Striptease is an art, you know, even if it's not what I should be doing, really.'

'Oh yeh? Well, you can do it, why not?'

'Where are you stopping tonight?'

Tom missed a beat. 'I rather thought . . .'

'Nothing doing, love. I have to get my beauty sleep.'

Tom had visions of having to sleep rough. She was really landing him in it.

'Fancy a drink?' he offered.

'Okay, I know a club where we can go.'

Tom's first thought was that it was likely to be a clip joint and expensive. 'Lead on,' he said cheerfully, covering his worries.

They hadn't gone a few steps when Halo, her body swathed in an expensive fur, hailed a taxi.

'Changed my mind. You come home with me, sonny.'

Tom was bemused by her behaviour. She was capricious, unpredictable.

After a mile or two, the taxi stopped, Tom wasn't sure where, and he found himself paying the driver while Halo stood impatiently at the door of a block of flats.

'You're a funny one, aren't you?' she teased him, when they'd opened a bottle of wine. Tom didn't know what to answer. If anybody was funny, she was surely the one.

It was a functional flat, rented, consisting chiefly of a bed and a sofa, it seemed. Halo's clothes were hidden in cupboards which had been carved out of the room space. The only other notable feature was the number of teddy bears and soft toys with which she presumably comforted herself when she was alone. Except that she also had a dog, a yappy little terrier which she obviously left on its own when she went to work. Tom took an immediate dislike to the dog.

He couldn't make Halo out. He didn't normally have any trouble dealing with women, and was certainly not used to having his advances rejected. Why was Halo so difficult? If she hadn't been so alluring, he'd have pulled out of the situation very quickly indeed.

It wasn't long, though, before they found common cause in their dislike of Grant Pickering. Halo had a well-developed down on the man who'd treated her so casually. It was more developed than his own. In fact, he felt quite moderate when he heard the spitting fire that came from Halo.

'You know what made me puke about the time he dumped me, and it wasn't the first time he'd just packed me off when he got bored? Because I didn't get my own back. There's things you can do, you know, to guys who treat you like a shit.'

'Like what?' Tom asked innocently.

'I'm a thrower. I'm known for it. I'll chuck anything – plates, books, goldfish bowls. Serve them bloody well right. Or you can let down their tyres, they hate that. There was one guy who I found was two-timing me. We'd been together two years when it happened. I cut all the legs off his trousers. He was hopping mad! Didn't have a single pair to go out in. Nothing. I won that one.'

Tom recoiled visibly at these boasts and began to wonder

233

how he came to be pursuing a woman capable of such spiteful, vicious behaviour. Cautiously he asked, 'What would you have done to Grant, if you'd had the chance?'

'Oh, smashed something, I expect. But he's a difficult one, in fact impossible. There's little you can do to annoy him. I'm still thinking about it, though.'

'You mean he's not forgiven yet?'

'Look, darling, no one messes me about and gets away with it. The best thing to do about getting your own back is to take your time. Wait till they think you've forgotten all about it. I'll get my own back on Mr P. one day.'

'Don't hurt Carly, though, will you. It's not her fault.'

'You're really soft on her, aren't you? Even after what she did to you?'

'Yeh.'

'Sentimental fool.'

'I can be.'

'Huh.'

Tom didn't feel much like making love to Halo after this recital; he slept on the sofa, and left the flat before Halo awoke. He went back to Liverpool with his tail between his legs, all the more disappointed because of the way his expectations had been aroused.

His rejection by Halo felt like a rejection by London. However insignificant a part she was of the showbiz scene, that was nevertheless the message she delivered to him. Showbiz was a foreign country.

In those months after his marriage to Carly, Grant Pickering was also much in the thoughts of Alan and Suzie Greenlee. It had taken some time for Suzie to extract from her husband precise details of that long-ago row.

'Why do you want to know?' he would always answer. 'Why are you so interested in the great Mr Pickering?'

Suzie wouldn't deny her interest. 'What if I am? He's got a damn sight more to offer than you have.'

Greenlee would frown but wouldn't lose his temper. He had no wish to enter that argument again. Suzie knew quite well why they had married, and sex had very little to do with it. She needed a man for protection and he, as husband and manager, was there to supply it.

'But what was it? What did you do? I need to know.'

Greenlee eventually caved in and told her.

'I was slow in paying on a tour once, so that comedian chappie, Rex Room, turned nasty. Did me over.'

'Beat you up? On Grant's orders?'

'I don't know about that, but I felt threatened, put it that way. It may just have been Rex getting all worked up off his own bat.'

'But why were you slow in paying? Your usual stingy ways, I suppose.'

'It wasn't as simple as that. I was going to pay, but there's a lot to be said for making clear to people how dependent they are on you.'

'Why?'

'Business, love. No need to worry your little head over things like that. That's what I'm here for.'

Suzie stopped quizzing him, though she was little wiser. But it was clear to her that if anyone had come out of it badly, it wasn't Grant. He was quite within his rights to be suspicious of her husband's devious little ways. She didn't understand why Alan had to be like that, but she wasn't going to stop him, so long as it worked in her favour.

Hers was a strange marriage. From the outside it was incomprehensible, unlovely. Greenlee was forty now, while she was twenty-three. It looked like opportunism. He had spotted her talent and had bound her to him with two types of contract. She was one of those entertainers who couldn't cope without an agent or manager and had accepted the terms of the deal.

Now, two years into the marriage, she was beginning to realize just what price she had paid. She had married in spite of her parents' objections. She had made a straitjacket for herself. She couldn't move, professionally or privately, without deferring to her husband.

The most tangible price he had exacted was in starving Suzie of sex. There had been a little of that at the very beginning, but it soon stopped altogether. It was Suzie, in fact, who had insisted on their sleeping in separate beds, but Alan had acquiesced without a murmur. It seemed not to matter to him. Outwardly it seemed not to matter to her either, and as she had no close friend to confide in, no one knew just how frustrated she was.

All she had was her talent, that bright, bold thing about which there was no question. All her waking moments were dedicated to the fulfilment of that talent. Would she find the right outlet for it? Would she ever escape from her gilded cage and find a different kind of fulfilment? Did she even want to?

Gradually, she came to realize that Grant could provide a way out for her. He was bursting to help. So she must give him a signal. If he mistook the signal for something else, would that really matter?

With uncommon ease, Grant found a West End theatre for *Acts of Folly*. The show would open, after a short pre-London run, at the end of May 1969. That is to say, within four months of Grant and Carly's honeymoon. The chances were that the first night would coincide with the birth of their child.

When Grant eventually heard the music, he was astonished. Any doubts that Carly might have sown in his mind about the suitability of the story were swept away. It was a brilliant score, so hummable you could catch it immediately, and it contained three potential hits. Grant carefully tied up the contractual arrangements so that his company, or rather companies now, would reap the rewards if the show was the success he felt it was bound to be.

236

Starfinders was to present the show in conjunction with two established theatrical producers. The director, Robert Mayne, had a good track record in legitimate theatre (including a spell at the National), and a talented team was hard at work on design, lighting, costumes and advertising.

Inevitably, there were moments when the project looked as if it would fall apart. Grant found there was much more to worry about in putting on musicals than anything he had attempted so far. But the rewards were potentially so much greater. A transfer to Broadway? A film? Spin-off singles and original cast albums? And, as soon as the show had broken even, those wonderful royalties trickling in for years and years.

Doubts about *Acts of Folly* took several forms. It proved hard to raise backing. The 'angels' were reluctant to put their money into a show whose chief producer had never worked in theatre before. Grant, in a mood of 'I'll show 'em', consequently had to put a great deal of his own money into the production fund.

Then there was the vexed question of whether the show's title was a selling one. In the middle of the night, Grant woke up in a sweat and turned to Carly, now hugely pregnant and sleeping on her back.

'I just know the title's wrong,' he whispered to her in the dark.

'Don't worry about it now, love,' Carly murmured, half asleep.

'I'm sure we should go for something more . . . more *grabby*, like *Scandal* or *Stolen Kisses*.'

'Leave it till the morning . . .'

One alternative that had already been chewed over was to call it simply *Follies*, but the opinion, strongly-worded, from the writers was that this might attract the wrong kind of punters. They'd come expecting a leg show. Another suggestion was to call it *Victor*, after 'Victor Wilmer', the chief character. But Grant didn't want the male role to be

237

built up to the detriment of the female. The agonizing went on. In the end, the title stayed as it was.

Then there were the agonies over casting. Trying to ensure that all the right people were available together at the right time was a juggling act that Grant had rarely encountered in the pop world. The part of Victor was to be taken by David Prince, quite a name in West End musicals, and a very good actor, well capable of handling the extremes of emotion the MP had to experience as his career was put to the test.

There still remained the question of who would play the three women, Caro, the MP's wife; Stephanie and Christine, the two victims of his 'assault'.

The writers and Robert Mayne were at first completely hostile to Grant's notion, adopted from Carly, that all three women should be played by the same actress. Arthur Friedmann said it would restrict the range of the songs if they had to be accommodated to the same voice. Barclay White said the book would have to be cut about too much in order that they never appeared on stage together. Grant managed to prove this wouldn't be too difficult to achieve, but Robert Mayne then claimed the actress playing the three women would be exhausted by so many quick changes.

Who, in any case, was the actress who could carry it off?

The writers began to behave oddly in order to sink Grant's proposal. They went 'unavailable' whenever he tried to get in touch with them. Then they lobbied Robert Mayne to oppose Grant. It was an exasperating time for everyone.

Whose musical was it anyway? A good question, thought Grant. He certainly didn't believe it belonged to the writers. It was everyone's and nobody's, except that he felt a good part of it was his. After all, he was putting up a lot of his own money and the Starfinders group of companies was not only co-presenting the show but also putting out the album on the new Paradise Street record label. And he'd had the idea in the first place. At least, he felt as though he had.

* * *

Suzie Paul wasn't known to Friedmann, White or Mayne, so Grant was going to have an uphill struggle to cast her in the show, but he was convinced she would be perfect for it. That experience of first hearing her sing in Australia hadn't left him. If she could have that effect on him, she could have it on others, too.

Grant arranged to meet Suzie and Alan Greenlee for lunch at the Ivy. It was a very theatrical restaurant where one quite expected Noel Coward to walk in at any moment. Suzie looked devastating in all her finery and sat modestly not saying anything while Grant made his pitch to her husband. It choked Grant even to look at Greenlee, but he gritted his teeth and got on with it.

'I'm convinced Suzie's right for the role or, rather, roles. I just know she can carry it off. And if she does, well, the sky's the limit from then on in. But it's not my decision alone. The writers, the director, they'll all take a hell of a lot of convincing. They've never seen Suzie act, never heard her sing, so if we're going to make this thing work, the three of us, we've got to lay on a little presentation.'

'Suzie doesn't do auditions,' Greenlee announced flatly.

Grant was taken aback by this, but wasn't going to be put off by any posturing from Greenlee. 'I know how you feel, Alan. But that's show business. No point getting on your high horse.'

'You misunderstand me, Grant. Of course, people need to know what they're getting. All I'm saying is that whoever makes decisions about Suzie's future should base that decision on an actual performance, and not on what she does in the usual cattle market.'

'I take your point. The question is, how do we arrange the alternative?'

Suzie continued to regard him, silently, sipping at mineral water and moistening the gloss of her lips. She found it a very pleasurable experience, two men fighting on her behalf. It was almost as good as having two men fighting over her.

'It's a question,' Grant went on, soberly, 'of arranging for everyone who matters to see Suzie perform. In public. Then they'll have no hesitation about giving her the role.'

'I still don't see why you can't force the issue,' said Alan. 'You're the big boss. You're putting up the money, as I understand it.'

'I have to carry everyone with me, Alan. You know the business. And the writers, frankly, make Doubting Thomas look like the Good Samaritan. Of course, they've got a lot riding on it, too, and they're entitled to be a hundred per cent convinced before they take such a risk.'

'I'm sure Suzie will happily go along with whatever you come up with.' Grant looked at her and she smiled benevolently. She seemed to be saying it would be all right. She knew her husband had been playing his manager's card a little too insistently.

'I have a plan,' Grant told them both, as though he had just thought of it. 'And you'll just have to say if you're willing to go along with it.'

Grant gave no hint that in making a play for Suzie's participation in *Acts of Folly* he was in any way gratifying his whim to have her around him, to be seen to be doing things for her. He appeared to be in it solely for the good of the show. He unfolded his plan.

As a sweetener, which would hold whether Suzie ended up with the lead in *Acts of Folly* or not, Grant offered her a contract with Paradise Street Records. It would be for three LPs made up of standards and new material. The first was to be released within the month, the other two over the following year and a half. He had it in mind that 'My Funny Valentine' would be one of the tracks, but he didn't mention it at this stage.

Secondly, on the launch of the LP, Starfinders would work with Greenlee to get Suzie more radio and TV dates. That would help promote the LP. The money she made wouldn't be important, and Starfinders wouldn't dream of taking any commission.

Thirdly, again tied to the LP, Starfinders Concerts would mount a couple of showcase performances – on a Sunday evening at the Palladium, say – which they would pack with a friendly audience. All this would in effect be Suzie's audition. Grant would make sure they'd be a triumph, with standing room only. A part in the musical would be impossible to withhold from her after this.

Greenlee was duly impressed, but it was his reflex action not to accept offers without quibbling. At the first sign of this, Suzie cut him off. She extended her right hand, the golden bracelet jangling against the wine glasses in the middle of the table, and squeezed Grant's fist as he thumped the table to underline his points.

'Dear Grant, I can't thank you enough. You've got too much faith in me, but I won't disappoint you. We'll accept, won't we, Alan?'

Her husband was speechless at first, then meekly said, 'You heard what she said, Grant. It's a deal.'

Like most people, Carly had never heard Suzie Paul sing. It came as a complete surprise to her when, thumbing through the papers, she came across an advertisement for two Sunday night concerts at the Palladium. It was adorned with a sensational picture of the singer, specially taken for the purpose.

'Hmm,' thought Carly, 'that's the girl who "starred" at our wedding.' The orchestra was to be the Royal Philharmonic. Goodness. Who was she? Where had she suddenly come from, and so quickly? Why was Grant presenting her at the Palladium when she wasn't even his client? Why had he made no mention of all this?

'Well, it's a little wheeze I have,' he explained to Carly, when she taxed him on the subject. 'We don't have a top girl singer on our books. Effie Dunne doesn't count, she's something else, more of a personality. And I can't sign Suzie up because she's bound hand and foot to Alan Greenlee.'

'But is she any good? It seems a big splash.'

'Oh, yes, she's good. She's very, very good, believe me.' He had to be careful not to show how very keen he was on her. It was a delicate matter of promotion. Not too much, not too little. Carly must never know quite what was going on inside his head with regard to Suzie.

Casually he mentioned that Suzie might be up for a part in *Acts of Folly*.

'Which part?'

'All three, actually.'

'So you like my idea?'

'Only if it works. That's one reason for the concert, so the Spanish Inquisition can take a look at her.'

'The Spanish what?'

'The writers and the director. I've got to convince them Suzie can do it. They're not exactly in a mood to agree with me at the moment.'

'You sound very keen on her.'

'Oh, no, not like *that*. Not at all.'

But Carly wondered. Grant seemed obsessed.

When the time came, Carly was unable to attend either of the Palladium concerts as she wasn't feeling too well, so Grant was left to his own devices. He was jumping up and down with excitement beforehand. It was a very expensive way to gratify a personal whim, if that was all it was.

The theatre was packed for the second of the two shows. Starfinders had many talents and hype was one of them. The tickets weren't too expensive, indeed it was more like a free concert. The chief aim was for Suzie to appear in a successful 'event' and create as much of a stir as she possibly could.

She shone and carried herself entirely without support throughout the evening. She sang a wide range of standards. 'My Funny Valentine' was naturally included and yet again Grant was convinced she was singing it direct to him.

The first of Suzie's LPs, 'Songbird', had been rush released and sold briskly at the Palladium during and after the shows. Two songs it did not and could not contain were called 'Fair Name' and 'Why Did It Have To Be Me?' from *Acts of Folly*. After jibbing a bit, the writers had allowed Suzie to give them a sneak preview, out of context, in her showcase. As Grant was publishing the music anyway, there wasn't a great deal they could have done to stop this, even if they had objected. As it was, the writers were delighted. The part looked like a shoe-in as far as Suzie was concerned. And then the director signalled his agreement. The showcase had done what it was supposed to do.

Grant covered Suzie with flowers, champagne and congratulations. Then he drove himself back to Montagu Square and excitedly rang Carly down at Quornford. 'She's got it,' he exclaimed exuberantly.

'Who has?'

'Suzie. She's going to play all three roles.'

'That's nice,' said his wife, sleepily.

Rehearsals for the out of town try-out of *Acts of Folly* began at Bristol in early May. Grant was driven up and down from London to keep an eye on them but failed to get a very clear idea of what the end result was going to be like. The musical theatre wasn't like the pop business he had grown used to. There were too many elements, and they never seemed to come together. The last pieces of scenery weren't arriving till two days before the show opened. The orchestrations were late. The revolving stage, vital for the large number of short scenes, was always threatening to jam.

Robert Mayne had chosen a new system for back-projecting slides and film to cover the off-stage 'real' events of the 1950s. At one point in the show, the real Sir Anthony Eden's voice had to be heard giving a Suez speech and later there was one by Harold Macmillan, so a short round-up of contemporary newsreels had been compiled to go with them. But at every rehearsal Grant saw, the films were too long, or one was away being re-edited, or else the projector didn't work.

As for the cast, Suzie was doing well but did indeed seem stretched by having to play and sing the three parts. The quick changes left her breathless, not good for singing. David Prince, the male lead, started getting stroppy at the amount of attention her difficulties were being accorded compared with his. He needed to be soothed, but this was not the director's way. Robert Mayne was all for confrontation; consequently a number of marathon shouting matches took place. Feet were stamped, doors slammed, and then grovelling reconciliations had to be arranged.

It was all very draining. On such occasions, Grant would silently slip away and worry quietly to himself. He was kept going solely by his faith in the talents of Suzie Paul and by his genuine belief in the excellence of the musical. If he was to expand his showbiz base, all these problems were just something to be endured. He wasn't, couldn't be, in complete control of a monster like this.

The first night at Bristol was, encouragingly, only moderately disastrous. A few lines were forgotten, but no one except the script-writer noticed; the revolve jammed once; the lighting managed to get one cue behind, but the back-projector worked faultlessly for the first time. The chief problem was that *Acts of Folly* lasted almost three hours.

The drama critic on the Bristol paper sharpened his pencil and told readers that '*Three* Acts of Folly' were too much for him, and he'd have gladly settled for two. But he admired the music and the writers' desire to expand the territory of the English musical to tackle a more adult theme. Suzie Paul rated only one line in the notice, however. It wasn't totally clear that the critic realized she'd played all three women. She consoled herself that this was a back-handed compliment.

244

Grant made what soothing noises he could, but started to feel the icy breath of failure on his neck. It didn't help that Alan Greenlee wandered about saying the whole show was 'going off at half cock'.

'Better than no cock at all,' Grant told him, with a meaningful look.

It was almost impossible to get Suzie on her own to reassure her. Greenlee was always in the dressing room spreading gloom and despondency. In the end, Grant left it to Robert Mayne to sort out, chiefly by ruthlessly cutting half an hour out of the show, and hurried back to London to attend to other matters.

On the Sunday halfway through the Bristol try-out, the cast was bussed up to London to record the album for Paradise Street Records. Everyone was worn out and desperately needed the day off. But they did good work and all was satisfactorily on tape by midnight. Grant had to pay a sweetener to ensure the record would be on sale before the first night in London ten days on.

It was about now that he was first heard to mutter, 'Never again'. He had allowed himself to be drawn into a game he didn't really understand. Robert Mayne gave him odd assurance on this point. 'With musicals,' he said, 'there's nothing to understand. Nobody knows *anything*. You have to make your own mistakes, the same ones every time round. It's not much of a way to make a living.'

'Thanks a lot,' said Grant grimly. He couldn't understand why it had to be so hard. Wasn't it supposed to be entertainment?

Carly was in no position to pass judgement on a piece she hadn't seen. Nor was she able to put much of an arm round Grant and comfort him, so close was she to giving birth.

'What'll you do if it happens on the first night?' she asked.

'Tear myself in two, so one bit can be with you, the other at the theatre. I dunno, I just hope it won't happen that way.'

'Me, too,' said Carly, a little sadly, knowing full well that a clash of interests was just what fate was likely to treat them to.

Not quite, as it turned out. Their son was born at 12.15 p.m. on the day *Acts of Folly* was due to open in London. 'Just in time for lunch,' as Grant remarked, giving his first spontaneous smile in several weeks. The boy was a bouncy bundle of 8 lb 5 oz. He had an extraordinary amount of dark hair. 'Just like wild heather,' the Scots obstetrician observed.

Grant and Carly were both jubilant. 'It's what it's all about, isn't it?' Grant observed, soppily.

'Oh, yes, yes,' cried Carly, hugging the small person with all her might. 'He's adorable.'

'Since he's a boy, it's Neville, like we agreed, right?' said Grant.

Neville Pickering it was.

'If only Mam could have seen him,' Carly said sadly.

'I expect she can, looking out of heaven.'

'You reckon?'

Then it was time for Grant to start worrying about something else as the big night approached.

CHAPTER 14

The first night of *Acts of Folly* at Her Majesty's Theatre in the Haymarket saw the birth of a new star. There was no doubt about that. Suzie Paul was universally acclaimed as a major discovery for the musical theatre. Grant was ecstatic that his faith in her had been vindicated. He was even able to be civil towards Alan Greenlee as a result. In a surge of high spirits after the show he went so far as to kiss him.

Whether the show itself had a similarly bright future was more in doubt. It had gone well, the technical troubles had all been smoothed out, the performances were fine, and the songs had begun to imprint themselves on the audience's memory just as they were supposed to. In any case, there was so much good will emanating from the largely invited first night audience that it would have taken a real turkey for them to have spent a bad evening.

Next morning, the papers took a more clear-headed view. The piece was duly praised for its treatment of a serious theme. It seemed to betoken a less candyfloss approach to life than had been the norm in English and American musicals for so many years. But almost all the critics pointed to a fundamental flaw. It was the aspect of the show that everyone from Grant downwards had chosen to ignore while they worried over casting, technicalities, and personal feuds.

This was that the subject matter, the basic idea of the show, was a non-starter. Who wanted to see a man being hauled over the coals for an alleged sleazy misdemeanour? Where was the uplift? Did one even care for the hero, or his three women? The public took the message. *Acts of Folly* wasn't much fun. To see it would mean a duty evening at the theatre, rather than an entertaining one. They started to stay away in droves.

Grant was still elated by the birth of his son, but the disaster being performed under his name at Her Majesty's Theatre each night nearly flattened him. How could two such conflicting events in his life happen at once? He was in a daze. The show had been his own act of folly. He had never been one to confide, to share decisions, and now he had to pay the price. And it was, literally, a price.

The second performance had only been half full, and that was with an audience which had booked before it knew what the reviews said. Not all of its members stuck it out to the end. The morning after, Grant's co-producers called him to a meeting and made him look at the facts. The show wouldn't go into profit for months, if not years. Meanwhile, the outgoings were huge. There was only one thing to do, close *Acts of Folly* at the end of the week and write it off as a loss.

It was a bitter moment and it had come with frighteningly rapid finality. So much work, so much faith, so much hope was going down the drain. It was the worst setback Grant had ever experienced, and he had to endure it alone.

Worst of all, he had to face a very public form of humiliation such as he had never experienced in the pop music business. The papers started running pieces about him, poking fun and casting doubts on his business acumen. They also came dangerously near to rumbling his obsessive interest in the show's female star.

Notices were issued to the company. The show would close on the Saturday after only seven performances. Grant doggedly watched all the remaining ones by himself. He couldn't see why the show had failed, there was so much that was good in it, wonderful performances, marvellous songs, nothing to be ashamed of.

Acts of Folly was good. It was just that Grant had

learned the hard way that musical theatre obeys no laws of natural justice. You just couldn't win, except when you did, and even then you wouldn't know what you'd done to deserve it.

On the last night he put on a brave face and went backstage after the show to shake every member of the cast by the hand. Finally, he knocked quietly on Suzie Paul's dressing-room door, expecting to find Alan Greenlee conducting another of his ritual post-mortems. Grant was surprised to find Suzie alone, apart from her dresser.

'I just wanted to say . . .' Grant's voice broke. The dresser took her cue and left.

Suzie stopped applying her street make-up and took Grant in her arms and hugged him.

He started once more, 'I'm sorry . . .'

'No, don't say that. You did everything you could, you've done *so much*.'

Grant broke free and looked at her. She had a shining self-confidence in her eyes, as though nothing had gone wrong. Indeed, she had done well out of his obsession with her. She would survive.

'You win some, you lose some, simple as that.' She laughed, a brittle, nervous laugh, to be sure, but her eyes blazed.

Grant cleared his throat, as though he now realized he was over-reacting. 'Where's Alan? I thought he'd be here tonight.'

'Yes, well,' Suzie sat down and resumed her make-up. 'He chickened out, couldn't face it. I don't blame him.'

'You mean . . .'

'No, he's not left me. He's just not here tonight, that's all.'

'I thought he would've been.'

There was an anxious pause through which sped a number of unspoken thoughts.

'We both need a spot of cheering up, don't we?' Grant

said, falteringly. 'I – I – just want you to know I'll do all I can to help you, never mind all this.'

Suzie turned a hard look on him, but what she said wasn't meant to be hard.

'I know, I appreciate that, Grant. But you've got Carly, and the kid now. You won't go short on love and affection. You don't have to waste any on me.'

Grant turned to leave. Had he lost more than money on the show?

'Oh, by the way, there was something I meant to say to you,' said Suzie. 'I hope you won't take it the wrong way.'

'What is it?'

'Just something I heard said about someone once, someone who was in a spot of bother like you.'

'Yes?'

' "In defeat he thought only of future victories." You should remember that,' she added firmly. 'Now, haven't you got a wife to go home to?'

'Yes, I have,' said Grant.

He leant over and kissed her on the cheek in front of the make-up mirror, surrounded by the bright, naked light bulbs.

Then he slipped away, remembering the talisman she'd given him.

Next day, on the Sunday, Grant picked up Carly and little Neville from the hospital and all three were driven down to Quornford in the Bentley. In the circumstances, it was at first a surprisingly happy day. Grant played obsessively with Neville and wanted to hold him all the time, only reluctantly handing him back to Carly when the boy needed a feed. The child made up for a lot, but *Acts of Folly* continued to gnaw at him. He just couldn't put the defeat out of his mind.

And with good reason. What nobody knew in as much detail as Grant was the extent of his investment. He had rushed into a high-risk business with a lack of caution that was more typical of amateur theatrical angels than of a supposedly experienced entertainment executive, even one who'd only just turned thirty. It was all right for frustrated, stage-struck investors to throw their money after bad shows, it gave them a kick, a vicarious involvement in the footlights and greasepaint world, but he had overstepped the mark.

When the accounts were examined, they would show that Grant had put up his own and Starfinders' money to the tune of 85 per cent of the show's funding. Investors had been slow coming forward so he had made up the shortfall. Now, certain clauses in the contract meant he was chiefly responsible for the huge outstanding debts left by the show's demise. It was a matter of some £120,000. The only way to get out of the payments was for his various companies to go into liquidation and possibly for him to be declared bankrupt.

Whereas he had risked all, a lot of other people had risked only their time and talent. The owners of the theatre would soon find a replacement show. The cast and the hire firms would all get paid for what they had done, even if they didn't get the months of work they'd been banking on. Grant would not get a penny for all the time and effort he'd put in.

Then there was the money he had spent building up Suzie Paul and the cost to his record label of the original cast recording. In the end, despite the sweetener, the record wasn't ready for release until after the show had closed. He would be able to sell only a few copies to theatrical curiosity seekers now.

The more Grant examined the books, the more he saw that he was probably ruined. He had brought it on himself by a combination of over-zealous investment and by reckless personal expenditure in the years before. All his fine and worthwhile achievements were now endangered by this unwise theatrical adventure. It was impossible at this moment to tell the true extent of the damage because so many of his companies were involved, but it was likely that some would have to go to the wall.

As he watched baby Neville lying in his mother's arms that afternoon, he also realized that Quornford itself wouldn't be his for very much longer. He decided to wait a day or two before breaking all this to Carly. Poor thing, she hadn't even seen the show, the cause of the disaster.

On the Monday, he was told the Bentley would have to go. And the Jensen Interceptor. And the E-type. This was really going to hurt.

Of course, there were those who were pleased to see the difficulties Grant had brought upon himself. He had rough-handled enough people in the business over the years to ensure this. His abrasive manner didn't endear him to many.

There were exceptions. Carly was a brick when he told her the full extent of the damage. She offered to go right back to work, there and then, and open another clothes shop in Chelsea. Grant said he'd have to think about it. Johnny Todd was the first to ring and reassure Grant he'd help in any way he could. Jan Ferry, his PA, emerged as a tower of strength, refusing Grant the opportunities for self-recrimination that he craved, forcing him to face the reality of his situation and do something about it.

But, in the short term, it was Grant's enemies who looked like winning. Then, the final straw. Gareth Trigger of the Wreckers was caught in a drugs bust by Manchester police. George Evans of Starfinders was also charged. Grant knew the likelihood was that they were both guilty. It was foolish to allege that the police had planted the evidence, as Gareth was claiming. Gareth and George would probably go to prison.

Grant could have been forgiven for thinking this was the end of everything, or for wondering whether life was worth living at all.

*　　*　　*

Alan Greenlee was in two minds about how to react to Grant's difficulties. He'd had to stand back amazed and grateful as Grant moved in and built up Suzie's name and career. His wife had come very well out of the *Acts of Folly* disaster. Whatever people thought of the show, no one had a bad word to say about her. But she had not been given enough time really to prove her worth. No achievement, however genuine, faded quite so fast as a flop that the world wanted to forget.

Greenlee had been suspicious, too, of Grant's motives. A man didn't do what Grant had done purely out of charity. It was obvious that he was badly smitten with Suzie. So Greenlee was secretly glad about the chastening experiences being suffered by Grant. Maybe he'd pant a little less heavily after Suzie now.

Indeed, Grant did not appear to be in a position to dabble in Suzie's fortunes at all, since Starfinders looked as though it was foundering. Greenlee could build on the very satisfactory foundations Grant had laid for Suzie's future and try to ensure that no bad odour clung to her. All this would be some compensation for the indignity Greenlee had suffered at Grant's hands so long ago and which none of the recent events had expunged from his memory.

If Grant had brought the Starfinders empire tumbling about his ears by his injudicious investment in *Acts of Folly*, perhaps there were one or two parts of the empire that Alan Greenlee could now snap up?

That fateful barbecue in Australia had also been the setting for the auspicious first encounter between Alan Greenlee and Quentin Saint. It wasn't purely a case of talent-spotting at first sight. Greenlee was drawn to Quentin as a person, too, but there was nothing he'd been able to do about that. Now, he thought of taking Quentin over and promoting him as Grant had done Suzie.

Greenlee and Quentin had encountered each other at the usual showbiz gatherings, most recently at the first night of

Acts of Folly, which Quentin had found deeply boring. The next time was at a special screening of the new film *Monte Carlo or Bust*. The film's distributors were holding various pre-release showings to small groups of interested people with a view to getting the 'word of mouth' started. Suzie and Quentin both received invitations but Suzie hadn't wanted to go, so Alan used her ticket instead.

After the screening, they chatted happily over the drinks supplied by the film company. Greenlee suggested they adjourn for lunch. Quentin insisted they go to a small Soho restaurant called Henrietta's. 'It's run by the most outrageous queen,' he said, 'but you just have to bear with her. The main thing is there's lots of little alcoves, honeymoon cabins they call them. It means you don't get pestered.'

So that's where they went, Greenlee insisting in advance that he paid. Henry, the proprietor, was quickly dealt a flirtatious kiss by Quentin while Greenlee looked on, a trifle awkwardly.

They fell to dissecting *Acts of Folly*.

'Suzie was the best thing in it,' Quentin said. 'You must be very proud of her.'

Greenlee didn't want to listen to discussions of his wife's talent, but was glad Quentin followed the general trend. 'I suppose you'll be looking for another vehicle?'

'Maybe, but I'm not rushing it. She's having a rest. *Acts of Folly* took a lot out of her.'

Greenlee noticed Quentin making quick work of the glass of champagne he'd ordered when they sat down.

'Like something else to drink?'

'Well, I never like to mix my drinks,' Quentin whispered confidentially.

'I'd better get a bottle of champagne, then.'

They drank on, Quentin putting away two glasses to every one Greenlee managed.

Greenlee started digging. 'How's the Starfinders thing affecting you?'

'Haven't had any of our weekly meetings since it happened, that's all.'

'What weekly meetings? With Grant? Sounds like going to a shrink.'

'Keeps me regular, that was the idea,' Quentin giggled. 'No, we've always had them, ever since I first met Grant. It's part of our agreement. I write a song a week, come rain or shine, and usually on Fridays I go along and sing it to him.'

'You still do that? How extraordinary! Aren't you a bit big for that now?'

'I don't know, it's a good idea, really. Keeps my nose to the grindstone, and that's when he hands me my pocket money.'

'You're joking! He gives you pocket money?'

'Oh, yes. I'm hopeless with money, you see. So he gives me what I need, which isn't very much.'

'What happens to the rest?'

'It's all bound up in his company somewhere. I don't really know the details.'

Greenlee sensed that if he dug any deeper he'd be forced to confront Quentin with the facts of life. He wasn't sure he was up to it. Grant had obviously been operating the oldest trick in the book on Quentin. Discovering him, signing him up, and then robbing him blind. How else to explain it?

'How much are you earning these days?' asked Greenlee, as casually as he could.

Quentin told him straight. 'A hundred a week.'

'A hundred quid! You're not serious?'

'Well, that's what Grant pays me. It's part of our agreement.'

'But you should be earning three grand a week! He's conning you, Quentin. And after what's happened, you may not get even that.'

'I don't mind,' Quentin smiled blithely, helping himself to more of the champagne. 'My needs are small.'

'Now look, Quentin, let me run my eye over your contract with Starfinders. I don't want to interfere, but it may not be valid anyway, if he's about to go bust.'

'It's sweet of you to offer, but I don't suppose it is valid.'

'Why not?'

'There ain't one. Not on paper, anyway. Our little arrangement is just between ourselves.'

Greenlee was astonished. How could a performer of Quentin Saint's stature, with earnings possibly in the millions, put his trust in a manipulator like Grant Pickering? It was beyond belief.

Greenlee couldn't begin to understand Quentin's simple trust in the man who'd built him up. He couldn't see the relationship – which was odd, as he operated something very similar with Suzie. He had made sure she was sewn up, tied to him inescapably.

All the same, if Quentin really had no contract, it would be that much easier for Greenlee to capture Quentin for himself. That was what he very much wanted to do. Grant's troubles should mean that Starfinders' artistes could easily slip away from him if they wanted to. A company in liquidation would be unable to honour the management contracts with its clients, so technically they'd be free to join other agencies.

Having consumed most of the bottle of champagne, Quentin was beyond caring. Greenlee paid the bill, decanted Quentin into a taxi, and directed it to the pop star's home in Hampstead. Then he went back to his office, still amazed at the preposterousness of Quentin's position.

That same lunchtime, Suzie Paul hadn't been off shopping or out chatting with her girl friends. She didn't in fact have many girl friends to gossip or bitch with. She was a curiously self-contained person.

Instead, she was on her way to see an equally self-contained person, who also had no close friends – Grant Pickering.

Grant knew that Carly was safely out of the way, down at Quornford with the baby, so he'd had no hesitation in fixing a discreet assignation with Suzie at the Montagu Square flat.

It was looking noticeably bare. The antiques on loan or on approval had all been sent back to the shops as part of the stringent savings imposed on Grant. He was beginning to wonder how much longer he'd own the clothes he stood up in.

Suzie, wearing dark glasses, approached the flat and rang the bell. Grant opened the door and she entered quickly.

'God, what have you done to yourself?' she asked, taking off her glasses. 'You look awful.'

'It's only a beard.'

'Trying to look like John Lennon or something?'

Grant made no reply.

'Well, don't I get a kiss?'

'Of course,' said Grant, his old shyness with women reasserting itself. 'I didn't think you'd come.'

He held her. She smelt ravishing, exotic, glamorous.

'Why didn't you think I'd come?' she asked, sinking on to the long, low sofa, and extending her silk-stockinged legs provocatively towards Grant. He crouched before her.

'Nobody's keen on being seen with me these days, now that I'm down.'

'Oh, come on.' Suzie took off her glasses and played with Grant's tie, tugging it to chide him. 'It's not the end of the world.'

'It feels like it, I can tell you.'

'You'll pick yourself up, I know you will. I can feel it.'

Grant had bought in a small hamper from Fortnum's – some habits died hard – and he reached for the bottle of champagne.

Suzie smiled. 'There, you see, where there's champers, there's hope!'

He looked at her. Here was the woman he was suffering financial ruin for. if he hadn't been soft on her, he'd probably never have got mixed up in *Acts of Folly*. Now she teased him, cajoled him, delicately trying to get him out of his morose state. He remained intractable, removed from the matter in hand.

As she worked away at him, Grant wondered why she'd bothered to come and see him now, when she'd held him at such arm's length before? Did she feel obliged to humour him? Was that it? Or was it that he was a defeated man? Did she prefer him that way?

Inevitably, they began to make love.

Grant unbent sufficiently to realize he was making love to a woman thousands of men had lusted after. Being on the stage or in the pop business was a form of prostitution, so they said. Performers sold their looks, their bodies, their sex appeal just as much as their singing or acting ability. But he had achieved the fantasy. He was in bed with her. It seemed a long time since he first spotted her as that newspaper pin-up, but this was the fulfilment of that dream.

'You're not really in the mood for it, are you?' she chided him.

'Lot on my mind,' he mumbled unnecessarily.

'Not been sleeping either, by the look of you.' Suzie smoothed the dark rings under Grant's eyes with a finger and felt the rough stubble of his beard. 'You must get your beauty sleep. Take pills if you have to.'

'Don't like to. Never have liked pills, of any kind.'

'That's silly, darling. As long as you don't *always* take them, it's okay. That's what they're there for. To make you feel better.'

Suzie, too, worked hard to make Grant feel better. She stroked, kissed, massaged. Finally, he relaxed. Then they really made love. Very rough, very strong.

Grant hadn't dared imagine it could be so good with her, nor that Suzie would be so desperate for it.

Afterwards, they lay together warm, exhausted, feeling much better.

258

To Grant, one of Suzie's chief attractions was her direct, almost aristocratic, manner. He found it immensely sexy. It was a considerable turn-on to a lower-middle-class lad like himself. A working-class girl like Carly had been equally arousing once upon a time, but this was something else.

'You know, Suzie,' he said softly as they lay in the shaded bedroom while the London traffic roared about its business in the distance, 'I really don't know the first thing about you.'

'Like what?'

'I mean, how did you come to marry Alan? You're a bit posh, you know, and he's very . . . well, he's Yorkshire, isn't he? You don't seem to fit together at all.'

'You're right, but I can't explain it.'

'How did you meet?'

'He saw me in a show, told me how wonderful I was, and we were married within three months.'

'What did your parents think? You have got parents?'

'Oh yes. They didn't think. I've not had anything to do with them since I was expelled from school.'

'Expelled? Boarding school?'

'Yes. You see, I always wanted to be in the business. When I was in the fifth form there was this show I desperately wanted to see in London but the school wouldn't let me go. So I just went, and they expelled me.'

'Your parents didn't approve?'

'No. Mind you, there were other differences.'

'Is Suzie Paul your real name?'

'Ah, well, not quite. Smith-Powell, actually, with a hyphen. And Suzannah, always Suzannah, never shortened to "Suzie" when I was at home.'

'You thought Suzie Paul was a better stage name?'

'Well, don't you? Sounds Jewish, too, though I'm not.'

'Amazing. I can't say I see very much of my parents either, but it's not a complete break like yours.'

'I suppose they'd say I married Alan to make up for not having parents around.'

'Your father especially. Very psychological.'

'What a gruesome thought! But I suppose there's some truth in it.'

They chatted on, in a way that Grant had rarely done after making love to his other women, not even with Carly. It perked him up; he found Suzie the ideal person to talk to. In the middle of the afternoon, having done what she could, Suzie put on her clothes and very quickly left him on his own.

Next time they got together was over lunch, in one of the alcoves at Henrietta's. Unfortunately, this time Suzie undid all the good work she'd done cheering Grant up by passing on a piece of tittle-tattle, only intended as a joke.

'How's Neville?' she asked, as if to show there were no taboo subjects.

'Neville? He's fine. He's down at Quornford with Carly. I'll have to sell up, you know, so I expect they'll come to Montagu Square on a permanent basis, if I don't have to sell there, too.'

'That's terrible, they're both such lovely places.'

'No alternative, I'm afraid. If Quornford has to be sold, that's it. It's not as if it's been in my family since the twelfth century. I mean, I'm not a Smith-Powell or anything.'

Suzie didn't rise to the bait. 'It would have been nice for Neville to grow up in the country.'

'No, honestly, he'd be as much of a worry there, once he starts walking. There's the lake and a hundred other places he could get into trouble.'

'There was a picture of him in the paper, wasn't there?'

'Yes, in a colour mag. You saw that?'

'Mmm. Alan showed me a picture of a baby and put his hand over the caption and told me to guess whose it was.'

'And?'

'I said it was just like that chap we saw at your wedding.'

'Which chap?'

'Neville's the spitting image of him. The one who wrote "Tantalizing".'

Grant blanched. 'Tom Sheridan!' He was deeply shocked at the inference. He had never noticed any resemblance himself. His mind raced to examine the unpleasant implications. Were other people going around saying the same thing, that his son looked like Tom? Were they even saying that Tom was Neville's father?

'Suzie, what are you telling me? Why even mention such a thing?'

'I'm sorry.' She had completely underestimated Grant's reaction.

'You're telling me I'm not really the kid's dad! Oh yes, you are, that's the suggestion, isn't it? God help us, what a thing to say!'

'I've said I'm sorry, Grant.' Now she earnestly tried to calm him down. 'I didn't mean . . . I mean, I didn't know you cared so much.'

There was a long silence while Grant sat running his fingers through his hair and pulling at his beard.

'You weren't to know, I suppose,' he said at last. 'But, you see, Tom and I have been rivals since the day we met. Carly's been at the centre of it, of course. But I was the one who actually married her, and the reason we got married, or the occasion of it, rather, was that she was pregnant.'

'Oh, I see. And there's a possibility . . .?'

'I just don't know.'

'Don't you think you ought to talk it over with Carly before jumping to conclusions? It might be coincidence.'

'No! It's so obvious what's happened, once you think about it.'

He flushed deep red.

CHAPTER 15

The news from London filtered through slowly to those whom Grant Pickering had left behind in his rise to fame and fortune. Tom Sheridan gathered that the company which handled his songs would most likely be bought up by a large music publishing house and that he would receive any future royalties through them.

Tom couldn't help being glad that Grant's progress was checked, and he wondered how the collapse of Starfinders would affect Carly. For all that he had been humiliated by her leaving him, he still thought her wonderful and desirable. The only person he blamed for what had happened was Grant. If Carly had really gone after Grant because she was dazzled by his wealth and possessions, was it not possible that, without them, she might once more respond to Tom's attentions?

After his experience with Halo, Tom needed something to restore his confidence, but he did wonder whether in some strange way the woman had managed to wreak her revenge on Grant. He wouldn't put it past a witch like Halo to bring a man down the way Grant had been brought down.

Still, Tom didn't really know what had happened. If he had known that Grant's fall was in part precipitated by his passion for Suzie Paul, that would only have made matters worse. If Tom had known that Grant was now being unfaithful to Carly with the self-same Suzie, he would have been hard put to it to restrain himself from violence. If he'd known that he was the real father of Carly's boy, he would probably have *exploded*.

But he didn't know these things. He was away from it all,

still spending his days at large in Liverpool, no clear-cut aim in his life. The 'old days' of five or six years before were now sufficiently far away for him to be nostalgic about them. Tom, like so many others in the big city, had now formed a heroic view of his part in the city's sudden explosion. So much had been said and written about it that Tom could no longer quite make out whether anything he said about those days was true. Had he ever met the Beatles, or even set eyes on them? It was hard to tell, but he always said he had, because that was what people wanted to hear.

He still received royalties from the songs he'd written for Johnny Todd, a good wage by the standards of the city, but would he ever write another No. 1? He didn't want a nine-to-five job; occasionally he earned a few pounds talking to education groups or taking part in poetry readings, and he still sang with local bands. He was a personality in the city, the sort who always got put on the guest list for parties and press launches. He was always interviewed when the TV journalists and magazine writers descended on Liverpool for a quick programme or article.

His sex life was busy. There seemed a never-ending line of art students or university students who were sufficiently charmed by his talk and impressed by his status as one of the few Liverpool poets and entertainers not to have gone South to be happy to pop in and out of his bed, accompany him on his jaunts, and then move on.

He went through a brief period of dressing in a rather self-consciously arty fashion. He wore suits with coloured stripes on them, sometimes with waistcoats. He wore white shoes, a long scarf, and sometimes a fedora. He experimented with beards and moustaches, and with a ring in his ear. In this period, he gave very much the impression of a clown who'd been left behind by the circus.

In time, though, he went back to wearing the jeans, T-shirts and leather jackets in which he'd always felt most at home.

He held court in the Philly. Shortly after hearing about the Starfinders crash, he happened to meet Denis Northington, the drummer from the Offbeats whose group had been stolen from under his nose by Grant.

'I suppose you've heard the news?' Denis said, slipping into the seat beside Tom and his bed-mate of the week, a mute blond art student called Elspeth.

'It was bound to happen, wasn't it?' replied Tom. 'Overreached himself, did our Grant. Not shedding any tears for him.'

'Ah well,' said Denis, with that combination of moroseness and sentimentality that is pure Liverpool, 'we had quite a good run for our money. It was fun while it lasted.' He stared at the froth on his beer.

'Waddya mean, Denis? You've had a terrible time, and it's all down to that prat, Pickering. I know what he did to you. Took you over, turned you into a backing group, sucked you dry and spat you out.'

'No, we didn't have what it takes.'

'What's come over you, Denis? Stop making excuses. The fact is, you were no longer any use to that megalomaniac. He probably only kept you on his books for old times' sake. Now he's gone bust and you're out on your ear. I'm lucky, I got away before it was too late.' Tom was appalled at the way Denis was rewriting history in order to cushion the blow.

'I know Grant used us,' Denis was saying, 'but I bear no grudges. He didn't lose all his money just in order to dump us!'

'I wouldn't put it past him,' Tom snorted.

Elspeth looked on intently, hardly able to follow all the talk and wanting to get Tom on his own again.

'Well, it was an experience,' Denis concluded. Tom saw it was a lost cause, trying to make him angry over what had happened. Denis was accustoming himself to the notion of failure, to spending the remainder of his days living off memories of a few years on the coat-tails of a phenomenon. He'd leave him to it.

'So what'll you do? Can you go on as a drummer?'

'Doubt it. I'll always play the drums, one way or another, I suppose. As an amateur, if I have to. But I think I've reached the end of the line. I'll have to find something else to do. I might have tried teaching once, but it's a bit late for that now. Being with the band put paid to qualifications, and all that.'

'Yeh, well, there it is then. What about Paddie and Roger?'

'They're in the same boat. I expect they'll look for work round here as well. Rod says he's staying on in London. He thinks he can get work as a session guitarist, but I'm not so sure.'

'It's a bit like the end of a dream, isn't it? Bloody Grant Pickering. He deserves every headache he's got now, the way he's shat on everyone all these years. I hope he rots in hell.'

'He'll be all right, I expect. And you'll be all right, won't you, Tom? For all your calling him names, he's put a bob or two your way, hasn't he?'

'Nothing very much.' Tom wasn't going to allow anyone to spoil his dreams of eternal damnation for Grant Pickering. 'But how d'you mean, Grant'll be all right?'

'He'll pick himself up,' said Denis. 'People like that always do. He's a businessman, isn't he? Company goes bust, some get laid off, some don't, but he's free to set up a new one.'

'And cock that up, too.'

'Maybe. But he'll be back, he's that type.'

'I wish he'd just go away. I never want to hear of him again. Or have to meet him either. He gives me the creeps.'

'You're only jealous because he married Carly.'

'No, I'm not,' Tom said emphatically.

Elspeth showed a little more interest now. She had never

heard of this woman. 'Who's Carly?' she asked.

'A girl who used to live around here.'

'Used to run a shop. Grant pinched her from under Tom's nose,' Denis helpfully explained.

'How did he do that?' asked Elspeth.

'He had more money, and she sold out,' said Tom.

Denis took a sip of his pint. He'd said enough. He could see that Tom was still sensitive on that subject but, as was his way, acted as though he could simply put anyone who'd got the better of him out of his mind.

What Tom would never admit to the likes of Denis and Elspeth was that he still had a romantic idea he might be able to reclaim Carly one day. He just hoped that Grant's business crash would help bring this about.

During the long weeks of uncertainty following *Acts of Folly*, Carly kept as calm as she'd always been. Neville was an adorable baby, very good-natured and no trouble, but there was a limit to the fun to be had spending all day with him.

Mrs Pugh, the housekeeper, had always pressed Carly for household decisions about what to buy and cook, while Carly would have been much happier doing it all herself. So, one of the first changes after the crash was that Mrs Pugh was laid off, together with all but one of the domestics.

With no staff, Carly was even more lonely and cut off. She missed, too, the company of her friends and workmates in Liverpool. If ever she had dreamed of being mistress of a great house, she found the reality quite a letdown. If she had ever dreamed of giving up her shop and sitting at home all day, she discovered the reality had as many disadvantages. She hardly saw anyone, she was stuck out in the middle of the Berkshire countryside, and saw Grant only at weekends.

They had hardly had a chance to begin enjoying each

other's company, so quickly had his financial difficulties followed on their marriage. Grant was now working all hours to sort out the mess his companies were in. Carly had absolutely no idea what the future held for the three of them. She sensed they were in danger of losing everything they had together.

One day in September, just after his lunch with Suzie, Grant rang Carly, as he dutifully did when they were apart, and announced, to her surprise, that he was coming down to Quornford mid-week. He would cadge a lift from Johnny Todd. Carly noticed something odd about his voice. She was used to his sounding tired and grumpy. That had always been the way with Grant. Now there was a hint of menace.

'I've got some things to tell you,' was the only explanation he gave.

Carly braced herself for the worst. Was there something he hadn't told her about his business troubles? He hadn't confided in her much, but Jan Ferry, with whom she got on well, had taken the trouble to explain what was going on in language that Carly could understand, so she wasn't totally uninformed.

Eventually, there came the crunch of Johnny's Rolls on the gravel. She watched from a window as Grant got out. It appeared that Johnny wasn't stopping. As he drove away again, Grant bent down to pick a weed from the verge.

Carly found Neville and took him down to the entrance hall to greet his father. Grant kissed Carly a shade perfunctorily, she thought. He put down his briefcase and took hold of Neville saying, 'Let me look at you . . .'

Grant went ahead into the sitting room, carrying the boy, who seemed delighted at his father's unaccustomed attention. Carly followed, her flat shoes clacking on the marble floor. She was a little puzzled by Grant's behaviour but, if anything, more concerned by the undoubted deterioration in her husband's physical appearance since she'd seen him the previous weekend. Apart from the beard, which she didn't like, his hair had gone suddenly grey at the temples. He was only thirty. Were his losses having such a traumatic effect?

Carly settled on the sofa while Grant stood with his back to the fireplace, still holding Neville.

'You know what they're saying, don't you?'

'What about?'

'About Neville. He looks like Tom, so Tom must be the father.'

So *that* was what had been eating him. Carly had noticed the resemblance early on, and had considered the possibility but, naturally enough, hadn't said anything. She spent so much time looking at Neville's face it wasn't surprising if she saw all sorts of people in him – her mam, her dad.

'Well . . .' she hesitated. 'That's absolute rubbish. Tom couldn't have made me pregnant before you . . . you know . . . asked me to stay on.'

'Why not? All too likely, if you ask me. And I'm made to look a right Charlie, aren't I, on top of everything else?'

'Who's noticed, anyway?'

'Just people, when his picture was in the paper.' Grant certainly wasn't going to mention that one of them was Suzie Paul.

Carly continued hotly to deny the charge, whatever suspicions she might have had herself. 'It really can't be true, Grant. I don't believe it. I was so *sure* I conceived with you that night . . .'

Grant had thoughts of ordering blood tests to establish Neville's paternity, but that wouldn't make much difference to his peace of mind. The child *was* Tom's, because it looked like Tom.

'There's not much to be done, I suppose,' he said, finally.

'I know that. But I just wanted you to know that I knew.'

'Is that why you came, specially to tell me that?' she asked.

'No, there's one or two other things you ought to know.'

Grant handed Neville back to Carly. He moved close to her.

'You don't have to tell me now, you know,' Carly said. 'Why don't you *relax*?'

'Sorry, yes, I didn't mean to bite your head off.'

'Oh, Grant, never mind.' She ran her fingers through his hair.

'I'm going grey,' he said.

'Only a titchy bit. Anyway, I like it like that.'

'I'm not bloody surprised, though. It'll be white by the time I'm forty.'

'Rather that than bald. Very distinguished.'

'That's my Carly, eh?' He kissed her.

'Want a drink? I'll fetch you one.'

'No, I've just decided I'm on the wagon. If I take to the bottle with all this hanging over me, I'll never stop.'

'No wonder you're so stroppy.'

'Sorry.'

Gradually, Grant did relax and put the worry over Neville to the back of his mind. He was conscious of the cosy domesticity, warmed to it and responded, but he knew even that was in jeopardy.

In due course, he broke it to Carly that Quornford would have to go. Carly had known it was a possibility all along. She didn't really mind. It had never really been 'their' house. It was much too grand for her and, anyway, she preferred to live in the city. Grant thought they could just about hang on to Montagu Square, but they might have to settle for a more modest home in the suburbs.

'Only until I get rid of my debts, you understand.'

'And how'll you do that?'

'That's the tricky part. What it involves, basically, is running down the companies, ceasing trade, then setting up new ones. That's what I'm in the middle of now. I spend all day with the solicitors and the accountants sorting out the mess. The risk is we'll lose clients in the process. I've already told some I don't want them. The Modds were the first to go. Sad, but it had to be done.'

'Oh, the Modds . . .' Carly sighed. 'I never got used to that name. They were always the Offbeats to me. First come, first go. That *is* sad.'

'Johnny'll stay, of course. He's made that clear. Anyway, for heaven's sake, he needs me to look after him. As for the others, I don't know. There are plenty of vultures up on the roof.'

'So when do we move out of here?'

'It ought to go on the market this week. God knows how long it'll take to get rid of. Not everyone can stump up half a million, just like that.'

'Half a million?'

'Yep, that's what it's worth.'

'Jesus.' Carly thought about it for a moment. Then she was reassuring. 'I'll look after the move, Grant. I'll close up here. We'll make Montagu Square nice and comfy. When you've lived in a two-up, two-down most of your life, like I have, you can manage without all this.'

'I thought you'd say that. It's just I won't be happy till I've got another one.'

'You're the end!' exclaimed Carly with something like delight.

Grant even managed one of his rare smiles, but it only disguised a darker thought she wasn't privy to.

In defeat he planned only future victories. That was the motto Suzie Paul had given him. But who was going to share those victories – Suzie or Carly?

Slowly, brick by brick, Grant Pickering rebuilt his shattered empire. The old companies were closed, the old offices sold. The name Starfinders was no more, tossed aside like a faded sixties dream, and in its place began to rise a new talent agency, more mundanely entitled the Grant Pickering Organization.

The GPO, as it was instantly nicknamed, was set up largely with money Grant had wheedled out of Sir Edgar King, the former Tory minister with whom Tom Sheridan had had the famous brush on television. It was an unexpected alliance but Grant had cleverly worked through the lists of theatrical investors and identified Sir Edgar as a man with a soft spot for showbiz ventures. He had made a loss on *Acts of Folly* but didn't seem to mind. You won some, you lost some.

The clincher was that, like Grant, Sir Edgar had more than a soft spot for Suzie Paul. Grant brought the two together for a lunch at which Sir Edgar was able to ogle her. He also suggested, half in jest, that the best thing for the new GPO would be if Grant could sign up Suzie. Grant wholly agreed but explained to Sir Edgar the problems such a proposal would present.

The Grant Pickering Organization established itself in modest offices off Wigmore Street. One or two faces remained from the past. Mickey Clinch, still loyal, had sat out the enforced lay-off in his curiously unambitious, contented way. Jan Ferry surely deserved some humanitarian award, having worked for Grant without pay since the crash. This was an act of devotion that Grant would never be able to repay amply, but it showed not everyone looked down on Mr Pickering. He was capable of inspiring loyalty. It was one of Grant's most vulnerable points, that so many of his actions could be seen by different people in totally different lights.

There was the question of whether he had been genuinely supportive of Quentin Saint since discovering him, or whether he'd been exploiting him, milking him for all he was worth.

Whatever other people thought, Quentin still had faith in Grant. He was on board with the new company, the only difference being that this time, as Grant noticed, he had asked for a formal contract. This was most un-Quentin-like and Grant wondered if he'd been put up to it. Johnny Todd re-signed, together with Rex Room, and one or two of the other acts. The Wreckers, also, though Gareth and George were still awaiting trial on the drugs charges.

It was a perfectly respectable stable and a fittingly slimmed-down version of Starfinders. All the GPO had to deal with now was the small matter of finding hits for its artistes to record.

The one new artiste Grant most desperately wanted to attract to his banner was, naturally, Suzie Paul. But on what grounds could Grant go to Alan Greenlee and ask to take over his wife? Particularly since she was now busy establishing herself as Grant's mistress.

Suzie was exotic and different. She had nothing in common with Grant, the way Carly had, such as background and upbringing. And, unlike Carly, she was obviously a woman of talent and achievement. The qualities of support and intuition which Carly provided in abundance were as nothing compared with the apparent charms of a woman like Suzie. In having her, Grant felt he possessed a much more tangible commodity. If, and when, they ever went public with the relationship, people would be able to see at a glance what Grant had found in her.

For her part, Suzie was grateful for what Grant had tried to do for her. She also saw him as the husband she should have had, the man Alan Greenlee so obviously was not. No one suspected any of this, not Greenlee, not Carly, not even Jan Ferry, who knew everything else Grant was up to and was capable of anticipating most of his actions and feelings.

Grant would slip away from the office at lunchtime, always with a plausible excuse, and go over to the Greenlee flat in a large thirties block on Kensington High Street. Suzie's engagements as a singer weren't many just now so she was free to indulge her affair with Grant uninterrupted.

She kept cheerful, but it wasn't easy. On the days when she had no bookings, she still had to keep up appearances and not let herself go to seed by sitting around. She exercised, maintained her hair and make-up, and went for singing lessons. A little of her spirit and determination rubbed off on Grant. He knew he could talk to her in a way he couldn't manage with Carly. Suzie understood. Grant was desperate to do something for her in return, but what? She didn't appear greedy. He had already done far too much for her, and brought himself down in the process.

Their love-making was probably not the most important part of their relationship. The excitement of being part of show business was. Yet, if anyone had observed the two of them, their 'affair' had all the hallmarks of the real thing. They revelled in the secret assignations, the excitement of keeping them a secret, the pleasure in being sure that only they knew what they were up to.

One lunchtime in November, Suzie was due back in the apartment at one o'clock to let Grant in. She had actually had a small job that morning, recording a jingle for a Cornflakes commercial. It paid well, it was anonymous, and even if no one recognized her distinctive, sunny voice, it might have some subliminal effect on people. Nowadays, Alan Greenlee no longer accompanied her on jobs like this. He had come to realize that producers didn't take too kindly to having 'my manager' and especially 'my husband' hanging around while they were trying to work.

'I'll probably have lunch near the studio,' she told him breezily, giving nothing away, but Greenlee had taken note.

When Suzie returned to the apartment, without having stopped for lunch as she'd told her husband she would, she waved cheerily to the doorkeeper and rushed past him to the lift. Approaching the frosted-glass front door, Suzie noticed at once there was a light on inside. It was most unusual for her to forget to switch the lights off. In any case, if she did, Alan was so fussy he would go round turning them off. That was something he had in common with Grant.

Her heart missed a beat. Was it burglars? But the door hadn't been forced. Maybe they'd come in the back way, up the fire escape. She didn't know what to do. She began to move back towards the lift, hoping her high heels wouldn't tap on the linoleum. The porter would be able to help.

Then she thought better of it. There was no noise coming from the flat, no one moving about. She would only look foolish if she dragged anyone else into the affair. She fingered her door key. Then she breathed a sigh of relief. She heard the whirr of the lift starting up again from the ground floor. Slowly, it came up to the fifth and stopped.

Out stepped Grant.

'Thank God you've come,' she whispered.

'What's the matter?' He kissed her cheek. 'What are you out here for?'

'I'm not sure. When I got to the door, I saw a light on inside. I didn't want to go in.'

'We'll soon see what's up,' said Grant. 'Give me the key.'

They went to the door. Grant turned the key as quietly as he could. They moved slowly into the small entrance hall.

Soundlessly, Grant made an expression of puzzlement.

'Wait!' she whispered, holding a beringed finger to her glossy lips, and quietly opened the door to the main room; there was no one there.

Then, unmistakably, there was the sound of coughing.

'The bedroom,' Suzie gasped, and made for the door.

She opened it, with no idea what to expect. What she did find was thus a total and shocking surprise. Grant closely followed her gaze.

In the bed were two men. One, not knowing quite how to handle the intrusion, was Alan Greenlee. It took a little time for the other man to extricate himself from the position he was in and turn to face the newcomers.

'Oh, hello, Grant, fancy seeing you here,' said Quentin Saint.

CHAPTER 16

Suzie began to scream and shout. 'You filth! What do you think you're doing? Get out, both of you!'

Grant was just as stunned by the revelation, but not so hysterical. 'Don't you think it would be better if we –'

'Get out, you two,' she sobbed. '*Get out!*' She stormed into the lounge.

Grant lingered.

'Well,' he said, 'here's a how-de-do.'

Quentin was now lying with his hands behind his head on the pillows, looking quite pleased with himself. Alan Greenlee was sitting up, also apparently cool and unrepentant.

'The point is,' he said to Grant, 'the point is, Pickering, I know what *we're* doing here. But what are *you* doing here? That's what I'd like to know.'

'Ah yes,' said Grant. 'That's a very good question.'

He quietly closed the door and went to join Suzie.

It was a measure of how stunned she was that she begged Grant to pour her a gin. Normally, she didn't touch the stuff. Now she sank the measure in one gulp and demanded another.

'I know what they said,' she snuffled, 'he'd stick his arse out to get any kind of business, but I never thought I'd actually find him at it.'

Grant poured himself a gin.

'Okay, the sex between us was never very important. Never very good either,' she went on, her voice firmer. 'It was separate beds from the word go, but that's not always an indication, is it? And he was able to *do* it, you know. It just shows, doesn't it? You never know what's really going on –'

277

'Well, I wasn't sure Quentin ever *did* do it, so that makes two of us.'

'He's always been on about how wonderful Quentin is, ever since they met in Australia. I should have smelt a rat.'

'And there was me thinking Quentin had no sex life to speak of, however much he liked to camp about.'

'Christ, I tell you how I feel, I never want to be in the same room with him ever again, let alone the same bed. But he's my bloody manager, isn't he, for God's sake, as well as my bloody husband. What am I going to do, Grant?'

Quentin and Alan were still in the bedroom next door, equally unable to sort out the mess they'd made but not inclined to obey Suzie's order to leave.

Quentin was taking a blithely unconcerned view of the matter, only vaguely wondering what effect it would have on his working relationship with Grant. Greenlee was rapidly thinking ahead, wondering whether, now that matters had come to a head, he could force the pace and get what he really wanted.

'A nice little dance we've got here, haven't we?' said Greenlee. 'It might as well have been me finding her in bed with him. She said he was besotted with her, but I thought she just meant in business.'

'Makes you think, doesn't it?' Quentin put in, not very helpfully.

'Think what?'

'Well, if he's so keen on your wife, and you're so keen on me, you could do a straight swap. You manage me, and he can have her.'

'I don't think he'd buy it.'

'Why not?'

'Well, I'd still be married to her.'

'Would you buy it?'

'Come on, Quentin, you're jumping the gun.'

'Just a thought.'

'Anyway, I can't see Grant swallowing it. You've got your royalties from your songs, Suzie's got none of that.'

'Grant might be only too glad to get rid of me. If he got her, he might think he'd done rather well out of it.'

'All right. We'll put it to them. Clothes on, and make yourself respectable.'

Greenlee knocked on the lounge door and cleared his throat. Grant looked at Suzie who made a face of revulsion.

'Come on, Sooz. Let's get it over with. Come in,' he called out when she didn't respond.

Greenlee and Quentin crept in quietly.

'Let me put my cards on the table,' Greenlee began. 'It won't have come as a surprise to you that Quentin and I have a great regard for each other. I think I can say that, can't I, Quentin?'

'Sure, sure,' said the singer, studying his fingernails.

'Quite apart from the other thing, which I won't begin to talk about or try to explain –'

'Good,' said Grant.

'It's obviously going to be awkward for the four of us from now on, so I want to help find a solution. There's something between you two as well, of course?'

'Yes,' said Grant, without even looking for permission from Suzie to say it. 'We won't pretend.'

'Good. That makes it easier, perhaps. Look, how's this for an offer? You manage Suzie, and I manage Quentin.'

There was a pause which expanded.

Suzie's brain was spinning.

Then Grant said firmly and bluntly, 'Out of the question.'

'Why do you say that?' asked Greenlee.

'I can't discuss it with both of them sitting here.'

Grant laid a comforting hand on Suzie's to show he was thinking of her.

'Well,' Greenlee began again, undaunted, 'how about this then? I manage Quentin and you keep his songs.'

'I suppose that's a possibility.'

'God, I could scream!' Suzie suddenly erupted. 'You're taking it all so calmly. Suddenly changing the whole basis of . . . of *everything*! I feel terrible.'

'Sorry, Suzie,' said Grant soothingly. 'But there's got to be some changes made. We can't possibly continue as though nothing's happened.'

'Thank you, Grant, that puts it very well,' said Greenlee. 'So what are we going to do?'

To the already complicated quartet of personal alliances and working relationships that existed between Grant and Suzie, Alan and Quentin was now added a fifth factor: Carly.

When she moved up to town, Carly was less isolated, but soon became bored. There was a limit to what she could do about the flat, and she felt excluded unnecessarily from Grant's world. It wasn't like the early days in Liverpool when she could pop into the office and help him. Now it was all so *important*. Her views wouldn't be listened to, there were others in the way. Her influence over Grant, an influence he'd once been happy to acknowledge, had dwindled to nothing. She even had to make an appointment to speak to him – if it was on a business matter.

She still wondered about opening a boutique – Paradise Plus she would call it – but Grant didn't seem keen and kept asking where she'd get the money. She took to going out by herself, leaving Neville with the nanny. She went to the pictures on her own, in the afternoon, joining the other human wreckage that found itself free to do the same. She went window shopping along Bond Street and Knightsbridge, she read, she listened to records, but she had to be careful about spending any money. She forced herself to make clothes as she'd always done. But it wasn't the same when she wasn't making them for a specific purpose, out of a creative urge.

She also took to dreaming, and remembering the past.

One day she spotted an advert for a poetry reading due to take place at one of the trendier entertainment pubs in the East End. Should she, shouldn't she go? She wrestled with the thought for some time, knowing how annoyed Grant would be if he found out. Finally, she told herself not to be so stupid, said goodbye to Neville and the nanny, and set off by Tube and taxi to the remote venue.

The White Swan was in an unfamiliar part of London's docklands. The area had a deserted air; many of the houses were derelict, the warehouses empty and run down. The taxi left her at the end of a dark alley. She paid the driver and picked her way over the awkward cobbles, white boots beneath the velvety, mauve miniskirt she'd bought at Biba before the crash.

She went into the pub. She hated being on her own and felt the eyes of the male drinkers swivelling towards her, giving her the once-over.

'Eh,' she began to ask the barman, suddenly aware of her Liverpool vowels, 'where's the poetry happening?'

'Upstairs, darlin'. Go out and in again through the door on the right.'

'Ta.'

She did as she was told and found herself climbing a steep staircase and paying five shillings admission at the top. The man who took her money had long hair and an unkempt beard and was probably smoking something illegal. Carly took her seat in the small, barely half-full room. She was self-conscious, being on her own and too well-dressed. She very much wanted to see and not be seen so moved behind a pillar.

The evening's 'happening' was due to begin at eight o'clock. At about a quarter past, a small jazz group shuffled on to the makeshift stage. Without apologizing for the late start, it launched into a modern jazz set. It was much too avant-garde for Carly and she began to be uncomfortably aware of the hardness of the seats, as well as the attentions of some of the male members of the audience who kept looking her up and down.

After the jazz, there was another unexplained pause until a host of sorts shuffled on and thanked the band. It was all very shambolic. How Grant would hate it, Carly thought. It was so far from his slick showbiz world. But if anyone had pointed out the unpunctuality and lack of polish, they would have been told it was all part of the happening. She began to wonder whether she should have come at all, but decided she would sit it out, now that she had come all this way. She had, after all, come for a special reason.

Grant returned to Montagu Square early that night. The business with Suzie and Greenlee and Quentin had sent his pulse racing; it was yet another in the long series of shocks to his system that were beginning to wear him down as well as add grey hairs to his head.

'She's gone out,' the nanny told him. 'Didn't she tell you?'

'No, she didn't,' Grant snapped. He was annoyed that Carly wasn't there. What was she up to? He had decided to tell her about the Suzie–Quentin swap that had so rapidly been agreed, but not to explain why it was happening. That could wait. He had screwed up his courage to tell her that much and now he felt cheated.

He went into the kitchen to pour himself a drink and caught sight of the *International Times* in the letter rack on top of the fridge. The paper was folded at the Forthcoming Events listings and, not really conscious of what he was doing, he ran his eyes down the column. He spotted a familiar name and instantly knew what Carly was up to, where she was:

White Swan, E1, Thursday 8:00, Happening.
Liverpool poets inc. singer/songwriter
Tom Sheridan, plus jazz support.

Trust Carly not to be able to leave that shit alone. Grant was furious. Impulsively, he rang Mickey Clinch at his flat in Camden and told him to get over to the White Swan and bring her back. 'No arguments, just get her. I mean, no argument from her . . . yes, I'm sorry, I didn't mean . . . it's very kind of you, Mickey . . . soon as you can.'

The touring Liverpool poets had finally turned up an hour late. Each casually walked on and read his poems with a curious lack of animation. An earnest-looking girl in the front row, with large teeth, said things like 'Wow!' at the more obvious sentiments in the poems. The rest politely clapped at the end of each piece.

Then on came Tom. Carly was delighted to see how well he looked, how little he had changed. Still the jaunty air, the ready smile. Still the hair tumbling over his forehead, the standard uniform of jeans, check shirt and old leather jacket.

Carly hid as best as she could so that Tom wouldn't be put off if he saw her. He was a good deal cockier than the others, she noticed. Because he sang songs and played the guitar as well, his verse had more impact. Carly was delighted to watch him again. It was so long since she had actually seen Tom perform. He had matured. His delivery was more polished. The audience loved his poem about the recent moon landing, describing it in the vocabulary of popular songs. If only he could escape the confines of such a ramshackle show, he'd have quite a future in this sort of entertainment.

It was odd knowing him so well, his body, his mind, to watch him charming the audience and winning them. He had a gift. She realized how much she missed having him around. And she wanted him, physically.

When he read a sequence of three love poems which she knew had been written to her, she had a quiet snuffle to herself. Then, so eager was she to see his every move, she emerged from behind the pillar and, as he sang, he spotted her across the smoke-filled room. He played a wrong note, swore, smiled and then sang on, obviously cheered.

The clock on the wall ticked past ten. Carly began to wonder about getting home. If it went on too late she would miss her chance to say hello to Tom.

At about ten thirty the evening seemed to be petering out and the performers looked intent on getting back to the bar before it closed. With the audience, they adjourned downstairs. Carly noticed the girl who said 'Wow!' had reached Tom before her and was busy telling him how wonderful he was. There had always been hangers-on around poets. She had been one herself – with Tom – in a manner of speaking.

She pushed her way towards him and made sure he averted his eyes from the other girl long enough to register her.

'Oh, hi, Carly!' he shouted, and embraced her, still gripping his pint pot in one hand. 'I saw you. What an honour!'

The large-toothed girl took one look and scuttled.

'Hiding behind your pillar!'

'Tom, you were fabulous.'

'Give us a kiss then.'

With his free arm he scooped Carly up and pressed his lips to hers. Then he put her down and moved the palm of his hand up and down her back and over her rear. Carly didn't mind. Here was someone wanting her, telling her she was sexy, making her feel good. They'd been apart a long time, and old feelings were returning; Tom was working his famous charm upon her.

By the time Mickey had found out where the White Swan was in the East End and had steered himself over there in his little car, it was all but closing time. He feared he would miss Carly.

He just made it. His small, stocky form was soon pushing its way towards the bar.

'Well, look who it isn't!' Tom exclaimed, catching sight of the person he regarded now as Grant's hatchet man. 'It's the mighty midget himself. What brings you here, Hopalong?'

Mickey affected not to have heard and spoke to Carly. 'Grant sent me. He says you're to come home.'

'Why, what's happened?' asked Carly.

'I don't know. He just told me to fetch you. Sounded annoyed.'

'Well, since you're here, how about a lift back to town?' asked Tom.

'Yeh, sure,' Carly told him. 'I suppose we'd better go.'

Tom drained his pint. Mickey wasn't sure about taking him. He knew Grant wouldn't approve. Still, if Carly said so, who was he to argue?

They nosed back across the City and into the West End. It became apparent that Tom had no definite destination.

'Can I kip on your floor?' he asked.

'Yes, of course,' said Carly, without hesitation.

Grant would be furious, she knew, but it was unavoidable, unless you were as ruthless as he was.

By the time they reached Montagu Square, Grant had had plenty of time to brood. It was largely his own fault. If he'd only told Carly what time he had expected to come home she would have been there. But he hadn't, so she wasn't. He was very irritable by the time Carly finally walked through the door. He almost burst a blood vessel at seeing Tom behind her, ambling in with his canvas holdall, Mickey bringing up the rear.

Mickey gave a gesture meaning 'Sorry, I couldn't help it' and went right out again.

'So you *were* there,' he said crossly to Carly. Without looking at Tom, he gave him an offhand hello.

'I don't have to have your permission, do I?' Carly shot back. 'You were out, so I made my own arrangements.'

Grant was aware he was on difficult ground.

'Well, was it a good evening?' he asked, suddenly polite.

Before Carly had time to answer, Tom answered: 'Yes, ta muchly. One of the best. Say, swell place you got here. I thought you were supposed to be broke.'

Grant snorted. 'Yes, well, everything's relative, isn't it?'

'No chance of a drink, I suppose?'

Grant frowned again. 'Of course, help yourself.'

'Thanks. Where do I have to look?'

All Grant's carefully-laid plans had been thrown into chaos by Tom's arrival. That kind of thing seemed to have been going on for as long as he could remember.

'Where's your kid?' Tom asked.

'He's asleep. Let's not disturb him.'

'Okay.'

'I'm going to bed,' Grant announced abruptly, and left the room. He wouldn't be able to talk to Carly tonight, that was clear.

Carly and Tom chatted until late, drinking and indulging in a little playful touching in front of the warm fire.

Suddenly, Tom said he wanted to see Neville, that very moment.

'We'll only wake him,' Carly pleaded, but Tom was insistent.

The flat was on two floors, and in a moment Carly was quietly opening Neville's bedroom door. A small night-light in a saucer cosily illuminated the bed. There, soundly asleep, was the little boy, a thumb stuck contentedly in his mouth, his wild hair dark against the pillow.

Tom's exuberance was stilled by the sight.

'He's lovely, isn't he?' he whispered delightedly to Carly. He stared intently at the baby, then lent down and gently kissed him. The boy seemed to smile in his sleep but didn't wake.

'That's a good head of hair he's got. Where did he get that from?'

'Don't ask me,' Carly answered with a nervous laugh.

'Well, bugger me, isn't he just the spitting image of someone you know?'

'And who would that be, Tom?' whispered Carly, unconvincingly.

'Oh, my sweet lord, what a thing! Is it possible? Could *I* be his dad?'

'Don't be silly.'

'But what if I *am* his dad? It's possible, isn't it?'

'No, Tom, no, no, no . . .'

Carly gave Tom some blankets so he could sleep on the sofa. He slept in his jeans. She tucked him up.

'I'll not change me mind,' Tom insisted. 'It makes sense to me.'

'I have to tell you,' Carly eventually admitted, 'you're not the only one to wonder.' She gave him a goodnight kiss. 'But you must promise not to go on about it.'

Tom said nothing to that.

She left him to turn out the light and went upstairs to face Grant. Happily, he was asleep.

In the morning, it would seem less complicated. Nothing would need to be resolved, as long as no one insisted on its being resolved. Tom would wander off to his next poetry happening, at the University of Hull, making no demands. Grant would go to work. And Carly would be left to fill another day as best she could with her child. Never mind who the father was.

CHAPTER 17

Within a week or two, new contracts were drawn up. Suzie went to the Grant Pickering Organization; Quentin signed on, as performer only, with Alan Greenlee Management. Grant was reluctant at first to bring to an end the weekly sessions when Quentin turned up to sing his latest song, but that was rather a quaint custom and sentiment couldn't be allowed to prolong it.

He would still get his lucrative share of Quentin's writing royalties – past and future. They would still pass through the GPO, but without Grant having to worry about the more costly and time-consuming performing side of Quentin's activities. He only hoped that Quentin would be able to keep on turning out the hits under Alan Greenlee's extremely personal management.

Grant threw himself with a will into rescuing Suzie's fortunes. She was scarred by the revelation of her husband's true leanings and found it very difficult to have anything more to do with him. She rented a modest flat in Swiss Cottage.

At first, Grant could find nothing to suit her in the West End. She wasn't keen to audition for the replacement cast of *Hair* – that wasn't her thing at all. Then, in the old tradition of show business, the girl who was going to play Eliza Doolittle in a touring production of *My Fair Lady* fell ill just before rehearsals began and Suzie was perfectly placed to step into her shoes. It was never intended that the production should reach the West End but it was to have a full-blown provincial tour. It was money, and it was work.

'You'll enjoy it, won't you?' said Grant, never very sure whether he was speaking with the voice of manager or lover. 'And it'll give you a chance to sing, that's the important thing. Never let cobwebs grow over your larynx . . .'

Suzie was pleased. Grant also reflected that there was no harm in what she had just gone through in her private life. She had lived a little now, was less of an innocent.

'I think the public likes that in a singer,' he told her. 'They want to feel when you sing of broken hearts you know what you're singing about.'

'There is such a thing as *acting*, you know,' she replied tartly. 'And I've had quite enough experience lately to last a lifetime, I assure you.'

'I know, I know. But the future's rosy, I can assure *you*.'

'Well . . .'

'You must believe that.'

Suzie rehearsed and went on tour. The production packed audiences into theatres all over Britain. Grant saw the show in six different places. One was Liverpool when *My Fair Lady* played a week at the Empire. Grant kept his head down. He didn't want anybody to know he'd been there. He certainly wasn't going to cross the Mersey to visit his parents. He also felt guilty about the long-standing debt he owed his Uncle Trevor in Waterloo. Grant wasn't even sure that the old man was still alive, but this wasn't the moment to be thinking of paying out money to anybody, however small the amount. Besides, he'd said he would make good the sum when he'd had his first stage success, and there wasn't any sign of that yet.

Having Suzie away on tour took a certain amount of pressure off Grant. The truth was, he'd begun to find her less desirable now she was under his wing. There certainly wasn't the same need to pursue her.

He started paying more attention to Carly again and spent more evenings at home. On one such occasion he picked up a book Carly had left lying about.

A postcard fell out of it. Grant saw it was from Liverpool,

turned it over and saw the words 'Your loving dad, Tom' at the bottom. Then he saw that the postcard was addressed to Neville.

So Carly must have told Tom – admitted he was the boy's father. Grant thought for a moment, then slipped the postcard back in the book.

Carly still hankered after work in some form, but Grant discouraged her. Life wasn't too bad, though. One day she met up with Virna Todd for lunch. Virna and Johnny had made it legal shortly before Starfinders crashed. Carly had been unable to accompany Grant to the small wedding because she'd been so pregnant with Neville.

Now it was Virna's turn. They arranged to meet and swap notes. The two showbiz wives could still enjoy a good gossip, even if Carly did wonder whether it meant she was turning into the sort of bored wife whose high spot was her lunches with friends.

Carly was glad that Johnny had settled on Virna for his second wife. She seemed to know what she was doing. She was a bright one, not a moaning minnie like Maureen back in Manchester. In fact, Virna seemed every bit as easy going as Johnny was himself.

She drove up from the Todd mansion, which they still maintained a few miles from Quornford, and Carly taxied over from Montagu Square. They had lunch at the Hungry Horse, the small but fashionable restaurant in the Fulham Road. It was Virna's idea to eat there. 'Then we can wander down to the King's Road and strut our stuff,' she said.

The two women went downstairs and were greeted by waiters in striped mini-aprons. They were shown to a small table alongside the pub mirrors and prepared to tuck into the menu of Continentally-flavoured English cooking.

'Wine?' asked Carly.

'Oh no,' said Virna. 'I'm not supposed to drink with this lump inside me, or smoke. It's terrible.'

'You're as strict as I was.'

'You bet.'

'Half a bottle of red for me then,' Carly smiled at the wine waiter. Virna was surprised at this. Carly had always held back on the wine before.

'You're looking wonderful, V.,' Carly told her. 'Everything okay?'

'Sure. Everything's just fine. Best thing I ever did, getting married.'

'How about Johnny?'

'I think he's pleased about the baby, though it's not his first, of course. But men are funny, aren't they? You can't really tell.'

'Is he, you know, all right otherwise? Grant never tells me anything about what's going on, but I know Johnny was wonderful over Starfinders. When Grant told me of the letter he'd written, I burst into tears. It was so *nice*.'

'Yes, it was,' said Virna, with a laugh. 'I wrote it.'

'You didn't?'

'Sure. I can help him like that. But Johnny's so dependent on Grant. If Grant dropped dead, heaven forbid, Johnny would fall apart. So I was just making sure.'

'Mmm, good for you,' said Carly. 'It's about time Johnny made another splash, isn't it? Trouble is, Grant's been so busy building himself up again, his clients have had a bit of a raw deal.'

'Of course,' said Virna, pointedly, 'there are clients and clients . . .'

At that moment, the waiter brought their chicken and mushroom pie.

'I mean,' Virna went on, 'Grant seems very devoted to that new female songbird of his.'

'Suzie, you mean?'

'I gather she gets a lot of *personal* attention from the management. Mind you, she is pretty striking, isn't she?'

Carly felt her stomach turn to jelly.

'A bit peculiar all that, wasn't it, swapping Quentin Saint and her? Johnny said he couldn't understand it.'

'It was peculiar,' said Carly thoughtfully, as if to show she hadn't given it too much thought previously. 'But it's just a business arrangement, you know.'

'God, you're so naive, Carly. What did he want to give away Quentin to a creep like Greenlee for? So that he could take on Greenlee's wife.'

'No, I don't think that was –'

'That's what Johnny thinks, anyway.'

'Mmm,' said Carly, hiding her distress in mouthfuls of pie. 'Well, let's not talk about it. I expect there's nothing in it.'

'Tell you what,' Virna leant over, confidentially, realizing she'd upset Carly, 'isn't it time you started on your second one?'

'Second what?'

'Baby, silly. Keep 'em coming, my mother always used to say.'

'We haven't really thought,' Carly replied vaguely. In fact, they hadn't talked about it at all.

But she liked the idea. Maybe it would help clear the air over Neville. The trouble was, Grant had been practising the best contraception of all with her. They hadn't made love for weeks.

The two women finished eating at about three thirty, paid the bill, and were just leaving the restaurant when Carly suddenly stopped. Seated in a corner were two women, one white, one black. The black one was Halo, the dancer Grant had once carried on with.

There was no avoiding her lethal gaze. Carly fumbled to keep Virna by her, for strength.

'Well, fancy seeing you two again,' Halo began. 'It's been a long time, hasn't it?'

'You know Virna, of course,' said Carly confused. 'Now married to Johnny.'

293

'Oh, really?' said Halo, coolly. 'By the way, this is my friend Sacha. Sacha von Sachs. We work together.'

Virna was itching to get up the stairs and away, but there was no escaping Halo.

'What work's that?' asked Carly. 'A show?'

'In a way. We've each got a spot at Raymond's Revuebar.'

'Oh, fancy.'

'Yes.' Halo was enjoying this. 'In fact, we had a visit from a friend of yours not so long ago. That Tom Sheridan.'

Carly blushed. 'Tom? What on earth would he . . .' The question died on her lips.

'He's keeping well.'

'I know. I saw him, too, quite recently, at one of his poetry happenings.'

'I spoke to him the other day on the phone. He gave me all the news from Liverpool. I gather your Grant's been up.'

'Has he?' Carly was getting ever more uncomfortable. 'Perhaps he has. I don't know what he's up to half the time.'

'Tom said he was with that Suzie Paul. She's great, isn't she?'

Carly felt she would scream if she didn't get away quickly. 'Well, nice to have seen you,' she said untruthfully, and rushed to join Virna going up the stairs.

'Nasty piece of work,' Virna remarked when they were both outside in the Fulham Road. 'Stripper, eh? About her level, I'd say.'

Carly wasn't interested in going into all that. She gave Virna a big kiss before hailing a cab.

'I must ask Grant what he's going to do about Johnny,' she said.

Virna looked at her. They both knew that what Carly really meant was, 'I must find out about Grant and Suzie.'

*　　*　　*

The photographs of clients that once lined the corridors had had to be reduced in number following the shake-out which led to Starfinders becoming the Grant Pickering Organization.

Now they were all in Grant's own office and often Jan Ferry would find her boss pacing up and down in front of them, deep in thought. The photographs served as a reminder that he must keep finding things for his clients to do, reshaping their careers, giving them purpose and direction. He had to justify the significant proportion of their incomes he creamed off, and his survival anyway depended on them, just as much as theirs did on him.

Grant was well aware that what was required of him as a manager was perpetual restlessness. He could have sat back and waited for the phone to ring with work for his clients, but he wasn't like that. He didn't wish to hear that his clients had been belly-aching behind his back about his not pulling his finger out on their behalf. He had to provide the spark.

On this day, in late June 1970, he paused before the portrait of Johnny Todd. Johnny was the client most in need of a shot in the arm at the moment. He hadn't had what you'd call a proper hit for two years now. He popped up as a guest on TV shows – more chat than pop – and he was extremely popular in the clubs. But it was hard to see where he could go, how he should develop. Yet Johnny had been loyal to Grant and he must never forget that. The most obvious course was a change of image and a relaunch.

Grant paused next in front of a group shot of the Wreckers. They stared out, a mass of leather, denim and hair, like a Hell's Angels roadblock. Grant almost recoiled. They weren't really his cup of tea. He didn't enjoy the heavy rock that they played, but he couldn't ignore, nor did he want to, the substantial sums they brought in, especially from the United States.

Quite a few people thought the Wreckers were an American group, as though their Wrexham accents must be an obscure West Coast dialect. Indeed, they spent most of their time in the States now and were becoming cult figures. Just lately they'd been invited to perform at the Atlanta Pop Festival.

Gareth Trigger had been given a conditional discharge on appeal against his cannabis conviction. He might have had to spend six months or more in prison but he'd been very, very lucky. The police, over-zealous as always in drugs cases, had made a small error in evidence and Gareth, who was as guilty as hell, walked free.

Grant stood next in front of a newly-hung photograph of Suzie Paul, taken in performance during her Palladium showcase. The blond hair gleamed under a cluster of lights, the lips and teeth glistened. It was a magical pose and Grant reflected proudly that she was his.

He smiled contentedly to himself. His was an unusual stable: Johnny Todd, maturing pop star; the Wreckers, heavy-rockers; Suzie Paul, songstress, now pleasing provincial audiences in *My Fair Lady*. Something for every taste. It would have been even more of a mixture but for the light mark on the wall behind Suzie's portrait that showed where Quentin Saint's larger picture had lately been removed.

The decision that came to Grant now was based on a combination of various half-thoughts. Suzie was in Scotland for three weeks with *My Fair Lady*, so there was no chance of her pestering Grant for time together – time away he'd be unable to justify to Carly. So he would go to the US and see the Wreckers perform at the Atlanta Festival and generally keep an eye open for opportunities on the other side of the pond.

Much of the flavour had gone out of Grant's life following *Acts of Folly*. He had lost face. He began to think that, were he to look westward, he might find some soothing balm there, a solution to his professional and domestic problems.

Grant stopped off in New York. He was apprehensive, subconsciously aware he was looking for something – an escape, a new direction – but unable to see his way out of the mess he was in.

In the old days, Liverpool had been the great exit point for travellers to the New World. His route to the land of opportunity had taken him to London first but, in essence, he was making the same trip.

The journey westwards had been made easier for him and for everyone else in the music business by those first travellers of the modern age from Liverpool, the Beatles. In 1964, the Beatles had not conquered America for themselves, they had opened the door for British pop as a whole. Everyone who followed had to be grateful to them for that.

Grant went to see managements and record companies in Manhattan but soon realized he'd have to head further west if he was going to strike gold on his clients' behalf.

First there was the three-day Atlanta Festival. He took a plane down to Georgia and managed to root out the group, which was being looked after by George Evans. Dear, faithful George. He was permanently assigned to the Wreckers now. Like Gareth Trigger, he had escaped sentence on the cannabis charge. Now, as if keen to put Britain behind him, his wan, lugubrious Liverpudlian accent was overlaid with Americanisms.

He had also gone more than halfway to meet the group in appearance. His curly fair hair was now desperately thinning and, as if to make up for this, he wore a long prophet's beard. If nothing else, it served to cover up his bobbing Adam's apple.

'You'll have to wear your beads,' he told his boss laconically. 'Or you'll stick out.'

Atlanta was like fantasy-land. Grant felt he was a stranger

but also, curiously, as if he had 'come home'. He felt a charge. There were armies of performers and managers swirling about the festival and Grant made use of the occasion to compare notes and forge links. It was a very different world to the one he was used to, but gradually his nervousness wore off and he began to feel it was one he might possibly be happier in. The business seemed more direct than in Britain. People were more straightforward. They were wonderfully open as to what they were in it for, namely money, sex and dope, and you didn't have to deal with so many patronizing money men and old-school-tie managements.

The Wreckers were reasonably glad to see him, not least because they hadn't met since the Starfinders crash and the drugs bust. He set their minds at rest on both scores. They played their set early in the evening of the second day. It was rapturously received and Grant felt hugely proud of the group. For the first time, he actually enjoyed what they did. Records didn't convey the full force of heavy rock in performance. You needed that volume of noise to make your body tremble and get the flavour.

He sat for hour after hour watching the other acts: Jimi Hendrix, the Allman Brothers, Captain Beefheart, Procul Harum among them. For Grant, the festival became an emblem of another kind. In future years, he would date his conquest of America from this moment. The fact that his musical conquest, for the most part, took a different tone to what he was listening to now was neither here nor there. Atlanta was where, he later claimed, he'd felt the vibrations necessary to head him off in a new direction.

It was George Evans who really did it. They were sitting out a set by a folksinger. They were in one of the tents set aside for the use of managers and hangers-on.

'How's Johnny?' George asked. 'It seems an age since I saw him.'

'Johnny's just fine,' Grant replied. 'But you wouldn't

find him at a gig like this, now would you? I mean, just imagine, him and the Wreckers on the same bill!'

'I suppose he's more *commercial*.' It was true. Johnny was the commercial, showbiz, acceptable face of pop. The Wreckers were 'alternative', outsiders, raw, unpackaged, the real thing, as well as being commercial in a different way.

It came to Grant in that instant. No interfering with the Wreckers, that would be foolish. Keep them happy, make sure they didn't kill themselves or, worse, render themselves incapable of performing through drugs, and that was all they needed.

But Johnny, if he was ever to make an impression in the US, would have to aim for a different heartland. It was odd that the States were capable of embracing two such vast constituencies. At Atlanta, with flower children and hippies stretching as far as the eye could see, it was difficult to realize there were people of a different sort under the same heaven. But President Nixon's 'Middle America' was very real and a force to be reckoned with. It wasn't only made up of the middle-aged and conservative.

'Johnny would really appeal to them,' George went on. 'Tom Jones has started to do it. The blue rinsers are quite happy waving their knickers in the air, provided they're not frightened by a band or a singer. Now, Jimi Hendrix, never! The Wreckers frighten them, too, but Johnny could have them eating out of his hand. It's like with Elvis. Same thing. Dangerous rocker, sweet old balladeer. Johnny can do both.'

'But tell me, George, how do you get to where Tom Jones is over here, just now?'

'You need a good manager!'

Grant didn't mind the dig. 'He's got one, but what d'you think it takes for Americans to like a Brit who almost speaks a different language?'

'Well, Tom Jones is a good singer, and, like Johnny, he's got what it takes in the trouser area. Beyond that, he's got hits, so audiences know him before they arrive. And, just as important, he's got into the supper rooms, the dinner and cabaret circuit. That may be difficult. The rock world's tough, but you should meet some of the hoods who run Vegas and Reno and places like that. I'd be glad to help you, Grant, but I value my life.'

'Never mind that. What else does Johnny need?'

'An act. You know, forty-five minutes or an hour. Good orchestrations. A bit of chat between numbers. Tell a few jokes. He could do it, but he needs some help.'

'Trouble is, Johnny's always reluctant to go abroad. He's a bit like me in that respect.'

'Until now?'

'Yeh, that's it. I needed to get away.'

'Personal reasons?'

Grant looked at him. 'Yes. You know?'

'I don't hear nothing, but I pick up the vibrations. Trouble with the wife?'

'No, not at all . . . well, no more than you'd expect.'

'What did I hear about you and Suzie Paul, then? And a little whisper about your kid?'

'For Christ's sake, George, what's that supposed to mean? You said you never heard anything.'

'You'd be surprised. Word gets around.'

Grant looked unconvinced.

'Well, to tell the truth, Tom's been over.'

'Tom Sheridan? That shit?'

'We did once share a flat, you know.'

'Of course.'

'Anyway, he told me about you and Suzie Paul, and about him being Neville's dad.'

'Well, that's a load of cock for a start.'

'Tom seemed pretty convinced; very angry he was.'

'It's just not true, George. Or not provable.'

'And he said you'd been in Liverpool with Suzie Paul appearing at the Empire.'

'Oh, for God's sake! No one knew I'd been there.'

'So, that bit's true?'

'Don't ask me, George, don't ask me. Like I said before, matters are a little complicated. That's why I feel like trying my hand over here.'

That night, Grant fell into a mood of gloomy introspection while the music played. So, people realized about him and Suzie Paul? People 'in the business', that is. Well, of course they would. Gossip like that always spread. The point was, when would Carly find out? And what would happen when she did?

Grant kept postponing his return to London while he took a crash course in American middle-of-the-road music. He listened to the FM stations, watched TV chat shows to discover how singers could be promoted, and finally took a plane to Las Vegas.

He had no idea quite what to expect, but was given a hint when the stewardess announced as they came in to land at McCarran Airport: 'Please keep your money in your pocket till you're off the plane.'

The jet whipped up great gusts of sand as it taxied to the terminal. There was a burst of ninety-degree heat as the aircraft door swung open. The gamblers didn't have long to wait. There were fruit machines right by the door as they stepped out of the plane.

Grant took a taxi to the Sands Hotel – he liked the idea of staying at a place owned by Howard Hughes – and he arranged to see as many shows as he could. Then, in his English way, Grant went for a walk. As the sun began to sink lower over the desert and temperatures went down to moderate, he journeyed down the Strip.

He went into Circus Circus, which was like an old-fashioned fair, with high-wire acts, even an elephant, performing over the gambling tables. He went downtown and saw the great twinkling walls of neon outside the Golden

Nugget. He looked at the gamblers, the men and women who had sat all day before rows and rows of fruit machines in this and other darkened, subterranean caverns without ever straying into the desert heat, never leaving the chilly embrace of air-conditioning. Grant saw the little old ladies crouched over their chips, relentlessly plying the machines with coins and yanking the handles with all the strength they could muster. He listened to the endless clash of coins and bells ringing as jackpots were hit and winnings cascaded out.

There was one fat woman in particular he noticed. She pulled at the massive arm of a machine called Big Bertha and won $500. It didn't bring her much pleasure, judging by the look on her face.

Finally, he went to see Tom Jones perform in front of a thousand diners at Caesar's Palace.

Grant was happily anonymous. He was seated at a long table with a group of Americans who immediately fell on the fact that he was British. For once, they didn't ask where he came from in England. Then the show began. After a rock band called the Universe, a group of girl singers, and the comedian Pat Henry, on came Tom Jones.

Grant was torn. He felt curiously proud that a British entertainer could have made it this far. But he was also resentful. Why wasn't it one of his? What had Gordon Mills, Jones's manager, done to make it work for his client? After all, if Jones from Pontypridd could become 'Tom Jones Superstar' (as it said on the billings), why couldn't Johnny Todd, the warehouseman from Salford?

Grant studied, made notes. How would Johnny Todd ever get a TV series into America, as Jones had, so that the audience knew who he was, knew what to expect, before they reached the venue? Grant was fired with ambition to see his man pull it off. It was a feeling as intense as any compulsion to gamble. Oddly, Grant left Las Vegas without

302

having bet a single cent. The big gamble was to come. That was how he would get his kicks from now on.

Grant's new ambition weathered the journey back home but came under severe pressure the moment he set foot in Montagu Square at nine thirty in the morning after a night flight.

Baby Neville staggered forward to grasp him round the knees, but Grant met with little response when he kissed Carly. She lost no time in producing a copy of the *Daily Mail*, a few days old.

The article was accompanied by a photograph of himself and Suzie Paul. Each sentence was encrusted with old background information, about his marriage to 'former shoe-shop assistant, brunette Carly', the *Acts of Folly* crash, Suzie's husband and manager Alan Greenlee, the apparent 'swap' with Quentin Saint. It made a good few paragraphs. There was only one sentence of 'news' in it: Grant was having an affair with Suzie.

'Why is it the wife who's always last to know?' Carly cried, forcing Grant to pay attention. 'I mean, how could you, Grant? It's so *cheap* – doing it with a client. Have you got no taste? And how long has it been going on? You really are the pits, you know, cheating on me like this.'

Grant tried to explain, but Carly kept pouring out her pent-up anger and disgust. In the end, he tried to hug her, to get her to stop. She froze, pushed him away.

'When did it start?' she asked.

Grant swallowed. 'After *Acts of Folly*. She was very good about all that business, considering what a kick in the teeth she'd had. And I was on the ropes myself. That's when.'

'But I tried to help, didn't I? What'd she got I hadn't?'

'How can I answer that? It's difficult to say.'

'I want to know. Is it the screwing? What'll she do that I won't? Some kink I don't know about?'

'No, none of that.'

'I suppose you took her on knowing she'd be more than just a client?'

'Will you listen, Carly? I didn't tell you everything about that. The fact is, Alan was carrying on with Quentin.'

Carly was genuinely shocked by this revelation. 'You're kidding?'

'No. And it gets worse. She actually walked into the room when they were in bed together. So you can understand how she must have felt. That was why we had the "exchange of prisoners" and why it happened so quickly. She couldn't wait to get away from Greenlee, and Greenlee couldn't wait to get into bed with Quentin. In more ways than one.'

Carly was shaken. 'God, that's awful! I thought it was odd, but I had no idea . . . And what about now? You've been away from both of us for a few weeks. What do you feel about her now? What do you feel about *me*?'

Grant hesitated, found it hard to look his wife in the eyes and explain.

'I suppose you'll say you want to have us both.'

'I know that's impossible.'

'At least you've got *some* sense, then. That's one of the great fairy stories, isn't it? A little fantasy you men invent for yourselves, that you can love two women. Really what you mean is you love one, the wife or the bit on the side, but you haven't got the courage to tell the other.'

'If it comes to that, I should've thought you had some experience.' There was more than a hint of Grant the agent making a negotiating point. 'Aren't you a little bit in love with two men. Me and Tom?'

Carly was thrown by the suggestion, as though she'd never faced up to it before, but she denied it vehemently.

'No, I'm not in love with Tom. And if this is love with you, I'd rather it was something else.'

Grant threw away his negotiating hand.

'Carly, let's not mess about. I've behaved really shittily. There was a reason, but I promise you I'll stop. Believe me, please.'

He tried to hold her in his arms once more, and now she didn't resist.

'Why the hell do we have to get into these messes? Why can't life be simple? Why?'

CHAPTER 18

Rex Room felt left out in the cold. He had been with Grant since the beginning, but had hardly shared in Grant's success. All Rex could claim after seven years was that he'd kept in work – of a kind. He was too old now to compere pop concerts; the new breed of disc jockeys had taken over, so for him it was the humble round of smokers, masonics, barmitzvahs and after-dinner speeches. But always with a smile on his lips, a ready quip to hand, a smart, flashy suit on, and a too large handkerchief in his breast pocket.

Rex had never made it anywhere near the big time, although he had played a week, somewhere down the bill, at the Palladium. And it was true he had appeared on television, but always as a guest on other people's shows. He had never had a show of his own and no one had ever asked him to prove he could act in situation comedy.

At the age of forty, he was simply a stand-up comic. Of late, he had put on a good deal of weight, so that he now had a substantial paunch which projected oddly from what otherwise would have been quite a handsome figure. He used the paunch to rest the hand which held the microphone. The other hand clasped the microphone stand. Occasionally, he would lift the microphone to the side of his mouth, like an electric shaver.

He told gags. Very seldom would he make a satirical remark about a politician. For that you won applause rather than laughter, and applause wasn't a coin Rex was keen to accept. Mostly he pretended to bare his soul, cataloguing the largely imaginary disasters of married life. He had been married twice to what could loosely be described as showgirls. 'And, as showgirls go, they could certainly be

307

described as loose,' he would have added. Trina and Catherine had both been blondes, nice enough in their way, with long legs. They had been drawn to the comic in the way women often are drawn to funny men. 'Funny is money' was the Hollywood saying. 'Funny is sexy' could equally be true.

It took neither of Rex's wives very long to discover that behind the beaming, white-toothed smile, the ready quip and the confident chatting-up lurked a human being who was a good deal less than amusing. He was a totally different animal when denied an audience. He could hardly be said to exist when he wasn't in front of one. People who met him offstage were shocked by the steely, flinty side to his character.

Although Rex contrived successfully to project something akin to warmth when he was in the spotlight, by no stretch of the imagination could he be described as warm when he was out of it. Stories abounded of his stand-offishness. At dinners where he was supposed to mingle with the guests before doing his turn, he would huddle in his hotel room until it was time to do his act, rather than have to press the flesh. At other times, he would get drunk and abusive. Grant's agency would subsequently have to waive the fee.

In fact, oddly for one who was supposed to make people laugh when they met him, Rex had a disturbing tendency to make people angry.

Rex was also noted for the type of company he'd begun to keep when he moved South from Liverpool. At the time of his second marriage, he bought a bungalow in Essex. It happened that one of his first engagements was in the East End. He learned, as he was about to start his act, that two well-known criminals were in the audience. He trod carefully and was later honoured with an introduction. He was photographed with them. He was a toughie himself. He had learned how to survive in one of the meanest parts of

Liverpool. Now here he was breaking bread with Eric and Harold Bramley and getting quite a kick out of it.

In turn, the Bramleys seemed to get a kick out of mingling with the likes of Rex, the comedians, the singers, the showgirls. It was altogether satisfactory to everybody. The Bramleys gave night-clubbing a certain edge. For their part, they made sure that Rex kept getting bookings. He was grateful, very grateful.

Little of this was grasped by the bookers at the Grant Pickering Organization. They just believed Rex had found his natural constitutency, took their percentage, and left him to get on with it.

Rex was both flattered and regretful at this turn of events. Although he retained a certain fondness for and loyalty towards Grant, this didn't prevent him from belly-aching about his lack of top-line success. Why was he condemned to minor league bookings? Why was he never on TV these days? Why wasn't the GPO doing anything about it?

Rex decided to find out who was at fault.

Like many other comedians, he combined the anarchism of his routines with straightforward right-wing political commitment. To him, most of the population (and, it therefore followed, most of his 'lovely, lovely' audience) was made up of shirkers. It would do no harm if National Service was reintroduced, and hanging, too, for that matter. But the greatest curse of all, in Rex's opinion, was homosexuality. So vehement was he on the subject that it didn't take anyone very long to get round to wondering whether he was bent himself.

He was not, and the reason for his hostility was very simple.

'You know why I don't get bookings on TV, don't you?' he was fond of asking his fellow professionals.

'No, why?' his reluctant listeners would reply.

'Well, it's like this, see. All the bookers and TV producers

309

are bent, see? "Gay" they call it now, but people less gay it'd be hard to find. They don't fancy straight talent like mine.'

'So what are you going to do about it?'

'I've been thinking about that . . .'

Rex's plan was to get an agent who was gay and who would thus, he reasoned, have an influence over that alien world, could talk to the suppliers of work in their own language. The trouble was, so alienated was he from the world he despised, he had no idea how it worked or even who was part of it.

With a bit of neck, he decided to put his cards on the table in front of the man from whose organization he wished to break; namely, Grant Pickering. Grant appeared exceptionally relaxed about it all. He could long ago have dispensed with Rex's services if the comedian hadn't been earning enough, but if Rex was saying he wanted to go elsewhere, that wasn't really a problem. It was all right by Grant. Rex didn't bring in much money for the GPO and would never be a star. He was only around for old times' sake.

'I agree with everything you say,' Grant told Rex with a smiling but concerned look. 'I can see you might do better with a different type of agency. We're more of a music outfit here. You could well be right about the TV crowd. Like you, I'm not . . . that way. I find it hard to deal with people who are. I get terribly dull and straight as soon as I feel a guy's about to stroke my knee.'

Rex gave him a half-smile.

'You know Alan Greenlee?' Grant went on.

'Of course I know bloody Alan Greenlee. You've not forgotten how I got that money off of him?'

'Of course not, Rex. But just listen. I don't think he's handled a funny man before. If you rule out Quentin Saint, of course! Alan and I recently did a deal. I took on Greenlee's wife in return for Quentin.'

'What does that mean?'

'Well, I think Greenlee would fit the bill along the lines you suggest.'

'He's *one of them*?'

'He's gay, yes. Do you want me to give him a ring, without, of course, explaining why I'm giving away another of my valued clients?'

'Yes. Takes a thief, eh? Clever idea, Grant. Thanks a million.'

'I'll get on to him right away. If he'll take you, I'll just have to ask you to sign a letter releasing you from our agreement.'

'That was painless, wasn't it?'

Grant flipped open the lid of the cigar box on his desk and tucked a large Corona in Rex's top pocket.

Grant was as good as his word. He rang Alan Greenlee and offered to make him a present of Rex. Greenlee was keen to broaden the base of his agency and a comedian would fit the bill, so it was agreed that Rex should move across. All three parties were pleased, though one of the three had no idea why he had been blessed with the deal. The thought, 'What is Grant up to?' briefly crossed Greenlee's mind, but no answer presented itself.

Suzie ended her tour of *My Fair Lady* and returned to London. Grant managed to book her TV and radio spots in sufficient number to keep her happy. When they talked now on the phone it was usually about business. Grant had been pulled up sharp by having to reveal to Carly what had been going on. He didn't feel inclined to slip between the sheets with Suzie any more.

'Have you lost interest?' she asked him. 'Why?'

Grant hedged, denied he had, but would explain nothing.

'Carly knows? Is that it?'

Grant thought for a second, and then said, 'Yes. I told her, after it'd been in the paper. Had to, didn't I?'

'What's she going to do about it? Leave you?'

'Why do that, for Christ's sake?'

'Doesn't she mind?'

'Of course she minds.'

'So, you've told her you'll not see me?'

'Well, yes, I did.'

There was a pause. The telephone line crackled. 'But you *can't* not see me . . .'

'I know.'

'So where does that leave us?'

'In a hell of a mess, that's where.'

Some forms of entertainment vanish into thin air at curtain fall; all that remains is a few torn posters, a faded photograph or two, and memories. But records do not fade. They are always around somewhere, being played to bring back bygone moments, recreate atmosphere.

So it was with Johnny Todd's record of 'Tantalizing'. In the spring of 1971, at the tail end of the boom in British film-making, which had started in the sixties, the song was used on the soundtrack of a film that was particularly successful in the US. Its producers negotiated rights to include the song in a soundtrack LP. From there, it was released in the US as a single and shot up the charts.

Without doing anything at all, except anticipate the royalties, Johnny Todd had his first American No. 1.

Grant sent Johnny over to make capital. At last, Johnny had what he needed to start conquering the US, a label, a tag, a peg, some identifiable reason for people to remember his name. Grant, eager for any excuse to put distance between himself and his domestic problems, decided to accompany Johnny on the tour.

Doors opened to Grant now, doors that had remained stubbornly closed before. He was Johnny Todd's manager. 'Yes, we'd be pleased to talk business with you, Mr Pickering . . . A booking for Las Vegas? Well, I'm not sure about that . . . but let's *talk*, by all means.'

Grant had the bit between his teeth. He wheedled, cajoled; he wasn't going to let this one get away from him. And, in time, it happened. Johnny Todd had his name above a hotel on the Strip in Vegas. He was going to pack them in. He musn't mind, Grant forewarned him, if audiences were eating their dinner as he sang, or even if they talked right through his act. They didn't mean to be rude. It was only natural. They were enjoying themselves really.

'Sure, sure,' oozed Johnny, who was getting ever more relaxed the older he got. There was one point in his shows when he let rip with a rock 'n' roll medley, but for the most part he sang sugary ballads and middle-of-the-road standards. The mix seemed to work.

Grant was quietly jubilant that all his planning and observation had finally paid off. He felt a new man, physically excited, unable to sleep, in no need of Carly or Suzie. Not even to share his triumph.

After two shows one Saturday night, Grant sat in the star's dressing room, waiting for Johnny to come offstage. The champagne was cooling in a bucket. Virna Todd was elsewhere in the hotel complex, no doubt eagerly waiting for her husband to climb into the marital bed after arousing so many fantastic hopes among the women in the audience.

Virna also had to look after Dylan, born eight months previously. Johnny's second son, their first, Dylan had been brought to the States at Virna's insistence. She realized perhaps that Johnny might need reminding of his family obligations as the American version of fame took hold of him.

There was the sound of a commotion outside the dressing room. Then the door was flung open. Johnny's face fell when he saw Grant sitting there, waiting. It wasn't hard to see why. On his arm he had a statuesque showgirl. So statuesque, indeed, that Grant's first reaction was to admire the extensive silicone deposits she carried around at her breast.

'Look who's beaten us to it,' Johnny grinned, dropping a hint. Grant took it, embarrassed at being in the way of whatever Johnny had planned for the girl.

'This is Sharon,' Johnny explained, unnecessarily.

'I'm sorry, I'll go,' said Grant. 'We need to talk, Johnny. I'll be in my room – 2002.'

'Okay, I'll be on to you.' He winked.

Grant slipped away, thinking to himself that this was quite like old times. People didn't change. Not for marriage, not for his new baby boy, would Johnny forgo the pleasure he was about to receive from Sharon's skilled tongue and lips. The only difference was that his wife and son were now but a stone's throw away.

Grant knew he wasn't exactly in a position to lecture his client on the sin of adultery. It was hard, however, for him to be understanding about the infidelities of others. He retreated alone to Room 2002 and waited. He knew that Johnny would eventually come.

When he did, it was knocking on midnight. Johnny looked as sheepishly triumphant as after any of those groupie gropes in the jive-hives of Merseyside long before. But Grant wasn't going to hold a post-mortem.

'Help yourself to a drink.' He waved at the polished chestnut cabinet, the size of a coffin.

Glass in hand, Johnny lowered himself on to Grant's bed while Grant sat in an easy chair.

'I think we've got to decide,' Grant began, intently.

'What?' Johnny looked as if he was about to go straight to sleep.

'We're in this together, but I think it's a must.'

'What are you talking about, Grant? I don't follow.'

'Put it this way, Johnny. I don't want you to go home.'

'To England? You mean never?'

'Exactly. You've shown you can do it here. This is where it's at. I want you to milk it. No more piddling around back home. This is the biggest record market in the world. You

314

can be big, really big, over here. I've absolutely no doubt about that.'

Johnny was struggling to keep awake now. 'Do we really have to talk?'

'I just want you to know how pleased I am with everything.'

'You're telling me I've got to come and live here, right?'

'Not telling you, suggesting. It's the only way to make it work, Johnny.'

'But I like it back home. I like you being there, looking after everything.'

'I'm prepared to make you a promise, Johnny. I'll move here, too. Run the organization from here, or LA. Anywhere. I need you just as much as you need me. And, anyway, I've had enough of Britain. It was all right a year or two ago, but the scenery's shifted. I mean, why pay those taxes? This is where we'll make it, Johnny – together. How about it? Give me your answer, and then I'll let you get some sleep.'

'Oh, all right, yes. But you'll have to ask Virna what she thinks.'

Out Johnny went, like a light, but Grant had never felt more awake than he did just then. After trying to work out what to do with Johnny's body, immovable on top of the bed, Grant fished in Johnny's jacket pocket for his room key, found it, and stealthily crept out, leaving the superstar snoring.

In a minute he was tapping gently on the door of Room 9000, the Presidential Suite, and letting himself cautiously in.

'That you, Johnny?' said a muffled voice.

'It's me, Grant. You decent?'

'Sure. Come to seduce me? Where's Johnny?'

Grant entered the vast room, draped in swathes of purple velvet. Virna was wearing a skimpy nightdress and lay sprawled invitingly on an enormous bed, toying with a

315

handful of paperbacks and a packet of Marlboros. Muted cries came from Dylan in another room.

'No, have to seduce you another time, I'm afraid. Johnny fell asleep on my bed, sleeping the sleep of the just,' said Grant, not with total accuracy. 'We were discussing a rather important matter and he just keeled over. Silly of me to try.'

'What was it?' asked Virna, waving him over to sit on the edge of the bed.

Grant could see her breasts and most of her body through the nightdress, but didn't want to think about all that just now.

'I need you to help me,' he told her. 'I've put it to Johnny that he should stay over here. Really crack the market. Not go home. Live here. I think the ball's at his feet.'

'But what about . . .?'

'What about what?'

'Me and Dylan? And you, would you stay on?'

'Yes, I would. Run things from here. It's been coming for a long time. This is the break we've all been waiting for.'

Virna surprised Grant with the swiftness of her response.

'Yes, I'd love to live here – on one condition.'

'What's that?'

'You bring Carly and Neville. I wouldn't want to sit around on my own, I'd need company. Carly and I get on fine. So that's my condition.'

'Johnny was just awake enough to say it all depended on you.'

'That's it then. You have my answer.' She leant forward and kissed him, which was a surprise. 'Now you'll have to drop that other woman, won't you?'

Grant looked up from his hands, which had been the object of close scrutiny. Virna was being very assertive. Was she saying that on Carly's behalf, or her own?

'Suzie? What's she got to do with anything?'

Virna was amused by his bluster.

'Quite a lot, I should think,' she said with a wry grin. 'If you lived here, she'd be a long, long way away. I expect Carly would like that.'

Grant didn't rise to the bait, but was aware that Virna's hand had touched his leg. He bounced up from the bed as if to go. It was the first time any hint of physicality had passed between them, but Grant was in no mood for complications with Johnny's wife. If that was what moving to the States was going to mean, it was more than he could cope with now.

Having won Virna over so quickly, there was not much more to do that night. 'Mind if I sleep on the sofa?' he asked. Virna gave him a surprised look. 'No, on second thoughts, I'd better go back to Johnny. When he wakes up he'll wonder where his key is.'

'All right, love, but don't lie on the bed next to him. We don't want you doing an Alan Greenlee, do we?'

'Virna, some things will *never* happen and that is one of them.'

'Goodnight, Grant. Send him back to me as soon as you can.'

He leant forward and kissed her. She clutched him. There was a hint of desperation in it, but again Grant refused to respond or even wonder at the reason.

'I think it's a fantastic plan,' she told him, 'I really do. But I'm not kidding. Either Carly comes, or I don't.'

'You've got yourself a deal, Virna. I can't see Carly saying no. Can you?'

'No, I can't,' said Virna, simply. 'If you need any arm-twisting doing, you know where to find me.'

'You're an angel.'

Grant slipped quietly out, found his way back to Room 2002 and, ignoring what Virna had told him, lay on the bed two or three feet away from the snoring Johnny Todd. He put in his earplugs and was soon soundly asleep by the side of his star. It was going to be all right.

When he woke next morning, Johnny had gone, safely back to Virna. Or so Grant assumed.

Grant flew home to London in a bid to persuade Carly.

'Don't you think it's a great idea? It'd help us solve all sorts of problems.'

'Such as?' asked Carly doubtfully. 'What would I want to live in Los Angeles for? Or anywhere else? I haven't got used to London yet.'

Nothing was as powerful as an idea whose time had come, however. Grant was in no mood for opposition, and Carly saw that she would have to go along with his plan.

'There's one thing that might appeal,' he mentioned, almost as an afterthought. He remembered what Virna had said. 'If I'm in the States that means there'd be a helluva lot of space between me and you-know-who.'

'That woman?'

'That woman. Right.'

'As long as she doesn't follow us. Wouldn't put it past her.'

'Carly . . .'

His argument did make sense, however – or seemed to. Carly began to see the move as a way of re-establishing their marriage, of putting the past behind them.

Next evening, Grant came home and found Carly in the middle of a long phone call to Tom in Liverpool. Tom was, naturally, doing everything he could to make her stay. At Grant's arrival, Carly rapidly extracted herself from the conversation.

'Well, of course you had to consult Tom,' said Grant with heavy humour. 'After all, he's always given you such good advice.'

'Don't be such a beast, Grant.'

A move to America, Grant concluded quietly to himself, would mean that she, too, would be putting miles between herself and Tom Sheridan.

* * *

318

Suzie took the news badly. 'So you really are dumping me, aren't you? You said you couldn't, but you've found a way.'

Grant hated that cat-like look, which women assumed at bad news. How they could change. To which Suzie added her posh, superior air.

'No, I'm not dumping you,' he insisted, his voice flat. 'I still love you very much.'

'Tell me about it,' Suzie hissed contemptuously.

'And we still have a professional relationship,' Grant went on, unabashed. 'I'll still work *very* hard to make sure you do all right.'

'But *how*, for God's sake? How can you do that from across the Atlantic? It's impossible. Don't kid me, Grant.'

Then Grant said what he would never have admitted to Carly, Virna or Johnny.

'Believe me, Suzie, if there was a way of taking you with me to the States, I'd have thought of it. If Johnny can make it over there, so can you! You know I think you're capable of anything.'

'Fat chance. You've ruined my marriage, you've dropped me professionally. You stink!' She ran at him and tore at the flesh on his face with her long fingernails, drawing blood.

It was an unexpected gesture, almost as unexpected to her as to her victim. At once Suzie was contrite and burst into tears at what she'd done. Grant dabbed his face with a handkerchief and then picked Suzie up, gently stroking, bluntly consoling, with such words as he could muster.

Grant felt foolish sitting there beside her while she sobbed. He had known she would take the news badly but, somehow, not this badly. He spoke up in his own defence. How it was foolish to blame him for the break-up of her marriage to Alan. Far from ruining her career, Grant had done everything he possibly could to promote it.

The waves of resentment kept coming towards him. He

worried about leaving behind him an embittered woman. Who was to know what form her spite might take? He didn't like what he was doing, but what other way was there?

Suzie still showed no sign of coming out of herself and talking to him sensibly. With sudden briskness, Grant stood and said, 'Goodbye. Jan Ferry'll be in touch.'

He closed the door and left. It was like closing a door on the past.

CHAPTER 19

Los Angeles seemed to stretch as far as the eye could see under the thick yellow rind of smog, but the people round the pool appeared none too worried. It was quite like old times: ostentatious luxury in a house which even had a sign saying 'Quornford West' on a carved post just inside the electronically-operated gates.

That Sunday, it was Johnny and Virna's turn to drive over in the Rolls from Malibu. They would have lunch and sit with Grant and Carly by the pool at the Beverly Hills mansion. Juanita, the Pickerings' Mexican maid, had prepared an elaborate trolley-load of salads, fish and meats, and Grant administered drinks from his newly-installed poolside bar. The Californian sun squeezed through the LA smog and they were as happy as millionaires could be.

It was May 1972, less than a year since both families had decamped to California.

'We've come a long way, haven't we?' said Johnny, his lean, trim, deeply-tanned body well worthy of the celebration it was currently receiving in countless glossy magazine articles.

The statement was a kind of ritual. One or other of the exiles was bound to say it before the end of the day.

Johnny broke into a contented but sufficiently self-deprecatory peal of laughter. You weren't supposed to crow and yet, why not? All this, Grant's house in Beverly Hills, Johnny's ranch at Malibu, with neighbours who were household names around the world, the pool, the cars, the sunshine – it was a very long way from what they'd all grown up with.

Grant was, as ever, less well-tanned, more pasty

complexioned, and had gained a little weight. It was all right for Johnny: his work schedule meant he could look after himself and sit in the sun most days. Grant's problem was more of catching cold in the air-conditioning at Occidental Tower where he had his offices. He was paler than he should have been, but he still looked chunky, and Carly had fallen in love with him all over again.

She looked more beautiful than ever. She was relaxed, her hair lustrous, her skin lightly tanned. She adored Neville, now almost three: every bit as sharp as his legal father, every bit as charming as his putative father. Carly was relieved, too, that the bad times were behind them. They had been through a lot since getting married – the crash, the business over Neville's paternity, losing Quornford, Grant's playing around with Suzie, the pulling up of roots and the move to America.

'Yes,' Grant said, swirling the fruit around in his drink. 'I never imagined it turning out like this, but there we are.'

Virna kept up her efforts to get Dylan to play with Neville, without their both falling into the pool. Then she said: 'Mind you, I think the past happened to someone else. It feels like that.'

Grant wasn't having it. 'Nonsense, we're still the same people we were ten years ago. It's just the scenery that's different. And thank God it is, too. I'd had enough. The way they taxed us into the ground, the weather. No, we're the same, it's Britain that's changed. I think we left at just the right time.'

There were no dissenters, merely a quartet of mild self-congratulation. The least likely to succeed, maybe, but they had done exactly that.

'And there's more to come.'

It had not been an entirely smooth ride. The success had not been totally predictable. What success ever was? But now the risk could be seen to have paid off. The Grant

Pickering Organization was firmly based in Los Angeles. The London office was very much alive under Jan Ferry, but the future lay here on the West Coast and Grant found it increasingly hard to bother himself over the small potatoes he'd left behind in Britain.

The fact was that Johnny Todd had become a very big star indeed. The American public had taken him to heart in a way only Grant had believed it could. Johnny had made a successful television series. He had performed in almost every major city. He was a name everyone knew. They were walking on dollars. And Grant was for ever puzzling over what Johnny could do next.

There were several options. He could keep on doing what he was doing now, for ever. He could try to break into films. Or he could take part in stage musicals. Broadway was now a lively place with rock musicals scoring heavily. Grant was still wary of musicals, however. He had burned his fingers so badly over *Acts of Folly* that he never again wanted to get mixed up with that difficult business. There was another reason, too. He had grave doubts as to whether Johnny Todd could act.

For the moment, though, it was lotus-eating time. The loyalty between Grant and Johnny had been tested by the collapse of Starfinders and found to be rock-solid. Even if he had no other clients, Grant could live very handsomely on his 25 per cent share of Johnny's earnings. He also had his share of the Wreckers. He had offloaded Quentin Saint while retaining his share of Podge's ever-growing song catalogue. He was completely free of minor talents like Rex Room. He could be satisfied that all was for the best.

Johnny dived impressively into the pool. Grant declined to follow him. Pools were for doing deals round, not for swimming in. Besides, it was the poolman's day off and Grant wasn't sure the filter was working correctly.

He turned to Virna and began to flirt with her while Carly looked on, thinking it was harmless.

323

'What on earth are you wearing that button for?' he asked her.

Virna fingered the 'McGovern for President' badge on her white cotton bikini top.

'Because he ought to get the nomination.'

'And what can you do about it? You haven't got a vote. None of us has.'

'Maybe not, but we all live in a country at war, a war that should be stopped. He's the one to do it.'

'You've been talking to the wrong people,' Grant teased her. 'Didn't you see the President on the box last week? He seems to know what he's doing.'

'Oh, don't talk politics, for God's sake,' Carly interrupted. 'Nixon gives me the creeps. There's a church, you know, called St John's. I went past it the other day. The main doors are locked and won't be opened until America leaves Vietnam.'

'Ah, still the good Catholic, eh, Carly?' said Virna.

'It's nothing to do with being a Catholic. It's Episcopal, anyway. I think that's what they call it. And I'm not a good Catholic. I've been corrupted by all these showbiz people I live with.'

Grant grunted. 'There's nothing to stop you going to church. We have a driver who'll take you. You can go pray with the Mexicans if you're that keen.'

'See, Virna? See what I have to put up with?'

Carly stretched out and touched him, a gesture that Virna noticed. She was slightly jealous to see how Carly and Grant were apparently so happy again together. It was always difficult to tell what was going on in Grant's head, he was such a dark one, but everyone knew how he'd behaved before and Virna was not uninterested in how he might behave again.

Indeed, if there was a speck of dark in the haze-filled cloud, it was over Virna's head. The trouble was, she felt that as far as the world was concerned she didn't exist.

Since taking up residence in the US, the public relations consultants had descended on Johnny. He was no longer portrayed as the honest working lad from Salford made good, the warehouseman turned star. If he was to be an idol, then roots were unimportant, immaterial. His publicity didn't play on the fact he was a Mancunian, or even English. To study his act would lead most audiences to believe his birthplace was a small rock in the middle of the Atlantic.

Along with the discreet reticence over origins – they weren't denied, just not emphasized – came an absolute blackout on his marital status. If it was mentioned at all, it was in the past tense. He 'had been' married but divorced 'a long time ago', which was true. The fact that he had remarried and fathered a second child was carefully not mentioned. There were certainly no photographs of Johnny and Virna canoodling together in connubial bliss.

There were sound reasons for this approach and it was more subtle than the blanket denials of marriage which had been the order of the day for most pop performers in the sixties.

It did make Virna feel odd, however. It was not as though she was a wife Johnny felt embarrassed about, which had been the case with Maureen. In fact, Virna was almost as radiant as Johnny, with matching tan. Today she looked at her best, delicious cream and beige pants, cotton top, and several thousand dollars' worth of jewellery distributed about her person. Her hair looked more coppery than ever. But what did she do, what was she, to justify looking like this? She was no more and no less than Johnny Todd's wife, and the publicists wouldn't even let her whisper that.

Her McGovern button was the smallest of indications that she wanted to be different, to be her own woman. If Johnny supported anyone it was Nixon. Indeed, plans were in train for him to sing at a White House supper quite soon. Virna was just letting him know where she stood.

She found a certain resistance when she claimed to be 'Mrs Johnny Todd' around Beverly Hills, even though the name was printed on her credit cards. People thought she was trying it on. It was as though she didn't exist.

Like Virna, Carly was almost always in her husband's shadow but, for the moment, didn't appear to mind. Like her husband, she was not flamboyant. He, in any case, although part of show business, was not a performer. To most people he was no more than a name, if that. His appearance counted for little. Indeed, such power and authority as he had was not reflected in it.

Carly lived through Grant, or at least through him and Neville. There was no hint of resentment in her on these grounds. She could see the logic of the set-up she had chosen. Unless someone disturbed her into thinking differently, she wasn't going to change her ways. Virna had given her the paperback of *The Female Eunuch* and told her to read it. As yet, there'd been no reaction.

'Come on you two, eat up,' said Grant, hustling them towards the trolley. 'This is all good stuff we've got here. Mighty fine.'

'Listen to him – "mighty fine", indeed.' Johnny put a wet arm round Grant's shoulders. 'In six months, I'll bet you'll have a totally American accent. You're halfway there already.'

'Well, I can't help it,' explained Grant. 'I always end up talking like the folks I'm with. I translate English into American, in case they don't understand me.'

'I can still tell you're from Liverpool,' Virna said, reaching for the Thousand Island dressing.

'And how's that, Miss Sharp?'

'It's the way you say one word. It's one you use a lot.'

'What's that?'

'Singer. We say "singer", you say "sin-ger". It's a giveaway.'

Carly smiled. There was no mistaking where she came

from. Hers was more than an accent, it was a way of life. The reckoning was she'd never lose it.

'Tell you a sign I saw the other day.' Johnny drew Grant away from the others. 'It was outside a roadhouse. "100 Topless Nude Go-Go Dancers Nitely".'

'You went in to count them?'

'Nah. But it makes you think. It was in some tacky district. Where do they find one hundred topless go-go dancers?'

Grant had no answer.

Gustavo, the Mexican servant, came over, thrust another steak on Johnny's plate, and went away.

'You'd better be careful, superstar,' Grant warned, 'he likes to fatten people up. I mean, look at me.'

'Then he tries to frighten you to death.'

'With stories about last year's 'quake?'

'*Si!* You've heard? How he saw electricity transformers glowing red and exploding?'

'Yeh. That one. And the man in the plane at five hundred feet seeing the earth ripple, and telegraph poles riding up and down.'

'Horror stories. D'you think they're trying to drive us out?'

'It'd take a lot more than that,' said Grant. 'It hasn't rained since December, and rain is something that *could* force me away.'

'You don't have to tell me. I come from Manchester.'

'That's what's nice about this place,' Virna was saying to Carly, 'there's none of that class nonsense, making you feel small.'

'Balls,' Grant turned and corrected her. 'Of course there's class here. There's two of them: rich and poor. And God help you if you're poor.'

'But it doesn't matter how you talk,' Carly suggested.

'As long as you talk simple,' Grant said. 'Most Americans can hardly speak English because they've all come from somewhere else. I mean, Juanita and Gustavo, I can't make out what they're saying half the time. That's why songs have to be simple here. They've only got a limited number of words. You've got to be straightforward, specially if you're a singer.'

'There you are, "sin-ger",' shrieked Virna, prodding the rim of fat round his waist.

'That's why a *sin-ger* has to appeal to the lowest common factor.'

'Denominator,' corrected Virna.

'Piss off.' He tried to catch Virna's eye, but her face was hidden behind shades.

Carly went over to the trolley and forked more healthy pieces of salad on to her plate.

'Let me help you to some more of your own champagne,' Johnny offered.

'No, thanks, Johnny. I'm very West Coast now, mineral water all day long. I'm very healthy, and I'm always having to pee.'

'Ha!' Johnny exclaimed. 'Miserable!'

'Anyone heard Bill Ballance on the radio?' Carly wondered out loud.

'Yeah,' swooped Virna, 'he's fantastic.'

'Some of us have to work, you know,' said Grant. 'Is he the DJ who talks dirty?'

'Sort of,' said Carly, surprising her husband with a topic they hadn't shared before. 'He does this show every morning called *Feminine Forum*, on KGBS. All the housewives phone him and tell him what they've been up to in the sack. You'd never hear anything like it back home. On Friday there was this short-order waitress telling how she'd had to resist her boss who was a lezzy. And there was this other woman on how she seduced blokes. With one, they'd poured wine over each other. And Bill Balance asks, "Did he lick it off, honey?" It was great!'

Grant gave Johnny a wide-eyed look; the singer just laughed.

'Eventually, he couldn't make it with her because it was his first time not with his wife.'

'There's a moral in that somewhere,' Grant added quietly.

'I heard something else about that show,' Virna said. 'There was this woman describing how she'd been having it off with a lover, and her husband was listening and recognized her voice!'

'Well, just you be careful when you ring in,' Grant advised her in a would-be kindly way.

Virna gave him another look, less kind. Grant noticed, and wondered. The devil found work for idle hands to do.

Many months later, and far away from the warm delights of Los Angeles, Rex Room was shuffling forward in a queue. The London rain lashed against his cheeks, but he didn't have an umbrella and he'd never been one to wear a hat. He thought of chucking it in, but he'd queued for so long it would have been a waste to stop. He waited on as the crowd, with aching slowness, moved nearer the entrance to the exhibition.

Rex's calculated move to Alan Greenlee Management had, up to a point, produced the effect he'd wanted. Greenlee had agreed to have Rex on his books when Grant Pickering came on at his most persuasive. Grant didn't reveal, of course, what lay behind Rex's move or how glad he was to get the minor-league comedian off his hands.

'I'll do what I can for you, Rex,' Greenlee had assured him, had even offered not to charge commission for the first six months, an offer which Rex gratefully accepted, unmanly though it might seem to do so.

After the meeting, Rex had wandered back to his flat. The phone was ringing even as he came through the door. It was Greenlee with a booking for a guest spot on a TV quiz called *The People Game*. Rex did rather well on it and cherished hopes of a new career as a professional guest.

Which was why he was a little disappointed, standing there in the rain outside the Tutankhamun exhibition, when no one appeared to recognize him. They said eight or nine million watched *The People Game*. Surely *some* of them must be in the queue?

It was first time Rex had ever been near the British Museum. He had made several jokes about it in his time, of course. Mummies were more fit for puns than to satisfy any genuine historical interest on his part. Tutankhamun was different, though. The exhibition was all the rage. He had to see what the fuss was about.

Besides, if you were a comedian, there wasn't a lot else to do during the daytime. Life began at eight in the evening. You usually had to be on your best form at about eleven. So, you had to be careful not to do anything too tiring until then.

Rex wrote down jokes he'd heard from other comedians in a school exercise book. His spelling wasn't very good and quite often he just wrote down the start of the joke, and then lost interest. He would be furious with himself later for not having put in the punchline. At other times, he wrote only the punchlines but left out the gags which he then had to reconstruct. On the whole, though, he had a good memory for jokes. Give him a subject, however obscure, and quick as any computer he would be able to deliver one about it.

His was a rough and ready mind, often in turmoil about the world. He looked sad. He looked like a comedian. He was restless, dissatisfied. He aspired as much as he perspired, and that, if for no other reason, was why he was queueing with hundreds of others for a glimpse of the Egyptian treasures which had come to London for the first time.

Once inside, he pushed his way past people sticking their noses into the lesser exhibits, until finally he did what he had come to do. He stood in front of the massive gold funeral mask of Tutankhamun.

'Christ!' he swore quietly to himself, profoundly impressed. Who could fail to be moved, touched, enthralled, excited, by the sight? Rex felt very pleased with himself for having made the effort.

Then he bustled back to Streatham. With no booking that night, he went out, bought a bottle of malt whisky, and settled down in front of the television.

Towards ten thirty he'd drunk quite well of the whisky and was nodding off. But, although he put on his worn, old pyjamas and turned out the light, he found himself incapable of sleep.

It was awful being on your own and without a woman, but the last leggy blonde had moved out four months ago. Or had he kicked her out? He couldn't remember. And he hadn't had any of that since then, despite the impression he liked to give in his act and to the men down the pub.

His mind reeled and slid in and out of all kinds of superficial dreams.

The one image that was never far away was that of Tutankhamun. That serene, mystifying, silent, maddening stare. It was almost as though Rex was still standing in front of it, so clear was the image.

It would take a little time to form and grow, but the experience gave him an idea.

It was only to be expected in Johnny Todd's royal progress to superstardom that he should appear as a guest on NBC's *Tonight Show*. Johnny Carson's programme was taped in the afternoon for showing on late-night TV all over America. Johnny T. well knew that Johnny C.'s was the ultimate accolade.

Johnny's musical director and accompanist, Dustin Heaven, would be with the singer to liaise with the resident band. Grant also detailed a publicist called Joe Concho to travel to the studio in the limo and help Johnny hone his ad libs. Johnny kept forgetting them and Concho grew increasingly nervous, even to the point of ringing Grant to tell him it was impossible to deal with Johnny.

But there was no need to worry. As always, Johnny won through just by being himself. He sang a song and chatted amiably to the brilliant Carson who brought out the best in him. Whatever he said seemed to bring a warm and enthusiastic response from the studio audience.

It was a triumph. Johnny Todd moved further up in the pantheon. The song he sang re-entered the American charts and stayed there for another six weeks on top of its original ten. He was becoming the golden boy of American popular entertainment. In fact, thought Grant, he looked golden. His tan had a gold edge to it. He wore gold bracelets and rings, there was gold in his hair.

Johnny watched his interview go out, lying in bed with Virna alongside him. He was on a high watching himself and laughed in anticipation of his jokes. The success made him feel quite horny. At the end of his spot he switched off, using the remote control, and turned to fondle Virna.

She had other ideas. She wasn't playing.

'Hey, what is this?' he asked, puzzled.

'You're the great lover, you should know,' Virna told him, sharply.

'What d'you mean?'

'The world knows what a stud you are. So it's up to you, isn't it?'

Was she hinting at his one-night stands? That was a subject never discussed.

'Come on, love. What's the matter?'

'No!' She shrank from his touch.

Johnny pulled back and had to let his ardour cool.

'I've had enough of you ignoring me, except when your cock's up, that's all,' she told him over her shoulder.

'Virna, what's getting you?'

'I'll tell you.' She turned round to confront him full face. 'I've had it up to here, your going on TV, oozing sex over everybody. And I never get a mention. You're married to me, so why not admit it?'

Johnny dozily realized he'd have to provide her with coherent arguments. He wouldn't be able to rely on charm.

'It's not that I don't love you, or anything. You know that, Virna. It's just that my fans don't want to think about me being married. They have to have a fantasy that I'm available. I don't deny I'm married. I just don't shout about it all the time.'

Virna singled out the word 'fantasy': 'How do I know it stays as "fantasy". I don't know what you get up to when I'm not around. I dread to think.'

Johnny lay back against the pillows and covered his naked flesh with the silk sheets. If his usual way out of quarrels – jokes and sex – wasn't going to work on this occasion he would just have to leave things as they were. They said you should make up your quarrels before going to sleep, but he couldn't see a way out of this one.

'Thanks very much for spoiling my evening,' he told her churlishly, turned over and apparently went to sleep.

This annoyed Virna all the more. Why wasn't he as upset as she was? It was like water off a duck's back with him. Fancy being able to sleep in the *middle* of a row . . .

It was many hours and cigarettes later before Virna passed into something approaching sleep herself. By this time she had worked up a considerable hatred of Johnny Todd and removed herself to a spare bed to get away from him.

How had she got herself into this position? The prospect before her was of being a virtual prisoner in their high-security Malibu ranch while Johnny swanned around being famous and having everything his own way. What could she do about it? How could she escape? In the long hours of sleeplessness she thought hard. She had to decide whether she really wanted to pull out of the marriage, or whether to try and get her way within it. It was a difficult problem, with so much money at stake now.

She reached a decision. If Johnny was going to go on

refusing to acknowledge her in public, then she would have to break the rules herself. Maybe he was screwing all the women who threw themselves at him, maybe he wasn't, but she would have to take things into her own hands. She would take what sex was available and would make as much mischief as she possibly could by seducing one particular man. That would teach Johnny a lesson. That would stir things up.

She wondered what Grant was like in bed.

CHAPTER 20

Rex always had to put on a show of being busy in order to convince himself he was a success. So he was a great one for making appointments with 'my agent', 'my bank manager', 'my accountant', even if there was nothing really to discuss. There were other rituals, too, like listening to the radio news at 6.00 p.m. for topical gags and, for the same purpose, buying the evening papers. All this helped to fill up his day.

In the first week of 1973, he had rung up Alan Greenlee's assistant and fixed to come in and see 'my agent'. He erupted through the door, at the top of an old building in Regent Street, and as usual started telling gags to the receptionist where she sat at her typewriter. She dutifully tittered and made Rex feel good. He was concerned to see that there was still no photograph of himself in the entrance lobby, whereas there was a large colour one of Quentin Saint. Perhaps I'd better get some new ones taken, he thought to himself, and have a large one made for Alan Greenlee. Then he'd have to put it up. But that would cost a great deal and why, in any case, shouldn't Greenlee pay for it?

Greenlee came out and greeted him with a handshake and a clutch round the shoulder. 'Happy New Year, Rex! It's going to be a great one.'

Rex shrank perceptibly, and they went into Greenlee's pokey office.

Greenlee knew there was no reason for Rex to be there. He had just come, as ever, to remind Greenlee of his existence, to chivvy him along, but with nothing particular to talk about.

'So what else have you been doing? Have a good Christmas?'

Greenlee was chatting, rather wishing Rex would go home.

'Oh, yes, yes. I keep busy. Go to the pictures a lot, you know. Reading. Always reading. Gives me ideas, you see.'

'Good. Really?'

'And, I tell you what. I went to that Tutankhamun show just before it closed.'

'Ah, you got in? Missed it myself. Have to queue long?'

'No. No more than a day.'

'What . . . oh, ha ha! Was it worth it?'

'Worth it!' Rex leapt up and stood with his thumb in his top pocket as if about to launch into a routine. Greenlee had noticed before how Rex couldn't sit still for a minute. He was much happier on his feet. He couldn't tell an anecdote or a joke without doing all the gestures, and this was easier done standing up. 'Worth it! A knock-out. You've never seen anything like it. Tre-mendous. No, really. I tell you, I was so excited I couldn't sleep.'

'You make me sorry I didn't see it.'

'You should've, Alan. You'd have really liked it.'

Greenlee surreptitiously looked at his watch. He was due to meet Quentin Saint for a New Year's lunch, though this wasn't a piece of information he was going to give Rex. He might get ideas in that direction.

Rex spotted the gesture. 'Not keeping you, am I?'

'No, no, sit yourself down, Rex. Can I offer you a drink?'

'That'd be nice. G and T?'

'Sure.' Greenlee fussed over the drinks cabinet but pointedly poured out nothing for himself.

'Now, what can I do for you, Rex?' he asked.

'Ah, yes, thank you.' Rex took the drink, saw the gaping chair and realized to his surprise he was still standing. He sat down, a little shamefaced. 'Thing is, I think it's awfully important for you and me to keep in touch, agent and client, eh? That's what was wrong with me and Grant Pickering. Never talked to me. It's through chatting that the ideas come, isn't it?'

'Oh yes, right.'

'Well, Alan, what have you been doing? I expect you go to lots of shows, yes?'

Greenlee instinctively rested his hand over his watch as though reading the time by Braille. 'Yes, well, the last thing I saw was that *Jesus Christ Superstar*. At the Palace. I'd been a bit reluctant to go when it first opened. You know, I thought, like everyone, it wasn't my cup of tea if it was all religious. But it was nothing like that at all. It's like a rock musical, you know. Very good. That's where the future lies, as I said to Quentin.'

'Quentin?' Rex pretended not to know which Quentin he was talking about.

'Quentin Saint.'

'Ah yes. Used to be with Grant . . . as well.'

'Yes. Anyway, I told him it was about time he wrote something like that. He's so good at writing single songs, but a musical, think of that! I think he was really impressed. So he's looking for a story.'

'How about King Tut?'

'What? I don't know. Sounds a bit unlikely. I don't see a lot of ancient Egyptians dancing about to rock music, do you?'

'You could call it *Rooty-Tut*! You'd be amazed what people write musicals about. I mean, I saw one at the Roundhouse the year before last. Someone must've sent me a free ticket. Called *Maybe That's Your Problem*. It was about premature ejaculation. I ask you!'

'Didn't make it to the West End?'

'No. Came before its time.'

Greenlee laughed and hit the desk with his fist.

Rex went on: 'But no, I don't mean King Tut. I mean the way they discovered the treasure. It was quite a big story. I remember my Dad telling me about it. There was a curse or something. All the people who dug it up died off one by one.'

'Well, I don't know.' Greenlee fiddled with the papers on

his desk. 'But it's a thought, Rex. I'll mention it to Quentin and see if it strikes any chords with him. Strikes any chords, ha!'

'Remember I want a part if it ever gets done. Make sure he writes one for me. Everybody's doing it these days, turning to acting.'

'Comics are usually over the hill when they do that, Rex, but yes, I'll mention it to Podge.'

Rex blinked at the nickname.

'There's a lot of money to be made in musicals,' Greenlee went on. 'And lots to be lost, as a certain mutual acquaintance of ours found to his cost.'

'Grant?'

'Yes. Didn't hold him back for long, though. Now, you'll have to forgive me, Rex, but I've got a lunch date. Lovely to have you pop in like this. Any time you want a chat, just give my assistant Barbara a ring.'

It seemed the opposite of an invitation, the way he said it.

'Or perhaps we could have lunch one day?' Rex suggested.

'What a good idea. Must fix it . . .'

Rex stretched out his hand and shook Greenlee's firmly, to try and show who was really in control. Then he bowed out, popped his head round the door of Barbara's office, told another joke to the receptionist, who again dutifully laughed, and made a noisy showbiz exit. He didn't have anything to do for lunch, or for the rest of the day, but when he left the lift at the bottom he took out his diary and consulted it.

Alan Greenlee waited as long as he could in the office, not wanting to share the lift down with Rex.

'I think we'll have to be a little busy when Mr Room comes calling in future,' Greenlee said to the receptionist.

'Yes, Mr Greenlee.'

'Now, I really must get round to the Caprice, otherwise

Quentin'll be in a panic. He hates being left alone at tables. Back about three thirty.'

In April 1973, almost a year since they'd arrived in California, Carly gave birth to her second child. It was another boy, and this time it was perfectly clear that Grant was the father. He had Grant's intense look combined with her own large eyes. They called him Steve.

'They'll all be falling for him one day, won't they?' Carly said, holding the bundle.

'Give him a chance,' said Virna Todd. 'Give him a few years before he gets into all that.'

Carly thought Virna was getting on her hobby-horse again and she wasn't in a mood to be preached at.

'Here, you hold him,' Carly said, passing over the baby. 'And don't drop him in the pool.'

Carly had been home from the hospital three days and was taking it easy. That wasn't difficult. Her life now seemed to revolve entirely round the pool. Grant was out from before breakfast to midnight. The Mexican couple did everything about the house. Now that Steve was born, all Carly had to do was sit in the sun and cultivate her tan. Just like Virna.

'Is he a "Steve"?' asked Virna.

'How do you mean?'

'Solid and reliable. It's in the name, don't you think?'

Carly tried to think of the Steves she'd known. 'Yes. I suppose he is. The thing is, I think they grow towards the names you give them. That's why it's so important to choose the right one.'

Virna smiled, feeling Carly was a bit eccentric for thinking such things. She was a simple soul. Virna sometimes wondered what Grant saw in her.

'Will you stay for lunch?' asked Carly.

'Salad, you mean?'

'Yeh, boring, I know. I'd give anything for a good scouse right now.'

339

'Scouse? I thought that was talk.'

'No, it's food as well. Lob-scouse they used to call it. Stew to everyone else. But, of course, we're not allowed to have it here. It's either lettuce leaves or Mexican stuff.'

'Well, you're the boss. You should tell them what you want.'

'Yeh, but can you see Juanita and Gustavo knocking up scouse or Lancashire hot-pot? They don't even know what a kipper is. It's a different world. I'd like to visit the Pool and stuff me face.'

'You'll feel better when you've got your body back,' said Virna, coolly.

Juanita duly brought the expected salad.

'Funny, Americans,' commented Virna. 'I mean they always give you so much. You ask for a piece of bread with your soup and they bring you a whole frigging loaf.'

'They don't like to appear mean,' suggested Carly.

'And you try getting your coffee at the end of a meal. They always give it to you as soon as you sit down. They just won't be told. I've tried, it's impossible.'

'Ha!' said Carly, who was still able to enjoy these national differences. She weighed into the coleslaw.

Steve fell contentedly asleep in his basket, apart from the occasional parp. Neville, almost four, was at school now and would be brought home by the security guard in the afternoon.

'Tell me,' Virna asked casually, 'do you think Grant is always straight with you?'

'What about?'

'Sex.'

'Oh yes,' said Carly, without a blink.

'In spite of what he got up to with Suzie Paul?'

Carly frowned, but she wasn't going to let her good mood be spoiled. 'He said that's finished, and it clearly has. I mean she's not here in LA, is she?'

'No.'

'So, why do you ask?'

'Oh, nothing. Except that I fret about Johnny.'

'You mean about other women?'

'I don't know what he gets up to.'

Carly was faced with a dilemma. She felt like saying, 'Of course he plays around, you fool,' but she didn't. She had heard from Grant what went on, that Johnny was never one to turn down an opportunity. And here was his wife making out she didn't know. Was she genuinely innocent?

'I don't know,' said Carly, uneasy. 'But he must get tempted, mustn't he? I mean, you can't be the No. 1 heart-throb and not get offers?'

Virna bristled. 'So what? He's my husband. It's his duty to be straight. It's just fantasy. That's what he's always said.'

'You've talked about it then?'

'Yes. In passing.'

Carly noted an undertow of bitterness that Virna was reining in.

'I wouldn't worry about it, if I were you. Grant wandered away from me. And now he's wandered back again. That's all that matters. You can't marry into this business and worry about it, or you'd never stop.'

'I wish I felt the same.'

'Oh, come on, Virna, what is this?'

'Well, I tell you, if I ever found out Johnny was betraying me, I'd . . . I'd . . . well, I don't know.'

'Enough!' Carly said, with unusual firmness. 'We're not going to spend any more time sitting around worrying about our husbands. What the hell if they do screw around? As long as they've enough left for us, we should worry.'

'I wish I could feel the same,' said Virna for the second time.

That was how the conversation ended. As far as Virna was concerned it had merely confirmed her suspicions. Carly was obviously part of the male conspiracy. A sympathizer. Well,

Virna would have to show her, show them, in the only way she knew how.

Tom Sheridan crept, as it were, stealthily towards Lime Street Station. He slipped aboard the London train and hid behind a copy of the *Daily Mirror* until he was satisfied no one he knew was in the carriage with him. He only relaxed when the train had crossed over the Mersey bridge at Runcorn.

Tom had finally decided to leave Liverpool. He had held out longer than most. Grant, George and Mickey, Carly and all the others had long gone South to London and then, of course, far, far West.

He had thought about it long and hard. There weren't the opportunities in Liverpool. The caravan had moved on. The city was dying on its feet. Apart from which, there was nothing and no one to hold Tom in the city. He hadn't found a woman he'd wanted to live with for more than a few weeks. The only woman he really wanted was several thousand miles away in LA.

So he had decided to live in London. That was where people had to go. Nowhere else would do. He would look for a flat. Buy a copy of the *Evening Standard* and tramp around. He had money in his bank account and there was always the next royalty payment from 'Tantalizing' to look forward to. It always seemed to be getting sung or played somewhere in the world.

It wasn't long before he discovered the wisdom of his move. An advert for a flat in the paper sent him south of the river. Clutching his shiny new *A to Z*, he took the Northern Line and headed for Waterloo. The Tube was a new experience. Everything in London had an edge of excitement for the newcomer. The *women* on the Tube, just panting for it, or so he imagined . . .

Then he saw someone he thought he recognized, someone off the telly. Well, that was London for you, stars

342

everywhere. You never saw any in Liverpool. Then he realized he knew the man both from TV *and* from Liverpool. He moved over and parked himself by his side.

'I know you,' he began. 'You're Rex Room. D'you recognize me?'

'Yeh, half a tick. Aren't you Tom?'

'Tom Sheridan, yeh. What are you doing here?'

'Going home. Live in Streatham.'

'Ah well. I'm going to see a flat. I've just come down. Came yesterday.'

'For a holiday?'

'No, for good. I've decided London's the place. Liverpool's had it.'

'They all come round to it in the end. Welcome to the unemployed.'

'Bad as that?'

'Only kidding. But it's not exactly paved with gold. Least I haven't found it so.'

'Well, fancy meeting you. Still doing the patter then?'

'Oh, yes,' replied Rex. 'Haven't you seen me on the telly?'

'Sorry. Don't watch that much.'

'What about you? Still the poet?'

'Still the poet, singer, songwriter. Anything I can lay my hands on, frankly.'

'Got an agent?'

'No fear. Not after the trouble I had with Grant-ruddy-Pickering.'

'I was with him, too, but I changed. Good move, I reckon. Man called Alan Greenlee.'

'Handles Quentin Saint?'

'That's the one.'

'Is he any good?'

Tom Sheridan went to see Alan Greenlee to find out what the agent could do for him. The first thing Tom did was tell Greenlee he'd once been with Grant Pickering.

'Oh dear,' said Greenlee with a mock sigh, 'this is getting to be like Pickering-in-exile. I've got Quentin Saint and Rex Room. Now you're wanting to climb aboard. Frankly, I don't see much money in poetry readings, or whatever it is you do.'

'Don't think of me as a poet. Think of me as a writer. I'll write anything. I've had hits, you know.'

'I know you've written one hit song,' said Greenlee testily. 'But that's no use to me if you're still obliged to Grant Pickering for those. Am I right?'

'Well, yes.'

'Same deal as with Quentin. I've got an idea, though. I've someone who's looking for a writer. There might just be wedding bells between you.'

'So, who is this person?'

'I'm Mrs Johnny Todd,' Virna announced to the guard at the entrance of the Occidental Tower. 'I've come to see Mr Pickering.'

'Is he expecting you?' the black guard asked, casually but firmly.

'No, he isn't. But he'll see me, I'm sure.'

'Just one moment, ma'am. Take a seat.'

Grant was surprised by Virna's call, but immediately tried to be accommodating. Virna was shown up to the seventeenth floor, then found her way to the office of the Grant Pickering Organization, following the pointing finger signs – a flying finger being the company's symbol. She had to wait for a moment, sitting below a wall-sized photo of her husband in one of his raunchier poses. Then she was shown into Grant's office.

'Virna! This is unexpected.' He kissed her on both cheeks and gave her a squeeze. It wasn't something he could recall doing before in all the years he'd known her. Oddly, it was the first time they'd met without their spouses being present – at least, not since the night in Vegas when he told her about leaving England. 'Like a drink?'

'You bet. Whatever.'

'It's nice to see a woman drink. Carly was off it for months when she was expecting and doesn't look like ever starting again.'

'Steve's a beautiful boy,' announced Virna, in best bulletin style. 'You must be very pleased.'

She didn't have to say what she meant.

'So what brings you to world headquarters?' Grant asked, looking at her closely and giving her his full attention.

'Grant, I want you to tell me something. You may wonder why I ask, but it's important.'

'Shoot.'

'It's this. How much does Johnny screw around?'

Grant swallowed, stood up, began to study the view of downtown LA through the picture window.

'Why do you ask?'

'Just tell me, yes or no, Grant. It's important, like I said.'

Still Grant didn't answer. 'You must tell me why you want to know before I give you an answer. Johnny and I are such old, old pals . . .'

'I think you've answered,' said Virna with a snap. 'By hedging, you've given me the answer.'

'No, I haven't,' insisted Grant, fixing her with his stare once more.

Virna was chilled by the power behind Grant's voice. She had never encountered his frightening side head on. It was something she'd heard about. It was very different from the easy-going evasiveness with which Johnny contrived to sail through life.

'I know I'm not married to Johnny,' he said quietly but firmly, 'but if it means anything, and I think it does, I've known him far longer than you have. Seen him come from nothing to this, so I'm not prepared to do or say anything that will hurt him or our relationship, at work or in private.'

Virna shrank from meeting Grant's eyes but listened intently to his words.

'You've asked me to say something which no woman should ask another man about her husband. But, since you ask, I think you'll find Johnny's okay by you. What does he need to screw around for? He's got you. He hasn't any hang-ups that I know of.'

Grant knew that he mightn't sound very convincing, but he wasn't going to rat on his friend.

'I don't believe you,' Virna lost no time in snapping back at him. She was suddenly angry, tearful. 'Tell me this then, Grant, if he hasn't any hang-ups, why isn't he poking me?'

'Oh, I see. It's like that, is it?'

'Yes, it bloody well is. What's the point of him being the world's greatest lover if I don't get any of it?'

'I see. Well, Virna, you've got to work it out for yourselves. Shouting at him won't help. You need to talk to him. Really talk.'

'Did you talk to Carly when you were screwing Suzie Paul?' Virna delivered her taunt bitterly.

Grant made no reply, but gave Virna a look of distaste.

'It makes me feel so . . . so inadequate,' she went on. 'Mind if I smoke?'

'No, go ahead.' Grant rarely smoked himself but was unusually tolerant of the foible in others.

'I tell you what I hate most, it's when I'm not mentioned. It's as if I didn't exist. I'm not afraid of the publicity. I won't let him down. I can make myself look presentable, but I can't take being ignored.'

Grant said: 'I can understand that. I'll give it some thought and have a word with the publicity boys. Johnny's so big at the moment I think we can afford to take a risk or two. I see no reason why a well-placed article in a good magazine about your marriage and what it's like being Mrs Todd should do any harm. Leave it with me, Virna.'

She stood up, crossed over and threw her arms round him. 'Thank you, Grant. You're a good man. If only it had happened before.'

'Yeh, I know, I'm sorry. I expect we just didn't think. Sometimes in this business we forget we're dealing with people who are married to other people. You're a *real* person, Virna, I know that.' He kissed her on the forehead, she tightened her clinch, then he indicated by a movement that they weren't to continue.

He put an arm round her shoulders and took her to the window.

'There you are. There's the world.'

'No, Grant, it's not as easy as that if you're a woman. I'm Mrs Johnny Todd. Nothing else. And until just now I wasn't even able to claim that.'

'Never had any ambitions?'

'Hardly any less than Carly, I expect. I wanted a child. I've got that. I wanted a husband. I've got that. And I wanted a bit of fun. I've had that.'

'You never wanted to do anything really big?'

'I haven't the talent. I'm just a woman.'

'Carly doesn't have your worries.'

'Are you sure, Grant?'

'Yes.'

'Then you're a lucky man. I expect that's why you went after Suzie Paul. Because Carly never complained. Suzie Paul's ambitious, isn't she?'

'Yes, of course she is.'

'So why did you marry Carly?'

'She has her ambitions, too. I married Carly because she's talented, quite as much as for any other reason. She ran her own shop. She's a marvellous cook. And you've seen her photographs? That's her latest hobby. She's really good at it. So whether she's got more or less talent and ambition than Suzie doesn't really enter into it.'

'Have you got talent, Grant?'

Grant laughed and turned his head away. 'Not really. That's why I mix with talented folk, manage them, exploit them! If I have got talent it's in that direction.'

'You wish you were a performer?'

'Used to. I wanted to be John Lennon, I think. But there came a point early on when I had to see I hadn't got it. It's like languages. You've either got the knack or you ain't. And I was useless. So I found myself something else to do to keep me off the streets.'

'You're doing all right.'

Granted noted Virna's compliment and, like most Englishmen, didn't know how to respond to it. 'So I've been able to do something for you?' he asked, moving from the window and bringing the meeting to an end.

'Yes. Thank you, Grant.' She sensed he was keeping her at a distance, felt keen disappointment that he didn't take her bodily and resolve her problem that way.

It was only when Virna was outside the Occidental Tower again that it hit her that Grant hadn't helped her at all. He'd sided with Johnny. Well, what else could she expect from a man?

What more could she expect from that particular man, from Grant?

She wondered.

CHAPTER 21

Tom Sheridan would never have admitted it, but he was nervous. He had lived his life so far without having to rely on nerves as a spur. But now they had caught up with him and he was exceedingly annoyed with himself for it.

At first he put it down to the London cold, or to what he'd had to eat and drink the night before, but in the end he had to face up to it. He was nervous about meeting someone who was an established success, when he himself was not. The man was also probably gay and that had always slightly disconcerted Tom. He was frightened that, in a way, he was going to be judged. What success he had had to date was due largely to bluff and to luck. That was quite normal in show business, but now he was going to have to pull out all the stops to show he could genuinely deliver the goods.

He carried a satchel containing four heavy books, a foolscap file and a bundle of scrap paper. When he emerged at Hampstead Tube Station he looked at the map and then began to climb the steep, narrow passage until he found the house he was looking for. It was a curiosity, a Gothic folly out of a Hammer horror picture, but set down amid the more conventional dwellings of left-wing politicos, shrinks and literary folk.

Tom rang the bell. There was the distant barking of a small, yappy dog. Tom didn't fancy meeting that. Then the oak front door opened and a woman he half recognized stood before him.

'I'm Tom Sheridan,' he said. 'Come to see Mr . . . Saint.' It sounded silly calling him 'Mr Saint'.

'He's expecting you, Mr Sheridan. Come in.'

Tom had had no idea what to expect. What sort of house

349

was a gay rock star like Quentin Saint supposed to live in? It was eccentric, to be sure. Purple walls, purple everything, yet it was curiously homely. That was better than he'd anticipated.

'Come this way,' the woman said.

'Excuse me,' he asked, following her, 'haven't I seen you before somewhere?'

'Indeed you have. I used to be Mr Pickering's housekeeper at Quornford. As you probably know, he had a spot of trouble. Mr Saint was looking for someone, so my husband and I came here instead. It's different, of course, but very nice.'

'Oh yes, very nice,' said Tom, intrigued by this shuffling of servants around the pop world. Mrs Pugh had been at Quornford that dreadful weekend with Carly and Halo.

She showed Tom into a room at the end of a long corridor.

There, seated at the piano, was Quentin Saint.

'Hello,' he twinkled. 'I've got something for you.'

He started playing a tune which, of course, Tom recognized. It was a new arrangement of 'Tantalizing', quite unlike any he'd heard before. It turned the song into a haunting ballad, giving it quite a different complexion.

Tom sat next to Quentin on the piano stool. It was the highest compliment Quentin could have paid him. It was also Quentin's very clever way of introducing himself, of breaking the ice.

'I thought you'd like that. It's a smashing song. I've done it at one or two gigs.'

'When are you going to record it?'

'We'll have to see. Like something to drink? Coffee? Champagne?'

'Let's talk first. I'm curious.'

Alan Greenlee had been the matchmaker. He had an idea about doing a musical on the discovery of the Tutankhamun treasure. It sounded good to Quentin, but he only wrote songs. He needed someone to provide a framework for the show, to write the book, and maybe help with the lyrics.

Then Tom Sheridan had walked into Greenlee's office, courtesy of Rex Room, and appeared to provide the perfect solution. He could write. He needed the work. It would all be wonderful. Provided he could get on with Quentin. Greenlee prayed that he would.

'It's a wonderful idea, isn't it?' Quentin said. 'Trouble is, I haven't a clue what to do with it. Do you know anything about it?'

'No, but I've been reading. I got some books from the library.' He opened the satchel and tipped them out.

'This is by Howard Carter, the archaeologist. He was about fifty when they discovered the treasure. But we can make him younger. Then there's the Earl of Carnarvon who paid for it all. Big house in the country, bit dotty. And he's got a daughter, Lady Evelyn. So love interest there.'

'With Carter?'

'Yes. Even if there wasn't really, it won't do any harm.'

'Hmmm. The only bit I've thought about is the finding of the treasure. It'll look sensational on stage. They enter the tomb, and *bong*! Suddenly, larger than life, there's this huge head of King Tootsie all in gold. And there's this music.'

Quentin swivelled round on the stool to face the piano and struck enormous chords, faintly oriental, haunting and mysterious. After a few bars he stopped abruptly.

'That's as far as I've got.'

'Great,' cried Tom, almost as excited as the archaeologist in the story. 'But you must see this.' He picked up Carter's book. 'This is how he describes looking into the tomb: "As my eyes grew accustomed to the light, details of the room within emerged slowly from the mist, strange animals, statues of gold – *everywhere the glint of gold*."

'How about that, "everywhere the glint of gold"? Then it goes on "I was struck dumb with amazement, and when Lord Carnarvon inquired anxiously, 'Can you see anything?'"

it was all I could do to get out the words, 'Yes, wonderful things!' " '

' "Wonderful Things"?' Quentin played with the words and reached for the keyboard. 'There's a title for you!'

'Could be amazing. Everyone'll think it's about a load of boring old archaeologists, but there's more to it than that. You've got the crazy old lord, the love interest, and then the curse. Everybody dropping dead. Eight people who were connected with it. And the newspaper fighting for the story. *The Times* bought them all up. I think it could work.'

'Of course a hell of a lot'll depend on how it's staged,' Quentin remarked. 'But that's not our problem. It's got the makings of something, though. Great possibilities.'

'And "everywhere the glint of gold" for us, if we pull it off?'

'Right. But can you afford the time? Nothing up front, I'm afraid.'

Reluctantly, Tom said he'd give it a try. He'd been wondering about the money. 'I'll have to, won't I?'

Quentin gave him a little pat on the hand. 'I need to get in touch with Grant Pickering's woman. Jan Ferry, you know. All my writing still has to go through Paradise Street Songs.'

Tom froze. 'You mean, if we write this show, it'll have to go through Pickering? He'll get a whack?'

'Yes. I don't mind. It's worked out fine for me. Alan only handles my performing. Grant held on to the rest.'

'Fuckin' 'ell! That man is the bane of my ruddy life. D'you know anything of what he's done to me, Quentin? He ran off with my woman. They have my kid – yes, the kid I'm father of. The man fucking haunts me. Here's this thing I really want to do and now you tell me he's going to get his greasy fingers on a share of it. I'll *never* get him off my back.'

'Look, love,' said Quentin, soothingly, 'if you want to do it at all, it's got to be done this way.' Then a smile. 'I want you to, Tom. Isn't that enough?'

'Well, we'll see.'

'That's better. Now I can't do anything until you sketch out a story. I can fiddle about, but how soon can you let me have something?'

'I've got nothing else on. A week?'

'Fine. I was expecting you to say six months!'

Tom started putting the books back in his satchel. Quentin walked him to the door. He was keener than he was letting on. To compose a musical would give him a status more solid than any number of one-off hits. It would also bring him back in touch with people, having to work with a team. He was a lonely soul. The sex with Alan Greenlee had been fairly perfunctory and had come to an end, anyway. They were still chummy, but it was a working relationship now. That was why Quentin was so pleased that Tom had been suggested. Tom was very attractive. It would be nice to work with him.

'We can't begin to interest anybody until we've got something down on paper,' Quentin emphasized as they dawdled down the long corridor. 'Then we'll have to do a demo and go out and find a producer and all that. I've never done it before, but I've got a nice feeling about this.'

'I'm glad you have. I'm petrified.'

'Don't worry, love. It'll be all right. Believe me. Hear from you . . .'

Briskly, and with a friendly wink, he was gone and Tom was heading back to his flat with a sizeable task in front of him. He knew neither how to do it, nor how to organize himself to do it. But he knew he must find a way.

Grant found he couldn't concentrate for the rest of the day after Virna had made her surprise call. He had important meetings to attend. The Wreckers were signing with a new label, and he was in for a session with the accountants. He felt he would burst as the corporation men droned on hour after hour; he repeatedly had to force them to talk language he could understand.

The meeting with Virna had taken Grant unawares, and that was something he didn't like. He had also been disconcerted by the undercurrents to the conversation. Virna was challenging – that was her nature – but she had an uncanny knack of making Grant feel uncertain about his work, his marriage, his whole existence.

His mind kept wandering away from the accountants' talk. What was she really up to? If she wasn't careful she would spoil Johnny's success with her whingeing and moaning. Grant had made her an impulsive, grand concession, about making her married state better known, but he had a feeling it wouldn't be the end of the matter.

Grant even wondered whether Virna was trying to make a play for him, to teach Johnny a lesson, to give him a dose of his own medicine. Surely not. That would involve hurting Carly, and Virna was supposed to be a good friend, her only real friend in exile.

Grant couldn't resolve the problem and was annoyed with himself for being so upset. As soon as he could after the accountants and lawyers had packed away their yellow pads, he escaped and rang Johnny.

The singer was appearing at the Hacienda in Reno and, as it was 6.30 p.m., could probably be reached in his dressing room. He liked to arrive early and relax before a performance. There was even a little terrace, covered in Astroturf, where he could sit out and watch the sun go down. That was where Grant found him.

'Oh hi, Johnny. It's Grant. Hope I haven't woken you?'

'No, you haven't.'

'Listen, Johnny. I had a caller today. Virna.'

'What did she want?'

'Looking for a shoulder to cry on.'

'I might have guessed. She's been playing up a lot. I put it down to the usual.'

'Well, that's as may be, but she was sufficiently worked

up to come and see me. You know what she wanted to ask me? Whether you screw around.'

Johnny paused. 'She asked you *that*?'

'Yes.'

'I thought she knew. We just never talk about it.'

'Well, I denied it. Whether she believed me, heaven knows.'

'Thanks, Grant, you're a good fella.'

'I had to make one concession.'

'Oh, yes?'

'She's worked up because she hates being hidden away.'

'Oh, that.'

'Yes, really hates it. I told her I thought we could make a change. There's no harm, I don't think, in being more open that you're married. It might help.'

'Hey, I'm not so sure about that.'

'Well, think about it. I'm coming round to the idea. I think it might help. You're so bloody big and doing so well, nothing can stand in your way now.'

Johnny made a noise as though not convinced.

'And, for God's sake, be *nice* to her. Give her one, or something. She was complaining.'

'She's always complaining.'

'Johnny, think about it. I'm only your manager. I'm not the fucking Samaritans, but you owe it to her. Okay?'

'Okay.'

'How are things otherwise?'

'Oh, great. Good houses. Full last night and tonight. Bit of a cough, but I'm okay.'

'Good, glad to hear it. Speak to you again in the morning.'

Johnny left the phone off the hook. He was in a bad mood now. He didn't like to be disturbed like this before a show. Grant was meddling, there was no other word for it.

That night he gave only a competent performance, less good than he'd given for a very long time. He was irritated. He drank with his cronies until it was time to collapse into

355

bed. He didn't ring Virna in LA. She would have to wait for reassurance.

Grant had a way of assuming loyalty where it wasn't always to be found. He ignored the fact that sometimes people worked for him not because they particularly wished to add to the greater glory of the Grant Pickering Organization but because they needed the money and had to work for somebody to get it.

This applied in particular to his old Liverpool mates, Mickey Clinch and George Evans. Arch hangers-on from the old days, they had followed Grant down to London and then across the Atlantic. They would both describe themselves as 'Grant's dogsbodies' when wanting to appear sour, 'fixers' or 'road managers' when they wished to sound more elevated.

They carried out their ill-defined duties well. Nevertheless, they'd never quite lost the air of two Scouse lads who'd hit the big time. They had a wide-eyed approach to being in the United States. It was still like a dream.

Grant gained strength from having two such able lieutenants. He himself sometimes appeared to be the provincial lad who'd stumbled into the big time. He still felt an outsider in the American showbusiness world. In Mickey and George he had two friends who had travelled the long road with him. With them, he could indulge in sentiment for the past and nostalgia, highly selective, for the days back in Liverpool when they and the world were young.

Not that Mickey and George were with Grant in LA every day. They were usually out on the road, George with the Wreckers and Mickey fussing over Johnny Todd. George appeared genuinely happy tagging along in the wake of the heavy rockers, provided he was able to get his fix of the drugs that freely circulated in those parts, and which the brush with the law back home had failed to put him off.

Mickey was a more complicated character. He had never

really grown up. He had never needed to. From his first days out of school he had managed to latch on to other people, culminating in his long-running adhesion to the fortunes of Grant Pickering. He was a perpetual schoolboy, doggedly loyal, treated like a pet. Grant even had a way of patting him on the head and putting his arm round him.

His interests appeared to be restricted to food and beer. He had long ago filled out his T-shirt and jeans. No one drew attention to it but he seemed to have no relationships with either women or men. The days were gone when he would pick up some of Johnny's cast-off groupies. Mickey was good to have around, but no one really knew what was going on in his mind or what his ambitions and desires might be. No one stopped to consider whether he even had any.

Johnny found Mickey very useful as his gofor. If you were a big name like Johnny, to pop down to the hotel lobby and buy yourself a newspaper or a packet of cigarillos was fraught with difficulty. You would get mobbed, asked for your autograph. On one occasion Johnny had gone to get some gum and been treated to a round of applause from a lobby full of blue-rinsed fans. It was equally painful to do it through Room Service. That always took an age and bellhops always lingered, wanting to chat or fish for tips. Johnny had never got used to giving tips, never knew how much to give. He left it to Mickey to look after the tips.

Mickey was useful in that way, and continued to be so in another, more important, one. He was still pimping for Johnny, more or less discreetly.

In return, Johnny would make sure Mickey had enough cash. But what such sweeteners could never totally remove, however large they were, was a feeling of resentment. Why should Johnny have all the luck, with fame, money and women? He was the same class as Mickey, after all. What was it all about?

Mickey worried over these matters but wasn't bright enough to resolve them into a satisfactory world view. So, he felt it necessary to get his own back, not so much on Johnny himself, but on the whole set-up Grant Pickering had established.

He began to steal. He didn't need to, of course. His pay from the Grant Pickering Organization was good; he had Johnny's 'tips', but that wasn't the point. It was a cry for help. In Reno, Mickey began to put the theft on a grander scale. All it needed was a willing accomplice, equally interested in making a few bucks at the expense of his employers.

Joseph Noriega III was a clerk in his early thirties. By dint of hard work he was now in charge of the box office for shows in the Hacienda auditorium. Mickey quite easily fell in with him. He often had to pop in to arrange 'house' seats, complimentary ones for guests of Mr Todd or Mr Pickering. However much demand there was for tickets, house seats were always kept back until the last possible moment in case important guests turned up to see the show.

Mickey was impressed by Noriega's efficiency, his brisk 'Yes, sir, no, sir' manner, so different from his own mole-like mumble. One afternoon they slipped into the hotel coffee shop for a natter. Mickey had a doughnut and a milkshake, Joseph ordered a herbal tea.

'Tell me,' Mickey asked him innocently, 'what happens if more people turn up for a show than you've got seats for? It happened again last night. Do you just turn them away?'

'No, sir,' replied Noriega. 'We try *very* hard to seat everyone.'

'But how? Lay on extra tables?'

'Yes. Or squeeze them on to other tables. People don't mind. Even if it's twenty dollars a plate for show and dinner. People understand.'

'So there's never a problem?'

'Never has been yet.'

Noriega wondered why Mickey was fishing in his territory.

He tried to head the conversation off with money talk of another kind. He was star-struck and would much rather have had Mickey's job, able to rub shoulders with Johnny Todd.

'How much would you say he earned a minute, your Mr Todd?'

'Shit!' exclaimed Mickey. 'I've simply no idea. And I'm certainly not going to ask him. Two thousand a show? Work out how much that is a minute.'

'Two thousand a show? Five, more like. Dean Martin gets four.'

'Well, I wouldn't know.'

'Is he a regular guy, like he seems?'

'You want to meet him?'

'Really I would, yes.'

'Well, no problem. Can be arranged. But tell me . . .'

Then the conversation lurched back to the workings of the box office and slowly Mickey managed to prise out of Noriega the information he'd been inching towards.

'I'm told people in the box office stand to make a lot of dough.'

'Who told you that?' Noriega shot back, suspicious.

'You hear things. But I can't work out how it's done. I mean if you take money from people, you give them a ticket, and that's that. How do you make money on the deal?'

'Well, I'll tell you. And I'm not saying I do it myself, right?' Noriega dropped his voice so low, Mickey could hardly hear what he said.

'It is possible, and I'm not saying anyone here does it, to do one of two things. There's usually a rush before the show starts. You're trying to fit in as many people as you can. You can order up extra tables, like I said, or put twelve people on a ten-seater. You can take their money, but you don't have to give them a ticket. The ushers show them direct to their seats. The money may be diverted, you see, because there isn't a ticket.'

He winked at Mickey who was enjoying this.

'And the other way is more obvious. It has to do with the demand for tickets. When there's a big demand, the price on the ticket still doesn't rise. So there's no way to profit legitimately from that.'

'What about touts?'

'Well, that's it. I couldn't go out and tout tickets myself, so what I have to do is make sure the tickets get sold to touts rather than direct to the public. If it's a twenty-dollar ticket, I sell it to the tout for fifty, sixty. He sells it for eighty or a hundred. That way we both make thirty or forty. The management still gets the twenty, so everybody's happy.'

'That's clever,' said Mickey with a grin. 'Wouldn't do for the GPO to get to know, would it?'

'Nor the hotel. But there's no way they would. So long as you sell to the right people, there's no way it can get out.'

'How can you be sure? There might be plants.'

'I can tell,' said Noriega confidently, tapping the side of his nose.

'Of course, I could make some house seats available for selling,' said Mickey. 'As they're free anyway, you could charge anything you liked for them.'

'I can see you're a man I can do business with,' said Noriega, squeezing his arm.

'Good,' said Mickey.

'But first you introduce me to Johnny Todd, eh?'

CHAPTER 22

Quentin Saint and Tom Sheridan worked hard at the Tutankhamun musical. In the case of Tom, harder than he had ever worked before. But they didn't know what to call it.

'*Tutankhamum Superstar!*' suggested Quentin, making one of his little hand gestures.

'Trouble is,' Tom quibbled, 'nobody can spell Tutankhamun. There seem to be about six different ways. I doubt if he knew how to spell it himself!'

'As long as people know how to pronounce it, and they do . . .'

'How about *The Magic Tut?*'

'We'll think of something.'

'Or *Tutankhamun* exclamation mark.'

'You've got to be careful with exclamation marks.'

'Why?'

'Think of those Lionel Bart shows, *Blitz!* and *Twang!* They all had exclamation marks and they were *awful*.'

'But so had *Oliver!* and that was marvellous. And what about *Oklahoma!* and *Oh, What A Lovely War!* They didn't do too bad.'

'And *Oh! Calcutta!* That's got *two*, and that's *terrible*.'

'We'll think of something.'

Tom had found no difficulty in mapping out a two-act structure for the show. It was only loosely based on the events of the 1920s. If there was likely to be any trouble from the descendants of the real people involved they'd just have to change the names. The gist of it was Howard Carter's drive to prove himself an archaeologist, his extracting from Lord Carnarvon such funds as he could lay

361

his hands on, and his pursuit of the buried treasure and Carnarvon's daughter while the curse took its toll.

There was to be a sub-plot about journalists cutting each other's throats over the story, and that was to become a sort of chorus, together with the Egyptians fretting over *their* treasure being dug up by their colonial masters. It had everything, drama, excitement, spectacle, and a wonderful set of songs by Quentin. It wasn't yet a proper score but it was heading that way. It was rock-flavoured but at times symphonic, so they'd need a larger than normal theatre orchestra, and there were delightful twenties pastiches for the journalists to sing.

'I think my boys are really on to something big,' said Alan Greenlee, unusually excited at what he'd helped set in motion. He was always saying it, so few people paid much attention. Nevertheless, he managed to persuade a small group of influential folk to make the trip to Quentin's house in Hampstead for the first 'performance'.

It was an all-male gathering and, come to that, an all-male cast. Tom sang the male parts, Quentin the female. Tom was complimented on his singing by the man who'd produced Quentin's last two albums – a compliment he took amiss, as he was *supposed* to be a singer, after all. The whole evening went exceedingly well. The emphasis was totally on the songs.

'But just imagine the scenery and the costumes,' Greenlee piped up. 'We need someone like Sean Kenny to do the sets. Have a sandstorm on the stage, that sort of spectacle. All things are possible.'

The record producer wasn't concerned. 'I think the songs are so good we ought to do what they did with *Jesus Christ Superstar*,' he said. 'Instead of putting the LP out after the show's opened, put it out first, so the audience comes into the theatre humming the tunes.'

'It would be a gamble,' said Quentin cautiously.

'An LP might kill the show before we got it staged,' Tom pointed out.

'Better that than lose thousands on a flop,' said Greenlee.

'Let's talk about it,' said the record producer. 'I'll see what my people think. I'm keen to do it. I'll resign if they say no.'

'Oh, don't say that!' exclaimed Quentin. 'There's enough melodrama around here without that. They'd call your lovely little bluff.'

'Well, there's no avoiding it now,' Greenlee said rather heavily. 'It's time I talked to Grant. He has the rights to Quentin's work.'

'Gawd strewth!' cried Tom. 'Do we have to? Why does he have to stick his ugly mug into everything. He's had nothing to do with this. Why should he have a slice of the action?'

'There's no avoiding it, as I said,' Greenlee pressed on. 'If you fancy litigation to the end of the century, *and* you're willing to pay for it, then by all means . . .'

'Well, at least let's make sure he doesn't get involved in producing the show,' Tom pleaded. 'He's had one almighty disaster, we don't want *Tut* to be his next. He hasn't a clue about these things.'

'Does anybody?' asked Greenlee, but didn't wait for an answer. 'I can only talk to Grant and sound him out.'

'Well, I hope he's too busy in the States to come over and mess us about.'

'Let's just see, Tom. Let's just see, shall we?'

Virna Todd's magazine interview was no help. She was supposed to be telling the world what it was like being married to a top singer and how glamorous it was. But she was unable to speak with conviction and even the cosmetics applied to the marriage by the journalist failed to disguise the cracks. Of course, all the right things were said, how she was devoted to him, how he was an excellent father and husband, how there was never any trouble between them over his female fans . . .

It was thereabouts that the readers' credulity evaporated.

The protestations of Johnny's faithfulness didn't ring true. And if they were such a united couple, why hadn't the magazine been able to bring them together for a photograph?

Johnny saw the article and smiled enigmatically. 'Well done,' he told Virna, 'very nice.'

Virna had failed, even if the piece was recognition of sorts that she was his wife. She would have to think of something else if she was ever to find peace of mind.

'Do what you like, my love,' said Johnny, breezy as ever. 'The world is yours. I'll pay.'

Virna bridled at this approach. It was the worst thing the great lover could have said. Once more he retreated into his own private space to get away from her. He eagerly took up a last-minute booking for two weeks in Las Vegas, knowing she wouldn't follow him there.

Grant was glad of this; he wanted Johnny to put himself about. He negotiated an even better deal for him than he'd got in Reno. And, further down the line, Mickey was glad too. He'd be able to milk the GPO of more of its profits, line his pocket, and get his own back on life in general.

Virna was furious that Johnny was to be away once more, though what she would have done with him had he been at home she couldn't say.

The taunting of Johnny Todd began with a few practice sessions he was unlikely to become aware of. With nothing else to occupy her days, or nights, Virna began cruising. She went after anything in pants, while Dylan was parked with his nanny.

Delivery boys, truck drivers, policemen on or off duty, all could hardly believe their luck as this mad Englishwoman made for them, caressed their genitals, and allowed them to have their way with her in a variety of positions, mostly pretty basic.

Few of them believed her when she told them who she was. 'I'm Johnny Todd's wife,' she would say as they zipped themselves up and stumbled off, not knowing what had hit them.

'Yes, ma'am,' they would say, thinking this was some deranged fantasy she was imposing on them.

'If you don't believe me, look at this,' she'd say, diving into her handbag and producing a much-pawed copy of the magazine article about herself.

That only served to make her conquests even keener to get away.

But still no word reached Johnny, many miles away, insulated by fame from almost every kind of rumour.

One of the first to hear of Virna's behaviour was Carly Pickering. The British colony in Los Angeles was liable to buzz if one of its members behaved exceptionally. Carly was at Vidal Sassoon when she discovered that the man doing her hair was also from England.

'Small world, eh?' he said. 'Are you in the business?'

'No, just married to it.'

'Meaning?'

'My husband runs something called the Grant Pickering Organization.'

'Oh, 'scuse me, should have guessed by your name. Well, indeed, he *is* the business, isn't he? Very nice, too.'

'Thank you.'

'Now, just remind me – Johnny Todd, doesn't your husband manage him?'

'You're well-informed.'

'We had that Mrs Todd in here once.'

'Virna, yes.'

'You know her?'

'Why? Are you going to dish the dirt?'

'Well, I don't want to tell tales out of school, but we did have a teensy-weensy spot of bother. This Mrs Todd had one of us go do her hair at home. Some people prefer it that way. Anyway, our fella came running back to say she'd gone for him. Trouble was, she'd picked the wrong guy. Hadn't been able to come up to expectations. Terrible business. Anyway, when the others got to hear, they were queueing up to take her on. She made them very happy I believe. They gave her a nickname.'

'What was that?'

'Martini.'

'Martini?'

'Yes, you know, "Any time, any place, anywhere . . ." '

What interesting things you hear at the hairdresser's, Carly thought.

Gradually she received reports of Virna's behaviour from other sources and concluded that they must be true. Carly didn't fancy meeting her after this, but they were due to have a barbecue at the Todd ranch the following weekend.

I must tell Grant, she thought, but something else intervened and she didn't have a chance to warn him that the wife of his top client had obviously flipped her lid.

What intervened was Grant ringing from the office to tell her he was coming home for dinner. That was unusual enough, but he added that he wanted Carly's advice on a business matter. This was most unusual these days. It had been long ago, in Liverpool, that he relied on her taste, judgement, and good sense. Why had he suddenly thought of her again?

Grant jumped out of the Mercedes with a spring in his step, took the stairs from the garage to the porch two at a time, gave Carly a big kiss, and whirled Neville round. He had long ago decided that, never mind Tom Sheridan's claim, Neville was his son. He adored him, and managed somehow to overlook the growing resemblance to Tom. As for the infant Steve, there wasn't a smidgin of doubt, and Grant was devoted to him. Whatever else he might be, Grant was a good father, conscientious and dependable. Everything, in fact, Tom Sheridan would not have been. Carly was perfectly aware of this.

He gave the boys back to Juanita for safe keeping. Then he tapped the parcel he'd brought home with him from the office.

'You won't believe this,' he said. 'You've just got to listen to it.'

'All right, all right,' replied Carly, matter-of-factly, 'drinks first, then dinner, then you tell me.'

'Drinks first, yes. Margueritas please, Gustavo. But I must tell you *now*. I've said pretty rough things about Tom in my time, but he's finally pulled something off. And he's moved to London, at long bloody last.'

'I know.'

'How d'you know?'

'I can't remember how I heard.'

'Anyway, him leaving Liverpool is about the most unlikely thing since God knows what. What's more, he's got himself hitched to Alan Greenlee, who's set him on to writing a musical with Quentin. And *this* is the fruits of their labour.' He tapped two tape boxes and a bound script with the words *'Tutankhamun! – A Musical'* visible through a window on the cover.

Carly was intrigued. 'What does Tom know about Tutan-thing?'

'It's been all the rage in London – the exhibition. It'll soon be on in Washinton DC. It's a *very* good idea for a musical, the hunt for the treasure. There was a curse, too, you know. I have to take my hat off to Alan for bringing Tom and Quentin together. Seems to have worked a treat.'

'Dinner first,' said Carly, firmly, and rang for the Mexicans to bring it in. They had rice with peppers, tomatoes and tortillas. Apricot ice-cream to follow. They went to kiss the boys goodnight and then they listened to the tape right through.

Even with Tom and Quentin singing the songs, there was no doubt the musical had possibilities.

'That's great, really great,' Carly told Grant as the final chord died away. 'They've got a winner there.'

'Not so much of the "they've got". Quentin's songs come through me.'

'But they're Tom's as well, and he won't want you within a million miles.'

'Tough shit. He's got no alternative.'

'Grant, that's not fair!'

'Yes, it is. I'm not letting Greenlee have it all, even if the idea was his.'

'Hmm.'

'I thought I'd bring you in on this, Carly, because I didn't have your help with *Acts of Folly*. Now you approve of this, I'm going to get *really* involved, as I'm perfectly entitled to.'

'They'll put it on in London, will they?'

'*We* will, Carly. Yes, the West End, I expect. Then Broadway. Who knows?'

'Who'll be in it?'

'How about Johnny as Carter?'

'Johnny, an archaeologist? You're joking. He can't even act.'

'We'll see about that. I'm going to make sure my people get involved in this. It'll make up for *Acts of Folly*, and how.'

A thought struck Carly, but she held back from expressing it. She supposed that Grant would find a part for Suzie Paul.

This was exactly the point Grant had reached himself.

CHAPTER 23

Grant was on such a high over the proposal from London that it was impossible to talk to him about anything else, anything that would diminish his mood. So, Carly shrank from telling him the tales about Virna. She told him, however, that she, too, had had an idea. She was completely over her second baby now and was looking for a project on which to focus her attention. Any thoughts she might have of opening a boutique in Beverly Hills she knew would be sat on squarely by her husband, but she had to find something to do.

'Grant,' she said. 'It's almost two years since we got here. What about a party to celebrate?'

'Yes, great idea, but on one condition. You lay it on.'

'Okay by me. Can we hold it here in the garden?'

'Sure. Get a tent. Have the caterers in. The organization'll pay. Oh, and one other condition.'

'What's that?'

'We have a balloon.'

'Only one? We'll have lots, if that's what you want.'

'No, not party balloons, a big balloon – the sort you can go up in. You can have them made in different shapes, like ads. If we had one in the logo –'

'The Flying Finger?'

'Or the Fickle Finger of Fate, as everyone seems to call it, yes.'

'Thy will be done, but I'll need a budget.'

'How about fifty grand. Would that cover it?'

'For Christ's sake, Grant, it'd better.'

During Johnny Todd's two-week engagement at the Main

Event in Las Vegas, he'd had Mickey Clinch working overtime, fetching women he fancied. Half the fun was supposed to be in the chase but Johnny had forgone that pleasure for the near-certainty that Mickey would deliver what he desired. There was still an element of chase involved, even so. He still had to say 'Take your clothes off' to the women who were brought to his door.

Only occasionally did one say 'no' and leave in tears, possibly to have a complex for the rest of her life about refusing Johnny Todd.

Mickey plied his trade briskly, efficiently, wordlessly. Yet his resentment still mounted. It reached such a pitch in Vegas that he was no longer able to sleep and had resorted to tablets to put him out. The distinction between day and night began to blur for him.

He would never have dared express his feelings to Johnny, but he wondered whether he should say something to Grant about what he was being required to do. He had no idea what his boss's reaction would be. Grant might bark back that it was what Mickey was paid to do. The job description 'personal assistant' could cover anything. He might tell Mickey that if he didn't like what he was asked to do, he should go home to Liverpool.

Alone in a still strange land, Mickey was apprehensive of Grant. So he kept on expressing resentment in his own way. At Las Vegas he found another Joseph Noriega.

Hooper Phillips was his name and between them they creamed off a sizeable sum from Johnny's shows. Mickey was aware he was playing with fire, but he felt justified. It was no more than the kind of minor fraud exercised daily by disgruntled employees the world over, the non-business phone calls, the stealing of equipment, from computers to paperclips, the dealing with grudges that no pay-hike or incentive bonus could relieve.

What was more, no one noticed. The Grant Pickering Organization and the local promoters in Vegas continued to get their cream. Who were they to worry that the cream was fractionally thinner than it should have been?

Telexes flowed between the GPO in LA and Alan Greenlee Management in London over the Tutankhamun project. Greenlee found a new excitement in life with planning the show which he'd been so instrumental in setting up. He was gratified that his enthusiasm appeared to be matched by Grant's.

He was gratified, too, that Grant was keen to be involved in producing the show and not just with publishing the compositions of Quentin Saint and Tom Sheridan. Grant might still be associated in some people's minds with a musical flop, but he must have learned a lesson or two from that, and he knew a darn sight more than Alan about musical theatre, which was precisely nothing.

It was becoming obvious that Grant would have to pay a visit to London in order to put the whole project on a more businesslike footing. There was still a long list of questions to be dealt with: about casting, whether to put out an album in advance of the stage presentation, and so on.

Grant promised to make the trip, 'but not before my party, Alan,' he said, over the phone. 'A pity you can't join us. My wife's organizing a big bash. All the Brits'll be there.'

'I'm sorry, too, Grant,' Greenlee oiled graciously. 'May we have a repeat performance for the first night of *King Tut*?'

'Good idea. Let's think about it, Alan.'

Greenlee thought how like a showbiz promise that sounded. Grant had been in LA less than two years, and he was already sounding like a native.

Carly drew up lists of possible guests for the party, about three or four hundred at the first count. There was the staff of the various Pickering companies, mostly based in the

Occidental Tower, and there had to be glamorous British guests from the movie community. She weeded out those who were hostile to Grant's organization in some way, and then had to put a few back in.

Then there was the balloon. Carly managed to find a company which manufactured large inflatable structures in any shape desired. It would be costly, but it would be deductible. After all, a flying advertisement would be seen by many more people than were actually invited to the party.

Jed Vallance, the constructor, was puzzled, and mightily amused at first, thinking Carly wanted a flying finger that pointed vertically, whereas the GPO logo went horizontally.

'Oh, I'm glad of that, lady,' he told Carly. 'Might have been kinda lacking in taste, the other way.'

'Don't worry,' said Carly, 'every dirty crack you can think of has already been made about that finger.'

'Why have a finger at all?'

'It's a talent agency, so it's supposed to represent direction, determination, foresight, and all that. Trouble is, my husband's name being Pickering, everyone thought it was to do with picking his nose! That's why we turned it sideways in the first place.'

'Okay, lady, I get you.'

'How much are we talking about?'

'How'd ya settle for twenty thousand? And that includes inflating and piloting on the day of the party.'

'I think we could agree to that,' smiled Carly, reaching for her cheque book and pen.

If standing had been allowed at the Main Event in Las Vegas, it would have been standing room only for the entire two weeks of Johnny Todd's engagement. It represented the high point of his showbusiness career to date. Not only had he been breaking box-office records, his latest album was at No. 1 in the US charts. In the press he was being described, inevitably, as a showbiz legend. Grant kept up a barrage of full-page advertisements in *Variety*, thanking all and sundry for making everything possible.

So, when Grant was told that Mike Fernandez, General Manager of the Main Event, was on the line, he assumed it was to tell him of fresh triumphs by his client. But it wasn't quite that.

'Mr Pickering,' Fernandez began. 'I thought I'd call you first before I called the cops.'

'I beg your pardon?' Grant, surprised, sounded at his most English and turned away from his view of the LA skyline in order to concentrate.

'You won't thank me,' Fernandez went on, 'but this involves one of yours and one of mine.'

'I can't imagine what you're talking about.'

'Call it fraud, embezzlement, a scam, whatever. The pickle is, we each have an employee who's been sticking his thumb in the pie.'

'For Pete's sake, say what you mean,' barked Grant.

'Okay, your guy, Mickey Clinch. He's Johnny's PA?'

'What's the matter with him?'

Well, I have a ticket-office manager called Hooper Phillips and between them I reckon they've been creaming off five or six K a week while Johnny's been with us.'

'That's a serious charge, Mr Fernandez. I've known Mickey for ten years now. He came with me from England, you know.'

'I dare say, but he's picked up some bad habits. He and Phillips have been working us over.'

'How do you know?'

'They've been selling tickets which don't exist to last-minute showers, putting over-payers on to specially laid tables, and so on. Another of my staff tried to get a ticket at the last minute, got drawn into the scam, and asked for a refund when his guest took ill. That's how we discovered the racket, because they wouldn't give him his money back. We

373

went through the records. Clinch and Phillips came clean.'

'Look, Mr Fernandez, I know this is asking a lot, but don't tell the cops.'

'Now, that's –'

'*Please*. There's no hurry. I'll be on the next plane to Vegas. And I'll bring my cheque book. This is a matter of . . . can I explain when I see you?'

'Mr Pickering, it's been an honour to do business with you and Johnny, and I've no wish to spoil our happy working relationship.'

'So you won't do anything until I get to you?'

'You have my word.'

'Till this evening then. I'll stay over if I may.'

'Be our guest, Mr Pickering.'

'Sure. I'd like that.'

Grant replaced the phone gently and sank back into the depths of his executive chair, once again pondering the LA skyline.

Sod Mickey! What did he need the money for, anyway? He was well paid. He hadn't anything to spend it on, unless he was gambling. Was there some other reason for his behaviour? Only by talking to him direct would Grant find out. He'd been right in his instant request to Fernandez to freeze any action.

Grant called in his secretary.

'Gloria, something's come up. I need to go to Vegas, by the first flight. Book me anything, doesn't have to be first class. Get Berkeley to the door to take me to the airport.'

'But when will you come back, Mr Pickering? What about the party?'

'The party's not till Sunday, that'll be all right. Johnny flies back after his last show tomorrow. We've laid on a jet for him, haven't we?'

Gloria nodded.

'I'll come back with him, then. We'll all be here like we're supposed to be, ready for the big day.'

Grant reached for the phone and called Carly.

'Slight change of plan. I've got to go to Vegas. Mickey's in trouble.'

'Oh?'

'Nothing serious. I mean, he's not dead or anything, but he seems to have a screw loose. I'll come back with Johnny tomorrow night. Won't be with you till after midnight.'

'Okay.'

'Sorry to dump you with the party.'

'No problem, the party was always mine. It'll be even more of a surprise for you, if you're away tomorrow.'

'You're a marvel, Carly. Love you. Can't wait till Sunday.'

'Take care. Oh, by the way, the Finger's arrived. They've laid it out on the big lawn. It's huge, even without the air in it!'

'Wonderful. Now I've got to point the finger at Mickey. I always had my doubts about the size of his brain, but now . . .'

'Be kind, Grant. Don't chew him up too much.'

'We'll see.'

'Does Johnny know?' Grant asked Fernandez as they sat atop the Main Event, knowing full well that the general manager's office was next door, but on a separate elevator, to the Imperial Suite where the singer was even now having his late-afternoon nap.

'I didn't think it right to worry him. I thought I'd wait till you were here.'

'I'm most grateful. He's easily upset by things like this. He relies on Mickey a good deal, you know.'

'I can imagine,' commented Fernandez, wrily. He could indeed.

'What's the position with the law? You have to report the crime?'

'No, but I can't close my eyes to it, if only because I can hardly keep Phillips on, can I?'

'No. On the other hand, I can keep Mickey on, and I fully intend to.'

A pause.

'I suppose you could say nothing's really been stolen,' Fernandez suggested, tentatively, 'because they sold tickets which didn't exist.'

'I see that. Can I make you an offer then, Mr Fernandez? I'd hate to have anything come between us, especially when Johnny's show's been so outstanding.'

'I agree. I support your view.'

'Right then. I'll deal with Mickey, if you don't go to the cops. I'm not sure what I'll do with him. Just want to talk to him and find out why he did it. You'll fire Phillips? No pay-off, just straight dismissal? And I'll pay you to cover what you've lost.'

'But as I said –'

'No, you *have* lost out. You fed people even if they didn't have proper tickets. You'll have to find a new ticket-office chief. I insist on that sort of . . . gift. Then we can call it a day. Do I have your agreement?'

Fernandez smiled from behind his moustache. 'I admire your spirit, Mr Pickering. I wouldn't have done what you're doing for one of my staff.'

'I don't suppose you would. But sentiment comes into it. He may have betrayed me, and I'm angry about that, but I can't turn him out to the wolves. He's kind of vulnerable. And I suppose I owe it to him, to look after him, as I brought him over in the first place.'

'Then shall we call it a day, Mr Pickering? It'll be as you wish. Let us not talk of it ever again. Now, tell me, would you like to see a show tonight?'

Grant wasn't thinking. 'A show?'

'Yes, by one of the great showbusiness legends of our time. It would give me great pleasure if you would be our guest.'

376

'Oh, *him*! You bet. Let's not tell Johnny I'm here. I'll sit in the audience and let him stumble across me.'

'I think that would be very agreeable.'

They shook hands. The pieces had been swept under the carpet.

That night at the Main Event, Johnny Todd gave one of his best-ever performances. He was unperturbed by what had been going on behind his back because he knew nothing of it. Grant and Fernandez sat at a prominent table right in front of the stage.

Johnny had just done his rock 'n' roll medley and swept off the stage to tumultuous applause and buried his bronzed face in a thick towel held out by Mickey. Normally, this would have been the moment for him to alert Mickey to the woman, or women, in the audience he was to chat up, but not that night.

'*Grant's here* . . . he never told me . . .!' These words were gasped breathlessly as Johnny threw the towel back at Mickey and took a sip of the special concoction of brandy, lemon juice and honey with which he lubricated his voice. Mickey made no response.

He knew there could be only one reason why Grant had come to Las Vegas.

When Johnny went out on stage again, Mickey hurried to the spy-hole which enabled him to see the audience. He soon spotted Grant sitting with Fernandez. He felt a chasm open in his stomach. Fernandez must have brought in Grant because of the ticket scam. What would Grant do? Would he sack him?

Johnny now slowed down the tempo of the show by singing a sequence of smoochy ballads. This was the first time he came down off stage to move among the audience. He took the opportunity to look at the talent on offer. To a girl with breasts bursting out of a low-cut frock he asked, 'When are you going to finish off that dress?' It was all thought out beforehand, this series of ad lib quips, but the audience gave each one a wild response. He kissed a few women, pressed the flesh of a few of the men – among them Grant Pickering.

He couldn't decide whether to draw attention to Grant's being there, as he normally did when he saw notables in the audience. He would get them up to take a bow in the spotlight. But he wasn't sure that the name Grant Pickering would mean very much to these people. In the end he turned it into a joke. He thrust the microphone under Grant's chin and asked, 'And where are you from, sir?' He held the microphone away and added, 'You old faggot!'

'Los Angeles,' replied Grant.

'Are you sure, sir? What's that accent you've got there?'

'Well, I was born in Liverpool.'

'Is that Liverpool, England, sir?'

'That's right.'

'And what did you say your name was?'

'I didn't, but it's Grant.'

Fernandez almost choked with laughter.

'And what do you do for a living, Grant. Are you a lawyer?' That was a safe bet with any man in an American audience.

'No, I'm your manager, Johnny. Have you forgotten? When are you going to shut up and sing another song?'

Johnny clapped Grant on the back, gave a signal to his musical director. He, in turn, cued the band into the forceful brass introduction to 'Bridge Over Troubled Water'.

At the end of the set, Johnny once more retreated into the wings.

'Fancy Grant being here, eh, Mickey? No fun tonight.'

Mickey looked back morosely, and said nothing.

After the show, Grant moved slowly backstage through the pass door, with Fernandez still at his side. It was never wise to hurry to the star's dressing room after the show in case he was taking a shower. Or, in Johnny's case, was otherwise engaged.

When they reached it, Grant politely knocked and announced, 'It's the old faggot from Liverpool here.' The door was opened by Mickey. He gave a half-smile to Grant but quickly suppressed it when he saw Fernandez bringing up the rear.

'We need to have a little talk, don't we, Mickey?'

'Anything you say, Grant.'

'Well done, champ!' Grant said to Johnny, throwing his arms round him.

'The Main Event is proud,' Fernandez added. 'You had them eating out of your hand, Mr Todd.'

'Thanks. So what brings you here, boss? Spying on me, eh?' Johnny laughed.

'No. Come to sort out this little bugger.' Grant swung round and pointed accusingly at Mickey.

'What's that?' asked the singer, genuinely not knowing.

'Don't worry, Johnny. It's all been taken care of. Just that our little friend here has unfortunately had his hand in the till.'

Mickey, at that moment, dearly wished for the ground to open up and swallow him.

'Mickey!' Johnny exclaimed. 'I'm surprised at you. He's a good fellow. You know that, Grant.'

Mickey shrank under Johnny's embrace.

'Well, don't you worry about him,' Grant chided. 'It's all taken care of. But we nearly had a scandal on our hands. Mr Fernandez has been most co-operative.'

'I'm grateful to you, Mr Fernandez,' Johnny said piously. 'But I'm still in the dark.'

Mickey could hardly wait to get out of the dressing room.

'I'll talk to him now,' said Grant. 'See you in a minute, Johnny. Want to eat?'

'Sure. A horse.' And he turned to remove the light touches of make up from his face, knocking over a small photograph of Virna and Dylan as he did so.

Grant indicated to Mickey that he should leave the room ahead of him. They tried to talk in the passage, but showgirls on their way home kept brushing past them.

Eventually, they found themselves alone on the stage which twenty minutes before had been ablaze with lights and music. Now, it was a heap of shadows. The auditorium was clear of stragglers and the waiters were clearing away the last debris of a thousand dinners.

'Why did you do it, Mickey?'

Mickey blew out his cheeks like a child, and said nothing.

'Oh, come on, Mickey. You can tell me, can't you? I've just got you off, scot-free. You might have been put inside. Why did you do it?'

'I'm sorry, Grant,' he finally mumbled, but that wasn't an explanation.

'You can't possibly be short of money.'

Mickey shook his head, indicating that he couldn't explain what he'd done. He certainly wasn't going to express his resentment of Johnny's demands, or the resentment he felt at being so close to the massive money-making activities of the Grant Pickering Organization.

'Fernandez is going to fire this Phillips guy,' Grant told him. 'I'm making up the lost money. Don't you think you owe me an explanation?'

That only made matters worse. Grant was adding to the trust Mickey knew he'd already betrayed.

'I'm not going to get you to say anything, am I?'

Mickey shook his head.

'Well, fuck you, sunshine. But I tell you this, Mickey: if there's ever anything else like this, you'll be on the slow boat back to Liverpool, understand? I'm not a fucking charity, you know.'

'Yes,' said Mickey.

'Now, fuck off, and don't spoil the rest of my time here.'

Mickey stood frozen while Grant strode away, snapping

over his shoulder: 'You're still coming to the party?'

Mickey stared back.

'Well, you are. That's an order. I want you there, Carly wants you there, so you'll *be* there, okay?'

Grant went to collect Johnny. They would eat and drink till the small hours while Johnny unwound. Johnny was unable to shed any light on Mickey's behaviour. 'Always seemed such a happy little bugger,' he told Grant.

The date had already changed to Sunday 3 June before Grant was back at Quornford West. He had spent all Saturday by the pool at the Main Event, had taken in both of Johnny's shows in the evening, and flown back to LA with him and a still mute Mickey to arrive in the early hours of Sunday morning.

Carly was fast asleep when he slipped noiselessly into their bedroom. The clothes she was to wear for the party were hanging ready in the closet. She was sleeping soundly, exhausted by the preparations, but Grant would dearly like to have spoken to her.

He took off his clothes and folded them neatly over a chair. Then he got into bed and looked down at the sleeping form of his wife. Most women turned into hags as they got older, but Carly only improved. Motherhood had filled her body out a bit, but not too much. Her skin and hair were better than ever, or as good as money could make them.

Grant wanted her then. Why should he wait? What would it matter? Only a few minutes, then they would both get to sleep without trouble.

Slowly he slipped the silk sheet from her glowing form, lifted her legs apart and started kissing her until she, while half awake, became half aroused. He buried his head between her legs and licked away until he had produced a reaction.

'Oh no, I'm asleep . . .'

381

But Grant wasn't going to be refused. He took her forcibly and quickly came without her.

A minute after, he pulled himself away and soon fell asleep, leaving Carly awake now, disturbed.

So selfish of him, she thought.

So typical of her, he would have thought . . . if he had been thinking.

CHAPTER 24

They were woken by Neville jumping all over them. There was no opportunity to lie in that Sunday morning with the vans containing the caterers, staff and security guards already beginning to arrive by ten o'clock.

At noon sharp, the Flying Finger was inflated by hydrogen burners and the logo, fifty feet wide, lurched over the rooftops, pointing out towards the Pacific, as though detached from the body of some giant explorer.

If people had lost their invitations and directions, they would be able to find their way to Quornford West by following the Finger.

By the time the first guests turned into one of the designated car parks, the whole operation was moving forward like a mighty plan of battle. A spectator at the gate noted the arrival of a Bentley Continental, a Rolls-Royce Continental, a Rolls Phantom, a Rolls Corniche, and six assorted Mercedes and Porsches, all within the first fifteen minutes.

The guests in their summer clothes entered the front door of the mansion and then spilled out into the gardens at the rear where the sprinklers played. They walked among the camellias, oleanders, bougainvilleas and cypresses. They drank in the smell of eucalyptus and orange blossom. And then they plunged into the air-conditioning of the vast pink-and-green-striped marquees. These were filled with tables bearing lobster, salmon, Beluga caviare, cold meats, cheeses, fruit, cakes and puddings.

At the entrance to the first marquee stood Grant and Carly. He wore his white suit, she a dazzling turquoise silk dress that, for once, she hadn't made herself. The guests had to descend a flight of stone steps to reach them. It was rather like entering a TV chat show. Many of the guests were used to that.

A toastmaster took invitations as guests handed them to him, and barked out their names.

'Mr and Mrs Johnny Todd . . .'

'Sir Donald and Lady Wilding . . .'

'Mr Sammy Davis Jnr . . .'

'Mr Mickey Clinch . . .'

Then the guests moved forward to shake hands and kiss Carly and Grant. As they did so, a photographer caught the moment.

'Hi Johnny . . . Virna . . .' A big kiss for her. 'You can't have had more sleep than me,' Grant said to Johnny, 'and you're looking as fresh as a daisy.' It was true. Grant was surprised but gratified that his pet superstar was one of the first to arrive.

'I do what I'm told, you know that,' said Johnny, with a glance towards his wife.

Virna said nothing. Carly gave her an embrace, then added, a trifle formally, 'So glad you could come.'

Grant was already on to the next guests. 'Hope you have a really nice time.'

'Do we get to have a trip in the balloon?' asked Sammy Davis Jnr.

'For you, Sammy, anything.'

'Hi, Mickey. Glad to see you.' Carly leant down and kissed him as though she had no idea what had been going on.

'Hi, luv, thanks,' said Mickey and moved rapidly on, muffing his handshake with Grant.

'Enjoy . . . enjoy . . .' Grant was getting carried away already.

The guests spilled out of the marquees into the garden, having obtained their glasses of vintage champagne. They wanted to look up at the Flying Finger.

'I know the Finger is on Mr Pickering's notepaper,' said Lady Wilding, 'but why d'you think he chose a finger for his lurgi?'

'Logo, darling, logo. There are several reasons, mostly rather rude, but it could be because he wags his finger at people a lot. Or that's what I've been told.'

'Fascinating . . .'

The Preservation Hall Jazz Band of New Orleans had been flown in to provide the entertainment. The six wizened old jazzmen and one woman were seated on a raised platform in the garden. The woman was Billie Pierce who, with her husband De De on cornet, led the ensemble. They were survivors from the very dawn of jazz.

It had been Carly's idea to hire the main musical entertainment from outside Grant's empire. That way there would be no suggestions of favouritism, no jealousy. The band struck up with 'Peanut Vendor'. Much younger stars of the entertainment world stood awestruck at what they heard. Even those members of the Wreckers who were sufficiently together to make it to the party looked on in amazement at these creatures from another world.

Grant and Carly behaved liked royalty, as they were surely entitled to do at their own lavish party. They did not spend much time together but dutifully circulated, each talking to as many guests as possible.

'You seem well and truly settled in,' declared Sir Donald Wilding. 'Quite part of our little community.'

'Oh, yes,' replied Grant. 'No going back now. This is where you have to be in the music business these days. I like it here, anyway.'

'Good, good,' Lady Wilding told him. 'You're doing so well. Where are you from back home?'

Grant wondered whether she was winding him up; surely everyone knew?

'Liverpool, I'm afraid,' he replied, on the defensive slightly.

385

'Oh, really,' Lady Wilding said. 'So many people are!'

Grant moved on, eager to find more congenial company

'Come on, Mickey, you can tell me what's going on.' It was Carly pumping him where Grant had failed. 'Aren't you happy? Would you rather be back home? I'd quite understand if you would.'

'No, it's not that,' said Mickey. This was more explicit than anything he'd said to Grant two nights before.

'I quite often wish I was back in the Pool,' Carly told him. 'You can keep most of this, frankly. I'd much rather be living off chip butties in Liverpool 8 on a wet Monday in November than have all this.' She made a gesture round the mansion.

This encouraged Mickey.

'It's all right, I'm glad of the work. It's interesting.'

'So what is it you don't like, Mickey?'

'I can tell *you*, can I? You won't tell Grant?'

'No, why should I?'

'It's Johnny, you see.'

'Johnny? What's the matter with Johnny? You've known him long enough.'

'I have, but I don't like having to do his dirty work for him.'

Carly looked at the sea of showbusiness talent talking animatedly in front of her and sensed that Mickey felt no more part of it than she did.

'You haven't always felt like this?'

'Just lately I've grown to hate it.'

'Do you want me to have a word with Grant? Or Johnny?'

'No!' Mickey looked disturbed.

Carly made a mental note to do something, whatever Mickey said.

By one thirty almost everyone who was going to arrive had done so. It seemed that all three hundred guests were squeezed into the marquees at once, to enjoy the air-conditioning and to pile their plates high with food. Everyone had a tan, though the English expatriates still lagged in this respect and the Wreckers were as white and pasty as ever.

There was a bank vault's worth of jewellery being worn by the women and what seemed like an equivalent amount of medallions and bracelets worn by the men. The Hollywood women must have been up since dawn doing their make-up. Their husbands, balding, portly, cigar-chomping, were not nearly so appetizing to look at, not unless you were a gold-digger and could X-ray their wallets.

Grant presided over the party with quiet assurance, only shrinking when some American male clapped him on the back and told him how wonderful he was and introduced him to yet another bored and bewildered wife. Though almost everybody was part of 'the business', Carly was still interested to see how they reacted to the presence of celebrities. Back home in England it would be a case of, 'Don't look now, but isn't that . . .?' Here in the States, celebrities were people to be hailed, cheered and applauded without restraint, even at a private party.

Carly added to the celeb-spotting when she fetched her camera and ran off several rolls of film. It might not be quite what was expected of a hostess but she very much wanted to record the occasion by snapping her famous guests in informal poses.

Grant looked hard at the guests, too, especially the women. He was trying to find someone he liked, fancied even, but he didn't. There was an obviousness about the sexuality of these people. In such matters he felt a foreigner still or, worse, a member of another race. It was, as always, the wine which was making him think he ought to feel randy.

The nearest he came to it was when a black girl, he wasn't sure who she was, came into view. He didn't speak to her, didn't introduce himself, just looked on longingly while she flirted with another man. A song-plugger prattled distractingly in Grant's ear.

The girl was wearing a pair of pale blue denims. So tight were they that Grant reckoned she couldn't be wearing anything beneath them. She had the most beautiful rounded rear. Below it, she had shapely thighs and long graceful legs. On her feet she was wearing platform shoes which pushed her knees ever so slightly forward. Grant sighed to himself. What an invention tight jeans were. They could bring water to a man's eyes. He couldn't look away. The sight made him feel happy, sad, nostalgic. He remembered Halo, the one he'd so briskly despatched when Carly came back into his life. He felt a whisper of remorse. He knew he had behaved badly towards Halo, but all was fair in love and war, and she *was* a bit of a bitch.

But what was he doing feeling like this? He was married to Carly, a remarkable woman, mature, exciting, the mother of his children. He must go and be with her, tell her so, reassure himself and her.

She was out in the garden, surrounded by a group of admirers, a fact that Grant could only note and joke about. He took Carly's camera from her and led her away.

'Well, you've done it,' he said with a grin. 'It's marvellous. You got everything just right. I couldn't have done this.'

Carly laughed, pleased by her husband's compliments. Her capability as an organizer hadn't been put to the test since Paradise closed, but there had never been any doubt that it still existed. Since the earliest days, she had been capable of making food, making clothes, of quietly and efficiently doing whatever had to be done. The party was the first occasion in a long while that she had stepped out of the domestic scene and achieved something in public. She was quietly pleased with what she'd done.

But she felt no great need to prove herself. She had this capability, but what was the use? She couldn't see what more she could do to give her life meaning. She was a wife and a mother, and that seemed to be that. Yet the loose end flapped, and now Grant seemed to be hinting she should harness her talent and energy in a more appropriate way. But how?

The one thing he would never suggest was that she join him in the organization and develop her skills there. If Grant had thought it through at all, he would probably have realized he didn't wish to have his wife in the office with him. He still had his secret side, he still liked to do things by himself and then show them to his woman for her approval. And if Carly had gone to work with him, she might have been too good and shown him up.

'Now, love,' she said to him, 'there's someone you've absolutely got to meet.'

'Who is he?'

'It's a she.'

'Do I know her?'

'We'll see.'

She took Grant by the hand and led him through the crowds of people waving 'Hi' and 'Great party' and stood on tiptoe to spot the person in question.

They hadn't shaken hands with everyone at the entrance; there were some late arrivals, and the woman Carly was searching for was one of these.

'There she is.'

Grant didn't need encouraging to look at the small, svelte blonde who weaved towards them, turning heads as she came. She was balancing her food plate and champagne glass precariously in one hand. He thought her face seemed vaguely familiar, but couldn't be sure.

'Well, hi,' he said, going into automatic.

'Now you have to guess who it is,' Carly giggled, the whole thing a girlish joke.

'Have we met before?' he asked, embarrassed. It was his usual chat-up line.

'Yes, we have,' came the reply in a precise English accent.

'You're from England?'

Carly giggled again, tickled by her husband's unease.

'What do you do?' Grant persisted.

'I'm a singer. I'm sorry you didn't know that.'

'Oh, well, I –' He was going to say, 'I meet so many', but stopped himself in time.

'Come on, Grant, you can do better than this,' said Carly. 'I'll give you a clue. You once turned her down at Starfinders.'

Now Grant was squirming. He hated it when he was confronted with past decisions, especially when they involved rejection.

'I give up, you'll have to tell me, but clearly I made a terrible mistake,' he added graciously.

The blonde smiled, flashing beautiful teeth.

'I'm Fawn.'

'Christ al-bloody-mighty! Fawn Flack!'

Carly doubled up with laughter.

It was indeed dumpy Fawn, all the way from Liverpool. The folksinger and would-be star had been brought to the party by a man from a rival talent agency. She was over on the Coast looking for work and had managed to get herself signed up.

'I've an LP out at home,' Fawn told Grant. 'I'm surprised you haven't seen it in the charts.'

'Under your own name?'

'No, just Fawn.'

'Ah, well, I wouldn't have put two and two together.'

Fawn was a new person. She had been given a complete makeover. It wasn't just the teeth. Her granny specs had been replaced by contact lenses, her make-up professionally applied. Her hair had been completely restyled, longer, blonder. She had lost half herself in weight. And, though it wasn't obvious then, she'd also found someone to teach her to sing.

'This is *amazing*,' was all Grant would say. 'So you're still singing?'

'Oh, yes, that's why I'm here. I've got myself an agent. Here he is.' A small Jewish-looking man stepped forward.

'Hi, I'm Harry Emanuel, glad to know you.'

'So there's nothing I can do for you?' Grant said, almost relieved.

'Well, no. Not unless you've got any projects going. Films, musicals, specials, I'll do anything. I'm not choosy!'

'Not just at the moment. But this is wonderful. So you've really made it? I wonder if there's anybody left back home.'

With fulsome promises of further meetings and undying affection, Grant and Carly moved on royally from Fawn and Harry.

'Well, bloody 'ell, who'd have thought it?' Grant whispered to his wife. 'What a renovation job!'

'You were always too hard on Fawn.'

'Oh, come on. She's had a nose job, too, I wouldn't be surprised.'

Johnny Todd had a number of things in common with Grant, apart from their North of England upbringing. There was a curious way in which they copied each other, rather than behaved like rivals. If one had an article of clothing which the other admired, or a gadget, it would only be a day or two before the other quietly obtained one. This was reflected in their private lives, too. It was no coincidence that Johnny's remarriage had followed so close on Grant's wedding. Grant's marriage had been precipitated by Carly's pregnancy, but Johnny's and Virna's had been a straightforward copy, designed to supply

Johnny again with that useful domestic gadget known as a wife. Hence, too, the fact that each man had a mansion and both automatically followed each other's choice of new cars.

Fortunately, they couldn't compete at career level, and Grant wouldn't try and top Johnny's score of extra-marital flings. His dalliance with Suzie Paul had been quite different. Grant was a one-at-a-time man. Johnny's cheery promiscuity was not for him, though he pretended to be amused by it, so long as it caused no trouble. But they were drawn very largely to the same type of woman, whether it be the domestic Carly and Virna for wives, or, as now, the black girl, the vision in tight jeans. Yet, whereas Grant had been satisfied to look on from afar, in a moist, nostalgic way, thinking the girl unachievable, Johnny bowled over and started working his unmistakable charm on her as though she were a woman in an audience he could flirt with publicly and lay privately.

The girl flaunted herself and it wasn't long before Johnny was gazing deep into her eyes, his hand resting on her rump, his mind fuzzily wondering where he could go with her to peel off the skin-tight jeans.

It was not to be. Johnny became conscious of a jabbing on his upper arm. He turned and his face lost most of its smile. It was Virna, at her most harpie-like, saying, 'What's going on here?' She spoke loudly, so everyone could hear. 'You haven't got enough for me, so what do you want with her?'

The black girl allowed herself to be released from Johnny's grasp.

'Come on!' bawled Virna, taking her husband by the arm. 'You've got a date with Carly. She says you're going up in the balloon.'

At this Johnny burst into a grin once more, turned to apologize to the girl, and docilely followed Virna towards where the Flying Finger hovered over its basket, having been brought down to ground level.

Carly greeted Johnny, introduced him to Jed Vallance,

the pilot, and Grant was told to use Carly's camera to take a photograph of the three in the basket before they cast off.

'It's perfectly safe,' Grant called over to Johnny. 'I've put up your insurance.'

Johnny laughed. 'I hope so, man.'

A waiter handed glasses of champagne to the trio.

Then the jets were turned up, the balloon was cast off and, slowly, it rose above the garden, until the shadow of the Finger crossed the pool, where some of the guests were already pushing each other in. It hovered right over Quornford West itself. It was quite something, thought Carly, to be able to look down on your home like this.

As they gained height, other guests tipped out of the tent to stare and point skywards.

Jed Vallance did what he had to do to steer the balloon. It was a brief ascent they were making. They would return within the half-hour, landing back near the house again, with any luck. If not, then out in the scrub, or on someone else's land or, least happily of all, in someone else's pool.

The curiously-shaped balloon edged away from Quornford West and into the smog-tinged sky.

Down on the ground, the Preservation Hall Jazz Band struck up 'St James's Infirmary'. Grant beamed. It was only right that Carly, whose triumph this was, and Johnny, Grant's top artiste, should be the ones to make the first ascent.

Grant was still looking up, shading his eyes against the sun to see Johnny and Carly waving from the basket, when he felt a hand go round his waist and squeeze him. He turned to look at the woman by his side but had already recognized her by the scent. It was Virna.

'They make a fine pair, don't they? Just like you and me.'

Grant was thrown.

'Er, yes,' he replied.

393

'How long'll they be up there?'

'I don't know, twenty minutes, half an hour.'

'Okay, I've got something to show you. Can we go in?'

Grant didn't know what to make of the request. 'If you want to.'

They walked away from the crowd, still craning heavenwards, back through the near-deserted marquees, and into the house. The security men relaxing in the main entrance hall suddenly stood up and hid their cigarettes when they saw Grant approach.

Virna made for the stairs.

'What is it, then?' Grant asked.

'I'll show you.' Virna stretched out and took him by the hand.

Grant felt a tingle of excitement, but didn't allow himself to think what it foreshadowed.

'Where's your bedroom? Is it this one?'

Virna turned the doorknob and found she had correctly identified the master bedroom. The bed with the mirrored headboard loomed large with a white quilt upon it. Through an arch she could see a circular bathtub on a raised platform.

'Lock the door,' she told Grant.

'What is this, Virna?'

She smiled and turned to face him.

'Lock the door, and I'll tell you.'

After Grant had obeyed, he turned back to her. With a quick gesture, Virna removed the silk top of her sundress. She was wearing no bra and her evenly-tanned breasts swung out before her, the nipples already erect.

'There. I told you I had something to show you. It's odd you've never seen them before.'

'What is this, Virna?' he said again, though the answer seemed obvious.

'Nothing. I just thought, seeing how Carly's up there showing Johnny the sights, I might as well show you mine.'

394

'Virna, you're not suggesting they're . . .?'

'With the pilot on board? Of course not, that's not the point. The way Johnny ignores me and chases after any tail he can stick himself into is the point, though. I think it's time I had my share. If he can't spare me any, perhaps you can.'

'Virna, this is most embarrassing . . .'

'I want you to fuck me. No one'll know. It'll serve Johnny right. Come on.'

'I don't think it's a very good idea. I like you very much, Virna, but it'll only spoil everything. And I owe it to Carly . . .'

But as he spoke, Grant could tell his body wasn't listening. He stirred, and back came all the stifled feelings he'd had for Johnny's wife over the years.

Virna advanced and pressed her breasts against his shirt front, nestled her hair against his face, slid her hands down to his slacks and tugged at the belt.

'Come on, Grant. If you don't, I'll just have to rape you.'

'I think you're doing that already.'

Grant lost his footing and toppled backwards on to the bed. Virna moved on top of him.

CHAPTER 25

Mickey Clinch was one of those who had chosen, or been persuaded, to fall in the pool while fully clothed. Several of the younger women had cooled off in this way and were now drying off with their assets exposed to the gaze of the talent scouts who had caught on to this aspect of the afternoon's entertainment.

Mickey was not one to display himself, however, so sat, not far from the pool, wearing soggy T-shirt and jeans.

It was in this forlorn state that George Evans found him and sat down.

'Like a smoke?'

'God, no,' replied Mickey crossly. 'You know I'm not into that.'

'You should be. It'd relax you. Still, how's tricks?'

Mickey confessed to his trouble over the ticket scam in Vegas. George took in the information without comment, certainly with no indication that he'd ever been involved in similar milkings of the Grant Pickering Organization while in the company's service.

'How did Grant take it? You've been forgiven, or you wouldn't be here.'

Mickey nodded.

'That's Grant all over, isn't it? He'd do anything rather than have a row. Always buys himself out of trouble. Still, it's one way, I suppose.'

Mickey grunted, still distracted, and in no way opening up.

George brought out a cigarette paper, rolled it between his fingers, and took grass from a small leather pouch. 'You remember Fawn, the fat one from the Pool?'

'What about her?'

'She's here, but you wouldn't recognize her. Half the size, different colour hair. She's been done over from head to foot. Incredible. Quite fanciable.'

Mickey wasn't interested in the news, only in brooding. George could see there was no way of getting through to him. He couldn't think what to do about it and disappeared into a grass-induced haze. Mickey sat, staring into space, his wet clothes slowly drying.

The distant sound of the Preservation Hall Jazz Band brought him back to consciousness after a few minutes. For a moment he could not think where he was.

'Do you usually fall asleep afterwards?'

Oh God, he was in bed with Virna . . .

Grant panicked and then realized it was too late now to do anything about it. He had fallen for Virna's little plan. Whatever it was – teaching Johnny a lesson, teaching him a lesson for having 'created' Johnny, unfinished business between Grant and Virna – whatever it was, there could be no going back, no pretending it hadn't happened.

'Did you enjoy it?' she asked, persistent still.

'Sure, sure.' Grant knew he mustn't collude with her, otherwise the matter would get totally out of hand. 'Tell me. Are you really saying he's stopped, you know, making love to you?'

'More or less.'

'Well, he's a bloody fool, that's all I can say.'

Virna smiled and relaxed. 'You tell him then,' she said. 'Go on, I dare you.' She lit a cigarette.

'No, Johnny mustn't know, Carly mustn't know. Secret between us. Promise?'

'Promise.' Virna seemed to melt. She had proved something to herself. She wasn't sure what it was, but she had.

They lay in silence, then Virna needed an ashtray.

'We don't have those in here,' Grant told her. 'Neither of us smokes.'

'I'll put it down the john.'

Virna smartly got off the bed and swept into the bathroom. Grant watched her go. She was in very good nick. Johnny didn't know what he was missing . . . and yet, how could one tell other people what to feel about sex? Johnny was probably bored with her, bored with her for being a wife and for always being there. Perhaps she was right to look for her own pleasure where she could find it. Grant didn't see them as the sort of couple to split up. Or, if they ever did, it would be with the most bloody divorce the world had ever known.

'Hey, Grant, come and see.'

'What is it?'

'They're coming back.'

Grant got off the bed and went into the bathroom. Virna was looking at the balloon containing her cuckolded husband and Grant's betrayed wife. Yes, it was unmistakably coming in the direction of the house.

'We'd better get back to the party.'

They dressed quietly and straightened the rumpled bedcover together.

'There,' Virna said with a smile, at last, 'no one would ever know, would they?'

'No,' said Grant, and volunteered a simple straightforward kiss.

The Flying Finger overshot the garden and the basket touched down in scrub, demolishing a few bushes before tilting over and precipitating Johnny, Carly and Jed on to the ground. No one was hurt; the only casualty was the Finger, which now collapsed, shrivelled up, over a tree. It would be the devil of a job to retrieve it without further damage, but it had served its purpose.

Johnny and Carly dusted each other down and climbed back towards Quornford West. They were admitted through a break in the electric fence and greeted with cheers, ever so slightly tinged with derision, as though they'd just completed a first crossing of the Pacific or similar heroic deed.

Grant greeted his wife with a kiss. Virna, to Johnny's surprise, similarly planted a greeting upon her husband's cheek and appeared curiously attentive to his needs.

Towards 3.30 p.m., the Preservation Hall Jazz Band played its last set. Carly suggested to Grant he ought to say a few words, so he went on to the small stage and took the microphone. It was the nearest Grant had been to 'performing' before an audience in a very long while.

He was determined not to be showbiz and schmaltzy. He paid tribute to the elderly, dignified members of the band from New Orleans, thanked everybody for coming, and pointed out that the party was to celebrate the Grant Pickering Organization's second year of operation in the US. It was also a celebration of Johnny Todd's preeminent position in 'the business' which was just wonderful. As he said it, he realized he sounded like an Academy Award winner and told himself to shut up. He was about to put down the microphone when he remembered his duty.

'I'd just like to say one final thank you. This whole day, right down, or up, to the Flying Finger, has been laid on by Carly.' He held out his hand for her to come up and join him on the stage. She did so, he kissed her and gave her a hug. 'In fact,' he went on, 'she's made such a good job of this, I'm sure you'll agree, I think we ought to call it the Grant and Carly Pickering Organization. She's treated the whole thing like a major production. And all I've had to do is approve the budget.'

There were supportive shouts all round.

'So God bless you all. Take care now . . .'

Virna Todd observed this touching tribute with curious pleasure. She had had Grant, got what she wanted, and it wasn't going to end there. Johnny noticed his wife's change of humour and, ignoring the black girl in jeans who had excited him so earlier, he decided he and Virna should leave early, which they did.

He was going to take his wife home and lay her. Virna seemed to have an unmistakable aura of sex about her, the like of which he hadn't sensed for a long time.

As the shadows lengthened in the late afternoon, guests left in twos and threes. Then the caterers moved in and cleared up every speck of rubbish so that Quornford West became as it had been before, as squeaky-clean as Disneyland. The balloon was retrieved, folded up and stored for another day.

Yet still there were hangers-on round the pool. Grant and Carly went over towards them. They were mostly Wreckers who lay around stoned, under a haze of smoke. George was still 'minding' them, and there were various loose women, assorted wives and girl friends, who had become detached from the men who'd brought them to the party.

As ever, Grant felt ill at ease with the Wreckers' line-up, but he tried to make conversation and show willing. More drinks were ordered up for those who needed them.

Suddenly, Grant froze, his stomach fell away. He was staring down the barrel of a gun.

'What the . . .?'

Behind the gun, twitching nervously and sweating visibly, was Mickey Clinch.

Grant asked huskily, 'What is it, Mickey?'

Grant had turned white. Carly saw what was happening and stepped forward without thinking and touched her husband's arm.

'Ha!' laughed Mickey, mirthlessly.

Then he pulled the trigger, the gun still pointing towards Grant's stomach.

'No!'

There was a sharp crack.

Grant could see something emerging from the end of the barrel. But he could feel nothing. If this was being shot, it wasn't too bad . . .

Then he saw what it was.

Out of the barrel had come a small white flag on which was written the word 'BANG!'.

There was a terrible silence, broken after a second by Mickey's uncomfortable laughter. This was taken up nervously by one or two of the onlookers.

'You fucker, Mickey,' cried Grant, deadly serious. 'Give me that thing!'

He tore the pistol out of Mickey's hands and threw it away. It described an arc over the pool and landed in the shrubbery beyond.

'What the hell did you do that for?'

'Only a joke, Grant. Can't you take a joke?'

'No, I fucking well can't.'

'You idiot, Mickey,' Carly chipped in. 'There are some jokes you just don't play, and that's one of them.'

'Get out, Mickey.'

Mickey did not move.

'You heard, Mickey,' Grant bawled. 'And don't bother to come into the office, until you're sent for.'

'Shit.' Mickey spat out the word at no one in particular. He turned and walked miserably away from the pool.

Grant and Carly watched him go while those around them looked on in awkward silence. Then there were mutterings from some placed more distantly, that Grant appeared unable to take a joke.

'Let's go in,' Grant said to Carly.

The party was over.

They didn't set foot outside the house for the rest of the day but sat quietly indoors and played with the children.

Grant was unable to get the shock of the incident out of his mind. It wasn't that he couldn't take a joke, it was the fact that this particular jape came from someone who was prone to instability at the best of times.

'It just shows you can't be nice to people, doesn't it?' Grant said. 'I get him out of the scam and this is all the thanks I get.'

'I tried to get him to talk early on, but he wouldn't give,' said Carly.

'He must have flipped his lid, finally. One thing's certain, I'm not having him around any more.'

'You can't just dump him,' Carly protested. 'Not after all this time.'

'I can, you know. I don't let people do things like that to me once, let alone twice. He doesn't deserve care.'

'You can't send him home. You owe him that, for old times' sake, however badly he's behaved.'

'Well, that's my business,' Grant told her, sharply. 'I'll decide what's to be done with him in due course.'

Carly hated it when Grant talked like this. It was stern, unbending, unforgiving of him.

Grant meant it. Mickey Clinch was never again to receive hospitality at the Pickering mansion. And, although Mickey wasn't fired from the Grant Pickering Organization and continued to draw his salary, he never again set foot in the company offices.

When it was time to turn in after the tiring day, a day full of highs and one almighty low, Carly went into the bedroom and instantly noticed something. Her first thought was that intruders had disturbed it, though nothing was out of place. In any case, the security staff had sealed off private rooms in the house, so that should have been impossible.

Then she realized what it was. There was a faint smell of cigarette smoke and she was sensitive to that. She went into the bathroom and noticed a cigarette butt floating in the lavatory bowl.

'Someone's been smoking in our bedroom. Can you believe it?'

Grant took a deep breath.

'Must have been one of the security men. No one else has been up here.'

'That must be it.' Carly troubled herself no more on the subject.

She read for a little while by the side of her husband, but he soon turned out the light and rolled over. Then Carly put out her light and snuggled down between the sheets. It was odd, she thought sleepily, her pillow gave off a scent just like Virna had worn that day.

Grant wasn't really asleep. He chewed over Mickey's gesture, re-experiencing over and over the icy shock of having a gun turned on him.

What had he unleashed in Mickey when he sorted out his misbehaviour? Grant couldn't begin to fathom it.

Then he started agonizing over the incident with Virna. Had he made a terrible mistake? It had been so totally unexpected, but perhaps she would keep her word and not tell or boast to Johnny about what they'd done. Grant would certainly manage not to tell Carly, but could he trust a woman like Virna who was screwy enough to do it in the first place? If she told Johnny, heaven knows what might happen. He might react irrationally, go off to another agency.

It was all too unpleasant for words and, worst of all, it had spoiled what was supposed to be a day of celebration.

Towards one o'clock in the morning, Carly woke up.

'Grant?' she whispered.

He made no reply, except for a grunt as though in the depths of sleep.

In time, he genuinely slept. He had resolved to leave within the next few days for London. He needed to see how *Tutankhamun!* was coming along. Besides, it was about time he revisited old haunts. And Suzie.

PART THREE

Our sails are loosed and our anchor secure
So I'll bid you goodbye once more.
The Leaving of Liverpool

CHAPTER 26

No sooner was Tom Sheridan's initial draft of the script for *Tutankhamun!* going the rounds of potential producers and backers than the rumour mill began to suggest that the production could well turn out to be as ill-starred as the actual opening of the tomb of Tutankhamun half a century before.

Tom was convinced that he and Quentin had been lumbered because Grant Pickering had taken over from Alan Greenlee as the main producer. 'It's not just that I don't like him and think he's a shit,' he would say, 'but anyone who could put on a turkey like *Acts of Folly* has already had his nine lives and doesn't deserve another go.'

Others were equally unsure of Tom's own contribution to the show. Tom had, after all, only ever written one hit song before, and that was of a completely different kind to the sort of lyrics required for *Tutankhamun!* Nor had Tom ever written a play, or had any other experience of the theatre.

The biggest question mark hung, however, over the subject matter of the piece. Hundreds and thousands of people might have queued for a glimpse of the treasure in Britain and the United States, but would they necessarily want to see a musical about it? And not about the treasure itself, but about the group of dotty archaeologists who dug it up in the twenties, most of whom ended up dead as the celebrated curse took its toll.

On the other hand, the show had two things going for it: Quentin Saint's score was unlike anything he had done in the limited field of the three-minute pop single and was certainly light years ahead of his 'Rhubarb Song'. His facility for playing anything put before him in his days as a rehearsal pianist had led Quentin to an excellent line in parody. But what he wrote was not just pastiche, it was good music in its own right. *Tutankhamun!* was a rounded piece in the newly-emerging rock-opera mould and everyone was confidently predicting that three of the songs, 'Wonderful Things', 'Do You Think That We Should Do It?' and 'One More Year' were potential hits.

The other factor the show had going for it was the scenery. The days when sets had consisted of canvas and wood flats hauled up and down by ropes had begun to give way to electronic and computer-guided systems which would revolutionize the way shows looked on the stage. West End Theatre Corp. had brought in Daniel Calverley, a set designer who enthused over the prospect of constructing an all-purpose set which would change from Highclere Castle (Lord Carnarvon's home) to the offices of *The Times* and to the desert in Alexandria, from the exterior to the interior of King Tut's tomb. All this would happen at the flick of a switch, almost as quickly as cutting from one scene to another on film.

Daniel Calverley also wrestled enthusiastically with the problem of creating a sandstorm that wouldn't bury the orchestra and first dozen rows of stalls in a tomb of their own. The only trouble was, these scenic flourishes were costing as much as all the other elements of the show put together. And there was grave doubt as to whether they would all actually work.

Grant Pickering's flight to London after the unfortunate ending of the big LA party in June 1973 turned out to be but the first of a dozen or more journeys back and forth before the curtain was finally to rise on *Tutankhamum!* three and a half years later.

There was no real reason why he should have become so

involved in the production. He was based in California now, the clients who really interested him were all in the States, and he had suffered the utmost humiliation over his only other venture into the field of stage musicals. But he was snared by the idea of creating a new one on the theme given and was lured on, just as the original treasure-seekers had been drawn to the tomb of Tutankhamun.

He began to see possibilities for getting his own way, leaving his personal mark on the production – in other words, making sure his clients had a slice of the perform-ing action. From the very first performance he'd heard sung on tape by Quentin and Tom he had known that Suzie Paul would be right for the role of Lady Evelyn. It was the main female role, held the top romantic interest, and it was well within her capabilities. In addition, he owed it to her.

More of a problem came with the casting of Howard Carter, the penniless archaeologist whose dream it was to discover the treasure but who depended on Lord Carnarvon for backing. The character's age had been reduced from his mid-fifties to mid-thirties and Tom Sheridan had left open the possibility of Carter's being more working class than had in fact been the case. This was in order to give more drama to his digging into the old aristocrat's pockets and to his pursuit of Lady Evelyn.

Brewster Grieve, a leading Shakespearian director, had been approached, tentatively, with a view to handling the show. He might seem a little up-market for the project but he had experience in dealing with complicated scene changes and was highly regarded.

During one of several working lunches at Luigi's in Covent Garden, Grant raised the question of who should play the role of Howard Carter.

'You know I manage Johnny Todd, don't you?' he said, looking meaningfully at Grieve.

'Yes, of course,' replied Grieve, leaving the hint where it lay.

Grant put it more clearly. 'In the life plan I've drawn up for Johnny, I see it as important he should take in a musical pretty soon.'

Nothing could have been further from Grieve's thoughts. If anything, he saw the role of Carter as being taken by an actor who could sing rather than by a singer who might just be able to act.

'I'm afraid I've not seen him give a dramatic role,' Grieve told Grant airily, to Grant's annoyance. What was all this about 'giving'? Grant wondered. Surely you *played* a role?

It was one of Grieve's unconscious little affectations: he always talked of Olivier 'giving' his Othello, as though it were a gaily-wrapped present. It was a small point, but it seemed to underline the gulf between their two branches of show business.

'I know, but it would be quite something, wouldn't it? I mean, Johnny would fill the theatre even if there wasn't a show.'

'But would his fans enjoy a story about archaeologists, that's the point, isn't it?'

'No reason why not. It's commercial.'

Brewster Grieve took a large mouthful of ratatouille to give himself time to think before going on.

'Do we know whether Mr Todd is even interested?' he asked eventually.

'He and I are very close. He'd love to do it. I mean, he wouldn't be able to do it for very long, six months at most, otherwise he'd have tax problems, but I can assure you he'd leap at it.'

'Hmm.' Grieve took a long swig of red Corvo. 'Is there a chance I could meet Mr Todd?'

'Sure, sure,' Grant said expansively. 'We could fly you to LA. Or Vegas or Reno, wherever he's on.'

410

Grieve was at once flattered and repulsed. He liked the idea of being jetted about at his producer's expense but he was sure Las Vegas wasn't his cup of tea.

There was another uneasy pause. The director was proving difficult. Well, he'd have to watch it, he wasn't even signed up yet. Grant didn't like obstacles, particularly those erected by so-called 'creative' people. If he, as producer, thought Johnny was good for the part, he saw no reason why he should have to haggle with anybody over the decision.

The silence lengthened. Grant played another card. 'Did you have anyone in mind for the role yourself, Mr Grieve?'

At this, Grieve looked up from his plate. 'Well, yes,' he said, putting his hands behind his head and leaning back. 'Have you ever heard of Andrew Farb?'

'Can't say I have. Don't suppose the punters have either.'

'He's been with the RSC and the National. He's got a sort of brooding, intense quality. He'd play a fanatic rather well. They tested him once for the James Bond role, if that's of any interest.'

'And he can sing?'

'Rather well, actually. Strong tenor voice. Could be put through a voice coach.'

'I ought to see him then.'

'I'm sure that can be arranged.'

Then it was time to talk about Suzie Paul and the role of Lady Evelyn. In all the time Grant had been away in LA, his professional interest in Suzie had remained unabated. He was always on the phone to Jan Ferry in London asking to have lists of Suzie's engagements, to receive tapes of her performances. Whatever there may have been between them personally, Grant was as convinced as on the day he'd first heard her sing that she was 'significant talent'. And when *Acts of Folly* temporarily halted Suzie's

411

progress, Grant had felt obliged to see that she would do all right in the end.

The part of Lady Evelyn, in that sense, was the answer to his prayers. It was as though it had been written expressly for her. She was the right age for it and the right class; she was perfect.

The bargaining between producer and director-designate continued like shadow-boxing with very little signed and sealed by the end of lunch, except that Grieve had apparently accepted that there was no arguing over Suzie Paul. Grieve knew her work, saw the logic of casting her, and had no desire to fight that decision. But he was determined Grant wasn't going to win right down the line.

Weeks passed and nothing seemed to happen. Grant was always in Los Angeles whenever Alan or Quentin or Tom or West End Theatre Corp. wanted to settle anything. He was never by his phone when they called from London. On the rare occasions when he phoned them, he had adopted the Californian habit of ignoring the time. He always woke them in the middle of the night when they were too sleepy to get their way with him.

The delays weren't really Grant's fault. Having been locked into an arrangement with West End Theatre Corp., the *Tutankhamun!* producers were obliged to use the Theatre Royal, Drury Lane. But that venue was doing very nicely with a long-running show which seemed unlikely to fold. It was the only theatre large enough for the special effects that were planned, and capable of seating an audience large enough to pay for them.

Grant, impatient as ever, revived the original idea of putting out the music on record to test the water and, with luck, create a demand for the staging of the show. 'After all, it worked for *Jesus Christ Superstar*, why not for us?'

Then the haggling began over who should appear on the

album. Grant immediately asked for Johnny Todd, Suzie Paul and others known to him, but it was at this point that Quentin Saint dug his dainty heels in. Whether he had been leant on by Brewster Grieve was hard to say but Quentin told Grant that, on the record, the music must have priority. Only the right *singers* should be allowed to take part. So, neither Johnny Todd nor Andrew Farb won the Carter role. It went to Ned Alexander, a popular tenor. Suzie Paul sang the part of Lady Evelyn. The rest of the cast was filled with 'proper' singers. Quentin himself even took a cameo role as a newspaper reporter, but that wasn't something he'd do if – no, when – the show was actually staged.

During the recording of the album, Tom Sheridan began to take an interest in Suzie Paul. Grant immediately spotted that there was something going on. In the studio, Tom was always sitting with her, apparently giving her notes about her performance. He was ever eager to bend his lyrics to suit her wishes.

With Grant constantly on the way from one meeting to another, Tom and Suzie were left to themselves for most of the time. Anyway, Grant's interest in Suzie was now supposed to be purely professional. He had more important things to worry about. But in the short time he allowed himself to think about it, he wondered just what Tom and Suzie could possibly see in each other.

Tom knew what he saw in her. She was a very sexy lady, remote and unattainable. That was always a challenge. The more women put him off, the more Tom was driven to pursue them. There was, too, an element of cocking a snook at Grant. Tom knew, as everyone did, that Grant and Suzie had been carrying on together before he went to the US. Whatever the state of the relationship now, Tom saw any playing around with Suzie as, in some way, a means of annoying Grant.

It was not to be, however. Suzie seemed determined to

keep any relationship on a purely business footing. One evening in the studio when Grant had long since departed, Tom seized his chance and asked Suzie out to supper.

'I beg your pardon?' she answered haughtily, with the inbred disdain of several generations of Smith-Powells.

'I just wondered if you'd like a meal, like?'

She knew what he was really asking. 'Oh, please, not that,' she said and laughed, damningly and witheringly.

Tom choked over the response. It contained so many putdowns at once. What did he, a common lad from Liverpool, think he was doing trying to get mixed up with a nob like Suzie? But she'd gone for Grant once, after all. What was the difference?

He muttered 'bitch' under his breath as Suzie swept off in her fur coat to the waiting car. Probably a Grant present, that coat.

The double album of *Tutankhamun!* complete with printed lyrics and background notes was released to only moderate interest in 1975. The record reviewers didn't really know what to make of it. The pop critics searched in vain for the type of Quentin Saint hits they were familiar with. The experts in musicals couldn't pigeon-hole it either, and damned it with faint praise.

It was only when 'Do You Think That We Should Do It?', Suzie's duet with Ned Alexander, was released as a single that interest began to stir. It climbed to No. 8 in the British charts, providing Grant Pickering with much satisfaction. Even Alan Greenlee cheered his ex-wife's success. It was his project, after all.

The sale of the single had a positive effect on the LP. That, too, began gradually but definitely to rise in the charts. At first it appealed to a minority taste. Although it never reached the Top Twenty albums, it stayed solidly in the lower register for several months. It would take even longer before anyone heard the songs sung as they were intended to be, on the stage.

It was only when the single made it to the charts that Suzie began to allow Grant to pay court again. She had taken his departure for the States in 1971 very badly. He had abandoned her, personally and professionally, and it hurt to be treated that way.

Now he was back in London, not permanently to be sure, but very frequently tipping off the flight from LA and, away from home, in need of female company. He had taken to wining and dining Suzie once more, giving her expensive presents and, of course, dangling before her the prospect of real fame and fortune when *Tutankhamun!* eventually opened.

Grant was very concerned as to what Carly would make of this, if she found out. Thank God she still hadn't heard of his one-off with Virna Todd. He loved his wife, of course, but he couldn't sort out what he was really going to do about any of the women in his life.

To begin with, his interest in Suzie, and hers in him, remained professional. Then came the single. It was proof to Suzie that Grant had made up for his earlier failures with regard to her, proof of his continuing faith. Just as sales of the single warmed up the LP, so it had a similar effect on their relationship.

He bought her a flat in St John's Wood. In time, he spent most nights there.

There had been developments, too, at Quornford West. Within a month of the big party in 1973, Virna invited Carly over for lunch at the Todd ranch in Malibu, which was rather more flash than Quornford West. The children of each family were now at school and so well looked after by nannies and security men that it was possible for the two mothers to talk in peace.

Virna made lunch as the cook was ill. It was Caesar salad, inevitably, and a bottle of Californian Chablis which Carly declined in favour of Perrier water. She was still guarding her figure, and well, too.

'Grant away again?' Virna asked, spooning out the salad onto large wooden platters.

'Second time this month.'

'London?'

'The musical again. He's like a little boy with a new toy. He's obsessed by it. I hope it's not another *Acts of Folly*.'

'Johnny says Grant wants him to appear in it.'

'Would he like that?'

'I would. It'd mean we could go home for a visit. California's all very well, but it's hard to get all the, you know, *English* things. I'm desperate for proper tea!'

'God, I know. I'd like to go to Liverpool and have a bag of fish and chips. Or scouse. I've tried making it here, but the vegetables just aren't the same. And Gustavo is always shoving chillis into everything.'

'You ought to tell him not to.'

'You try. I'm hardly allowed in my own kitchen. I tell you, I'm not cut out to have maids and such.'

'Oh, I am. I love bossing them about. I was obviously born to it.'

Virna dived into her handbag and fished out cigarettes and a lighter. Carly watched the ritual.

'Well, I'm pleased to tell you,' Virna went on between puffs, 'things have taken a decided turn for the better with Johnny and me.'

Carly had already guessed as much from Virna's less fraught manner.

'That's good. I'm very glad for you.'

'And you're all right? With Grant?'

'Yes.' There was slight hesitation, but she got it out.

'Well, that's that, then.'

'Except he's always away. Something snapped after the

party. I don't know what it was. He got this enthusiasm for the musical and he's been preoccupied ever since, or so it seems. I hardly ever see him. I sit in Quornford West behind the electric gates and go quietly off my head. Nothing to do except have my hair done and feel lonely. And there's a limit to how often you can have your hair done, isn't there?'

As Carly said this, a vague memory stirred in her about Virna's activities with visiting hairdressers and she wondered if she still got off with them.

'And then again,' she went on, 'I so miss England. Just little things like walking on pavements, and having early-morning mists, not smog. And being near a river. The pool and the ocean just aren't the same.'

'Well, we'll have to find you a walker,' said Virna.

'A walker? What's that?'

'A bloke who can take you out when Grant's not here, but who's trustworthy. Won't jump on you, if you don't want him to, that is.'

'How do you find one? They must be fags or past it.'

'You never know.'

'I'd like to meet some new people. How do I do that, living behind an electric fence, surrounded by security men?'

'Use cunning.'

Virna would have loved to tell Carly that she'd slept with Grant. But she could not, would not, and Carly gave no hint that she knew. Virna went on, mischievously, to test the water.

'Do you ever talk about us, you and Grant, I mean?'

'Well, yes, we often talk about other people. Married couples do, don't they? It's one of the pleasures, pulling other people apart.'

'So that's what you do? What does Grant make of me, d'you think? Does he fancy me at all?'

This was an impossible question for Carly to answer. Whatever she replied could offend.

'Oh, he likes you a lot. Thinks you're wonderful for Johnny.'

Virna was sure from this remark that her secret with Grant was safe.

'What the hell's she doing here?'

'She's in the chorus.'

'How did that happen?'

'I thought she was right. She dances, she sings well, and she doesn't need to black up.'

Grant gave a snort. 'Well, Brewster, I wish you hadn't. I'm not going to make an issue of it, but she's a bad lot, that girl. I know.'

'You've dealt with her before?'

'Ex girlfriend of sorts. Before I married. Bit of a nutcase.'

'I'm sorry,' Brewster Grieve told his producer with a wave of the hand, 'I can't be expected to know everything.'

Halo was a natural to be a member of the dark North African chorus in *Tutankhamun!* But Grant, sitting in the stalls during rehearsals, was taken aback by her reappearance in his life after so long. Her casting was another decision that had been foisted on him without his prior knowledge. He did not approach her.

Tom Sheridan did. He passed in and out of rehearsals, ostensibly to be on hand in case any rewrites were called for. Really he just liked to be in the theatre; he found the atmosphere heady, glamorous and exciting.

In a coffee break, he made a beeline for Halo.

'Tom,' she said, 'where've you bin?'

It was a different woman to the spitting cow he'd failed to bed successfully after that night at Raymond's Revuebar. Perhaps being in proper work was good for her.

'So, you've gone legit?' he smiled.

'Yes, it's great. And I *love* your show, Tom. I didn't know you were so clever.'

Tom didn't know how to take that. He asked her what she was doing for lunch.

'I expect you're going to feed me.'

'You're on.'

He looked forward to taking up with Halo where he'd left off.

CHAPTER 27

The first day of February 1977 was the date fixed for the opening night of *Tutankhamun!* Rehearsals went well and almost everything was in place now. Grant had bowed to the inevitable and not pushed Johnny Todd into the Howard Carter role. Ned Alexander, the singer from the LP, was signed up instead.

Then Grieve threw a wobbly and went back on his agreement to have Suzie as Lady Evelyn. His reasoning was that Suzie, good singer though she was, hadn't sufficient acting ability. The result was a desperate confrontation, with Grant abusing the director for ignoring the publicity value of Suzie in a role she had created on the LP and the hit single.

Grant won. Then he pushed his luck by suggesting another old friend, the reconstituted Fawn Flack, for the part of Lady Evelyn's girlfriend. She had rather a good song in Act Two. Grieve gave in on that, too, but, unfortunately, in the first week of previews, the show played for over three hours. Grieve decided the song was one of the essential cuts. There was no point in Fawn hanging around with nothing to sing, so in the end her whole part was cut. Grant was very upset about this for Fawn's sake, but he lost the battle; she had to go.

So it went on, tempers fraught, confrontations raging, histrionics on and off the stage. Choreographers, orchestrators, dancers and technicians positively queued up to engage in the lowest forms of warfare with the producer, the director, and with each other. Brewster Grieve went through the walking-out stage, and for a while demanded his name be taken off the posters. Then he relented and once more took charge.

The next thing was that a number of previews had to be cancelled when the special scene-changing device jammed. Audiences had to be given their money back.

Grant was better in that sort of crisis. In his opinion, the best way to deal with a recalcitrant machine was to kick it. Trouble was, in the theatre, you couldn't always find what to kick, so you had to cut your losses and say nothing. Every day that went by, Grant was getting better at doing that.

By the first night, the show was finally in good shape and possibly capable of justifying the £150,000 that had been spent on it.

Grant arranged for a Daimler to take him, Carly and Virna to Drury Lane. Carly had insisted on flying in for the first night. She wasn't going to miss this opening for anything. No babies this time. She brought Neville and Steve over from California. Virna came with Dylan. Johnny stayed away.

The Theatre Royal was dwarfed by the *Tutankhamun!* logo. This was an outstretched hand reaching for the famed golden mask of the boy king. The parts of the hand nearest the mask were splashed with gold.

In the foyer, Grant paused to shake hands with Sir Edgar King, the former Conservative minister, and pose for a photograph together.

'Carly, come and meet Sir Edgar,' he called. She came over. 'Sir Edgar is one of the shining knights. He's not only a principal backer of *Tut!*, he's even forgotten *Acts of Folly*.'

'Don't remind me!' Sir Edgar chuckled.

Carly shook his hand. 'You must be very brave,' she told him.

'Or very foolish. No, Mrs Pickering, just quietly confident. There are some shows one instinctively knows will be all right.'

'I hope you didn't say that about *Acts of Folly*.'

'Carly!' Grant chided her.

'Don't you worry about me, my dear,' said Sir Edgar. 'I can look after myself.'

'There's drinks backstage during the interval, Sir Edgar, and you're coming to the party?'

'Wouldn't miss it for the world, dear boy.'

It was hard to imagine the old buffer being disappointed by anything, thought Carly, even losing his money. But he was such a sweetie he deserved to have the show succeed. Carly was very tempted to mention the last time she had encountered Sir Edgar – when Tom Sheridan had punched him on that TV show in Manchester.

Then, abruptly as ever, there he was, Tom Sheridan himself. The same old Tom with his serious smile and his wild hair. Would she never be able to meet him without melting?

'You're looking nice,' was all she could think to say. It was unusual, if not unique, for Tom to be wearing a dinner jacket. Carly couldn't take her eyes off him. Then remembering who she was with, she said, 'You know Virna, of course.'

'Hi,' he said.

'And you know who this is.'

'My God, Neville, you're a big lad.' Tom looked at the boy who was probably his son and ruffled the hair which was so like his own.

'Nervous, Tom?' Grant asked.

'Not arf. Pissing meself.'

'On your own, are you?'

'She's busy tonight.'

'Oh, yes?'

'She's in the show.'

'Not Halo?'

Tom nodded, and Grant laughed.

'Trust you, Tom! Keep her off my back, won't you?'

A round of flashbulbs popping heralded the arrival of Quentin Saint. He was wearing tails, a purple T-shirt and silver sandals.

'Hi, Podge,' said Tom.

'Hello, Podge,' said Grant. 'Well, this is it, eh?'

They joined the audience as it trudged through to the stalls. They took their seats, and, a little later than advertised, the lights dimmed. Grant had been going even greyer with worry during the ten-minute delay while latecomers drifted in. Had the scene-change device stuck even before they started? Had one of the performers not turned up? Had Brewster Grieve staged another walk-out?

All that could be seen at first were pinpricks of light on the orchestra's music stands. The curtain quietly rose. Dim forms moved on the stage, the smell of theatrical make-up wafted out into the auditorium. Then, accompanied by ancient-sounding choral music, the first of Daniel Calverley's stupendous visual effects was gradually revealed.

Even if most people in the audience knew the LP of *Tutankhamun!* backwards, they didn't have any real idea what was going to happen in the stage version. Nothing could have prepared them for what they saw now. As the music rose, so did a crimson sun above a re-creation of the Valley of the Tombs of the Egyptian kings. As the 'Theme of the Boy King' crashed with cymbals and gongs into its infectious four-note motif, to be repeated throughout the show, a slow procession appeared, ancient Egyptians carrying objects into one of the tombs. Across the cyclorama was projected a series of vividly-painted hieroglyphics – lions, cobras, chairs and coffins.

Tom looked hard to see if he could spot Halo in her costume, and finally his eyes lighted on her elegant, familiar form.

The prologue over, there was a sudden switch to the very different splendours of an English stately home in the 1920s. Howard Carter, the fanatical, hot-tempered Egyptologist, was pleading with Lord Carnarvon, his patron, to finance one last season's dig to see if they could locate the tomb of Tutankhamun.

The song 'One Last Chance' reflected this plea but also Carnarvon's own position. He looked back on the frivolous, wasted life of an immensely rich man, and hoped to be allowed 'one last chance' to achieve something recognizable before he died. Carter announced, defiantly, that if Carnarvon withheld the money, he would go back to Egypt and finance it himself.

Grant, sitting in the dark, gripped Carly by the hand. The yearnings of the characters on the stage were feelings he could well understand. He hadn't realized the parallels between the story and his own life until that moment, but now they moved him.

A little later, Carly noticed he lightened his grip on her hand and took it away. That wasn't surprising. On stage now was Suzie Paul, playing Lady Evelyn Herbert, Carnarvon's daughter. She was pleading with her father to assist Carter, poorly disguising her infatuation with the archaeologist. Finally, Carnarvon gave in, and the scene changed back to the Valley of the Kings.

Tom could stand the tension no longer and slipped out of the theatre in search of a drink.

He found a pub nearby where he sat alone with a pint of bitter and worked his way through a half-dozen cigarettes, looking incongruous in his dinner jacket.

He glanced at his watch. Where would they be up to now? Back in the desert with Carter and his 'No. 2', Pecky Callender, probably, singing 'Four Thousand Years'. He had been forced into writing that one. It was felt there should be a song expressing just how old the treasure was. People had no idea. He had wrestled with the problem for days, if not weeks. At last he had come up with lyrics of which he was extremely proud. He reached for another cigarette. Would they be up to the song 'Pharaoh's Curse' yet, the one about the fate of those who would disturb the dead?

Tom looked at his watch again. It was going to be a long

wait until it was all over. They hadn't even reached the interval yet.

It was strange for Carly, sitting next to a husband who had invested so much energy and worry in this project. Strange, and almost unbearable, too, to be sitting next to him as he listened to Suzie Paul singing her heart out as Lady Evelyn.

In fact, Grant was preoccupied with another of his worries at that moment. The real Lady Evelyn was still alive and there had been lawyers' letters to deal with when it had reached her ears that she was to be portrayed on stage. Grant was keeping his fingers crossed that her spies, who no doubt were present, wouldn't be reporting back to her unfavourably. Tom and Quentin had had to juggle with all sorts of facts to make the 'book' of the show, but they believed they'd not exaggerated anything too much, except possibly the 'affair' between Carter and Lady Evelyn.

Now, on stage, as Carter peeped through a hole he had made in the entrance to the tomb and was asked what he had seen, he cried, 'Everywhere the glint of gold . . .' It was the song 'Wonderful Things'. Lord Carnarvon took up the words, and then Lady Evelyn. It was clear that what she saw as a 'wonderful thing' was the Egyptologist in the dashing jodhpurs and broadbrimmed hat.

The quartet of Carter, Carnarvon, Pecky and Evelyn sang 'Do You Think That We Should Do It?' as they debated whether to explore the tomb on their own, or wait for a more formal opening. On that cliff-hanging note, with none of the treasures actually revealed, Act One came to an end.

During the interval, in a small room covered in flock wallpaper, the principal backers and producers gathered for champagne. There was Grant and his party, Alan Greenlee fussing over Quentin Saint and quite unable to express his pleasure at the way things were going, and tight-lipped figures from West End Theatre Corp.

'Well, what do you think?' everyone was asking everyone else.

'Darling, it's wonderful!' said the more ebullient.

The more cautious chose the formula, 'I think it deserves to be a hit, but you just can't tell what those shits in the papers will say about it.'

A Theatre Corp. man brought over a squat, bald American and introduced him to Grant.

'This is Hymie Silverman of the Ambers.'

Grant immediately knew he must stand to attention. The Ambers owned half Broadway.

'Hymie's flown over specially.'

'We are honoured, Mr Silverman,' Grant said. 'I'd heard you were coming, of course. You're enjoying our little show?'

Silverman through years of experience knew not to give away any hint of what he thought.

'Great promise, great promise.'

Did he mean the show had promise in West End terms alone, or was he hinting it would have to be stood on its head and rewritten if it was to work on Broadway?

'You're not going to tell me it's too British in tone, are you? People used to say that about our musicals, but it's just not true any more. This isn't *Salad Days* or *Charlie Girl* or any of that crap. And the story's just as appealing to Americans as it is to Brits. You've had the Tutankhamun exhibition . . .'

Silverman raised his hands to fend off the onslaught.

'Mr Pickering, please. You anticipate. I know all these things. You've got a great little show here, believe me.'

The bell rang and it was time to return for Act Two.

By now, Tom Sheridan was chatting happily to fellow

427

drinkers in the pub. He boasted openly that he had written a musical with Quentin Saint.

'It's very good round about now,' Tom said, playing with his watch and slurring his words. 'You see, Lord Carnarvon and this Carter fellow start –'

'What about the curse?' a drinker interrupted him. 'The curse of the mummy's tomb, wasn't it?'

It was the one thing everybody knew about.

'Ah, well,' began Tom, raising his finger in a schoolmasterly way. 'That comes into it, of course. At the hour of his triumph, Lord Carnarvon dies. And, d'you know, this is true, this bit, when he died all the lights in Cairo went out. And back home, in England, his favourite dog gave a howl, up-ended its legs, and died too.'

He intended his audience to be impressed and in a way they were. The strange circumstances surrounding Tutankhamun's discovery had long ago entered the popular imagination. But would that be enough to ensure the success of the musical?

Inside the Theatre Royal, the tone of the show had switched once more from twenties parody and revue-like sketch to an awesome evocation of that most exciting moment in the history of treasure-seeking.

Brewster Grieve had cracked the problem of how to open out the action when the excavators moved deeper into the four chambers. Beautiful objects, at four or five times actual size, shining with jewels and gold, were reproduced above the players on the stage.

Then when the words of Tutankhamun were deciphered, meaning 'I have seen yesterday, I know tomorrow', the chorus appeared on a separate stage as living hieroglyphics.

Grant looked down at his watch in the dark. It had to be a good stage show or movie for him to be able to sit for very long without looking at his watch. Tonight, apart from the critics worrying about their deadlines, he was the only man in the theatre to do so.

428

The climax of the show came all too soon for most of the audience.

The scene was set for the opening of the actual coffin in which Tutankhamun's mummy lay. The devastating moment had been held back till now – the moment when the golden mask of Tutankhamun was suddenly revealed beneath the coffin lid. The serene, beguiling face of the young king, picked out in jewels and gold, flashed up and dominated the stage, like a sphinx over the desert.

Then a living Tutankhamun appeared and glided wordlessly across the stage before the startled onlookers. There was a reprise of the song 'I Have Seen Yesterday'. Finally, Lady Evelyn sang of her love for Carter (a reprise of 'One Last Chance'), realizing she would never have him. He was in love with the dream of treasure, not her.

The show ended with the stage crowded with the glittering gold displays of treasure from the tomb. In one final coup, the stage was emptied of everyone and everything by a vivid and convincing sandstorm, leaving the Valley of the Kings once more deserted and undisturbed as it had been for four thousand years.

There was the slightest of pauses, then the audience broke into applause and cheers. The critics from the daily papers, impervious to this reaction, were already halfway up the aisles as they rushed to meet their deadlines. Most of the audience appeared to rise to its feet. The cast took curtain call after curtain call.

Carly felt a lump in her throat and soon there were tears streaming down her face. Virna squeezed her, then Grant. Even he had lost his usual control and his heart was thumping.

It was a magic moment for him, vindication of all the faith he had put into the project. It was a triumph sufficient to wipe away all memory of the last time he had tried to achieve this.

Tom Sheridan heard the cheers. He was standing,

marooned on a traffic island, just outside the theatre, a glass of beer in his hand.

There was only one thing bothering him. A brightly-lit sign for the show dominated the front of the theatre. His name as writer of the book and lyrics was prominently displayed along with Quentin Saint's as composer of the music.

But higher up, Tom noted the names of Ned Alexander and Suzie Paul in even larger letters. And even higher the poster said, 'The Grant Pickering Organization in association with Alan Greenlee Management and the West End Theatre Corp. presents . . .'

Grant Pickering's name was larger than any of the others.

Tom wasn't going to change into a producer overnight just to see his name in larger letters, but he did decide, there and then, that he had to succeed as a performer. Then people would believe him when he met them in a pub. Being an unacknowledged writer was not what he'd spent his life working towards.

The feeling was reinforced when a publicity man located Tom outside the theatre and pulled him round to the stage door. Alan Greenlee had carefully lined up Quentin to take a bow, but Quentin had refused to go on without Tom.

The applause was still running after seven or eight minutes when Quentin trotted on stage, pulling Tom uncertainly behind him. Everyone knew who Quentin was, only a few worked out who the good-looking but squiffy figure was by his side. Tom dimly realized this. It was good to have this success, but he knew it wasn't the kind he wanted.

The *Tutankhamun!* first night party had been arranged by Jan Ferry, who still loyally ran the Grant Pickering London office. It was held in a nightclub which had been completely taken over and decorated in gold in accordance with the show's theme.

At last, everyone could relax. The avoiding of eyes, the forced hellos and waves, usually such a part of a theatrical occasion, coupled with an extreme awareness of who is 'in' and who 'out', all evaporated. There was little doubt they had a triumph on their hands.

'Rock-solid, gold-bottomed,' was how Alan Greenlee put it, as though anticipating the following day's headlines.

Then the members of the cast arrived. They looked so much younger, healthier and brighter than the sober-suited money-men and showbusiness moguls. Humbler, too. They could walk on air now. They deserved to.

'Well done, Suzie,' Grant said to his leading lady, cautiously, as Carly stood next to him. 'A star is reborn, if I may say so.' He kissed her gently and received a trace of newly-applied lipstick on his cheek.

His wife noticed. 'I'm Carly,' she said, without bitterness. 'I thought you were wonderful.'

'Thank you,' said Suzie.

Grant behaved less well, obsessed once more with Suzie's beauty and talent. He monopolized her, not letting other admirers get near.

Virna made straight for Ned Alexander and told him he was wonderful. 'My husband wouldn't have been a patch on you. Not right for the role.'

Ned had no idea who Virna was. 'Oh, really?' he said politely. 'I'm sure you're wrong.'

Tom Sheridan, seeing how Grant was smitten with Suzie, went over to rescue Carly. Tom had been sitting on his own, ignored by almost everyone, waiting for Halo to arrive.

'Hello, famous writer,' Carly said. 'How're you feeling?'

'Fantastic!' She could see he was pleasantly inebriated. 'They tell me it was very good,' he burbled.

'Where were you then?'

'Couldn't stand it. Went to the pub.'

'Oh, Tom, you'll never learn.' She patted his knee. 'I like the gear. Suits you.'

In another corner, Alan Greenlee was holding court with Quentin Saint sitting perkily by his side.

'You know what they've been putting in the papers about a curse?' Greenlee was saying. 'Well, fingers crossed and all that, but I reckon we've beaten it. They all said a musical about Tutankhamun wouldn't work, we'd all be struck dead in our beds, but we haven't been, have we?'

'No,' smiled Quentin, happily anticipating the gold he would rake in from royalties if the show ran and ran, as much gold as any dusty archaeologist could recover from an ancient tomb. 'A lot of cock, all that.'

'So, how long do you give it, Podge?'

'Six months. That's as long as I can keep my fingers crossed.'

'Rubbish! This'll still be running two years from now. And on Broadway and round the world.'

'Oh, get thee behind me, Satan,' Quentin mocked.

'Believe me, nothing can stop it now. It's all turned out for the best, hasn't it? Who would have thought? *Who* would have thought?'

The apparent success of *Tutankhamun!* that night was no surprise to Rex Room. After all, he had thought of the idea in the first place.

To be sure, there was scope for disagreement on this point and nowhere more so than in the offices of Alan Greenlee Management. Alan was convinced he himself had thought of the idea. It was Alan who had put together the writing team of Quentin Saint and Tom Sheridan and it was Alan who had entered into the production deal with Grant Pickering, West End Theatre Corp., and the Theatre Royal.

Rex remembered it differently. On the one occasion he had managed to advance his case, just before the first night (to which he had not been invited and for which, therefore, he had to buy his own ticket), Greenlee had been dismissive.

'Oh, come now, dear boy,' he had said. 'That was an idea that could have occurred to anybody. Everybody was talking about Tutankhamun when the exhibition was on. It was an obvious story to tackle, and we were the ones to get there first!'

So, after the first night, Rex had to slink back to his flat in Streatham clutching the glossy souvenir programme he'd shelled out 50p for in the vain hope of finding his name in it. It wasn't there. Not even a 'from an idea by' credit. Rex was quite sick with anger. He tried very hard to rip up the programme, but found the paper too slippery and tough. That made him even more wretched. In the end he scrunched the programme up and stuffed it in the fire, where it gave off the most disgusting smell.

Tutankhamun! played to packed houses from the start – it was the 'hot ticket' – and the show seemed certain to recover its vast production costs and pass into profit quite soon. Rex Room became consumed by bitterness. He wanted to have it out with Greenlee. But Greenlee, despite being his agent, had put up the shutters. When Rex rang, he was always 'with someone', or 'on the other line'.

In any case, it was Greenlee's assistant, Barbara, who dealt with Rex's bookings nowadays. Greenlee had issued a veto on Rex's hanging round the office even before the chip on his shoulder about the musical had fully developed.

So Rex had no outlet for his frustration, no one to express it to. The wound festered. He had been cheated of his just desserts and he wasn't going to let them get away with it.

If Alan Greenlee persisted in fobbing him off, he'd just have to approach someone who really mattered. He would have to see Grant Pickering. After all, it was Grant who had put him in touch with Greenlee as an agent, and Grant would understand. He might even think he owed it to Rex to see him right, for old times' sake. Yes, he would ring and make an appointment to see Grant as soon as he possibly could.

Grant would surely see him right.

CHAPTER 28

It was tempting fate for Carly and Virna to visit Liverpool in a chauffeur-driven Daimler, but that is what they did. Grant said that he had no wish to accompany them, didn't have the time, though he did say there was a small task he'd be most grateful if they'd perform for him.

So, the two showbiz spouses set off up the motorway in the February cold, with Neville, Steve and Dylan in tow. It took almost five hours to reach Liverpool, what with various watering stops at motorway service areas, but at last the city came into view across the Mersey plain.

'There's the cathedral,' Carly pointed out to Virna, who'd never been further north than Watford before, not even to visit Johnny Todd's people in Manchester. 'I mean, the Church of England one. That other thing sticking up, that's the Catholic. "Paddy's Wigwam" they call it.'

'It's not what I thought, all this,' said Virna. 'I expected it to be all coal mines and slag heaps.'

'Well, it's not. If there's one reason I'm glad I was born here, it's because I don't have daft ideas like that. It's a smashing place.'

As the Daimler drew near to the city centre through the more middle-class suburbs, the three boys peered out of the windows at the strange landscape. They had been told, 'This is where the Beatles came from' – information they were still too young to appreciate. In addition, Neville and Steve Pickering, nearly eight and four respectively, knew that Liverpool was where their parents had come from, but they weren't sure what to make of that fact. It was different, it was strange, and it wasn't southern California.

They had chosen, at Carly's insistence, to stay at the

Adelphi Hotel on Lime Street. It was freezing cold in the vast, high rooms, and when Carly phoned down to room service to ask for additional heating, two very Irish chambermaids eventually arrived wheeling a radiator – an iron structure, surely dating from before the First World War and constructed like a dreadnought battleship. It would make no difference to the temperature of the room, Carly knew, just by looking at it, but she gave each of the chambermaids a large tip.

Around teatime, Carly roused the driver and asked him to take them to 23 Lily Street so that Virna could see where she had lived until her mam had died almost nine years before. They were like visiting royalty, and even when Carly thought she recognized a former neighbour, any greeting froze on her lips. Her children looked at the terraced houses and regarded them as American tourists might view Elizabethan cottages in Stratford-upon-Avon.

'Oh God, Virna,' Carly said, 'this was a terrible idea. I couldn't possibly come back to this. I've been spoiled. We have everything in LA, don't we? None of this belongs to me now.'

'I love it,' Virna reassured her. 'It's certainly different to anything I ever knew.'

That helped, and when the boys were tucked up in bed at the hotel, and the chauffeur had been given the evening off, Virna and Carly slipped out into the city and tried to crawl back towards the way things used to be.

Their disguise was not entirely successful. They dressed down, wore jeans and sweaters, but they couldn't lose their California sheen. Their jeans were far too smart and well cut. Carly's hair was expensively streaked, and Virna couldn't manage to remove her diamond ring which must have cost Johnny what some Liverpudlians earned in a whole year. She had to remember to keep her other hand over it.

They went in the pubs, were chatted up by young men

who fancied a bit of skirt but who were wary of the gloss upon these two women. Other men were puzzled by Carly's accent, which she laid on rather. Who were these women? On the game or summat?

Carly took Virna by the hand, and showed her where the Cavern used to be.

'You really came here?'

' 'Course I did, lots of times. That's where I first met Grant and Tom. The same day.'

'What happened?'

Carly sighed. 'Oh, Tom was impulsive, marvellous, mad, as he still is. He threw himself at me, and I fell for him straight off. Grant didn't dare, and stood silently fancying me. He only found me afterwards by chance. I was serving in a shoe shop round the corner and he came in to buy some boots or winkle-pickers, I can't remember which. That's how it all started.'

'What happened to the Cavern?'

'They said it had to go because they were building an underground railway, but I'm sure they didn't really have to touch it. I'd love it if it was still here.'

They went to more pubs, drinking and laughing, a couple of women who could just about pass as a pair of Liverpool judies the more they drank.

'You know something,' Virna told Carly, shrewdly, 'I don't see Grant fitting into all this.'

'Well, he didn't,' Carly agreed. 'He was, you know, a bit on the posh side. Lived over on the Wirral, not *uz* at all. But he sort of got involved with this group, the Offbeats, the ones who backed Johnny at first, and started managing them. The rest is history, and all that.'

'Amazing,' said Virna. 'I wish I'd been part of it.'

'Bet you don't really. It was a bit desperate at the time, I can tell you. It's only now that it's become kind of romantic. Now you've got buses taking tourists round on Beatles tours. I ask you!'

They ended up at the Pier Head, looking out through the night down the wide, bleak river to the bay and the distant sea while the wind whipped up their hair. There was a dark smell of mud and water. Beyond that, Carly smelt old smells, of grain warehouses, of cigarettes and beer in pubs, and she tried to put the memories aside.

Virna noticed and held her hand. She thought she understood. It was a small miracle in its way, what had happened to Grant and Carly. They had gone so far from this place; maybe it hadn't been such a good idea to return.

Next day, the Daimler took them out to Waterloo. Grant had asked Carly to settle an old, old debt for him.

There was no guarantee that Old Trevor was alive but Carly found his name was still in the phone book and decided to turn up unannounced. Virna took the boys off for a walk along the sands so Carly could visit the old man on her own.

She turned from the sea front and walked up the path. The garden was sadly in need of care, but people had to do it for themselves round here. No Spanish gardeners, no sprinklers, for them.

'Hello,' she said to the old man who shuffled out to open the door. 'D'you remember me? I'm Carly Pickering. Grant asked me to look you up.'

A gleam came into the old man's eye as he held the door between forefinger and gnarled thumb.

'You'd better come in, lass, and have a cup of tea.'

Entering the old man's den was like going home for Carly. It was what her own home might have been had her mother still been alive. There was a seediness, a clutter, such as the old often surround themselves with. There were yellowing newspapers, saved for long-forgotten reasons; objects stood within handy reach on small tables – so many tables it was almost impossible to move.

Old Trevor said nothing until he had produced a pot of tea and opened the biscuit tin.

'So you sailed away to Californ-i-a?' he smiled.

'Yes, it's been a long time.'

'Well, let's have a look at you. Not too bad, either.'

Carly blushed. It was the kind of thing they'd say in these parts, but she was no longer used to it.

'You haven't got a shop, then?'

'No, but I haven't forgotten how you helped me out.'

'I suppose Grant's got so much, you don't need to now?'

'There's something in that, yes.'

'He's not doing so bad, is he? I read bits in the paper about him. *Tutankhamun!* now.'

'Yes, not so bad. He asked me to come and see you and say he's very, very sorry but he couldn't come himself and that he's very, very sorry this has taken so long but he promised you he'd repay the money you lent him for Starfinders when he had his first success on the stage. Well, he just has.'

She opened her Gucci handbag and produced a cream vellum envelope which she handed to the old man.

Old Trevor reached for his glasses and applied them shakily to his nose. Carly noticed they were held together with Elastoplast. His skin was parched and yellow, his eyes weak and pink. After a pause, he looked up and said, 'Daft booger. There was no need.'

'I know. But if he says something, he sticks to it. Slow, but honest, that's Grant.'

Old Trevor seemed reluctant to accept the money.

'You gave Grant the money when he was desperate. A hundred pound. It's been owing you all this time.'

'Aye, as if I needed it. What use is this to me?' He held out the cheque.

'A hundred pound was worth something then,' Carly went on.

'But he's wrote a cheque for a thousand.'

'Well . . .' Carly shrugged. 'You had faith in him and he just wants you to know he hasn't forgotten.'

'He never comes to Liverpool these days?'

Carly shook her head, knowing this wasn't strictly true. He'd been when Suzie Paul was appearing at the theatre.

'Pity. I'd like to shake him by the hand. He's done very well for himself, ain't he? Mind you, his mum's not best pleased.'

'Ah no,' Carly nodded, 'you could be right there.'

Indeed, Grant had also asked Carly to pay a visit to his mother and father and show them the grandchildren they'd never seen. Grant's generosity and affection were disbursed with calculated favour, but at least he had made an old man happy.

Next morning, the boys were noisy and objectionable all over the Adelphi breakfast room, but it was largely empty, except for a few commercial travellers, so what did it matter?

Virna smoked and read the *Daily Express*.

'No comment,' she said, handing it across to Carly, the paper folded at a particular page.

Carly knew it would be unpleasant news. How typical it should be Virna who handed it to her.

The gossip column reported:

It's a showbiz rule that the leading man falls for his leading lady. If they're playing Romeo and Juliet, so much the better, but few stage romances are quite so appropriate as that between blond chanteuse Suzie Paul and ruggedly handsome Ned Alexander, twin stars of the million-pound blockbusting musical *Tutankhamun!*

In the show, Suzie plays an aristocratic gel who pants softly across the desert in pursuit of fanatic archaeologist Howard Carter. Finally, she realizes he's a mummy's boy and not for her. In real life, the sandal appears to be on the other foot. It is father of four Ned, long-estranged from Brit, his Swedish designer wife, who has been doing the panting after his leading lady.

He should tread carefully. Suzie, 27, used to be the live-in love of *Tut*'s millionaire producer, Grant Pickering, 38, who is unlikely to look kindly on insubordinate behaviour from a mere cast member when it comes to contract renewal time. Will Ned, 32, survive the fabled producer's curse? Watch this space . . .'

'How about that then?' Virna asked mischievously.

Carly smiled wanly. 'It's publicity. That's the sort of silly thing they get up to. As if they needed it . . .'

Grant was enjoying his London success. He was squatting in Jan Ferry's office, dealing with any problems that had to be dealt with, but was uplifted still by the glowing reviews *Tutankhamun!* had received. He had anticipated the worst and harvested the best.

Outside the Theatre Royal, Drury Lane, the press notices had been pasted up with only slight cosmetic editing: 'Brilliant' . . . 'A golden evening's entertainment' . . . 'I beg you to see this show' . . . 'The musical of the century on the treasure of the century'. It was extraordinary how co-operative the gentlemen of the press could be in providing quotable remarks. It was as if they enjoyed seeing their words and their names up in lights just as much as the actors.

Jan Ferry had delicately handed Grant a photocopy of the other kind of publicity, such as was contained in the *Express* piece. He hadn't blinked, merely muttered matter-of-factly, 'Absolute crap!'

Much more irritating was the arrival in the office later that day of a real malcontent. Grant tried to make the best of it.

'Rex! Well, I never!' he exclaimed expansively as the comedian, ex-client and old acquaintance was waved into Jan's office. 'And what can I do for you, old son?'

Rex was in no mood to be patronized. He quickly explained the grudge which had kept him awake since the brilliant opening of *Tutankhamun!*

'I think you owe me something, Grant.'

'Who does, Rex?'

'Greenlee, and the lot of you. It was my idea, you know.'

'What *are* you talking about?'

'There's no doubt about it. I thought of it first, I can tell you the date even, first week of January '73. I'd been to see the exhibition and I told Alan Greenlee what a wonderful idea it would be for a musical. He stole the idea.'

'Now, Rex,' Grant began carefully, seeing how overwrought the comedian was, 'let me get this straight. I was always under the impression it was Alan's idea –'

'He's a liar!'

'Just a moment, Rex, let's talk this through. I first heard about it from Alan after he'd brought Quentin and Tom in on it. He came to me because I publish Quentin's songs.'

'The shit!' Rex stared straight in front of him. 'It's worse than that. Tom would never have been involved if I hadn't put Alan on to him. Put them in touch, I did. Happened to meet Tom on the Tube, gave him Alan's number, and next thing I know they'd stolen my idea.'

'Rex, let me tell you a few of the facts of life.'

Grant tried to be conciliatory. He'd known Rex for a long time and he felt a certain obligation to help someone who came from the same background as he did.

'I believe you, Rex. I'm sure you did give the idea to Alan Greenlee. He's never had an idea in his life, though don't quote me on that. But there's no copyright in ideas. This business is full of people stealing. Even *comedians* have been known to steal off each other.'

Rex looked at his shoes.

'Hell,' Grant went on forcefully, '*Tut!* wasn't my idea but I've ended up producing the damn thing. You may have been used, Rex, but you've not been cheated. It might have been different if you'd come up with a concept for the show, if you'd written a scenario, but just the idea – well, who's to say? Ideas often occur to more than one person at the same time.'

Rex wasn't soothed. 'But I've seen it on films and things, "Based on an idea by . . ." and things like that.'

'True, but that has to be negotiated. It's not there out of any nice sense of obligation. Now, in the States, it's much worse. They have what are called "spoiling actions". If you have a hit show or movie over there – even if you just *invent* something and it sells – as sure as night follows day, some guy with a lawyer behind him will come along saying, "It was my idea, I want a cut".'

'Frankly, I'm disappointed.' Rex choked out the words. He knew he was presenting a pathetic, shuffling figure and he hated doing that. A comedian's success depended on his appearing confident, brisk, on top of everything, incapable of being taken for a ride by the world. And here he was, quite the opposite of that.

Rex had the choice. He could spend the rest of his life telling people he'd been hard done by. He could be 'The Man Who Had the Idea for *Tutankhamun!* But Never Made a Penny Out of It'. He could make a career out of it, like 'The Man Who Gave the Beatles Away'. Or he could insist on the score being settled. The issue had assumed such irrational proportions in his mind that he considered this was the only road open to him.

'I thought you'd be able to help me, Grant, but obviously you're not going to. So I'll have to do it on my own. I'll go and see that bugger Greenlee again, make him see sense.'

Grant stood up to see him out. 'Don't do anything stupid, Rex. It's just not worth it.'

The comedian grunted and left.

Grant raised his hands in a hopeless gesture to Jan Ferry who had listened to Rex's complaint without intervening. Now she said, 'I don't expect we've heard the last of Mr Room.'

'Pathetic thing that he is,' said Grant.

Within minutes, he was deep in his papers again, Rex completely forgotten.

Whatever Grant might say, the affair between the two stars of *Tutankhamun!* wasn't wholly a figment of a publicity man's imagination, though the romance between Ned Alexander and Suzie Paul was a trifle stage-managed and it fell somewhat short of full-blooded passion. It was simply what often happened between leading performers in shows and films.

The love-plant was well watered. Every night, Ned and Suzie had to act being in love, they had to sing to each other. They saw each other dazzlingly made-up, in circumstances strong with romance – from the wings, say, beautifully lit, or with haunting music in the air. It was difficult to tell where the illusion ended and real life began.

So, there were fumblings and kisses, long hours before and between shows spent idly chattering. And Suzie was intrigued by Ned. He was so different from the men in suits she'd known, like Grant and Alan, who always appeared so ungainly next to actors. Ned was boyishly handsome, self-contained, dashing. With Alan and Grant, Suzie always felt that most of whatever attraction they had lay elsewhere, in their power, in their bank accounts. But with Ned, what was there was *him*, his well-honed body, his voice, his spirit.

Ned, for his part, was more directly smitten by Suzie. She was glamorous. She was born to be in the spotlight, an object of admiration. He was slightly dazzled by her.

The publicity man did nothing to discourage the press

from running the story. It could hardly help the show do any better at the box office, where it was booked out solidly for the next six months, but it wouldn't do any harm either.

Charles Hampden, who played the part of Lord Carnarvon, was a veteran actor, in his seventies now, and a wise old bird. After reading the piece in the *Express*, he cautioned Ned.

'Take care, my boy,' he said, 'you're playing with matches. Suzie's an absolute sweetie, I know, but she's forbidden fruit, if you take my meaning. You'll do yourself a nasty injury if our lord and master doesn't like what you're up to. And he certainly won't like reading about it in the papers.'

Ned was indignant. 'Just because he's running the show doesn't mean he can run our lives, too.'

'But that's where you're wrong, dear Neddie. It means precisely that. The producer has first pick. Always has done, always will. And he's a powerful man. If he doesn't want you handling the goods, he could do you harm.'

'I won't let him. People can't behave like that. Anyway, he'll soon go back to America and leave us alone.'

'Maybe, and you'll frolic with Suzie until your contract's not renewed. Don't be such a foolish boy. And what about Broadway? Do you think he'll want you there if you've been putting it over with his girlfriend? Come off it, sweetie.'

'I expect the damage is done, so why worry? I'll let things take their course.'

Grant did not in fact think too highly of Ned in the show, thought him rather effete, wasn't totally convinced that the actor's masculinity was one hundred per cent, never mind the 'rugged good looks'. He still felt Johnny Todd would have been better in the part. But he decided not to make a fuss. Ned could have his schoolboy infatuation with Suzie. The publicity would do no harm. It took the heat off him as far as Carly was concerned, and it might keep Suzie quiet, too.

Grant was perfectly capable of being generous when it suited him.

The immediate effect of the gossip on Carly during her visit to Liverpool was to harden her resolve to visit Grant's parents. It was part of her essential good nature that she was uncomfortable with unfulfilled obligations and couldn't bear family feuds. She had never been able to get to the bottom of the long estrangement between Grant and his parents, her in-laws. 'Estrangement' was perhaps too strong a word; the relationship had been allowed to lapse.

'It all goes back to when we were starting out,' she told Virna. 'They were very possessive of Grant, his mum and dad, him being the only kid, you know, like me. They didn't encourage his music. Not surprising, really, when he didn't have any talent. But they didn't like him getting into the scene. Thought it was all disgusting and immoral. Then they got word he was going out with me and – me being Catholic – that was the end.'

'God, was that the reason? I don't blame Grant for not putting up with that.'

'Any road, he cut himself off from them. He got successful, and I s'pose he thought he couldn't go back. Then there was our wedding.'

'They were there, weren't they?'

'Oh, yes. He sent a car for them. But they might as well not have been. And they've never seen Neville and Steve.'

'Do you send Christmas cards, or anything?'

'I do, though I'm not sure Grant would. So that's the way it is. But I think we ought to go and see them. The boys should meet their grandparents, specially as there's none on my side. And Mr and Mrs Pickering must be interested in their own grandchildren, mustn't they?'

'Search me.' Virna shrugged. 'Do you want me and Dylan to come?'

'If you don't mind. Back me up!'

Carly was soon talking to her father-in-law on the phone, having tracked down his new number. His wife hadn't been well, he explained, and they'd moved to a small flat but, yes, he supposed they'd be glad to see Carly and the boys.

'I've got a friend with me from Los Angeles, is that all right?'

'Oh, yes, we'd like to meet him,' said Ted Pickering.

'No, it's not a him, it's a her, the wife of Johnny Todd. You know, *Johnny Todd*?'

'That'd be interesting. We'd be pleased to meet her, yes.'

Carly couldn't tell whether her father-in-law knew who Johnny Todd was.

The Daimler was sent for, Neville and Steve were primed as to whom they were going to meet, and the expedition set off to Hoylake, through the Mersey tunnel, in time for tea.

Mr and Mrs Pickering lived modestly, it was clear, but had gone to a small amount of trouble for their guests. Mr Pickering had bought a Swiss roll and a packet of ginger biscuits. While he dithered about making the tea, his wife sat immobile in her chair. She received Carly graciously and unbent sufficiently to kiss her grandsons and even Dylan Todd who'd gone along for the ride. She seemed visibly surprised that 'that woman', whom Grant had married and who was, of course, a Roman Catholic, had become so presentable. She was unable, either, to hide her curiosity regarding the boys. Carly noticed she was more taken with Steve than Neville. Probable because he looked more like Grant.

The boys quickly demolished the Swiss roll and soon became bored; they were set in front of the television to keep them quiet.

The purpose of the visit was never stated. They were

curious, these family silences. In Virna's own family, it was literal silence. Her mother hadn't spoken to her father for twelve years. This followed a dispute now lost in the mists and, anyway, always inexplicable. Quite how her parents managed to live like this under the same roof was equally inexplicable, but so they did. Other people's parents were easier to like. Virna liked Mr Pickering, especially. He reminded her of Grant.

Grant was genuinely pleased that the old wound had been tended, especially as he hadn't had to do it himself.

'How were they? Miserable as ever?'

'They were very nice,' Carly insisted. 'And they were pleased to see the boys.'

'As long as I don't have to go and prostrate myself and ask forgiveness.'

'Of course not.'

'Well, thank you.' He suddenly took her in his arms and hugged her as he hadn't done for a long time.

'How did Virna enjoy it?' He loosened his hold on his wife.

'She was curious about Liverpool, but her parents are even worse than Ted and May, what with their not talking, so I think she quite enjoyed meeting yours. Mind you, like she said, other people's parents are always easier to like than your own.'

'There are exceptions. Your mam was a bloody miracle.'

'Well, that was one of the love affairs of the century, of course, you and her.'

Grant laughed, and then teased her because she had pronounced the 'h' in 'her'.

' "You and her," eh? Gerring all posh now, are yer? What's wrong with "you an' 'er"?'

'Oh, gerroff, Grant!'

It had been a slow, almost imperceptible process, but both of them had grown away from Liverpool.

He changed the subject. 'Did you hear about Suzie and Ned?'

'Yeh, saw it in the paper.'

'People are so obvious, aren't they?'

'There's something in it?'

'Oh yes, but with actors the real surprise is when they don't!'

Grant chuckled and Carly wondered what to make of his good spirits. Still, she wouldn't be able to get at him over Suzie if the star of *Tutankhamun!* appeared to be busy elsewhere.

CHAPTER 29

Soon it was time for Carly, Virna and the three boys to return to LA. They had just settled into their seats on the Pan-Am flight, ready for the long haul and rather dreading it, when Virna spotted a passenger they both knew.

'I say,' she said, nudging Carly, 'isn't that Tom?'

Carly looked back. 'Christ, yes. Hey, Tom!'

Tom Sheridan looked up and smiled, pleased as ever to see her. They were separated by several rows and had their seat-belts on.

'Talk to you later.'

When the time came, Tom assured Carly he really *wasn't* following her.

'Are you coming to LA?'

'No, just New York.'

'What's on there?'

'Going to spend my ill-gotten gains.'

'Making lots, are yer?'

'Everywhere the glint of gold! I can't believe the cheque I get each week. It's oil, Carly.'

'I'm glad for you, Tom. At last! You're looking really well, too.' Carly's delight in his changed appearance was obvious.

'Yeh, success is good for me! Pity I had to wait so fucking long for it!'

'Is it true you're doing another show with Quentin?'

'Doubt it. Who told you that?'

'I don't know. You haven't fallen out with him?'

'I never really fell in with him. We were thrown together, we did what we had to do to make a baby, but that doesn't mean it's for ever. Any road, I hate working with other people.'

'So what will you do next?' Carly's eyes shone. Virna noticed how happy she looked in his company.

'I've decided it's got to be performing. Writing's all very well, but it's the singers get the fuss made of them. Ask Virna, she should know.'

'There's a lot of competition.'

'I'm not trying to be Johnny Todd. There's room for both of us.'

'Is that why you're going to New York?'

'Yes. Through *Tut!* I've met various people in the record business, so I'm going to see about an album, me singing my own songs. I threaten to do a cover version of "Tantalizing" if you don't buy me off!'

'Oh, Tom.' Carly blushed at the thought. 'So, Alan's looking after you, is he? He set this up?'

'He helped, yes. He's supportive. Better than some I could mention.'

'Won't you ever forgive Grant?'

'Maybe one day. First, I just want to *show* him, that's all.'

When Tom was back in his seat, Virna told Carly everything she wanted to hear about her first love. How wonderful he was, how sexy, how clever. Quite shamelessly, she stirred up Carly's affection for Neville's true father.

'I fancy him too, you know,' Virna added. 'He can pop out of his pants any day.'

'Well, not on the plane, please. I've never believed that mile-high stuff. Completely impractical. Besides, you're supposed to be a respectable married woman.'

'Ah, well, there you're wrong.'

Carly already knew that, and made no comment.

As the plane flew westwards, Carly sank into a reverie about the man she'd once rejected. She could hardly believe how he'd been improved by success. He looked handsomer than ever, as Virna had unfortunately noticed. He wasn't ageing like the rest of them. Did staying single do that for you? Whatever it was, thoughts of Tom danced in Carly's mind, and the sensation was not unpleasing. It would be lovely if she could see him from time to time. Otherwise, just knowing he would be there, in the same country at least, was curiously comforting.

Investors in *Tutankhamun!* soon had a return on their money. The risk had been spread among about a hundred people. Sir Edgar King had had his confidence in the project vindicated. Grant Pickering and Alan Greenlee saw their personal stakes bloom handsomely. Both their production companies did well, too, and Paradise Street Songs raked in the publishing royalties to pass on to Quentin and Tom. It was all very agreeable, and such a long way from the *Acts of Folly* agony.

There was a contrast in the degree of satisfaction that Alan and Grant allowed themselves to express. Grant was a worrier at the best of times and didn't allow himself the luxury of too much content. He had so many irons in the fire, he hadn't time to indulge in complacency anyway. He was already thinking ahead to Broadway.

Alan Greenlee was determined to enjoy his success. After all, he had put the show together. Never mind that, one way or another, Grant was taking a bigger share. Never mind if Quentin and Tom's royalties went through Grant. Never mind that Grant took fifteen – or was it twenty? – per cent of Suzie Paul's earnings. What's past was past. Nothing should interfere with his pleasure in the achievement.

Rex Room thought otherwise. He was still making an almost daily nuisance of himself. Greenlee had regretted taking Rex off Grant's hands long before this. It hadn't been a good decision. Rex produced only a trickle of income for Alan Greenlee Management. His earnings as a comedian were far from the top rate and his agent was only on ten per cent.

Now there was his preposterous claim of dreaming up *Tutankhamun!* After so long Greenlee couldn't remember how the idea had first arisen. It was quite possible that Rex had first mentioned it, but Greenlee certainly wasn't going to admit that possibility now. Besides, it didn't matter if Rex had or Rex hadn't. He had no claim.

But the matter sat upon Greenlee's conscience. He could never quite banish his uneasy feelings on the matter. He kept postponing any move to resolve the problem, but he began to think that something might have to be done. He was still Rex's agent and couldn't just sever all contact with the man, however much he might be able to channel day-to-day contact into the hands of his assistant.

Then Greenlee received an unexpectedly polite request from Rex to come and see him perform at a charity evening. Showbiz folk wore their hearts on their sleeves and were always eager to help deserving causes. Greenlee recognized an opportunity to make a conciliatory gesture. He hadn't seen Rex's act for a long time, either, so he said he'd go, and sent off for one of the most expensive tickets.

The theatre was a crumbling Victorian music hall off the Mile End Road. It had been a cinema, warehouse and bingo hall before being restored to its original role. It was now used by both amateur and professional groups, largely for one-night presentations. Pop groups and TV comedians used it for 'smash and grab raids', cashing in on their instant fame. For most of the time, however, the theatre remained dark, unused, and empty. For the charity 'Night of One Hundred Stars' it was light and full. 'One hundred' stars was, possibly, stretching it. There might have been a hundred people involved but not many could be described as stars, even in the loose showbiz way.

Alan took a taxi to the East End, settled into his seat on the front row of the circle, and watched as the local audience arrived in all its finery. He was irritated that people talked through the overture, and the very big man sitting next to him squirmed in his seat and made clear his boredom with many of the acts that followed.

Greenlee was mollified to notice, however, that the man really came to life when Rex Room did his eight-minute spot towards the end of the first half. The man laughed noisily and looked around frequently as though to ensure enjoyment among those near him.

Rex was on good form, to be sure. He had found his true audience and knew exactly what would appeal. His material was slightly blue, but not too much. He affected a camp approach which Greenlee hadn't known him use before, and it was extremely funny.

'I'm not as young as I was, you know,' he said. 'I was travelling on the Tube the other day and a small boy offered me his seat . . . no, *don't* be like that! Talking of which, did you hear about the dirty old man? Spent all day showing Boy Scouts over the road. What he showed them, I've no idea . . . Now, I went to this football match the other day . . .'

He took the microphone off the stand and rested it against his paunch.

'My, you should've seen 'em play! All those butch men running after a piece of leather! They should've asked *me* . . . I've got a cupboardful at home I don't need any more!'

The big man slapped his chunky thigh at this and elbowed Alan into joining in the laughter.

Rex went on, building to the inevitable climax of a sentimental song. Alan Greenlee found it hard to believe that this supremely confident performance was coming from a man who could be so twisted and bitter.

When the lights came up at the interval, the big man next to him was still chuckling. ' 'E's good, isn't 'e? Dead good.'

'I'm glad you like him,' Greenlee replied. 'I'll let you into a little secret. I'm his manager.'

'Are you now? His manager, eh? Well, not getting your cut tonight, I don't suppose?'

'Not tonight, not for charity, no.'

'Manager, eh?' The man brooded over this point and turned to the equally large person on his other side. 'This geezer says he's Rex's manager.'

'Really?' said the other man. 'Pleased to meet you, Rex's manager.' He leant across his mate to shake hands. 'You've got a good man there. 'E's very popular round 'ere, you know. Better look after 'im.'

'Ah yes,' said Alan, a shade uncomfortably.

'Yeh,' agreed the man sitting next to him, 'we always have a good laugh at Rex. Everybody always laughs at Rex.' It sounded like an order. Then, abruptly, he said, ' 'Scuse us. I think we're expected at the bar. Pleased to meet you.'

Greenlee stood up to let the two men squeeze past him, then sat quietly studying the souvenir programme. As it was full of whole pages from advertisers saying how proud they were to be associated with the event, that didn't take him long. There was nothing to read about the individual artistes taking part, just their publicity pictures.

The two big men arrived back just as the lights were going down for the second half. They seemed popular figures. Many of the audience waved to them or called out greetings. As they sat down, the big one next to Greenlee said, 'We'd like to ask you to a party after the show, seeing as you're Rex's manager. He'll be there, of course.'

'Oh, I see. Well, thank you very much. I was going to say hello anyway, of course.'

'Well, you come with us.'

Charity shows are always apt to run on a bit, so Greenlee had plenty of scope during the second half to wonder who these large men might be. He still wasn't sure what he

456

had let himself in for when the show came to an end.

'By the way,' said the big man, 'I'm Eric. This is 'arold. Pleased to meet yah.'

'Yes, and I'm Alan,' said Alan.

'We know that,' said Eric. 'You're Rex's manager.'

They guided him down through the foyer and out towards a large white Jaguar parked on double yellow lines near the theatre entrance. They climbed in and drove the short distance to a club which announced, in neon over the door, that it was the Alhambra Niterie.

Inside, Eric and Harold didn't appear to have to pay for admission, nor did Alan Greenlee. The club was half full when they arrived, but, in time, members of the audience and artistes from the 'Night of One Hundred Stars' turned up.

Greenlee sat uneasily at the table where Eric and Harold had parked him. When Rex appeared, his old cocky self, a space was cleared for him.

'Thanks for coming, Alan.'

'You were excellent, Rex! Really excellent.'

Rex didn't seem surprised to see Greenlee here at the party, sitting at the same table as Eric and Harold.

'Who are they?' he managed to whisper in Rex's ear.

'They're businessmen,' Rex explained. 'The Bramley brothers. They own the club and other bits and pieces. They've been very good to me. They call me court jester, so to speak.'

'And we book you here?'

'Oh, yes, Alan. Who d'you take me for?'

'Funny, just hadn't registered it, though of course I know you do a lot of clubs round here.'

Drink flowed freely, and Greenlee downed the several large whiskies that were ordered for him. There was dancing, but that had never been an interest of Alan's. Towards midnight, he looked at his watch and wondered how he was going to get back home.

Sensing this, Eric Bramley leant over and said, 'Don't worry, Alan, we'll look after you.'

Did they run a taxi business, too? he wondered.

By one o'clock, Alan was getting quite agitated; no one showed any sign of moving. Nightclub hours were not his cup of tea at all.

Then a man in a black suit came over to the Bramleys' table and whispered to Eric. Eric turned to Alan and said, 'Alan, this is Alan.' He gave a gruff laugh. 'He'll run you home. Just tell him where to go, and he'll take you.'

'Well, thank you very much, Mr . . . Eric. I'd best be going now. I'm much obliged to you. 'Night, Rex. 'Night, everybody.'

With obvious relief, he went out with his namesake and was shown into a dark blue Ford.

There was already another man sitting on the back seat. Greenlee was surprised when, having settled in beside him, this other man was also introduced to him as 'Alan'.

'Maida Vale, near the station, please,' Greenlee requested and they set off.

They hadn't gone very far and were moving along quite slowly when the 'Alan' sitting next to Greenlee put a leather-gloved hand on his thigh, just above the right knee.

Greenlee flinched. The man increased his grip and continued to press very hard.

'I say,' Greenlee protested, 'what are you doing?'

The man said nothing but continued to press. It was distinctly painful. He seemed to have the ability to maintain his grip without any effort. On and on it went, harder and harder, until Alan could bear it no longer. He tried to prise the hand away.

'For Christ's sake, what are you up to?' Greenlee cried. He felt the man's grip slacken.

'Ah,' said the other Alan, speaking for the first time, 'we'll have to tell you then.'

'Tell me what?'

'We hear you've not been entirely guv'nor.'

'Entirely guv'nor? What are you talking about?'

'I think you know, Alan. What you owe to a client of yours, who happens to be a very good friend of ours.'

At last, understanding dawned.

The man reasserted his grip. It was astonishingly painful. Greenlee let out a yelp, but it sounded like a laugh.

'This is no laughing matter, Alan.'

'No . . . no . . .'

It all fitted together now. Grant remembered how Rex had bloodied him all those years ago over the money due to Grant Pickering's clients. It was that all over again.

'What do you want me –' Greenlee gasped, '. . . to do?'

'Make it up to our friend. What you owe him. Every penny. Find a way.'

'Okay, okay, I'll do what I can, anything . . .'

If only he could get out of this intolerable trap, he would go straight to the police, report Rex, and make the most terrible fuss.

'And if you ever talk about this little ride we've taken, well, Alan, I'm afraid your life won't be worth living. I don't think you'd want to show your face in public ever again. Not after we'd finished with it.'

'Of course, of course.'

'Got the message?'

'Yes, yes.' The pain eased.

'Ever caught your fingers in a car door, Alan? Could be painful.'

'No!'

The man then leant across Greenlee, opened the door of the moving car, and made to push him out.

'No, no!'

If the idea had been merely to give Greenlee a nasty shock, and the embarrassment of wandering around the East End in the middle of the night, the man had misjudged.

The car was going too fast.

Greenlee was hurled into the gutter. He ripped his head open against the high, hard pavement edge.

The car lurched back into a straight line, the door swung shut, and the occupants sped off into the night, task completed.

CHAPTER 30

Rex Room didn't leave the Alhambra Niterie till past three o'clock that morning. He drove home to Streatham and went straight to bed, still elated after his performance but sufficiently tired to get right off to sleep. He had almost forgotten what the Bramleys had been told about Alan Greenlee and what they had said they would do.

He slept soundly till about nine, when the postman rattling the letter box woke him up. He knew instantly that he wouldn't get back to sleep after this, so picked the two letters off the mat and made himself a cup of tea. He opened the smaller of the letters first. It contained a bill which he slapped down on the table with annoyance. He picked up the larger letter, felt the expensive quality of the envelope, and ran a finger over the embossed gold lettering and the Flying Finger logo.

What could this be all about?

Rex slit open the envelope with his finger and opened out the letter. It was from Grant himself:

My dear Rex,

I hope you didn't think I was too unhelpful when you called to see me the other day. I have now had a chance to think a little further and also to have a word with Alan Greenlee.

We both feel you are sincere in believing that you suggested *Tutankhamun!* to Alan in the first instance. So, although there is no legal basis for any claim, in the interests of good will and, in my case, because of our long friendship, we have agreed that some sort of token payment should be made to you.

This would be a one-off, cash payment, without any obligation on our part. Nor would we be committed to advertising the fact. We are thinking of a figure of two thousand pounds. If this is acceptable to you, would you kindly let me know, and I will have the necessary letter of agreement drawn up and sent to you.

Cordially yours,

Grant

Rex suddenly felt a terrible weight drop from him. Never mind that two grand was peanuts compared to what he might have made from the show. That wasn't the point. Someone had made him a gesture. Good old Grant! He allowed a tear to creep into one eye.

Then a disagreeable sensation crept over him. Why had Alan made no mention of this offer in the club last night? There wasn't anything fishy about Grant's offer was there? He hadn't made Rex the offer without telling Greenlee, had he?

Rex worried at the thought and sipped his tea. Then he went back to bed for a while. At teatime, he went out to buy his copies of the *Standard* and *News*, as he always did.

And that was how he heard the worst.

'No, it's got nothing to do with any Pharaoh's curse. Never was such a thing anyway, and our show certainly hasn't got it. It was played up by the papers then, and here you are playing it up again now . . .'

Grant Pickering had quite enough bother on his hands as a result of Alan Greenlee's death. He had no wish to waste time talking to stupid journalists and speculating about the Pharaoh's curse.

'Alan's death is a tragedy and a complete mystery, but there's been nothing else remotely connected with *Tutankhamun!* to support your fucking stupid theory. No

462

accidents, no deaths, no nothing. So piss off, okay?'

The journalist had to hang up, but didn't drop his theory. He'd just have to wait for another calamity to befall the show before dusting it down again.

What Grant had said about the death being a mystery was true, nevertheless. The body had been found in the City Road by a police patrol car at 2.45 a.m. At Greenlee's Maida Vale flat, the police were able to establish that he lived alone and wasn't married. They had a quick look through an engagement diary and his address book. They noticed well-known names like Quentin Saint, Suzie Paul, and several others, but there were no obvious clues to shed light on what had happened.

Later in the morning, Barbara, Greenlee's assistant, told them about his visit to the charity show the night before. When told what had happened, nobody at the theatre remembered noticing him. There was a similar sound of people clamming up when the organizers of the event were consulted.

The death was reported in the evening papers. The words 'foul play is not suspected' were not used.

Two days of anxiety later, the police had a word with Rex Room at his Streatham flat. They saw that he was very upset over the matter. He had lost his agent, after all. Greenlee had been to see him in the 'Night of One Hundred Stars', he explained. 'We met for a drink afterwards.'

'Where did you go?' the detective sergeant asked.

Rex hesitated, fractionally, and then owned up to the Alhambra Niterie.

The detective knew the place. 'There were people there with you?'

'Yes, millions. Mostly been to the show. Alan got a minicab sometime after midnight, or one o'clock, I don't know. That was the last I saw of him. It's terrible, frankly.'

'A minicab, you think?'

'Yep.'

'You didn't leave with Mr Greenlee, then?'

'No reason to. He lived in Maida Vale someplace. I live here.'

'Did you see him leave with anyone?'

'No, he got a minicab, like I said. Cross my heart and hope to die, I've a million witnesses. I stayed till three and drove my old banger back here.'

The detective noted how haggard the comedian looked, a very different image to the one he projected in his act and in his photographs.

'Tell me,' he went on, 'are you aware of anyone with anything against Mr Greenlee?'

'Why, you think he was murdered or something?'

'Perhaps.'

'No,' Rex replied, a little too quickly. 'He was a great fella. Everybody had a lot of respect for him.'

'He was once married, wasn't he, to Suzie Paul?'

'That's right, but it didn't last. I'll tell you why. He was bent, you see. He liked it the other way. She came home once and found him up the arse of Quentin Saint. You know, the singer. He was another client.'

'I see, and Mr Greenlee had something to do with this *Tutankhamun!* show, in which this ex-wife appears, is that right?'

'Correct, yes. That's show business for you. No hard feelings. One big happy family.'

Rex laughed for the first time, but it was his stage laugh and it rang hollow.

The policeman went on doggedly. 'Of course, what you say about Mr Greenlee's leanings is known to us, but would you say he was a *busy* homo-person?'

Rex thought for a moment and then saw the point. 'Well, that's not my scene at all. I hate the lot of 'em myself, think they ought to lock 'em up. But busy? I should think so. D'you think he was done in by one of them?'

'If he was murdered, you mean? It's possible, but it doesn't bear the signs of homosexual murder. You don't find the body lying in the street with them. Tied up and covered in blood more like. I've seen a few and you wouldn't show them at a children's matinee, I can tell you.'

Rex pulled a disgusted face. 'I should think not.'

'It's a mystery, Mr Room. But I'm an optimist by nature. We'll find out what happened eventually. Thank you for your help.'

'Pleasure,' said Rex, 'any time you need to know anything, don't be afraid to ask. Always glad to help the police.'

After he had shown the detective to the door, Rex realized he was sweating profusely. His shirt was sticking to his back, his collar soaked. He went into the bathroom and saw that his face was covered in perspiration.

He felt something rising in his stomach, fell to the lavatory pedestal and sicked up his breakfast. When he was over that, he washed his face, towelled himself free of sweat, and then threw himself on the bed.

God, he thought. I didn't mean him no harm. I just wanted him taught a lesson. I didn't want those fuckers to *kill* him . . .

It took time before Alan Greenlee's body was released for cremation. When it took place, the funeral was quite a showbusiness affair. A small crowd stood by the gates waiting to catch sight of any stars who might turn up. They were favoured with a glimpse of Quentin Saint incongruously squashed into a sober black suit and dark blue cape. The glamorous woman under the veil was Suzie Paul, the ex-wife. She arrived on the arm of Grant Pickering.

There were floral tributes from the company of *Tutankhamun!* and from people connected with the various branches of the business Greenlee had been involved in over the years. A handful of showbusiness journalists sat in on the service and there were two policemen, in plain clothes.

After the ceremony, Grant Pickering found himself standing next to Rex Room.

'You got my letter?' he asked.

'Yes, thanks a lot, very sweet of you. I got it on the day he . . . died.'

'Ah, sorry about that.'

'He did know about it, didn't he? I mean, this wasn't just you being nice and friendly like?'

Grant frowned. 'Of course he knew,' he said unconvincingly. 'You saw what I said in the letter?'

But Rex still wasn't sure.

'Well,' asked Grant, 'are you going to accept?'

A worried look came into the comedian's face. He hesitated. 'No, no, I couldn't. Not now, Grant. Not after this. I would've done, but not now.'

'It's up to you. Think about it. It's there if you want it.'

Grant could tell that Rex was holding something back. 'Rum do, eh?' he remarked quietly. 'You're without representation now?'

'Yes,' Rex whispered hoarsely, almost hiding behind the turned-up collar of his coat. 'It's just one darned thing after another.'

'Need any help, just ring the office, okay?'

Rex looked at Grant, surprised again by the kindness. Why had he ever left him? It was just another in the long line of cock-ups they called Life.

'I appreciate that, Grant. But I might do my own bookings for a bit. I'll have to see.'

'The door's always open. Goodbye, Rex.'

Grant caught up with Suzie who was already waiting in the chauffeur-driven limo, anxious to get back to Drury Lane for the matinee. A hand gently tapped Grant on the shoulder. The detective sergeant introduced himself and asked if he could have a word. Grant requested that it should be away from the crematorium. A time was fixed for the policeman to come round to the office the following morning. It was his second visit.

When he came, he cleverly probed Grant's curious relations with Greenlee over the years, how they appeared to have been rivals in business and in love, but had worked together right up to the end.

'Right, yes, I suppose that does appear odd, but it's not so unusual. Sometimes you have to work with people in showbiz, people you don't like, people who've done you down, or perhaps you've done down. You can't choose to work only with people you like.'

'You're friendly with Mr Greenlee's former wife?'

'Yes. Or so I read in the papers.'

'That never caused any friction?'

'It had nothing to do with the marriage breaking up. That was finished anyway because, as you know, his sexual leanings were in the other direction. She became my client but quite a lot of horse-trading goes on over clients.'

'It's very involved, certainly,' the policeman commented. 'I gather Mr Saint was also one of your clients before he joined Mr Greenlee?'

'That's right. He may come back to me now, in the light of the unhappy event. I've already suggested it. There's also Rex Room, the comedian. You've spoken to him?'

'Yes.'

'Well, Rex'd been with me for many years and then went over to Alan.'

'Why would that have been, sir?'

Grant thought for a moment. He wasn't going to give the real reason, which was that Rex thought a gay agent would get him more work. 'Oh, I was increasingly tied up in the States and he felt he wasn't being properly looked after. The usual complaint. So he went. It was amicable enough.'

467

'Did it work? The move?'

'I think so, yes. Rex is never going to be top of the bill, but Alan kept him pretty busy in the clubs where he's very popular, and rightly so.'

'I've spoken to Mr Room. I got the impression he didn't like gays. Yet his agent was one.'

'Rex hates them. But that wasn't what made him angry with Alan.'

'What was it then?'

'Don't you know?'

'No.'

'Oh, I thought you'd have found out by now. You know we have this show called *Tutankhamun!*? Well, Alan and I and people called West End Theatre Corp. put it on. Rex was very peeved about that because it was his idea, or so he claimed.'

'And was it?'

'It's possible. He got quite worked up about it. All he could see was us making money and he wasn't. Came to see me quite recently to ask if there was anything I could do. I told him there wasn't.'

'Doesn't sound like a reason to *kill* Mr Greenlee, does it?'

'Kill? Good God, no. It wouldn't have done him much good if he had. He still wouldn't have got the money. Ironically, I'd just made him an offer to get Rex off our backs. He told me my letter arrived the day Alan was found. He also says he can't accept it now . . . in the circumstances.'

'I see.'

Grant had given the policeman something to think about. He would have to go back and talk to Rex.

Tom Sheridan heard of Alan Greenlee's death when he was in New York. Although he'd teamed Tom up with Quentin to write *Tutankhamun!*, Greenlee had done little to advance his career as a performer. In fact, he had done nothing, which was why Tom had set off, of his own accord, to the United States. He hadn't even told Greenlee he was going.

Things went well. He felt he was making progress among the managements and record companies he saw. He was surprised at how seriously he was taken in the States. Liverpool still carried some weight. No one minded if he evoked that, whereas back home it was old hat. Of course, he also had the reviews of *Tut!* to wave in front of people and *Variety* continued to headline the show's success in London.

Tom had got to the point of talking contracts with Rootstock Records, a considerable achievement for someone who had simply stepped off the plane with a few demo tapes under his arm.

In a rare burst of good sense, Tom had called up Greenlee to sort out the contract, and that was when Barbara told him the news. If nothing else, it freed him from his commitment to Alan Greenlee Management. He certainly wouldn't be transferring back to Grant Pickering who now, it appeared, was likely to take over most of Alan's clients. Tom was free to find his own representation in the States.

Just before leaving London, he had bumped into Fawn Flack who was still struggling to set a foot on the lower rungs of the showbusiness ladder. Her earlier trip to California four years ago hadn't, after all, resulted in any breakthrough. And she still lived with the disappointment of having had to withdraw from *Tutankhamun!* before it opened. She told Tom, however, that her agent in LA, Harry Emanuel, had been very sympathetic, so Tom made contact. He flew to LA, and signed with the agency.

Within a matter of days he had the Rootstock contract in his hands. It was all a bit of a miracle, but he deserved success – as he was always telling people. He said it to Carly again when he looked in on her at Quornford West.

With Grant still in London, Carly was happily relaxed

about having Tom to stay for a few days. She just liked having him around. They lay by the pool together. He played his guitar for her, some of the new songs he hoped to record for Rootstock. And he went on trips with Neville and Steve.

It gave Carly an image, even if a false image, of what it would have been like had she married Tom and not Grant.

'You've changed, you know,' she told him, 'since you left the Pool. You're a nicer person. More open. You're not always putting people down like you used to.'

'Well, that's as may be, but I won't really be a nice person until I've made it on my own. As a singer. I really want to show 'em, all those shits who've kept me down till now.'

'You mean Grant?'

'Yes, and plenty of others, not just him. Perhaps I don't have to hate Grant quite so much these days.'

'Thank heaven for that. But don't talk about hating him. What's over is over. You can be bigger than that.'

'Perhaps you're right. But I lost you to him, and I'm not likely to forget that, am I? You, the best thing that ever was, and look at you now – marooned here, with nothing to do, and him away in London most of the time.'

Carly wasn't going to let on how right he was.

That night he almost went mad being under the same roof as Carly but in a separate bed. He made to go and find her more than once but each time was kept back by the certain knowledge that she wouldn't let him make love to her.

Then he was gone, back to London, and Carly lost her bright star.

Tom's visit and her own brief taste of home reminded Carly of what she was missing.

Yet her nostalgic visit to Liverpool had made her feel an outsider there, too. She was now too moneyed, too pampered, to talk on equal terms with the people she'd grown up with. She could never think of going back now. She felt she belonged nowhere, neither in England nor America. The feeling was only deepened by Grant's dawdling in London where he seemed likely to be tied down for months yet. Then he'd probably make for New York and start planning for *Tutankhamun!* on Broadway.

Never one to complain much on her own account, Carly's restlessness was encouraged by Virna Todd. Virna had made a kind of pact with her husband. As far as Carly could tell, they had reached an agreement whereby they could both screw around, provided the other didn't get to hear about it.

That wouldn't have suited Carly. She believed in one man, one woman, and that was that.

Then, one day at the Todd ranch, among many days spent idling together, Virna finally let on. Afterwards, Virna couldn't have said why she did it. They were, as often, talking about men they fancied, and Virna said, 'Well, I don't understand why you passed up that Tom Sheridan. I think he's fabulous. What's he like in the sack?'

Virna was well aware that Tom had been staying at Quornford West. It was natural for her to assume that, with Grant away, Carly and Tom had become lovers again.

'He's smashing,' Carly admitted reluctantly. 'He was my first, you know.'

'And you enjoyed it?'

'Oh, yes. Never been better.'

Virna saw this as further confirmation that Carly and Tom had been at it again recently. 'Not even with Grant?'

'Well, Grant's better at other things, let's leave it at that.'

'I know what you mean.'

'*How* do you know?'

There was a terrible pause. Virna looked at her hands.

Then she came out with it, foolishly but frankly. 'I've slept with him. Honestly, love, you are a bit naive at times. Didn't you know?'

Carly felt quite faint. Could this be true? Had Grant really slept with Virna, or was she making it up?

'When did you . . . do it?'

'At the party.'

'The big party, in '73?'

'Yes. When you were up in the balloon with Johnny. It seemed a fair swap.'

Carly hated this. The nerve!

'How come I haven't heard about it till now? Four years . . .'

It was typical of Virna, the way she threw herself at anything in trousers – hairdressers, messengers boys . . . But Carly's own husband was a different matter. How *could* she have done such a thing?

Oh, heck, Virna thought, that's torn it. Shouldn't have let that one out.

Carly started to cry. Virna moved over to comfort her.

'I'm sorry, darling, really sorry. It was nothing. You know me, I pushed him into it, he didn't want to do it. That's the truth.'

But Carly wasn't to be consoled. She excused herself and left early to drive home.

It might have been a small thing to Virna. It might have been a small thing to Grant. But it was a big thing to Carly. She couldn't bear the thought, especially as it endangered her only friendship in LA, with Virna, quite apart from what it did to her feelings for Grant.

From that day forward, the Pickering marriage was under threat. Carly had little else to worry about during her long empty days. What was her marriage if she never seemed to see her husband, if she was marooned in a foreign land? What a chance she had thrown up by not making love to Tom when he'd been over. She found herself thinking about him more than ever, hoping that he would soon return for another visit.

Grant, still in London, continued to see his marriage in the old light. It was his wife's job to be faithful, as he knew she would be. She had the children, she had plenty of money, what else did she want?

As for himself, he had a wife and a mistress, and that suited him fine.

Suzie Paul had just recently come back to him from Ned Alexander. There had been a preposterous moment when Ned had seriously wanted to accompany Suzie to Alan Greenlee's funeral. When Grant heard of the plan he rang Ned and put him in the picture.

'There are one or two things you should know, Ned. Suzie and I have been through a lot together. Money troubles, marriage troubles, now Alan's death. The message I've got for you is hands off.'

'Don't you think you ought to ask the woman herself how she feels?' the actor answered.

'I don't need to ask. I know how she feels. As far as you're concerned, she's being polite because she has to work with you.'

'Making love is a curious way to be *polite*.'

'Just lay off, Ned. I don't want you or anybody else upsetting Suzie. It's a simple matter. You've got a job to do, and I want you to get on with it, without meddling with other people's property. Get the message?'

'There's a threat behind what you say, isn't there?' Ned said acidly. 'The producer gets his way.'

'You bet he does. You're not so bloody marvellous as Howard Carter that you can't be replaced, you know. Nobody's ever irreplaceable in this business, you should know that by now. I'll have to think very hard about your future with us if you persist.'

'You mean Broadway?'

'Not even that far ahead. The chances of getting both London leads on there are minimal. We're going to have a helluva fight with the Americans to get one of you in. And you know which one I'll be supporting. In any case, this show's bigger than its cast. It'd do just as well with two kids in your parts, and I mean that.'

Ned tried to sound tough, but he wasn't very good at that without a script.

Within days, Suzie had apologized to Grant for wandering away from him. She knew which side her bread was buttered. Grant returned to her bed that night. Two weeks later, Ned Alexander was bending down to pick up a newspaper and pulled a muscle in his back. It was a genuine accident, but it effectively ended his association with *Tutankhamun!* His understudy took over for a week, and then it was announced that he was to be replaced by another actor entirely. Ned was out of the cast permanently and his backstage romance with Suzie was as dead as Alan Greenlee.

'Nonsense!' was Grant Pickering's response to a newspaper call inquiring whether Ned's misfortune was yet another manifestation of the curse. 'Fucking nonsense,' he repeated. Then he laughed. 'You have absolutely no idea how incredibly wrong you are!'

When a piece of scenery collapsed, seriously injuring a stage hand, and when the revolve started jamming about one night a week, Grant's response was still the same.

The incidents, coupled with his co-producer's death, meant that more and more of the responsibility for the show devolved on Grant. There were daily decisions to be made, crises to be dealt with. His absence from the GPO's LA headquarters became pronounced. He was needed there. He seriously wanted to be there. But he was continually prevented from going.

There was, of course, one compensation. Suzie was blossoming in the part of Lady Evelyn and, once Ned

Alexander had been disposed of, Grant settled again into being her devoted boss and lover. The longer he was away from Carly, the less worried was he about being unfaithful. The more his original compelling urge to manage Suzie was fulfilled, the more he wanted her sexually.

Each night Grant would work at the office until ten o'clock. Then he would go to Drury Lane and, standing either in the wings or at the back of the stalls, watch enchanted as Suzie sang 'One Last Chance'. Now that she wasn't singing it to Ned Alexander it was all the more enjoyable.

Grant also enjoyed the main 'Revelation of the Treasure' sequence, as it was called. It never ceased to amaze him, and even after seeing it dozens of times he still wasn't totally sure how it was done.

After the two Saturday night performances, Grant would treat Suzie with great gentleness. They might go off to a restaurant, Le Caprice was a favourite, so that she could wind down slowly. Or they would drive out late to a cottage that a friend made available to them near Newbury. They would wake up to the sound of birds singing and church bells ringing on Sunday morning and lie in bed until it was time for lunch.

'Do you know,' Suzie admitted one such Sunday in a moment after they'd made love, 'all the time Alan was alive, I still felt I was kind of married to him. Odd that, isn't it?'

'Not really,' Grant told her. 'I can understand that. Or if I can't, I can imagine it.'

'Though we were divorced, there was a way we were still married. I'm not religious or anything, but there is a sense that once you're married to someone you always are.'

'Maybe,' Grant said, not sure whether it was wise to agree.

'But now I'm free. It's an odd feeling.'

'You'd better not tell the police. They'd be very suspicious.'

'Oh, Grant, don't tease.'

'Sorry, but you'd be amazed what nasty minds they have. I'm not sure his death was suspicious, but if he was murdered, I bet we never find out why.'

Suzie turned on her back and closed her eyes. Grant stroked her face with his finger, brushing his chest against her breasts. For the second time that hour he found himself stirring. For the second time he began the foreplay that Suzie liked and then they made love again. It took longer, but was better.

And then they talked once more.

Suzie always broached difficult subjects head on.

'Will you and I ever marry, Grant?'

It was not a totally unexpected question.

'Ideally, I want you and Carly. She's the mother of the kids and we've known each other so long, but I know it may not last for ever. It's not much of a life for her, sitting all day by the pool in LA.'

'I could manage it.'

'No, you couldn't. You've got talent. And if you've got talent you have to use it, or you're not satisfied.'

'And she doesn't . . . amuse herself with other men while you're away?'

'I don't know, but I doubt it. That's just her. What she believes.'

'Odd that, isn't it?'

'Do you mind having me, but not having me?'

'Yes, I do. I want you to myself. I'm greedy. But I don't do too badly, I have an awful lot of you. Did you know I can tell when you're there watching me, in the theatre?'

'You can see me?'

'You can see quite a lot of the audience, people stick out, but I just know when you're there. I'm upset when you're not. I wonder what you're up to.'

'I didn't know that. Well, can you bear with me for a while? It's not just my marriage that's at stake. It's your career. I don't want to do anything that would interfere with your going on Broadway.'

476

'I won't be too disappointed if I don't, it's not everything.'

'Yes, it *is* everything. You've got to believe that, Suzie! You've been through a hell of a lot, and we're going to get you that prize.'

'All right, Mr Starmaker. As you wish.'

It was odd how sexy ambition could be. Longing for success was like longing for sex. Grant was quite unable to distinguish between the two, especially when it came to Suzie.

CHAPTER 31

Virna Todd had hardly got back to LA from London when her husband decided he should head for Britain on his first visit there in a very long while. It was to be a 'private' visit, which merely meant that Johnny wouldn't be giving any concerts. But he would appear on TV chat shows, give newspaper interviews, and relentlessly plug his albums.

There were two additional reasons why Johnny wanted to go. He needed to talk to Grant, who appeared to have taken up permanent residence in the UK. And he wanted, above all, to see *Tutankhamun!* Virna had told him it really was as good as people said.

When the musical had hardly been written, Grant had muttered about there being a part in it for Johnny. He'd never heard any more of that and thought he should jog Grant's memory. Johnny had conquered almost every field there was, with the notable exception of the musical. He must do that one day. If *Tut!* came to Broadway, surely he must be in it?

Johnny arrived back home in style. The staff in the first-class cabin of the British Airways flight from LA treated him like royalty – Hollywood royalty, if not actual – and he was feted all through his stay at the Inter-Continental as though he were a visiting head of state. He gave a stream of interviews, and sensed he was being discovered by a whole new generation. People had even begun to think he was American, so long had he been away and so deeply was he dug into the entertainment scene over there.

Then Grant accompanied him to see *Tut!* Johnny loved it, raved about it, wouldn't stop talking about it. But

Grant wondered how much of the enthusiasm was put on. It sounded so Hollywood.

They went backstage after the performance and Johnny enthused all over again in front of Suzie Paul.

'You're so wonderful,' he told her. 'I've never seen anyone so talented in my life. You have the gift.'

Suzie wasn't going to turn down compliments of this nature; she began to think that Johnny was pretty wonderful, too. The three of them went out for dinner at Langan's Brasserie. Johnny made straight for Michael Caine who was eating, proprietorially, with his wife, and they exchanged a few words of banter as they always did whenever they met in LA. One of the other proprietors of the restaurant swayed over drunkenly and made a rude remark about Johnny's tan. Grant whisked his client away, explaining this was all part of the Langan's experience.

When they sat down, it struck Grant as odd to see Johnny without a female companion, but then he no longer had a personal assistant like Mickey Clinch to look after such matters. Had he lost the knack of finding company for himself?

Throughout the meal, Johnny kept up his song of praise for *Tutankhamun!* It was as though his singling out of details from the show was to demonstrate what close attention he had paid. Grant rather wished he would shut up. All this showbiz elation was hard to bear. Par for the course in the States, maybe, but inappropriate here.

Then Johnny made his pitch.

'You know, Grant, Suzie, I'd like to make a proposition to you. I believe the time is right for me to stake my all on a role in the theatre. And I believe that Howard Carter is the role. I'd like to play him when the show opens on Broadway, as it's bound to do, of course.'

Grant made to speak, then caught Suzie's eye, and let her flounder first with a reply.

'That would be wonderful, Johnny,' she said tactfully. 'I'm sure just having you in it would do so much for the show. I expect Grant'll want to discuss it with the Americans first . . .'

'They'd expect to have their say,' said Grant. Johnny could tell he was hedging.

'There'd be no problem, would there?'

'Nothing that can't be fixed, Johnny,' said Grant firmly. 'There'll be those who'll say you haven't sung in a musical before, never actually sung on stage. And that it's a difficult role. It's a *singer's* role rather than a pop role, if you understand me.'

'I'll have to get into shape for it, vocally, dramatically, I know. But I'll do whatever's needed. I'll start tomorrow.'

'Now, Johnny, this needs thinking about carefully. I'll set it in motion as soon as I can.'

Johnny was disappointed. After all, Grant was his agent. It was Grant who'd first floated the idea of his going on stage. Why didn't he sound more enthusiastic?

The fact was, now that Grant had viewed the show so many times, he simply couldn't imagine Johnny convincing anyone in the role of an archaeologist, however roughened up by the writers the character had been.

Suzie, too, was aware that playing opposite a pop singer in his first acting role would be no picnic, particularly if Johnny behaved like the big star he was. She kept glancing at Grant, waiting for signals.

At the end of the meal, Johnny went back to his hotel and Suzie and Grant drove home to Suzie's flat in St John's Wood.

'I feel like I'm being squeezed, you know,' he told her, slipping off his tie and loosening his collar, ready to undress for bed. 'If I'm not careful, I'll be setting up a Broadway deal with my best girl in one lead and my oldest client in the other. Johnny won't be able to keep his hands off you, and he could make an absolute pig's ear of the show. What am I supposed to do?'

'You'll just have to be blunt with him, Grant. Tell him he's not up to it, if that's what you really think. Or organize some pretty convincing opposition.'

'That won't be easy. He's bound to feel insulted. But I know I can't put the show at risk because I'm frightened of offending him.'

The chauffeur drove Johnny the short distance from Langan's to the Inter-Continental Hotel. It was good to be back in Britain. He could be more relaxed, even manage without a personal assistant. He strode into the lobby and picked up his key from the porter, chatted briefly to the bright-eyed, attractive receptionist, and then stepped into the lift to the top floor.

When he stepped out, a woman was waiting for him. He didn't know why or how she was there, so he said simply, 'Hi, honey, how are you?' without really thinking about it.

He fumbled with his key, unable to get it to turn first time.

'Don't you remember me, Johnny?'

' 'Scuse me?'

'Don't you remember me?'

Johnny stopped fiddling with the key and turned to look more closely at the woman who did indeed, now he came to think of it, seem familiar. Hadn't he seen her very recently, or was it a long time ago?

'Did you want to see me, or something?'

'Oh, come on, don't be such a shit-face!'

The harsh words startled Johnny. 'You'll have to tell me who you are.'

'You've been to see a show tonight?'

'Now then, wait a moment. You were in it?'

'Sure. And we've met before. More than once.'

She was black, which narrowed the field; of all the women, groupies, he'd ever laid, very few were black and he usually did remember their faces, if nothing else.

'I'm sorry, honey, you'll have to tell me who you are.'

'We met at Grant Pickering's house, in the country. You remember that?'

'Ah yes, the famous Halo. Of course. And you're in the show? Well, I really should've read my programme better, shouldn't I? Come on in and have a drink.'

Johnny finally managed to get the key to turn and courteously ushered Halo in, slender and elegant as he now remembered she'd always been, a fur coat thrown over those fine limbs and a bright scarf on her head. High heels, too, of course.

It was an uncomfortable chat they had over the drink. All it did was remind Johnny of that cat-like behaviour she'd indulged in years ago when Grant was playing hot and cold with her.

'So Grant got you a part in the show?'

That was not what he should have said.

'He had nothing to do with it. I got it on my own account. I 'spect he'd have blocked it if he'd known. But he didn't, not till it was too late.'

Johnny couldn't begin to understand where all this spite was coming from. Surely it was a long, long time ago that Grant had treated her badly?

But as Halo talked on, Johnny realized she was cracked. She seemed to be threatening some terrible act of revenge against Grant, long-planned, and for which getting into *Tutankhamun!* was but a preparation.

'I'm not sure how I can help you, Halo,' Johnny said wearily, eager to be rid of this madwoman; the last thing he wanted to do was lay her.

'Huh,' she laughed. 'Nobody'll stand up to him. Not even Tom Sheridan. I thought he'd teach him a lesson if anyone would, after what Grant did, but what does he do? Writes a show for him!'

'Well, Tom's a nice man, very talented.'

'Don't bullshit me.'

Johnny felt silent, wondering how he could get rid of her. Should he call down to reception, call the cops even?

Halo rambled on, and the more she pulled names out of her head, the more Johnny began seriously to believe she was bent on doing actual harm. But to whom? Grant? To him? To Suzie, perhaps? Yes, Halo was probably jealous of Suzie in some crazy, mixed-up way.

'Sweetheart, I think I know how you feel. Do you want me to put in a word for you? Something like that?'

Halo just stood, spat the word 'Jerk!' in his face, and made for the door.

'Wow!' Johnny muttered to himself as he slipped the security latch on the door. 'What did I do to deserve that?'

Next morning, Johnny paid a royal visit to the Grant Pickering Organization offices in New Bond Street. He went round shaking hands with everybody and kissing the secretaries, most of whom had barely begun their teens when he first hit the road to fame.

Then he settled down in Grant's office for a long chat. He told him first about the disagreeable encounter he'd had with Halo the night before.

'I think she's a basket case. I tell you, Grant, I was actually shit-scared when she was with me. I was just waiting for her to pull a knife on me, so tensed up she was. I thought I'd be safe in London, now I'm not so sure. You've got a lunatic in your cast. Don't say I didn't warn you.'

'I'll look into it. It'll probably blow over.'

'I doubt it.'

'Anyway, Johnny, that's not what we've really got to talk about, is it?'

'No.' And away he went into a further round of lobbying.

Grant didn't find it a comfortable experience and was alarmed when he heard Johnny reviving the old formula, 'I'm not very happy about . . .'

He actually claimed he'd had a lot of approaches from other managements in recent months. Grant couldn't be sure whether he had or not, but took on board the message that if things were not done the way Johnny wanted, he might consider moving to another agency. This, from Grant's oldest, biggest client, was pretty heavy. It had never been remotely hinted at before. Why had it come up now?

Johnny then started to put the boot in at the personal level. This was something he rarely, if ever, did. Grant listened unhappily as Johnny began to wag the finger at him.

'She's a fine girl that Suzie, isn't she? I can see you're very soft on her. But aren't you playing a dangerous game, having it both ways? Virna's been hearing a lot from Carly, how she's not happy in LA, doesn't like the weather, the food, the people. How she hasn't got anything to do, doesn't have any friends. Sounds to me as if she'd rather come home.'

'Rubbish, Johnny. You're talking rubbish. All that could apply just as much to Virna, and what's she going to do about it?'

'Well, you see, Virna's a different kind of woman. She finds things to do. In fact, she spends most of the time I'm not with her screwing around. I don't mind. I've a similar system myself. It seems to work.'

'Good for Virna,' said Grant, doubtfully. 'But Carly's different, and not just in that respect.'

'Virna tells me you fucked her once.'

'Now, Johnny. I don't like this. I don't like the way you bring that up. It didn't mean a thing.'

'Maybe not. It may not have meant anything to you. It meant nothing to me – I didn't know about it. But it might have meant something to her because she's always had a thing about you.'

'Oh, yes?'

'And then there's Carly.'

'She doesn't know.'

'I wouldn't be too sure. I think Virna told her.'

'When?'

'When they got back from London. Carly didn't take too kindly to it, I gather.'

Grant looked embarrassed at the news. He had thought Carly would never find out. But you couldn't rely on Virna. She was always surprising you, coming out with odd things, always embarrassing. Not as unstable as Halo, of course, but unpredictable.

Grant got the message, and Johnny relaxed.

Grant started lining up the opposition to Johnny taking the role. First, he rang Quentin. He was back on the books of the Grant Pickering Organization as a performer. He was rehearsing prior to a twelve-city tour of the States. Although reasonably well known there, he had never really cracked the market and Grant was keen, now that he was back on the payroll, for him to consolidate his reputation.

He hadn't managed to persuade Quentin to move to the US. 'I'm an English sausage,' Quentin had said, 'and I'm staying put.'

'Hi, sausage!' said Grant into the phone, 'how's it all going?'

'I'm bloody knackered. There was blood all over the keys this morning. Did a nail in, hurt like hell.'

'You take care now. We'll have to extend your insurance if you're going to cripple yourself. Anyway, I've got a question for you. I just want an honest opinion, no bull-shitting. Yes or no.'

'No bullshitting, eh?' Quentin laughed, adjusting his

486

kaftan, and spread out on the sofa with the phone still pressed to his ear.

'If I was to say that Johnny Todd was going to play Howard on Broadway, what would your feelings be?'

'Ah.' Quentin didn't say any more for a moment. 'You're putting me on the spot, aren't you, oh great leader?'

'Yes.'

'Well, I'd say the Pharaoh's curse had struck again!'

'For fuck's sake! *Please . . .*'

'I think he'd be bloody awful, frankly. Now, don't get me wrong, I think he's a smashing bloke, I like everything he does, but he just wouldn't be right for our show. I mean, he can hardly speak an intro to a song without making it sound like semaphore. I dread to think what he'd do with *Tut!*'

'Trouble is, he's set his heart on the part. Sees it as his way into musicals. I'm sorry I ever said that's what he ought to do next.'

'Well, Grant, I'd vote against. I'd even be prepared to dig my little heels in. But then you'd only tell me I'd no right to.'

'You've no veto, sure. But I value your opinion, it's as much your show as mine or anyone else's. What d'you think Tom would say?'

'The opposite of what you want him to say. You'd better ask him.'

'Yes, I will.'

'Tom, it's Grant. How was LA?'

'She was wonderful . . . and I like your house, Grant.'

Even over the phone, the niggling between them was almost tangible. Grant tried to ignore it.

'I want to ask your advice about *Tut!* We're thinking about Broadway. It's going to be a different show, redesigned, new director, and so on. I think Suzie'll probably do it.'

487

'What a surprise.'

'Now, Tom . . .'

'Okay, she's great, yeh . . .'

'But we need somebody really big for Howard. That's why I'm sounding you out. Johnny's after it.'

'Todd-o?'

'Him, yes.'

'Ah.'

There was a pause during which Grant hoped, and rather expected, Tom would express disapproval. But Tom was thinking, and he wanted to know what Grant was thinking before he expressed his view, so that he could oppose it.

'How about you?' Tom asked.

'To be honest, I don't know. There's a lot to be said for and against.'

'Who else have you talked to?'

'Quentin's the only one so far.'

'And?'

'He's against.'

'Well, he would be. Probably like to play it himself, dreadful old poof. The way he camps about makes Tutankhamun look positively under-dressed.'

Grant knew there was never much love between collaborators. From Gilbert and Sullivan on, the chemistry of lyricist and composer inevitably led in time to explosion.

'I tell you,' Tom went on, glad to get it off his chest, 'you've got a bloody monster of an ego there. He's about as modest as a crocodile. I'm not working with him again.'

'Sorry you feel that way, Tom. You've written some wonderful stuff, it'd be a pity if –'

'Look, never again, I said. The thought of spending more time locked up with our little Podge is about as appealing as a night out with Idi Amin.'

'Well, anyway, he's against having Johnny.'

Tom was right in there. 'Then I'm all for him. Why not?

He can sing, just about. He'll pack 'em in. Give him a few acting lessons. Why not?'

Grant saw that Tom wasn't giving a reasoned view, just spite. It didn't help resolve the question. He'd have to consult others.

'Oh, Tom, by the way, don't mind me asking, but do you have anything to do with our old friend Halo these days?'

'Not if I can help it.'

'So, we're agreed on that one, are we?'

'Why, what's she up to?'

'Gave Johnny a very nasty turn when he was over. Now he thinks she's going to take it out on Suzie for being pally with me.'

'I'd expect nothing else. Bloody nearly chopped my balls off not so long ago, so it's quite likely, I'd say. You certainly do pick 'em, Grant.'

'Not all of them, Tom.'

'Carl-o.'

'Tom, what are you ringing for? You woke me.'

'Just wanted to chat.'

'But it's the middle of the night.'

'Not here it isn't. So, you're in bed?'

'Tom . . .'

'Are you wearing anything?'

'Stop it, Tom!'

'I've just had that so-called husband of yours on to me.'

'What about?'

'Oh, great affairs of state, affairs of the heart.'

'Don't tease. Who is it?'

'Did you know about the cottage in Berkshire? Quite like old times.'

'You mean Suzie?'

'I didn't say anything.'

'I don't want to hear.'

'It's not his only spot of bother. He says the lovely Halo – remember her? – she's running around like a mad axe-woman, threatening to cut Suzie's tits off, or something.'

'That's terrible.'

'Only joking.'

There was a pause. Tom let the rushings and clankings on the transatlantic line continue uninterrupted.

'Carl-o.'

'Yes, Tom?'

'When the bleeding 'ell are you going to tell that fella to stuff himself and get your ruddy bum back here where it belongs?'

'No, Tom, I *can't* . . .'

Two weeks after this flurry of phoning, it was time for Grant to head for LA once more after his long spell in London overseeing the launch of *Tutankhamun!*, absorbing Alan Greenlee's agency, and pushing all his many European projects forward.

En route, he would go to New York for a few days and discuss *Tutankhamun!* with the Ambers. He had to see if they could agree on a Broadway director, and perhaps reach a decision over Johnny Todd.

Finally, he would arrive in LA, get driven up to Quornford West, and be reunited with Carly and the boys.

Jan Ferry had arranged everything for the trip, right down to the car to take him to Heathrow. He had been to pay a last brief call on Suzie in her dressing room at Drury Lane before the Thursday matinee. Whatever he might get up to, she had to keep on delivering the goods, nine shows a week. She mustn't lose her voice, catch cold, or break a leg. Just keep marching on.

'No, it never gets boring, really,' she assured him. 'Every time's a little bit different. You keep discovering things, and you never get two audiences the same. At least, I'm not bored yet.'

'You'd better not be, Sooz. You'll be singing those songs on Broadway into 1980!'

'Don't! I'd rather not think about it. I'll have a holiday first?'

'Of course. We'll talk about that when I come back next month. Look after yourself, pet.'

'Oh, Grant,' she said, slipping her arms round his waist, 'you're going back to *her*.'

'I know.'

'I need you with me, always. You see, you're everything to me – my manager, my lover, my friend. But I'm not everything to you. You've got her . . .'

Grant didn't know what to say. It was the first time she'd expressed it like that. She was confronting him with the unusualness of his position, shared between two women, trying to have the best of both. There was, too, for the first time, a hint of a threat.

Suzie knew how bound up her career was with her private life. How terrible it would be if it all broke down. If she lost Grant, she'd lose everything. She was telling him he'd have to seal his commitment to her, he'd have to choose between Carly and herself. But Grant seemed unable to leave his wife; she was so good in every way.

What happened next changed all that. Grant slipped away from Suzie's dressing room, their problem unresolved, after one last kiss. On the way out of the theatre he suddenly thought of Halo and knew he'd flunked telling Suzie to be careful to avoid her. But it was too late now to go back.

He went to New Bond Street to spend a couple of hours dictating letters and making phone calls before going to the airport.

When the phone rang, Jan Ferry picked it up. She gave Grant a funny look. With her hand over the mouthpiece, she whispered: 'It's Carly. I think she's . . .'

He took the phone. 'Where are you? What is it?'

Carly was very composed. He recognized the tone at once. It was the one she used when she left him for Tom – controlled, quite warm, but devastating.

'We're here,' she said.

'Where?'

'Me and the boys. In London. At the Hilton.'

Grant registered that, of course, she'd be at the Hilton. Such an obvious choice. He'd stopped using Hiltons ever since they lost his baggage in Amsterdam and weren't gracious enough about finding it.

'What is this?' Grant exploded. 'I'm just leaving for New York. I'm going to join you Friday.'

'I know. But I had to make a choice, and I've made it. I've had enough of living in paradise, thank you. I've had enough of you screwing around with Suzie – even with Virna, for heaven's sake. I've had enough of you being in London all the time while I'm stuck in Beverly Hills. I want to be in England. I've grown used to living without you, you see.'

Grant was completely thrown. 'Why didn't you tell me? We could have talked about it. Has someone put you up to this?'

Carly bit her lip and said, 'No.'

'I do have some say in what happens to the boys, you know. And what about money?'

'I can manage. I just want to sort things out.'

Grant panicked. He was never at his best in personal crises, particularly when there was a plane to catch.

'What do you want me to do?'

'Do you have to go the States right now?' It sounded to Grant as if she was backing down a bit, giving him one last chance.

'Damn you,' he said, 'I'm not going to be fucked about like this. I've *got* to go to New York. I'll come back here next week instead of going to LA, though, heaven knows, they're crying out for me there. And we can sort it out.'

'No, go to LA, do what you have to do. Don't mind us. We'll look after ourselves.'

'Oh, for heaven's sake, what is this, Carly? I can't believe this is happening.'

'You caused all this, Grant, but I'm going to straighten it out.'

'Carly!'

It was she who put the phone down on him, to prevent further argument.

'Something the matter?' Jan Ferry asked him gently, tactful as ever.

'Carly's out of her mind. She's brought the kids over. Seems to be staying for good. Be an angel and see if you can be of any help. They're at the Hilton. I'll let you know if I can come back from New York next weekend and deal with her.'

Grant picked up his bag, gave Jan a hug – to remind her he was human – and ran down the stairs to the waiting car.

His route took him past the Hilton, but Grant didn't look up from his papers. The flight to New York was delayed and he drank more than he should have done. He reached New York with a splitting headache which would take him three days to shake off. The Pan-Am helicopter service to Manhattan was cancelled, so he had to share a limo. It was one of the worst journeys he'd ever had over the Atlantic and he wondered if he could ever bear to do it again.

The following week, he went on to LA – not, as he'd promised, back to London. 'I just have to, I've been away too long.' He found Juanita and Gustavo forlornly presiding over deserted Quornford West. Carly had emptied the closets and taken most of the kids' toys. She'd said her goodbyes to the Mexicans. Her departure appeared to have been as final as she said it was.

Virna Todd had been taken almost as much by surprise as Grant by Carly's sudden departure. When Grant called her in Malibu for a chat, Virna admitted that she probably hadn't helped.

'I told her about you and me. You know me, always blurting things out. I never dreamt she'd take it so badly.'

'I knew you'd told her. Johnny told me. You shouldn't have done. You should've realized Carly's not one to bend with the wind.'

'Well, you've given her plenty to put up with, haven't you?'

'It could have worked. It works for some people. Look at you and Johnny, you're still together.'

'We're peculiar, that's all. He's away again, you know. As soon as he was back from London he went to Chicago. I don't know what for. But I don't care. I look after myself.'

Grant knew what she meant and was more concerned at what Johnny was up to. What had he gone to Chicago for?

'So what are you going to do?' Virna asked.

'I'll go to London and talk to Carly. If I fail to change her mind and she insists on a divorce and the kids, I'll have to go along with it.'

'You don't sound terribly put out.'

'I've had time to calm down. I've thought about it a lot.'

'And you've got solace, as they say, in the arms of another.'

'They say that, do they? Well, they're right. I haven't lost everything. Life goes on.'

'You're a bastard, Grant Pickering. Butter side up!'

'What do you mean?'

'Drop a piece of toast, and you'll see what I mean.'

'Thanks, Virna.'

'Hey, guess what came in the post today?'

'What?'

'The new Tom Sheridan album.'

'And?'

'It's great.'

'Must give it an ear sometime.'

'He's great, too. He was over, you know.'

So that was it. Trust Virna to slip him the pieces. Of course, Carly wouldn't have bolted if Tom hadn't been working on her.

'Yes, Virna. I know he was over.'

CHAPTER 32

The first night of *Tutankhamun!* at the Amber Theatre on Broadway and 42nd was even more of an occasion than the London opening twelve months before. The original production was still running at Drury Lane and was just into its third major cast change. It was gratifying for Grant Pickering to think that it was still playing six nights a week in London, ringing up the till, providing employment, lining angels' pockets, without his giving it a thought.

It was a different *Tutankhamun!* that Broadway theatre-goers were about to see. The new American director, Kevin O'Dare, had reworked the whole show. The most noticeable improvement was in the dancing. That was always slicker, more disciplined and muscular on Broadway, and there would be more of it. Even though the story didn't really lend itself to many dance routines, it was essential to have them, and if they weren't there, they had to be put in.

The show had been completely redesigned, too, from the special effects to the logo. The cast was all-American, with two exceptions: Sir Anthony Poplin was making a return to the stage after twenty years in Hollywood and on the international screen. The part of the world-weary Lord Carnarvon suited him down to the ground. No American actor could have matched him.

And, of course, Suzie Paul was to repeat her winning – and, indeed, award-winning – performance as Lady Evelyn. There had been the customary arguments with American Equity over whether she should play the role. Grant had had to wage war with the union in order to get it for her, arguing that the part was that of an Englishwoman and there really was no American singer-actress who was right for it. Equity had finally conceded and now even greater things were expected of her than in London.

The part of Howard Carter was to be played by an English-born singer who, until very recently, had never acted on stage in his life. For Equity's purposes, though, he counted as an American as he was domiciled in California and had established himself without doubt as a major talent in the American showbusiness scene. So desperately had he wished to land the role, he'd even considered taking out American citizenship.

Nothing to do with the show had given Grant a harder time than Johnny Todd's determination to win the, at first sight, completely unsuitable part of Howard Carter. Anyone less like an archaeologist than the one-time rocker would have been hard to find. But Johnny had been adamant and made sure that Carter's songs from *Tutankhamun!* were included in his album schedule.

And though he'd never acted on stage in his life, he had tried to forestall criticism of his abilities by joining a stock company in Chicago for a brief season. He played three parts in the full blaze of his fame as a singer and didn't do half badly. The audiences he attracted to the theatre were disappointed that he appeared so heavily disguised and didn't burst into song, but he achieved what he set out to do.

Grant and Kevin O'Dare had been invited over to Chicago to watch Johnny working out and were pleasantly surprised at how good he was. Johnny never quite allowed the audience to forget his origins, but he clearly had the makings of a reasonable actor.

So, in the end, Grant and the other producers caved in. Despite Johnny's craven public auditioning for the role, the logic was irresistible. The character would have to be a little rougher at the edges than he'd been in real life and certainly less dashing than Ned Alexander had made him in London.

'But the fellow can *sing*, for God's sake,' Grant exclaimed. 'And he'll put bottoms on seats, however badly he acts.'

Kevin O'Dare shrugged. 'He can only bomb.'

'Or go like a bomb, as *we* say.'

Quentin Saint fought a rearguard action. He didn't want to appear to be sitting on the chances of another singer who desired to extend his range. On the other hand, he felt very protective towards a show he'd written and of which he was immensely proud. In the end, he waived his objections but registered polite disapproval by having nothing more to do with the Broadway production and declining to be flown over by Grant for the opening night.

Tom Sheridan declined to attend for different reasons. He hadn't altered his initial approval of Johnny's casting, but he had no wish to be rubbing shoulders with Grant or Suzie at this time. It was nothing to do with *Tutankhamun!* It was more of a personal matter.

Grant sat in his seat at the Amber Theatre wearing a white tuxedo. His hands fiddled with the programme. He was desperate to have one of the cigarettes he didn't smoke, to soothe him. He felt the weight of the responsibility he carried for the investors and, in an odd way, for the late Alan Greenlee. How Alan would have loved to be there.

The production the audience was about to see was costing five times what it had in London. Grant thought of the battles he had fought in the West End, and then the battles he had fought in New York, to get to this point, even before the curtain could rise.

Mrs Myreen Amber sat on his right, next to her husband. She was wearing her best Dior gown and several thousand dollars' worth of jewellery. Grant found it hard to make conversation. He desperately wanted Suzie by his side, but that was impossible. She, after all, was about to appear on the other side of the footlights. God knows what she must be feeling.

Grant thought of what might have been, of having Carly by his side, as she had been for the London opening, but all that was in the past. They were waiting for the divorce. She was living with the children in London, determined never to set foot in America again. Grant wished it had been otherwise; he still believed it was possible to love two women as he had done. But that was a battle lost.

He turned from Mrs Amber to the woman sitting on his left. She moved to stroke his fidgety hands.

'Relax, Grant,' she said. 'There's nothing you can do about it now. It's up to them.'

Virna had flown in from LA to be at the first night. There was a slight frostiness between Grant and her these days since he felt she had contributed to the bust-up of his marriage. Yet there was to be no breaking of the circle. Her life was still bound up with Johnny's, in spite of everything, and Johnny's was bound up with Grant.

'Sorry,' Grant whispered. 'When I start shredding the programme, you'd better slap me.'

'It's going to be all right.'

'I bet Johnny's having kittens.'

'Better than one of the chorus . . .'

In the No. 1 dressing room, Johnny Todd was shaking with nerves. He'd never known anything like it. Suzie, dressed, made-up, but a good deal less petrified, was making a last attempt to soothe him.

'Once you're on, you'll be all right, love.'

'I know, I know. It's just not what I'm used to. I can't be myself. If I fuck it up, I can't make a joke the way I usually do.'

'There, there.'

Abruptly, Johnny stopped pacing up and down and sat

next to Suzie. He'd thought of something to take his mind off the terror that lay ahead.

'I meant to say this before, but I didn't like to.'

'What's that, Johnny?'

'About your face. Grant said you were worried it would show, but it doesn't. It really, really doesn't.'

'Oh, love, that's sweet of you. I know I acted hysterically, but it was so horrible, all that.'

'I felt so bad about it because I knew it might happen. When that Halo jumped me in my hotel – you know about that? – I knew she was so screwy she'd do *anything*. I told Grant, but he was having all those problems with Carly, and you were left to suffer.'

'I know all that, John-jo. Don't worry about it. I had a nasty experience, but much greater luck. If God was trying to punish me – for what I'd rather not think – he didn't make too good a job of it.'

'But they said your face was terribly marked, you had to have the surgery . . .'

'It's all over.'

'Thank heaven that bloody madwoman's where she can't do any more harm.'

'Sad, though. Grant certainly walked right into all that.'

'And Tom Sheridan. He was after her too, once upon a time.'

'Doesn't surprise me. He made a pass or two at me. Does he try it on everyone?'

'In your case, he had very good taste.'

'Stop it, Johnny. This old-world charm doesn't become you.'

'God, how long have we got?'

At last, the house lights went down and the orchestra began the overture. No one talked. Good, thought Grant, encouraging, encouraging . . .

Then out of the gloom appeared the Valley of the Kings.

There was an instant round of applause. In another moment, Suzie and Johnny were entering the Valley with Sir Anthony Poplin wheezing in their wake as Lord Carnarvon. Soon they were singing their first number together.

Virna reached in the dark for Grant's hand and gave it a squeeze. It was just to show she was thinking of him, and to tell him everything was going to be all right. Suzie and Johnny were singing together like larks. Grant's lover, Virna's husband. Nothing could stop them now.

During the interval, Mrs Myreen Amber and the wives of other backers and important folk surpassed themselves. They put on an act of expressing delight and concern for the success of the production that wouldn't have disgraced British royalty. A room at the back of the stalls was set aside with the usual champagne, but Grant hardly felt like touching it. He knew what the Myreen Ambers were up to, what their husbands were up to, too. They were keeping their true views to themselves until it was obvious which way opinion was going.

Grant tried hard to take the pressure off himself by drawing attention to Virna Todd.

'You know Johnny's Virna, of course. Such a performance he's giving . . .'

Grant enjoyed the slightly startled look this introduction produced. The women seemed to betray some surprise at Johnny having a wife at all. They'd never really thought about it before.

'His first acting role, I'm told,' Myreen breezily announced. 'So very brave of him, wouldn't you say?'

This left Virna uncertain whether Mrs Amber considered he'd been wise to try at all. She attempted to shift attention back to Grant.

'Mr Pickering has been a major force behind Miss Paul's career, you know. Without him, she'd be nowhere.'

Grant looked at his shoes and swallowed.

'How wonderful,' Mrs Amber concluded graciously, 'wonderful in every way.'

Grant and Virna made their way back to their seats for Act Two. 'I could have kicked you,' he muttered under his breath. Virna dug him in the ribs and told him not to take everything so seriously.

The cheers which greeted the end of the first night of *Tutankhamun!* were such as Grant had never heard before. Grant kept telling himself that everyone was given standing ovations these days, and he shouldn't depend on first-night audiences for reliable critical opinions, but still . . .

Later, at Sardi's, Virna and he were reunited with their partners. Johnny and Suzie were given another standing ovation by diners as they crossed the restaurant.

Nothing must be taken for granted, though. Nothing was secure yet.

'You were marvellous,' Grant whispered in Suzie's ear, drinking in her perfume and the warmth of her frightened spirit. 'Even better than London, I mean that.'

Suzie said nothing but smiled, wide-eyed and distantly, aware of so many heads turned in her direction.

'Well done, Johnny,' Grant embraced his old friend. 'You did it! There were those who said it couldn't be done, but you showed 'em.'

Then the first editions arrived.

The reviews couldn't have been better. The quotes seemed to jump out of the text as Grant drank them in. 'A jewel of a show' . . . 'Johnny Todd shows himself no mean actor and in astounding good voice' . . . 'Suzie Gold melts all hearts, just as she clearly melted Howard Carter's.'

'But my name's not Gold,' the lady in question observed.

'Never mind, love, it's the quote that counts,' said Grant.

Myreen Amber came over. She could really say what she meant, now that the papers had given the go-ahead. 'Mr Pickering,' she said, enfolding his right hand in her own bejewelled clasp, 'I just had to tell you what a wonderful little show you've got here.'

'Why, thank you, ma'am,' said Grant, smiling, 'I think you could be right.'

Very much later, Grant finally took Suzie back to his apartment. It was halfway through the night. They both stumbled into bed and lay in each other's arms.

'I think it's going to be all right,' Grant announced.

'Yes, and I've got to do it twice more today, then on and on and on.'

'I know, love, I know. And all I have to do is count the money.'

'Well, that's *your* Pharaoh's curse.'

Grant froze as he usually did whenever the curse came up. 'Please!'

'Oh, come on. You're out of the woods now,' whispered Suzie. 'You've won!'

Within moments of putting the light out, both were more soundly asleep than they had been in months. Grant was happy and satisfied. He had his Broadway show, he had his stars, and one of them was lying next to him.

Carly heard news of the Broadway triumph of *Tutankhamun!* She was glad, chiefly for Tom Sheridan's sake. He'd be getting his royalties. That would keep him happy.

It would keep her happy, too, for Tom and Carly were now living together. It hadn't taken Carly long to get herself organized once she had broken Grant's hold over her. She'd bought a large Victorian family house in Ealing. There was plenty of garden for the boys to mess about in.

Tom arrived shortly after this – simply arrived on the doorstep with all his possessions in bags and boxes.

'Aren't you assuming rather a lot?'

Carly's welcome wasn't quite what Tom had expected. The way she'd bolted from Grant so dramatically had led Tom to think it was all on account of him.

He had egged her on, to be sure, and the knowledge that he existed at all made the whole leap in the dark so much less of a gamble. But she had told herself to be careful of men from now on, not to rely on them, to be her own woman.

'I'm assuming that you want me, that's all,' Tom told her. 'If you don't, I'll go right back where I came from.'

'Oh, Tom, of course I want you. Get that stuff off me front step and come on in.'

So, Carly had the man she'd always wanted. She'd quite set her mind against marrying again – him or anyone – yet it was nice having him around. He was, after all, Neville's father, the bond seemed stronger than ever, and he didn't exactly have to sponge these days with all the money coming in regularly from London and Broadway.

So, happily unmarried, Carly and Tom settled quickly into a life of mild sixties bohemianism, although, in fact, these were the dying years of the seventies. They were both now well into their thirties but seemed caught in a time warp, listening to their Beatles, Stones and Dylan records. The furniture in the house was also very period. Large circular paper lampshades from Habitat, scrubbed pine tables and chairs, and even Tom's old waterbed patched up with a bicycle repair kit and stowed in the first-floor bedroom.

Carly was happier than she had been since . . . well, really since leaving Liverpool. She had married Grant too quickly and become trapped in an inflated life style that wasn't to her liking at all. She had never liked ostentation, it didn't make her happy.

It helped that Tom Sheridan wasn't obviously an achiever in the way Grant was. He wasn't short of a penny or two now but he gave no impression of riches. He still dressed as he had done when a penniless hustler in the Pool – jeans, faded bomber-jacket, scuffed boots. He still wore the same long, unruly hair. Carly felt happier with all this. Grant could keep his squeaky-clean executive clothes and luggage, and all those deodorants.

She encouraged Tom to pursue his performing ambitions, vaguely thinking they'd never be achieved. It was quite like old times, to be living with a man who was still striving upwards, not being driven there in a limousine.

The settlement with Grant was sorted out in reasonable harmony and so the course for the future was set. When the divorce became absolute, she wouldn't be rushing off to wed Tom. They would continue in their sixties commune, even to the extent of Tom smoking those hopelessly outdated cigarettes of his.

On arriving back in England, one of the first people Carly had tried to contact was Fawn Flack, her oldest friend from Liverpool days. She sought to recapture something of the old life.

Carly knew that, in spite of all the art expended on her person, the professional life of 'Fawn', as she now called herself more simply, had not taken off. She supposed Fawn was in London, though she couldn't be sure. She asked around, but drew a blank.

Now she said to Tom, 'Are you going into Beverly Hills Artistes at all?'

The agency in Regent Street was linked to the one in LA for whom Harry Emanuel, Tom's American agent, worked. It was through Fawn that Tom had joined Harry.

'Could be. Why?'

'Ask if they're still in touch with Fawn. I really would like to see her again.'

'Okay,' Tom replied distractedly. He never wrote anything down, so he was bound to forget, thought Carly.

But he did not. He had news of Fawn all right. He could hardly believe what he'd learned.

'Fawn's dead,' he told her.

'What?'

'Topped herself.'

'No!' It was a yelp of pain from Carly. 'How?'

'Sleeping pills. Happened last week.'

'Where was she?'

'LA.'

'Oh, if only I'd known. If I'd been there . . .'

'Yeh, well, she had a rough time. When she dropped out of *Tut!* she must've gone back there for another try.'

'But why didn't she get in touch with me?'

'Too grand, you were, Beverly Hills and all that.'

'But why Fawn? She's about the last person I'd have thought would kill herself, she was such a bloody fighter. And the way she lost all that weight and did herself over, that took real guts.'

'They said she'd started putting weight back on. She worried about never making it. It really was the end when her part got cut in *Tut!* It can't have been much fun for her the way it's gone on and on and up and up, without her in it.'

'God, she's the first of our little group to go, isn't she? I can't believe it.'

'It happens. Showbiz isn't all smiles, y'know. It's pretty bleak when things don't go well.'

'But if only we'd known, we could have talked to her, helped her.'

'It mightn't have made a scrap of difference. Once people make their minds up, all the love in the world won't stop them.'

'But Fawn, and in LA, too. It's as if she followed us out there.'

The sad news hung over Carly for days. She tried to find out what had happened and whether Fawn had relatives in Liverpool who might need help. She drew a blank, but it was typical of Carly that she both took it so badly and tried to do something about it. The death continued to haunt her.

* * *

Suzie Paul had to keep telling herself it wouldn't last, this success, but while it did she might as well enjoy it.

It was true, the phrase about being the 'toast of New York'. When you were up, you were definitely up. She was invited to the best receptions. She was bowed to in restaurants. She merely had to mention her name for doors to open. Even when she produced her credit card in a Fifth Avenue store, a card still bearing the name 'Mrs Suzie Greenlee', she was recognized by an assistant.

'Oh, my God, you're that *actress*!'

Suzie smiled and nodded.

'What's the show? Not *Chorus Line*? No. *Jesus Christ Superstar*? Which one is it?'

'*Tutankhamun!*' replied Suzie quietly.

'Of course it is. My, you're so wonderful.' The woman started to applaud in the middle of the store. American celebrity was like nothing Suzie had known hitherto, but she knew the invitations would dry up as soon as she was out of the show. It would be as though she'd never existed.

Suzie's success only added to her allure in Grant's eyes. He was positively proprietorial and saw her present status as the logical outcome of all he'd striven for since first setting eyes on her.

Could she go any further? Was there anything else for Grant to strive for on her behalf?

Two months into the run, Suzie had to break to Grant a piece of news, not knowing how he'd take it.

'I'm pregnant.'

Grant swallowed. 'Say that again. I thought you always –'

'Pregnant. It's confirmed.'

'God.'

He could be forgiven for a certain hesitation in welcoming the sudden news. He had, after all, married his first wife on the basis of what later turned out to be a pregnancy for which he wasn't actually responsible. He had no reason to fear being taken for a ride a second time, but he did stand to lose the leading lady of his show.

'When's it due?'

'Six months and a bit.'

'So you won't be able to go beyond your present contract?'

'Grant! We're not talking contracts, we're talking about *our child*!'

'I'm sorry, it just kind of puts a different perspective on everything, doesn't it?'

'Nothing else matters, you mean?' she suggested, romantically.

'No, I don't mean that,' Grant replied, and Suzie felt like hitting him. 'I mean, when are we going to get married?'

'Oh, Grant . . .'

After the following Sunday's performance of *Tutan-khamun!* – the last till Tuesday night – a small executive jet took off from New Jersey and flew across the United States. It landed at Las Vegas, Nevada, just as dawn was breaking.

Grant had long fancied a wedding at one of the little chapels on the Strip at Vegas. No reception, no frills. Not like the last time. And that was where Suzie and Grant were wed.

Mike Fernandez from the Main Event laid on the Presidential Suite for the wedding night. It was the one Johnny Todd normally took when doing his shows at the hotel. Fernandez also laid on a limo to take the newlyweds to the airport and he himself accompanied them. It had been a quick visit but Suzie had to be back for the show; no time for a honeymoon.

'Hey, Grant,' said Fernandez, 'you remember that spot of bother we had over the ticket scam?'

'Yes.'

'Well, that Mickey fellow you bailed out –'

'Yes. Mickey Clinch. What of him?'

'Dead, I'm afraid. An overdose. Somewhere on the Strip.'

Grant wiped his face with a hand, felt a sharp stab of pain. Another one gone. He'd only just heard about Fawn Flack. Now it was Mickey. The old gang was disappearing, one by one.

'But he never used to be a druggy. This must've been something new.'

'Maybe.'

'You know, I hadn't spoken to him since all that about the scam . . . except, well, just after, when we gave a party. He pulled a gun on me. It was a toy, one of those where a flag pops out, but, hell, how was I to know that? I overreacted, I suppose, and kicked him out. Kept him on the payroll for old times' sake, but effectively that was it between us.'

'Always bad to do anything for old times' sake, I reckon,' said Fernandez, turning back to look at the road.

'I suppose he must've hung about here, wasting the money I paid him. Why the hell didn't he go home?'

Suzie could see that her new husband's question was unreasonable. So, too, in a moment, did Grant. 'Oh, hell, life doesn't get any better, does it?'

It was not the happiest remark from a man who had just remarried.

CHAPTER 33

Carly did not intend to sit around in London living off the money from Grant's divorce settlement, nor was she going to make more use of Tom's income than she thought was fair. She had been inactive for far too long. She knew she must push out and do something.

There was no question of her going back to selling clothes, or indeed of running a shop of any kind. That was all in the past. Besides, in the winter of 1978–9, with Britain grinding to a halt amid a wave of strikes and stoppages, fashion of any kind seemed frivolous. Carly had always had a good eye for what was commercial and the talent had not left her. Now she knew exactly what she must do, especially to make use of all the contacts she had acquired during the 'dead' years of her marriage.

'I've had an idea,' she told Tom. 'I'm going to do a book of photographs.'

'Who by?'

'Me, stupid. You know how I'm always snapping away. I've got stacks and stacks of stuff going way back when. I think it's a goldmine, all the people we used to meet, in the business, everywhere.'

'Such as?'

'Well, just everybody. And I'll take some proper portraits, too. Write to people. Don't you think it's a good idea? Sort of behind the scenes of pop.'

' "Johnny Todd seen sharing a joke with Bing", you mean?'

'Johnny Todd in the nitty-gritty if it comes to that!'

'What'll you call it? How about "Pop window"?'

'I'll think of a title. Well?'

'You find yourself a publisher, then I'll tell you it's a great idea.'

Carly felt a mite put down. 'You don't think it'll work?'

'Put me on the cover and I'll love you for always.'

'It's a deal. Don't move. Let me get my Nikon.'

'But I ain't got me clothes on!'

'So? "Hunky Tom Sheridan fancying himself" – that'll be your caption.'

'Who?'

If having to wait for luck, having to wait for the break, was a necessary qualification for success, then Tom Sheridan was well qualified.

Partly on account of his own character, his impulsiveness, his fecklessness, Tom had pushed away success on several occasions. But now it seemed to be his turn.

Reunited with Carly and their child, he loved domesticity in a way he'd never imagined possible. It seemed to suit him. He had settled down. The fact that he wasn't formally married to Carly added an element of spice and uncertainty to their relationship.

But his future as a performer was still not clear. His first album had made little impact. It was no substitute, though a comfort, to have substantial royalties from *Tutankhamun!* coming in. The desire to perform his own work remained strong. At last, he found a way to do it.

Beverly Hills Artistes in London had a bright young agent on its staff called Lori O'Sullevan. She was a firm believer that talent was not the most important element in entertainment success. It was how an artiste was handled, projected and promoted.

All agents, not least Grant Pickering, paid lip-service to this view, but many agents (and, probably, not least Grant Pickering) got by much of the time through being handed talent on a plate, performers already well on the road to fame. The job of such agents was to recognize this fact and give it a helping hand in the right direction. A small but key function was also that they provided the artiste with a kind of legitimacy simply by supporting him. Unless he had an agent, the artiste didn't really exist, and no one wanted to do business with him.

As Lori O'Sullevan was astute enough to recognize, Tom Sheridan needed more than that to get him through. He needed careful handling and she decided, impulsively, that she was the one to give it to him. It helped that she, too, was Irish – rather more Irish, indeed, than Tom himself. She came from Dublin and now plied her trade in London with all the confidence of the expatriate and of her race. She was, if anything, younger than Tom, but that bothered neither of them. She bossed him around like a big sister and he didn't resist or resent.

Tom and Lori talked, and talked, but to a purpose. Lori knew that out of idle chat between agent and client came ideas. If there wasn't the idle chat, the ideas didn't come. It was during one of these cigarette- and booze-strewn sessions that Lori began to grasp key things about Tom's potential that no one had ever done before.

There was a simple reason why Grant had never noticed them: he'd never looked. He disliked Tom, maybe with good reason, and he had never been in a mood positively to help him.

Lori soon saw that one of Tom's chief motivations was wanting to *show* people like Grant how good he was. He wanted to be able to crow, 'I told you so. You said I'd never succeed but I have . . . and no thanks to you!' It was a motivating force with quite the same power as revenge and Lori saw no harm in it.

She pumped Tom for information about his life until she understood the complicated set-up regarding himself, Carly and Grant. Then she asked, 'Tell me about Johnny Todd, I've never been very clear about all that. It's not his real name, is it?'

'God, no. His real name's Geoffrey Perkins or Charlie Farnsbarns or some such. No, that was another of Grant Pickering's crimes, you see. There's this old Liverpool seashanty, 'Johnny the Sailor Boy'. It goes: *Johnny Todd he took a notion/For to go across the sea . . .* If you recognize the tune, it's 'cos they used it as the *Z Cars* theme. But Pickering pinched the name, like so much else. He stuck it on this guy from Manchester. Crime against humanity, if you ask me.'

'D'you know any other seasongs?'

'Do I wah? How about "The Leaving of Liverpool"?'

Tom had his guitar with him. He played, and he sang as much of the song as he could remember:

Fare thee well to Princes' Landing Stage,
River Mersey fare thee well.
I am off to Califor-ni-a
A place I know right well.

> *So fare thee well, my own true love.*
> *When I return united we will be.*
> *It's not the leaving of Liv-er-pool that grieves me*
> *But me darling when I think of thee.*

Now I'm off to California
By way of the stormy Cape Horn,
And I'll send you a letter, love,
When I am homeward bound.

I shipped on a Yankee clipper ship,
Davy Crockett is her name,
And Burgess is the captain of her,
And they say she's a floating hell.

> *So fare thee well, my own true love.*
> *When I return united we will be.*
> *It's not the leaving of Liv-er-pool that grieves me*
> *But me darling when I think of thee.*

514

Lori loved it. 'You should think of doing more like that, Tom.'

'But I'm not a folksinger.'

'No, more folk-rock, I appreciate that, but if you could get some of that *spirit* in your work, you'd really have something. I mean, how about a modern seashanty? Or what someone from Liverpool would sing about California today? Just think what that could be like.'

'Maybe. I've been there, but I'll have to ask Carly, she can give me the dirt.'

Tom had at last met someone who was prepared to work with him rather than against him. It helped that she was a woman. He knew you couldn't fool women. Carly had taught him that long ago.

At the end of her six months on Broadway, Suzie Paul bowed out of *Tutankhamun!* It was a pity, but four months pregnant was not the best state in which to skip about the stage eight times a week. Johnny Todd also came out after the first six months and looked forward to returning to the Coast to refresh his tan. He had proved himself as an actor. He had shown he could carry a musical. Now it was on to films.

The two leading parts were taken over by 'real' American actors. In Suzie's case, this somewhat contradicted the argument advanced on her behalf that only an Englishwoman could play the role. But, as everyone was always saying when faced with such a difficulty, 'That's show business . . .'

All was set for the Grant Pickering circus to trek out to California once more. Johnny would be reunited, in some fashion, with Virna. Suzie would discover the delights of poolside life and Mexican cooking at Quornford West. Grant would be able to settle for slightly longer periods behind his desk by the picture window on the seventeenth floor of the Occidental Tower and feel that that was where he really belonged.

Initially, as some compensation for her comparatively

short spell as a Broadway star, Suzie would be able to look forward to another glittering prospect – landing the role of Lady Evelyn in the film of *Tutankhamun!* Already there was plenty of speculation over the casting, with Liza Minelli, Shirley Maclaine, even Goldie Hawn being mentioned as probable rivals. Grant said he was adamant that Suzie should have the role.

As for Carter, Johnny Todd was being spoken of, but so were those other unlikely singing 'Englishmen', Robert Redford, Marlon Brando, and Robert de Niro.

'Sometimes I hope the film never gets made at all,' Grant said wearily at one stage. 'All those fuckers wanting to get in on the act.'

It could – surely – make a very good spectacular, however. Ken Russell to direct it, perhaps? David Lean would be better, but he was so old.

Whatever happened, *Tutankhamun!* had served its purpose now. It would continue to bring in money for many years, but those who had been most closely involved at the start began to look on it as a thing of the past.

They were looking forward to the next venture.

Grant celebrated his return to California, both domestically and professionally, with a PR exercise designed to project him as one of the new breed of super-managers. The message was to be very positive. Not only did he represent artistes, he produced shows, too. A film was to be his next project.

It was unfortunate that the business journalists who had been lined up to speak to Grant seemed just as interested in irrelevant tittle-tattle as their showbusiness colleagues.

The man from *Time*, researching a cover story on 'The New Californians', expressed interest in Grant's journey from Liverpool to LA, but only became truly excited at the mention of the Pharaoh's curse.

'Now, look,' Grant wailed exasperatedly, 'do me a favour. I'll give you all the what might loosely be termed facts and you tell me whether they add up. Okay?'

'Okay, Mr Pickering.'

'First of all, it was never proved that a Pharaoh's curse operated in real life at the opening of the Tutankhamun tomb. It was just coincidence. Now, as far as the London and Broadway productions go, there have been only three deaths and only two of those were of people directly connected with the show. Alan Greenlee, my co-producer and the show's originator, died soon after it opened. Then Fawn Flack whose part in the show was cut killed herself. She had a lot of other problems. And then there's a third, totally unrelated event, but I'm mentioning it just for the record. Mickey Clinch, one of my oldest associates, died of an overdose in Vegas. There'd been differences between us, but he had nothing to do with *Tutankhamun!*'

'Except that he would have done if he'd still been Johnny Todd's minder.'

'Oh, you know that? But, look, what sort of coincidence is that? If the Pharaoh's curse is supposed to have rubbed off on the show, it's a pretty weak sort of curse, I must say!'

The man from *Time* appeared open-minded, but Grant, as ever, worried at the interest he'd shown. He set Joe Concho, his PR man, on to the magazine. It was noticeable that when the glowing mention of Grant appeared in *Time's* cover story, there was no trace of any curse nonsense.

A significant change came over Suzie as her pregnancy advanced. For the first time in her life she wasn't obsessed with her career, her looks, or her voice. Her approaching confinement was the most wonderful excuse to let all that go hang. First with Alan, then with Grant, she had been driven to excel. Now, domesticity beckoned and she found that what ambition she had, she could quite easily put off beyond the happy event.

Suzie had no idea how she would survive in American show business. What would she do, anyway? Musicals were so compeititve, even if her husband was a leading agent and producer. She wondered whether she would ever find her nerve again. Perhaps she would be happy just to be a mother and Grant's wife and lotus-eat in southern California. It wasn't a change she would ever have expected in herself, but then she'd never been pregnant before.

Virna Todd attempted to get pally with the new Mrs Pickering just as she had, so ambivalently, with the first. Suzie didn't seem to want to know, however. She appeared to enjoy her own company. Perhaps she looks down on me because I'm not a performer, Virna thought. Perhaps she thinks I'm common, she's so grand.

Whatever it was, there was no housewifely liaison struck up between the two expatriate women. Virna went back to throwing herself brazenly at anything in pants. Her husband carried on in similar fashion with his women, though he had to admit his technique was getting rusty.

In the summer of '79, Tom's new album of songs was recorded in London backed by an *ad hoc* group of session musicians. It was to be called *Thomas Sheridan: Old World, New World*. Lori O'Sullevan had insisted on the 'Thomas'. It sounded more distinctive, so she said.

Working with Harry Emanuel in the LA office, Lori revived the dormant contract with the Rootstock label and the record was set for release first in the UK and then the US.

Carly greeted Tom's getting it together as a performer with immense relief. It had taken so long.

'You'd better be careful,' she joked. 'If you do well, you'll find Grant's bought Rootstock.'

'Aye, and destroyed all my records as quick as they can make 'em!'

'He'll be livid, won't he, if you do well?'

'What d'ya mean "if"! Let him be. There's no way he can lay a finger on any of this. He doesn't own a penny of me.'

'You're sure there's no old contract which says you signed away everything in 1965, just so you could afford a cup of tea?'

'Certain.'

'Well, roll on release day, that's what I say.'

'You'll come with me when I go to the States?'

Carly stopped what she was doing and looked very sternly at Tom.

'No, I won't. I'm never going there again.'

'There'll be all those dollies throwing themselves at me,' Tom told her cheerily. 'You'll regret not being there to scare 'em off.'

'I don't care. What you get up to is your own business. I'd saw me leg off without an anaesthetic rather than go back to that place.'

'All right. But I'll miss you.'

'Well, there's something called the telephone. Know how to use it?'

'Carly . . .'

'At least, I can rely on you to keep away from Grant and Suzie.'

'You can that. I'd rather saw my leg off without . . .'

'Well, at least we're agreed on that. Everything's just fine with Grant now. He pays the alimony and the upkeep, so let's not disturb him.'

'Let sleeping crooks lie.'

Carly stopped what she was doing, yet again. To Tom's surprise, she looked at him and did one of those setting-the-record-straight pieces she was so good at.

'Grant is *not* a crook. I know he behaved shittily to me and I know you hate him for all sorts of reasons, but that doesn't mean he's a crook.'

'Splitting hairs.'

'No, it's not, Tom. I've never had to deal with him in business, I admit that, but from what I've seen and heard, the general view is he's sharp, he's canny, but he's not a crook. So I don't want you putting that around.'

'He's still a shit.'

'You don't spend the years I had with him, the kids and everything, without getting to know a person. And I know Grant's not a crook.'

'I can see there's no arguing with you on that one, so I'll shut up.'

'That, Tom, is the best thing you've ever said on the subject.'

'Ta.'

'And another thing: don't drag me into the publicity, will you? I don't expect they'll want to know that the superstar's live-in companion irons his underpants, so perhaps you'd better not tell them.'

'I shall leave it vague, Carly. Remember all that nonsense there was over whether Johnny T. was married or not? I'll just say there's a "very special lady in my life", and not elaborate.'

'Good. I'm delighted at this burst of good sense, Tom. What *has* come over you?'

And Carly ironed his jeans and his socks and his underpants, just as she'd always done.

'Do I get dragged into the publicity over your book?' asked Tom after a pause.

'Wouldn't be fair, would it?'

'I'm still in it, aren't I?'

'Sure. One of the best pictures. They wanted to leave it out, though.'

'Who did?'

'The woman at the publishers.'

'Why? Not famous enough?'

'Something like that. But I told her: "By the time the book's out, he *will* be famous". It'll be out for Christmas, just after your album, so you'd better make sure that it's true.'

'You're still calling it *The Flip Side*?'

'Yes. No one can think of a better title. It says what the book's about, the other side of pop people's lives, so why not?'

'I suppose they don't think I have a "side" yet, is that it?'

'Stop feeling sorry for yourself, love, and tell the boys to come for their tea.'

June 1979. It was a girl, born slightly premature, but exquisitely small and delicate, and doing well. Grant, who'd just had his own fortieth birthday, was especially happy that it was a girl, after Neville and Steve. He suggested to Suzie they baptize her 'Lady Evelyn'.

'You can't do that,' she said. 'You can't call a kid "Lady".'

'Why ever not? There's "Duke" Ellington and "Count" Basie, why not "Lady" Evelyn Pickering?'

'That's different. Those weren't *given* names, they were nicknames.'

'That didn't stop President Johnson's wife. She was Lady Bird, wasn't she?'

'No. That was "Ladybird", one word, like the insect. Not the same thing at all.'

But Lady Evelyn Pickering she was named.

Lady soon caught up with her proper weight and provided Suzie with an obsession. Whereas Carly had never been at ease doing nothing, Suzie fell to it with a will. She rarely sang now, didn't even hum to herself. It was as though she'd never been in show business.

It was ironic that Grant had married Suzie at all, given how caustic he'd been in the past about singers who wed their managers. It was a pretty unappetizing spectacle, usually – unattractive, middle-aged money-men peddling

521

their wives' much younger flesh and talents. But here was Grant in that very position himself.

Lady still had to go back and forth to the hospital for check-ups during the first six months of her life. There had been a scare that she was handicapped. The doctors had lists that they ticked off and if the child was deficient in more than a certain number of ways, there was cause for alarm.

Grant and Suzie's baby had slightly ungainly movement in her right leg, but the paediatrician said it could well disappear once she started walking or when the leg had fully grown. There was also a problem with one of the tiny toes on her left foot. It was ever so slightly deformed, pushed half under another one. Suzie hated even this smallest imperfection but the paediatrician told her it was of no more significance than a facial mole. If need be, it could be sorted out later on.

In October of that year, Tom's *Old World, New World* album was released in the UK. Alas, it failed to create the stir that everyone, and not least Tom, had hoped for. The most unfortunate consequence was that the American release was put off to the following year. Tom feared this would mean indefinitely. Carly needed to exercise all her skill to prevent him getting terminally depressed.

It didn't help when her book of intimate glimpses of pop people 'off duty' came out the following month. She attracted rather more publicity than Tom had done and *The Flip Side* became a modest but lucrative best-seller in the run-up to Christmas. Tom had the grace to be embarrassed by his appearance in its pages when his name still cut so little ice in the pop world.

'Never mind, love,' Carly reassured him. 'You just wait until they hear you in the States. They'll be begging me to let them have more photies of you.'

'I wish I had your faith, Carl-o.'

'Come on, love. Faith doesn't grow on trees. It grows

on *you*, and you've got to water it. I just know you'll do all right, see? Don't ask me why. Trouble is, when you do okay, it'll be like being with Grant all over again.'

'Well, I'm not there yet, so you can enjoy me like I am for a bit longer.'

'I'll always enjoy you, whatever happens. Always have, always will.'

'I feel another song coming on . . .'

At the age of eight months Lady Pickering was playing in her tiny paddling pool. The main pool at Quornford West had had a low wire fence placed right round it so there wasn't the slightest chance of her falling in. There were going to be no tragedies of that kind in the Pickering household.

Assembled for a barbecue that Sunday in February 1980 were Grant and Suzie, Johnny and Virna, and two executives of the Grant Pickering Organization and their wives. It was a relaxed occasion and the pre-lunch Margueritas were going down fast while Gustavo tended the barbecue.

The sun was just visible through the orange haze and about the only thing that could have interrupted the idyllic scene was the long-awaited major earthquake.

It came, but not quite in the way geologists had expected.

Johnny was holding court from a sunbed. He had slipped off his tennis shirt to reveal a deeply-tanned torso. Otherwise he had on white shorts, white tennis socks and white Italian shoes. He was explaining to one of the executives' wives how glad he was to have his tan back.

'I mean, eight months in New York and I was looking really pasty. And I don't think stage make-up agrees with me, you know. On again, off again, it does strange things to your skin. I often had that rather puffy, pink skin. I believe it's make-up turns it like that. Or else too much time under the lamp. It's one or the other.'

'Well, you've got a fine tan now,' one of the wives told him admiringly, and he accepted the compliment with a smile.

Suzie was wearing a string bikini and was stretched out on her sunbed. Being genuinely blond and fair of skin, she had to be careful with the sun. Her body was now back in shape after having Lady, but perhaps a bikini wasn't what showed her off to the best advantage. She was more of an evening dress person, more exotic by electric light.

Gustavo put the meat on the barbecue where it produced clouds of smoke and the sounds of sizzling.

Grant flopped around in sandals and slacks. He still had his shirt on. Perhaps it was his upbringing that made him always a touch reluctant to bare his flesh. He was telling one of the executives how he'd first set eyes on Suzie at a barbecue. 'It was over ten years ago, near Sydney. I'd gone to give Quentin a little shove on his first-ever overseas tour. Lazarus, the promoter, invited us over one Sunday to a barbie just like this, and there she was.'

'Why was she there?' asked the executive.

'She was married to Alan Greenlee in those days. He'd taken her there to do some dates. A lot of British acts go there, you know. Australian audiences know them from TV, speak the same language, understand the jokes. And there she was. I fell for her right away. Corny, but true! Anyway, it took a long time to get where we are today.'

'Very nice,' said the executive. 'Very nice!'

After the barbecue came the fruit, the sticky pudding and the eight varieties of ice-cream. There was more desultory chat about the future. What was Johnny going to do next? What was Suzie going to do now she'd had the baby? If there was anyone present who believed you shouldn't mix business with pleasure, he shouldn't have been there at all. In these parts, to combine the two was as natural as thinking and breathing at once.

Around three o'clock, Johnny was the first to cast off

his shorts, revealing a red, white and blue striped swim-suit. He checked that he was wearing his waterproof watch and hopped into the pool. The executives, more gingerly, divested themselves of their suits and did likewise. In time, everyone was in the water except Suzie, who didn't feel like it. Or didn't want to ruin her hair.

They soon tired of splashing about and sat drying off by the side of the pool.

It was then that Grant noticed a curious thing, some-thing he'd not noticed before in all the years he'd known Johnny Todd. It was a very small thing. He looked again. Johnny was sitting with his great tanned, hairy legs still dripping onto the tiles. On his left foot, the fourth toe was ever so slightly curled under the third toe.

'Have you always had that funny toe?' Grant asked him.

'Oh, yeh, runs in the family. My mother had one. Brother, too.'

'What about Dylan?'

'No, he escaped. Lucky fella.'

Grant thought for a moment.

'It's odd, though, isn't it?' he said, rather seriously. 'Poor little Lady's got the same problem on her right foot. Come here, darling.'

Grant went over to the paddling pool and lifted his daughter out.

'No, it's not her right foot, it's on her left foot, too. Isn't that amazing?'

Johnny laughed. 'Bunch of cripples, that's what we are. When you have to fill in forms and it says "distinguishing marks", I always feel like putting "funny toe".'

There was a silence. Grant scratched his head – and noticed a look, a glance, flash between Johnny and Suzie.

Everything became immensely, blindingly plain.

CHAPTER 34

Grant had fallen for it again. He had married the woman he wanted to marry, but he had married her, in haste, for the wrong reason.

Talk about the Pharaoh's curse, what sort of curse was this?

Grant shot up from where he'd been beside Johnny, turned, seized his friend by the shoulders and pushed him and the sunbed into the pool. The low wire fence broke in the process.

Everybody except Johnny, Suzie and Grant was surprised by the sudden explosion. Even more so when, as the singer slowly climbed up the steps from the pool, Grant seized the initiative and yelled, 'Get out of my house! Go on, *get out*!'

Turning to Virna, Grant shouted, 'And you, too! If it's not you, it's him. You're a couple of vipers. Get out!'

Johnny, still dripping water, picked up his clothes and shoes and with what dignity he could muster went into the house, closely followed by a bemused Virna. She was still looking towards Suzie, trying to catch her eye. But Suzie had retreated behind her shades, and held her head in her hands.

Grant, his voice husky, turned to his other guests, and apologized for what had happened. He couldn't explain it just now, but he would another day. Please would they leave?

They picked up their belongings and shuffled away, baffled as to what the scene had been about. The executives began to wonder whether the row between Grant and Johnny would be bad for business in any way.

Finally, Grant was alone with Suzie and Lady. He bent down and straightened up the pool-protection wire so that it would be safe for Lady to play nearby once more. Then he sat down. There was a long silence. The only sound was happy mumblings from Lady as she played with her toys.

'I was right, wasn't I? You and Johnny?'

'Yes,' Suzie answered. 'I'm sorry, Grant, you don't deserve this.' The tears ran down her cheeks. 'It's just one of those things. I had no wish to cheat you, or make you unhappy.'

'When did it happen?'

'What?'

'When did you sleep with Johnny?'

'Only once. Really.'

Grant didn't know whether to be relieved by this or not. It didn't count for much, either way.

'You know what Johnny's like,' Suzie went on, between sniffs at her handkerchief. 'He must have done it a million times with other women. He just pushes you until you give in. It's not that he's irresistible, he's just unstoppable once he sets his mind to it. And he *was* my leading man. It was inevitable he'd try it on sooner or later.'

'And which was it? Sooner or later?'

Suzie gulped and looked away. 'You won't believe it.'

'I'll believe anything. Tell me.'

'The first night on Broadway. Before the show. Johnny was like a jelly with his nerves, absolutely scared out of his wits. I'd never seen anything like it. He'd never done a show like that before and there he was on Broadway. He came into my dressing room, we chatted about this and that, and we just sort of did it, to cheer him up.'

'No wonder the curtain was late,' Grant said grimly. 'And that was the only time?'

'That was the only time, Grant, I promise.'

'I suppose we're quits then. While you were fucking away in the dressing room, I was sitting in the stalls being soothed by Virna. Once upon a time, I was being seduced by Virna when Johnny and Carly were up in a fucking balloon.'

It was too bleak an irony for Suzie to laugh.

'How could it have happened to me *twice*?' Grant demanded.

There was no answer. Grant picked up Lady and held her to him, as if to reassure the child that it wasn't her fault in any way.

And yet, Grant held her differently now. There was no escaping it, she wasn't really his daughter and he would never ever be able to hold her again without thinking how he'd been cheated by his oldest friend and client.

It was more than most men could have borne, but although Grant had been cuckolded twice, or cheated, or however people might describe it, he wasn't going to let it affect his onward drive. At least, that is what he told himself. Nothing would be allowed to interfere with the advancing march of the Grant Pickering Organization.

Next day, he made a very short phone call to Johnny.

'Oh, hi, Grant,' Johnny answered expectantly.

'Did you explain to Virna what happened?'

'No, of course not. I've got enough bruises as it is.'

'Well, that's all right then.' Grant hung up smartly.

Johnny knew from this that he'd been forgiven and life was going to go on just as before. He smiled. His luck had held. He couldn't lose, it seemed.

The two executives who'd been at the barbecue were each rung personally by Grant and given an explanation of the row with Johnny which bore no relation to the actual facts. Grant knew that talk around the GPO had to be nipped in the bud. It was just one of those rows that erupt after the lunchtime drinks.

The rift between Grant and Suzie wasn't healed. He thought about it a lot, endlessly replayed the events in his mind, tried to tell himself it wasn't her fault.

But the more he thought, the more he began to think again of Carly. How foolish he'd been to let her go. Suzie was wonderful as a prize – which he'd won – but was she wonderful as a human being?

She had done this thing, hadn't warned him, hadn't told him, hadn't done any of the things she could have done to lessen the blow. Even if she had thought he wouldn't mind, she was guilty of deception.

Grant did what he always did when things went wrong, he busied himself at work, left Suzie increasingly alone with Lady at the mansion. And, in the autumn he started making foreign trips once more. 'Just to check up on the show, you know,' he would say. In addition to the West End and Broadway, there were now productions of *Tutankhamun!* running in Sydney, Tel Aviv, Rome and Tokyo.

Having herself been the other woman in Grant's first marriage, Suzie was afraid he would find a new comforter on his travels.

But Grant had finally changed. He knew where he had gone wrong. If there was to be one woman in his life, he knew which one it was to be.

Lori O'Sullevan was in the car that drew up outside the house in Ealing on the way to the airport.

'Just hold on, I'll dig him out,' she said to the driver.

She rang the doorbell of the big old house. It was quickly answered by a good-looking lad aged about eleven or twelve.

'He's just coming,' the boy announced in a mid-Atlantic accent.

Dear Lord, she thought to herself, and if that isn't the spitting image of Tom himself.

'Ask her in,' came Carly's voice from inside.

'She says to come in,' said Neville.

In the hall was one suitcase and two guitars.

'Is that all?' exclaimed Lori.

'He travels light. Make sure he sends his knickers to the laundry. Or buy some new ones for him when you're over there.'

'Don't worry, Carly, I'll look after him.'

Tom emerged from the kitchen, a mug of tea in his hand.

'Your carriage awaits, your grace,' Lori told him, sensing she shouldn't be around while Tom made his farewells.

'Good luck, Tombo. Let us know how it goes.'

'Ta, love.' Tom was in one of his quieter moods. 'And don't forget, you can always come and join me.'

'We won't go into that again, love. Take care of him, Lori.'

Tom kissed Carly goodbye and headed off down the path.

Neville ran to the gate to see what kind of car it was.

'It's only a Merc,' he noted.

'Don't come back till you've cracked it,' was Carly's final word. With a wave, and what might have been a tear, she turned.

It was the autumn of 1980. Rootstock had finally decided to release *Thomas Sheridan: Old World, New World* in North America. Tom was going over to do all that could be done to make it work. Lori O'Sullevan would hold his hand. Harry Emanuel would join them in New York.

Carly had insisted on staying put in London.

It was convenient that on Grant's next visit to London, in November, Tom wasn't at home with Carly. Grant had gone to the lengths of getting Jan Ferry to ring Carly under the pretence that there was some quibble over the alimony, in order to check that the coast was clear.

Grant should have realized, of course, that Tom was in the States plugging his album, but he hadn't thought of it.

He wanted to see Neville and Steve, as was his right. He

wanted to talk about their visit to him in California the following summer. He wanted to see Carly.

Grant's driver took him out to Ealing and was told to remain parked out of sight round the corner. Grant walked up to the front door of the slightly crumbling old house, thinking immediately how different it was to Quornford West.

The door swung open and there she was, confident and blooming, in a way he realized she hadn't been for years. Carly radiated happiness and content, and Grant could have slapped her for it.

They kissed politely and Carly ushered him past the bicycles in the hall and through to what she called the lounge, though, as it was joined to the kitchen, it would no doubt be called a 'living area' in California.

'They're at school,' she said, clearing away a mess of magazines and records, answering Grant's unspoken question.

'Will I see them?'

'If you're still here when they get back. Cup of tea?'

'Sure.'

Grant settled uneasily into the vast sofa and looked at the Indian paintings on the wall. There was a faint hint of joss sticks in the air. It was curiously evocative of a different world and a different time. It was a wonder how Carly had managed to create all that from just the few props she had left over from the old days.

'So, how's things?' Carly asked, arriving back with the tea tray and Grant's favourite chocolate digestive biscuits.

'Want to hear the good news or the bad news first?'

'I don't want to hear bad news at all,' replied Carly, instantly trying to head him off.

'All right, everything's wonderful, wonderful.'

'How's the baby?'

'Wonderful.'

'I thought it was great, calling her Lady Evelyn! I'd never have had the nerve.'

'Well . . .'

Grant wasn't about to tell Carly how history had repeated itself, how he'd been duped once again into marrying when the child wasn't really his. Carly would have been sympathetic, no doubt, but it was too humiliating to mention.

'What's Suzie up to? Is she working?'

'Not really. She's still waiting to see about the movie.'

'What's happened to that?'

'They're still talking. You know how it is.'

'Yes.'

Poor old Grant, thought Carly. Without saying it, he was telling her that all was not well between him and Suzie.

'And how about you?' Grant was on his best behaviour, remembering to be polite. 'You look very happy. Tom treating you okay?'

'Yes, lovely, but he's not here. You know he's in New York with his album? Trust me to shack up with another bloody success, who immediately troops off to the States.'

'You weren't to know. He's doing well then?'

'Fingers crossed.'

'I'm glad.'

'But you've never liked Tom.'

'I know. But he deserves success, and he's waited such a long time for it. They say his new album's very different. I haven't heard it yet.'

'You're kidding? It's been sitting around in the shops for nine months.'

'Well, you know . . .'

'But it's bound to do better in America.'

'I hope it doesn't go to his head.'

'He can't get more drunk, more stoned, or any madder than he is already,' said Carly with a giggle.

'I don't know how you put up with him.'

'I don't put up with him. I get on with my life and he's

sort of there. Least he was until recently. You've never understood about us and I don't suppose you ever will.'

Grant changed the subject. 'Your book did well. Thanks for the copy. And the dedication. I like it. It was very good. Very clever of you. What's next?'

'I'm doing a new one, all new pictures. About the flip side of people in public life. I went to Downing Street two weeks ago, to do Mrs Thatcher. You should see how organized I am. It's frightening!'

'I wish you well, Carly. I still love you.'

'I don't believe you. You may've thought so once, but not now.'

'You can't stop me thinking I do.'

'No, I grant you that. But I won't make it easy for you. The trouble is, you like things how they used to be. Same as everyone else that came out of Liverpool. You're living in the past, as though the Cavern and the Beatles were the Golden Age.'

'Well, it was.'

'Yeh, but we can't spend the rest of our lives being sentimental about it. Heavens, it's nearly twenty years since all that. They have these buses taking tourists round Liverpool showing where John and Paul used to live! That was the telephone box he used to use, that sort of thing. It's unbelievable. I mean, they were only four lads, they weren't Jesus Christ, for Christ's sake.'

'I know, it's terrible, but I love it. And where would we be without it?'

'Much happier,' said Carly, firmly.

'Yeh, and living lives of quiet desperation in Wavertree, or in Upper Parly Street, or whatever.'

'Whereas, Grant, we lead lives of quiet desperation in London, New York and LA. Very flash, but not a load of difference.'

'Oh, yes there is.'

It was a subject they were never likely to agree on.

They talked about Neville and Steve flying out to LA for

534

the summer holidays. She said the boys were excited at the prospect of going back to where they used to live, even though they didn't seem to mind having left.

'Don't you and Suzie spoil them, will you?'

'Of course we will. That's what divorced fathers and step-mothers are supposed to do.'

Grant was relieved he could still talk to this ex-wife as one human being to another. There was no rancour, but that was mainly due to Carly. She was a very special woman.

That was the trouble. He had never appreciated quite how special she was. She hadn't had a talent he wanted to manage, like Suzie. But now he could see that that wasn't what mattered. He had been chasing after the wrong rainbow. He'd been a fool to lose her.

When it was time to go, Grant gave the impression he was walking back to the station, but a moment after he'd disappeared round the corner, Carly wasn't entirely surprised to see him sweeping by in his chauffeur-driven car.

Poor old Grant, she thought, still grappling with it. Then she looked at her watch, wondered what had happened to the boys, and carried on with her life.

Grant sat in the Jaguar, not working but musing. Getting unshackled from Suzie would be a major operation and, even so, he wasn't sure he was sufficiently a bastard to do it. Maybe it was just a fantasy. He had enjoyed testing the water, but the thought must end there. If he was going to escape from his predicament, he'd have to find another way. One thing was certain, though. He'd never be able to win back Carly as long as she was tied up with Tom Sheridan.

Tom had responded to the strong-arm tactics of Lori O'Sullevan and Harry Emanuel. It was what he had needed all his life, someone to take his career in hand. Now it was all coming together.

Thomas Sheridan: Old World, New World began, ever so slowly at first, to climb the US album charts. At the first sign of movement, however, other possibilities presented themselves. Interviews, appearances on TV shows, a concert tour beginning in the New Year.

It was apparent that Lori had pinpointed precisely the right fusion of folk and rock to provide the successful formula that had eluded Tom for so long. She had also focused on Tom's masculine appeal. He was a hunk, he photographed well, and in the flesh those bright blue eyes were magic. Why had no one made capital out of these assets before?

By the first week in December, his album had reached No. 19.

Grant had taken to staying at the Connaught. Suzie's old flat in St John's Wood had long been disposed of and Grant had revised his view of London hotels. If the Connaught seemed sedate, well, that increasingly was how he felt. What clinched it for him, probably, was seeing David Niven in the lobby there one day. If one English exile found it right, so could Grant.

There was another change now. He kept himself to himself these days when he was away from home. He was going through a more respectable period. He didn't feel like picking up dancers from the show, or any other woman, just for the sake of it.

That night he dined quietly in the Connaught Grill at seven. He had acquired the American habit of dining early, and sat on his own reading *Variety*. His meal of petite marmite, roast pheasant, trifle, and half a carafe of red Bordeaux slipped down almost unnoticed. Then he went up to his room and flicked on the TV, as he always did, just to see what was on.

He had quite a surprise. At 8.30 on ITV, there was a game show called *Identikit* which he hadn't come across before. The usual mixture of professional quiz guests and 'real people' (members of the public) were having to establish the identity of a well-known person from a kit of clues provided by the chairman – height, weight, inside leg measurement, and so on. As they made the right deductions, the face of the person gradually formed, jigsaw-style, on a computerized screen over their heads. Cash prizes were involved somewhere along the line, but the rules of the game seemed excessively complicated, to no purpose, or so Grant thought.

It was like a hundred other shows of its kind, but Grant was riveted by the simple fact that *Identikit*'s genial host was none other than Rex Room.

So, Rex had finally made it! After Alan Greenlee's death, Rex hadn't come back to the Grant Pickering Organization. He'd presumably been taken up by another agency, unless he'd started representing himself, in which case getting this TV series was quite a coup.

Grant marvelled at what he saw: Rex, never the most personable of men, contriving to spin the show along and dispense bonhomie. He looked older than Grant remembered. His paunch had disappeared – probably on doctor's orders. He must be fiftyish now, thought Grant, but looks sixty. Not necessarily a drawback. The British adored their entertainers if they were survivors, and Rex was nothing if not that.

Grant hoped Rex had found something to make him happy at last – the brittle glory of the game-show host. He had never collected his *Tutankhamun!* pay-off, as far as Grant could remember. The matter rested, just as Alan Greenlee, the victim, did.

It was ironic that the show was called *Identikit*, given Rex Room's known associations with the East End criminal fraternity. Grant didn't wait to see how it developed. There was bound to be some 'twist' or 'mystery guest', but he had seen what he wanted to see, and flicked over to another channel.

Then, as abruptly, he switched back.

It suddenly became clear to him what had happened. Rex

537

must have persuaded his chums in organized crime to put the frighteners on Alan Greenlee, and they must have gone a bit too far. That was why he had been so embarrassed by Grant's offer of the two grand. It was obvious, when Grant thought about it.

Should he let on? No. What would be the point? Rex had suffered enough. You could tell that, just by looking at him, smile or no smile. Just fancy that, though . . .

Four days later, on Monday, 8 December 1980, Grant was in New York, heading for LA and making a regular check on the Broadway *Tutankhamun!* He was even prepared to concede that it was a better show without Johnny and Suzie, though the principals were far from household names.

It was time for him to get involved in a follow-up. He started reading proposals and auditioning scores, but he wasn't at ease with the process. He needed an Alan Greenlee to set things up for him. Grant's talents didn't lie in that direction. Above all, he needed stars to find jobs for, and at the moment there were no calls on him in that respect.

He heard the news from the limo driver. Grant had been picked up at the Amber Theatre after the show, to be driven back to his suite at the Pierre.

'Bad news, Mr Pickering. That Lennon's been shot. At the Dakota.'

The words went right through Grant.

'*John* Lennon?'

'Said on the radio he's dead.'

'But who . . .?'

The answer didn't matter. At the Pierre, he rushed up to his suite, picking up the copy of the *Daily Telegraph* that the hotel's British management had thoughtfully put under his door, but it was the previous morning's edition, so told him nothing.

He turned on the television and sat waiting to hear more.

Since the early days in Liverpool, John had been the unspoken ideal that Grant had hankered after. He had been a man with an extraordinary genius for expression, for a kind of leadership of his generation, and – it had to be said – for getting up people's noses.

Grant had once wanted to be John Lennon. For many years he had conscientiously followed John's changes in looks and clothes. Unfortunately, Grant had lacked the talent to go with them.

Now the man was gone, murdered, pointlessly, not a mile across the park from where Grant was sitting. Grant cried. A rare thing for him. But he was alone, so it did not matter.

The death of John seemed to be the end of so much more. Grant felt it was the end of everybody's youth, the final gasp of those desperately, dangerously lingering sixties, the expiry of many a hope and dream, especially of those who had travelled so far from their unlikely beginnings amid the grimy industrial nowhere of Liverpool.

There was no one to talk to. England would be asleep. He rang Suzie in California and tried to make her understand. She, in turn, tried to soothe him, over the thousands of miles.

He spoke to Johnny Todd in LA. Johnny was devastated, too, though he had always felt himself part of a different musical world. He had thought that Lennon despised him, and shrank from picking up any of the withering comments that Lennon levelled at his style. His chief concern over the killing was his own security. His brush with the mad Halo had triggered the worry and he now rapidly insisted on having a personal assistant/security man to replace the long departed Mickey Clinch.

Grant stayed on in New York until the following weekend. He got drawn into the ten-minute silent vigil in Central Park on the Sunday, opposite the Dakota building. He went down and stood in the crowd, alone and sad. They said there were fifty or a hundred thousand people there, many carrying flowers. No one knew who he was.

When he returned to the hotel, he was taken aback to find Tom Sheridan among those paying tribute to Lennon on television. It must have seemed logical to someone. Tom's album proclaimed his origins as much as Lennon had always done. He even managed to suggest that he and Lennon had once been buddies. Twenty years of embroidered reminiscence had clouded even Tom's mind as to whether he had or hadn't ever set eyes on the hero.

Grant wondered whether to make contact with Tom. The TV seemed to suggest he was in New York. In the circumstances it might be possible for them to have a drink together, express solidarity, tell sad stories of the death of kings. Grant could help Tom in some way, possibly, with his growing American fame. Talk about *Tutankhamun!* Or Carly. Whatever he liked.

His hand fell back from the phone before he lifted the receiver.

No. What he must do instead was overcome his reluctance and actually listen to Tom's record.

Grant wrapped himself up against the cold again, went out and found a 24-hour record store. He bought a cassette of *Thomas Sheridan: Old World, New World* to play on the new Walkman he had just acquired. Back at the Pierre, he poured out a bourbon and put the tape on. He listened to it right the way through.

When he had finished he turned over the cassette and listened to it all again. Was it just because of the circumstances, or did Tom Sheridan really remind him of John Lennon? Grant picked up the phone.

A meeting never took place. Next day Grant flew out of New York, heading for Quornford West. He was unusually uncertain what the future held, especially since a door had just been so resoundingly shut on the past.

John Lennon's *Double Fantasy* album soon swept to the top of the US charts. In the same week, Tom reached No.

10, as high as he would go. That both albums were within the top ten was fantastic, and he revelled in the fact.

Tom launched into his concert tour, beginning with indoor venues on the East Coast in the New Year, then outdoors in the west for the next few months.

By March 1981, he was high on experience and adulation but physically exhausted from the punishing schedule. He began to long for England once more. Even for Liverpool. He longed for Carly, too. She still stubbornly refused to accept any inducement to be flown out to join him.

He wasn't entirely faithful, taking his pleasures with such mature groupies as presented themselves, and even with Lori O'Sullevan on a couple of occasions. He also increased his dependence on soft drugs, alcohol and cigarettes. It was amazing he had any voice left at all, he punished it so. He would argue that the punishment made it what it was.

The last venue on the tour was to be Anaheim Stadium in LA. Just two nights, and then the wrap. He wondered whether Grant or any of the other California exiles would come along. He was pleasantly surprised to find it was Johnny Todd who made the move.

Johnny seemed personally to have tracked Tom down to his hotel and bamboozled his way past the switchboard, a supposedly impossible task. A large handwritten notice in front of the operator warned, 'No calls to Mr Sheridan, penalty of death . . .' But Johnny Todd could get away with that sort of thing.

'Hi, Tom, wake you up? Welcome to LA. It's Johnny Todd.'

'Hey, hey,' Tom whooped. 'You sound just like a local, Johnny!'

'I *am* a local, Tom. Welcome aboard! Say, what are you doing in a mean old hotel like that?'

'Orders. I've a minder and a manager who keep me under lock and key. I'm a prisoner.'

'Well, what are you doing after your show Saturday

night? You'll be free as a bird then. Come and stay at the ranch a few days.'

'What ranch?'

'Oh, it's just a name. Our place in Malibu. You remember Virna? She'd love to see you again.'

'I remember Virna. Well, thanks very much. That'd be great. Then I have to go home. I'm with Carly, you know. Haven't seen her for about six months, though. Can't get her out here for all the tea in China.'

'Shame, Tom, real shame.'

Tom looked forward to relaxing at Johnny's ranch for a couple of days. With any luck, he might even be able to avoid Grant Pickering.

CHAPTER 35

No such luck. The last, standing-room-only, performance was no sooner over than Johnny and Virna, Grant and Suzie were making their way down the concrete tunnels behind the Stadium. They burst into Tom's dressing area and pounded him on the back with their congratulations.

Johnny was shaking Tom warmly by the hand and not letting go, making sure his right side was presented to the flashing cameras. Virna and Suzie, less ostentatiously, went up and kissed him.

Then, lastly, with a grave quietness, Grant shook Tom by the hand and told him, 'You've done it, you old pro. I never thought you would, but you have. I haven't stopped playing your album since I got it. I'm going to say it, Tom – I should never have let you go!'

Tom, high as he was, noticed the difference in Grant and felt there was poetic justice in the compliment. He didn't have to say, 'I told you so'. It was written all over his face.

Shortly afterwards, Tom, the two couples, Lori O'Sullevan, Harry Emanuel, and a few hangers-on swept off in a motorcade to the Polo Lounge.

Tom stood out in the group. He was the star that night.

'You'll have to come and live here now,' Virna told him invitingly. 'Join the clan. You can't go back to England now. This is the place.'

Tom took refuge in his favourite tipple. 'I'm not so sure,' was all he could manage to say. 'I don't think I'll ever learn to like goat's cheese pizza.'

'Carly won't let him, I don't suppose,' Grant tried to say quietly to Virna, 'you've got to remember that.'

'Oh, he'll crumble eventually,' Johnny interrupted, loudly. 'After all, we did!' They all laughed in a very showbiz way.

'Want to bet?' Grant asked, a little seriously.

'No, I don't bet with you, Grant, you know that. I'll just be right, and tell you so.'

'There's a lot of that going on tonight.'

Tom pretended not to hear.

Indeed, the object of all this discussion was now attempting, with difficulty, to light another cigarette from the candle in the middle of the table, but was too unsteady to make it. Johnny fished in his jacket pocket and produced a diamond lighter. He lit Tom's cigarette. Tom slurred a 'Thanks'. Then Johnny slipped the lighter in the top pocket of Tom's leather bomber jacket.

'There. Keep it. A present. I don't need it, now I've given up the weed.'

'Ta.'

The more sober individuals chatted on, turning to Tom from time to time, to check that he was all right. Suzie saw how lonely he was and wondered if he would ever go back to Carly, or whether she'd even want him back after what he'd achieved. She chose not to remember her own swift rejection of Tom's advances in the early days of *Tutankhamun!*

The Pickerings made their farewells at 1.00 a.m. on the Sunday morning, and Grant paid the bill for everybody, as was his way. He told Tom that they should 'have a talk' before Tom left for home, but he didn't really take in the message. He was led to the Todd motor and helped inside where he sat between Johnny and Virna as they were driven out to Malibu. Tom's own limo came in the rear bearing his four guitars and other luggage. Rather more than he'd left London with.

544

At the ranch, Virna immediately said, 'Excuse me, Tom, I'm going straight to bed. Lie in as long as you like. We don't do nothing Sundays.' She gave him a kiss.

'Goodnight,' muttered Tom, 'and thank you.'

'Come into the den, Tom,' said Johnny. 'One last drink before we shuffle off?'

Tom lurched and Johnny took it as a nod in the affirmative.

His head was spinning but he could just about appreciate Johnny's 'den'. It was a long, low, panelled room with Venetian blinds over floor-length windows. Part den, part boardroom, it had an expensive polished table and high-backed lime-green chairs, probably for meetings that never took place. There was a very large easy chair by the artificial fire. On the shelves were small clocks and cut-glass lamps, unlikely to have been chosen by the room's chief occupier. Johnny's gold and silver discs covered the walls and numerous certificates and citations were pointed testimony to the work he had done for charity.

Tom swayed towards the original of Johnny's *Newsweek* cover and managed to articulate, 'I didn't know you'd . . .' before collapsing on to the big chair.

'Another malt? What's your choice? I've about eighteen to choose from.'

'Irish,' said Tom, and began the long process of lighting another cigarette for himself. Johnny genially had to point out that Tom now had the lighter in his top pocket.

Johnny poured out the malt, neat, and handed it to Tom. Then he began some curious confession that Tom couldn't really follow. About how he, Johnny, had been an absolute shit. He was really the father of Grant and Suzie's child, Lady. This made little sense to Tom and he thought Johnny must have a screw loose. He, Tom, was the father of Grant and Carly's first child, Neville. Was that what Johnny was on about?

Eventually, even Johnny could tell that the nightcap had been a mistake. He steered Tom towards a guest room on the ground floor of the ranch. Tom wasn't even sure there was an upstairs. He wasn't in a fit state to judge. The walls were revolving now. He just wanted to lie down.

Johnny opened a door in the wall. 'I'm just through here, should you want anything.'

Tom glimpsed the other bedroom before crashing out. He didn't register that Virna was nowhere to be seen in Johnny's bedroom.

Tom slept for two hours, or three, he had no idea really. He woke up with a pain in his head and an ever more pressing one in his bladder. The room was pitch black and it took him a moment or two to remember where he was. Then another three or four to find the light switch, which he couldn't make work.

He was still wearing the clothes he'd fallen asleep in. Painstakingly he yanked his boots off. He stood up and felt round the walls for other light switches. He couldn't find any. He then felt something heavy in his breast pocket, found a diamond lighter, wasn't sure how it had got there, but lit it. This enabled him to see where the door to his host's room was. He avoided that and went out of the other one in search of somewhere to relieve himself.

The ranch was in darkness and utterly quiet. The moon shone eerily through a fan-light over the front door. Tom clattered about, trying each door in turn until he found a bathroom.

Then there was the long journey back to his bed. He advanced, still holding the lighter before him. But which was the door to the bedroom? He opened one at random and found himself looking at the dim form of Johnny in bed. He was apparently sleeping alone, dead to the world.

Tom figured that the door on the other wall would take him back to his own room.

He crossed Johnny's bedroom, but began to feel the lighter getting very hot between his fingers.

So hot that he dropped it. He picked it up, re-lit it, and finally reached the safe haven of his own bed.

CHAPTER 36

By lunchtime on the Sunday, a group of fans had gathered, weeping, by the ranch gates. Armed security guards kept them at bay, somewhat pointlessly, while the ruins still smouldered.

The news was shocking. It wasn't like the death of a hero, as when John Lennon died, but death had taken away another idol and the suddenness of his passing shook everyone, even those who'd never called themselves fans of Johnny Todd.

It didn't take long for the papers to point out that *Tod* was German for 'death' and that Johnny had starred in *Tutankhamun!* which, as everyone was supposed to know, had been afflicted by the Pharaoh's curse just like the original treasure-hunting expedition.

This time Grant Pickering made no attempt to combat the rumours. It was enough that his oldest friend and client, the cornerstone of his showbusiness empire, had been so cruelly cut down in his prime.

The fire had somehow started in Johnny's bedroom and rapidly engulfed the bedclothes and the bed he'd been lying on. About a third of the ranch had been destroyed in the ensuing fire. There were no other fatalities.

Tom had woken to find his room full of smoke. He had managed to struggle out of the house through the hallway. Virna also managed to escape and raise the alarm. Their son, Dylan, ten, had been away from home on the night in question. The Todd staff also escaped unharmed.

Grant fixed everything. Virna came to stay at Quornford West. Suzie looked after her. Grant dealt with the police and fire department. It was a mystery. Johnny had given up smoking, so it was unlikely that he had set fire to the bed himself. Tom admitted he'd been terribly drunk and had no idea what might have occurred after Johnny had shown him to his room. Forensic tests were being made, though there was little hope of finding the cause of the fire.

After the forensic tests, what was left of Johnny's badly-burned body was put in a glittering coffin to await a lavish, showbusiness funeral. His fans continued to cluster around the entrance to the ranch, outside the security fence, for the first few days, but in time they drifted away.

Tributes were fulsome, including one from President Reagan, newly installed in the White House. Johnny's records were played non-stop on middle-of-the-road stations across America. The lights outside the Amber Theatre on Broadway were switched off in tribute to the man who had formerly played the role of Howard Carter in the highly successful but – so they said – jinxed production of *Tutankhamun!*

Grant organized the funeral. Almost five hundred people attended, filling the church to the door. In a moment of dramatic irony, real theatre, the true significance of which was lost on all but three of the mourners, Suzie Paul sang an arrangement of the song, 'I Have Seen Yesterday' from *Tutankhamun!* Neither she nor Johnny had actually sung it in the show, but it seemed the most fitting one to choose.

Tom Sheridan, who had written the words, sat in the front row of the congregation in an unaccustomed black suit and dark glasses. Since the tragedy he had stayed on in California in a daze. He had even gone to stay with the Pickerings at Quornford West.

He wasn't sure what would happen next. Renewed pleas to Carly, from him and from Grant, had failed to bring her over for the funeral. She felt it was none of her business. Just now, Tom desperately wanted a smoke, and kept fingering the large diamond lighter in his pocket.

During the short eulogy, Grant sat with bowed head. He didn't take in a word. He held Suzie's hand. Lady Evelyn was too young to attend her actual father's funeral. How would they explain it all to her?

Virna carried herself with dignity. What was she going to do now, a superstar's widow marooned far from home in southern California? Well, thought Grant, at least she won't be short of a dollar or two. Already people in the business were joking that Johnny had made a good career move. There was nothing like a good death to stimulate record sales. It would only be a matter of time before the *National Inquirer* burst into print and told its readers that Johnny was still secretly alive and had faked his death to reap the benefits.

But Johnny was as dead as dead could be. His body was buried as decorously as the funeral directors could arrange in a torrential downpour. Who said it never rained in California?

Black limousines collected the soaking mourners. Virna, Suzie and Grant held a small wake at Quornford West, but few attended. It seemed the end of everything, another mystery unsolved, another member of the Liverpool circus taken away. Another penalty paid.

In time, a large tombstone was lowered over Johnny's grave. It simply said:

JOHNNY TODD
singer
Born 1939   Died 1981
'I have seen yesterday. I know tomorrow.'

There was no mention that he had been born Michael Armstrong or that he had come from England to seek his fortune in America or that he had made it. The detail was irrelevant.

Grant paid a visit with Virna when the stone was in place.

'Are you happy with it?' he asked her.

'As happy as anyone can be. Yes. Thank you, Grant – for everything. I don't suppose we'll see so much of each other now.'

'Why not? You're not going away?'

'No, I'm staying. The old country's not for me. I'm just going to have to make it on my own now.'

'What'll you do?'

'What does any showbiz wife, or widow, do? I'll find something. And if I can't, I'll just have to go fuck for it.'

Grant turned away from the tomb, as if not wanting Johnny to hear this. Like everyone else, he had heard the rumour that Virna had contrived to seduce Tom Sheridan on the day of the funeral, but he dismissed that as just talk.

'We'll always be around to help,' he told her.

She slipped her arm in his and they walked away from Johnny's grave to the waiting limo.

'Whatever happens to you, Grant, you survive. Like when you lost that money, you bounced back. Like when Carly left you, you had Suzie. Now you've lost the living legend. But you'll be okay, the money keeps rolling in.'

'Maybe,' he said, distractedly. 'That's what people think. I'm the man who made a buck or two, even in Timbuktu. There's only one thing I haven't got, and I don't expect I'll ever get it now.'

'What's that, Grant?'

'I'm not telling you, it's too precious. I've been foolish about it, and that's that.'

'Tell me, Grant.'

'No, Virna. The day when you could tempt me and succeed is gone. Come on, let's get out of this place. I've had enough of death to last me quite some time.'

Virna laughed a small, throaty laugh. She felt the same

552

and didn't so much as give a last glance at Johnny's grave.

In the car, she sat in the seat next to Grant.

'It's Carly, isn't it?'

Grant looked at her.

'What is?'

'What you haven't got.'

Grant made no reply, but Virna saw that she was right.

'When I Return, United We Will Be . . .'

EPILOGUE

July 1981

'Look what the tide's brought in. If it isn't Grant Pickering!'

It was Denis Northington greeting him from the front seat of his taxi-cab.

'Denis!'

Grant smiled, both annoyed and flattered that his anonymity had been shattered the moment he stepped off the train from London.

'So this is what you're doing now?'

'It's a job. And there ain't too many of them in these parts . . .'

Grant sat back in the taxi with the former drummer from the Offbeats at the wheel.

'Show me the sights, Denis, as though I'd never been here before.'

Grant wasn't sure what he wanted to see. He just wanted to remind himself that it all still existed. Or some of it. Immediately, he realized how small it all was, how the places in the centre of Liverpool in which he had worked and played nearly twenty years before were so close together. Closer together than in his memory, anyway.

'No, changed my mind,' Grant instructed. 'Let's go to Mathew Street.'

'Ah, well now, I once played the Cavern, y'know.'

'Of course I *know*, Denis.'

The taxi inched along where the Cavern used to be.

'That's new. What d'ya think?' Denis pointed to a tribute to John Lennon up on the wall. 'They wanted to put up a statue, but they can't find the money.'

'Ah,' said Grant, noncommittally.

'Terrible thing that, eh? And then Johnny. Terrible, too. You must have felt terrible, eh? I tell you there'll be no one bleeding left the way we're all dropping off these days.'

'How's your mam?'

'She passed over a couple of years ago.'

'Sorry. Mine died last week. That's why I'm back. Funeral tomorrow.'

'Ah, I see. Sorry, mate.'

Grant half-smiled. 'Well, there you are. Will you take me to Upper Parliament Street?'

'You're kidding, Grant. Want yer balls roasting, or summat?'

'What d'you mean?'

'It's no-fookin'-go after last night. All over that way.'

Ah yes, the rioting. Grant had read about it in the paper on the way up in the train. But it was just an obstacle he'd have to overcome. He was back in Liverpool for a funeral, but with another purpose, too, and nothing, not even riots, must be allowed to get in the way.

He had come back to find a woman, the one who used to be his wife. For him, the most important thing ever to come out of this city, and he'd been foolish enough to lose her.

Then she was there. Beyond the police barriers, amid the flames and destruction in Upper Parliament Street. A sheet of flame enveloped the white facade of a shop and it collapsed in a shower of sparks and dust. Carly ran forward, almost pushed by the force of the blast. Yet she appeared cool. She was in control. As always. What was she doing there at all?

Grant didn't know whether to let her see him at first. In the end, he simply stood amid the noise, the heat and the terror, and she came towards him, almost as if she'd been expecting him.

558

She stood erect and let him kiss her. They held hands.

'So you've come?' she said, her words almost lost beneath the ringing of burglar alarms, the wailing of police sirens and the crackle of burning.

'What are you doing out here, love?'

'I came to look for Steve. Well, sort of. He wanted to watch what was going on. Don't worry, he can look after himself.'

'What on earth have we done to deserve this?' Grant shouted.

Carly didn't attempt an answer. 'Why are *you* here?' she asked.

Now Grant didn't answer, but asked Carly where she lived exactly.

'Just round the corner. Come on.'

They moved away from the scenes of destruction and within a minute were in a deserted square over which the tower of the cathedral loomed in the flame-lit sky. The square had once contained the most splendid and opulent of Georgian houses, but many of them were now boarded up. No. 18 looked in better condition than most and Grant noticed the substantial security locks all over the door.

'Here we are,' she said, revealing the key she'd been holding close to her chest. She opened the door. Grant sensed at once that the atmosphere was very like that of the house she'd left in Ealing. The boys' things were everywhere and traces of the sixties were as marked as ever. Murals, collages and fabrics covered every available surface.

'Cuppa?' Carly asked.

'You've nothing stronger?'

' 'Course. Help yourself, there's most things on the tray.'

Grant poured himself a whisky and settled into an armchair. Carly sat on a low stool and hugged her knees.

'Hey, you've got a mark on your shoes!'

'Where?' Grant was quite alarmed that anything should have interfered with the perfect white of his Gucci slip-ons. Then he smiled. Carly was teasing him.

'Should've worn my Beatle boots, eh?'

'Not the ones I sold you? You've still got 'em?'

'They're in the museum.'

'I hope you've got nothing embarrassing in there!'

'Not really.'

'So why've you come, today of all days?'

'Me mam's dead.'

'Oh, love, when's the funeral?'

'Tomorrow.'

'D'ya want me to come?'

'Up to you. It's in Hoylake.'

'I'll see. At least you're going, doing the right thing at last.'

'Maybe.'

'Where are you staying?' Carly asked.

'The Adelphi.'

'Of course.'

'Still terrible.'

'Oh, aye. You can stay 'ere, if you want to. I doubt if you'll get much sleep. The police'll be at it all night, I expect.'

'It's terrible, all that. I can't understand how it happened. I mean in LA, okay. They had riots, but this . . .'

'Yeh, well. It's been waiting to happen. And it's not just the black kids like they're saying. They're all in it.'

'You're not scared?'

'No more than in LA. The boys'll look after me – if they come home.'

'Do you wish you'd stayed in London?'

'No. Best thing I ever did, coming back.'

'And how's the restaurant? How long's it been open now?'

'Four weeks.'

'It's open tonight?'

'Oh, yes, but if anyone comes it'll be reporters covering the riot, I expect.'

'And you really call it Fingers?'

'Yeh. Came to me just like that.'

'Not Two Fingers, nothing to do with the Fickle Finger of Fate?'

Carly smiled one of her innocent smiles. 'You think what you want, Grant.'

'I wonder what you'll do next? You've had a shop, been a photographer. When're you going into showbiz?'

'Never, if I can help it.'

'I'm really pleased, you know. I'd never have thought of it, but it's perfect for you. You were always such a bloody good cook. And you could organize anything, standing on your head.'

'Anyone can start a restaurant. It's about the only business you can run however old you are when you start. And I don't really do the cooking, just the menus. I've this chef called Pedro. He does six nights, and he's not allowed to do tortillas or any of that Spanish muck. It's great!'

'You underestimate yourself. Anyone can run a restaurant, if they run it badly.'

Carly had finally found the best outlet for her undoubted talents. It was a smart restaurant, situated on the fringe of the city centre, catering for businessmen at lunchtime, people from the university and the theatre at night. In the midst of a depressed city, with the docks shrunk, factories closed, hundreds of thousands out of work or leaving home, it was the one business that could survive.

'I'd very much like to see Fingers.'

'You want to eat?'

'Desperately.'

'Okay, let's go down. I'll hide the key for the kids. We can walk. You remember how to walk, don't you?!'

Grant was about to answer seriously, and then saw she was teasing him again.

'No, I haven't brought the driver, if that's what you're thinking. Came up on the train. Guess who was driving the cab I picked up at Lime Street? Denis Northington.'

'I'm surprised he didn't run you over.'

'Denis never bore a grudge.'

Carly locked up the house, but as they were crossing the square, a voice called out, 'Hey, mom . . . hey, dad!'

They both turned, and there, running towards them, with blackened faces and dirty clothes, were Neville and Steve.

'Dad, what are you doing here?'

Grant hugged both the boys before answering.

'Well,' he said, 'your grandmother's died, so I've come for the funeral.'

'Oh.'

'What have you been doing?' their mother asked. 'Not getting into trouble, I hope?'

'No, mum,' said Neville, who did all the talking. 'It's fabulous, isn't it? Just like the movies.'

'You go home now and stay in. Don't go out again, you hear? We're going down to Fingers for a meal.'

'Will you come and tell me a story?' Steve piped up appealingly.

'Of course, of course,' Grant replied.

'Good,' the eight-year-old told him positively.

'Okay, boys. The key's in the usual place.'

'Tarar.'

Grant and Carly resumed their walk down the hill, past the Philharmonic Hall and the Philly, and down towards Fingers.

'God, Neville is *Tom*, isn't he?' said Grant. 'How's he taken it?'

'He thinks he's got two dads. Doesn't see anything odd in it. I've just bought him his first guitar.'

'Is he writing songs yet?'

'He will, he will.'

'Steve's a nice little chap. Quiet, though.'

'He'll end up with the money, then.'

'Not bad for a Sunday night,' Carly said, looking at the customers in Fingers. The main body of the restaurant was on two floors of an old house with the kitchen in the basement. 'Most people too frightened to step out, I expect.'

It was a light and airy place, in yellow and white. The tables and chairs were all of wicker. Large fans revolved slowly overhead.

The head waiter, an Italian with a Scouse accent, briskly took their orders and Carly told him to fetch a bottle of champagne.

'On the house,' she said.

Grant didn't argue. 'God, I'm so pleased for you. I know it's mad to be here tonight, like dancing in the Blitz, but this is so *right*.'

'As soon as I realized Tom wasn't coming back, after the business over Johnny, I just said, "Sod it". I was fed up with the men in my life being rich and successful and wanting to live the American dream in southern California.'

'It may be the American nightmare in Tom's case,' Grant added. 'He's got money, he's had another hit, but he's haunted by what happened to Johnny. And now Virna's after him.'

Carly looked down at her plate. 'That bloody woman.'

'She seems to collect 'em, doesn't she? But if she and Tom ever got spliced, she'd go off him, and go straight back to her old ways. She's just had her nose done, you know. Not that you'd notice. She probably paid through it and all.'

'I don't want to know, Grant. It's nothing to do with me. Tom had his chance. I always loved him, still do, I s'pose. But there was nothing I could do to change him.'

'You haven't got a . . . companion?'

'No, I haven't, just now, and I don't bloody well want

one, frankly. I've had enough of men. For the moment, anyway. I'm not without my fans, but I'm enjoying being *me*, not someone's appendage, and I intend to keep it that way. I've got other plans, you know. This is only the start. I might even open a shoe shop, so there.' Then, abruptly, Carly asked, 'You've left Suzie?'

'I've left Suzie, Suzie's left me. I made a mistake, we made a mistake. It was like they say, sometimes when you marry someone, they change. Sometimes a relationship that's fine outside marriage evaporates as soon as you tie the knot. It was a mistake. Mistakes? You name one, I've made it.'

'What's she doing?'

'I've no idea. She'll try to get going again in the business.'

'Under your management?'

'Oh, yes, but George'll handle her. He's come in off the road, now the Wreckers have split. He's a desk man now. Shaved his beard off, given up drugs. Dear old George.'

'So, you're all on your own-io?'

'Yes. Back to where it all began.'

The chicken in tarragon sauce arrived for Grant, the salmon with fennel for Carly. She topped up his glass.

He raised it and said, 'I've never seen you look so happy, Carly. Even if the world's coming to an end just round the corner, even if this is the worst weekend in the entire history of this goddamn city, I know *you'll* survive. I'm ever so glad.'

'You're a soppy date, Grant, but thanks, love, and cheers!'

'And the food's marvellous.'

They tucked in.

Carly hoped Grant wasn't going to say anything else embarrassing. Was he going to come up with a proposal?

He'd certainly thought of doing so. Everything had fallen out so that he could. But in the end he had to acknowledge that LA was still a very long way from Liverpool. It had always been a very long way from Liverpool. And there was no giving up LA.

It just wasn't going to be possible for them to forge a new way of life together, even if Carly agreed to it.

'I was going to say something, but I've forgotten,' said Grant.

'Probably as well.' Carly winked at him with one of those big, deep eyes of hers.

'Oh, *I* know' – he was acting now – 'when are you going to open a Fingers in LA?'

'For God's sake, Grant, what'd I want to do that for?'

'You won't rule out a return visit?'

'No. I suppose I'll feel up to it one day.'

An ambulance or a police car screeched past outside. There was the smell of burning, and it wasn't coming from the kitchen.

Carly saw she needed to head Grant off. 'You remember Old Trevor?'

'Of course I remember Old Trevor. What's happened to him? Gone the way of all flesh?'

'No. That's the amazing thing. He's still going strong. Even lent me a grand for here! I go and see him when I can. He's a nice old thing.'

'I ought to do the same. He had faith. I've never really told him what that meant.'

'Are you learning, then?'

'Learning what?'

'From everything you've been through? You've won every *thing*, but you've lost every *one*.'

'No, I haven't. I've still got . . . well, I've still got so much. I've got my clients. I've still got Quentin, even if he is getting married.'

'Quentin!?'

'Yes, I know. A woman, too. The age of miracles isn't yet past, so you see I'm not finished yet.'

'But you've learnt?'

565

'I may not have learnt, but I'm willing to admit any mistakes you want to tell me I've made. How about that?'

'Good.' Carly laughed. She was being so in charge, Grant wanted to hit her.

'Well, what I wanted to say was,' he started hesitantly once more, 'I'll know where to find you . . . when I come back to Liverpool . . . in the future, that is . . .'

'Yes, you will,' said Carly, her mouth full of food. 'That's right.' She smiled one of her smiles again. Confident, herself.

'Oh, fookin' 'ell,' exclaimed Grant, putting on the accent. 'What a fookin' bloody lot we've been through, eh? If only we could go back to the beginning and start again! Back to '63, when everything was possible.'

Carly took a sip of her champagne, swallowed, and licked her lips.

'All right,' she said exuberantly, 'you're on! When do we start?'

More Thrilling Fiction from Headline:

STEVEN FINK

**TO THE BROTHERHOOD
IT IS A COMMAND TO
BE INSTANTLY OBEYED –
NO MATTER
WHAT THE COST...**

THE BROTHERHOOD
OF THE CRAFT

A worldwide organisation of immense power
which commands total loyalty and complete
obedience from its members.

LEE SINCLAIR

A member of the Brotherhood, hostage in
the US Embassy in Tehran, has been seen to
throw *the hailing sign* – a secret call for help to
which the Brotherhood is bound to respond.

ALEXANDER MYCROFT

His reputation in rescuing POWs from the
Vietcong death camps is legendary. But it has
left him with a legacy of waking nightmare and
with an enemy as deadly as any he found in the
jungles of the Far East. Now the Brotherhood,
to whom he has pledged his life, want him to
rescue Sinclair. As Mycroft's enemy and the
Muslim fundamentalists form an unholy
alliance, one man attempts to do what a whole
nation cannot . . .

FICTION/THRILLER   0 7472 3175 3   £3.50

PETER WATSON

CRUSADE

**'The most compelling thriller
of its kind to come my way since
THE DAY OF THE JACKAL'**
Harold Harris*

Behind the scenes at the Vatican, the Pope offers
David Colwyn, chief executive of the international
auctioneering house of Hamilton's, a spectacular
deal. In an audacious and provocative scheme to raise
money for a crusade against poverty and injustice,
the Pope wants David to organise a series of worldwide
auctions to sell the fabled treasures of the Vatican:
Michelangelo's sculpture, Leonardo da Vinci's
painting, Giotto's altarpiece – all will go.

Despite protests, the Pope's plan proceeds and the
world watches as David, in the glare of publicity,
raises millions of pounds. But now powerful forces
range in fierce and treacherous opposition – and the
Pope's plans go disastrously wrong, perverted by
revolutionaries and international criminals. Soon a
furious battle of power politics rages, a battle that can
end only in a bloody and shocking climax...

"Crusade's real edge is that it could be next week's news."
Daily Mail

"Peter Watson's imaginative near-future thriller stands
out... classy entertainment."
The Evening Standard

"Non-stop action, an incredible vortex of
fights and frauds."
The Guardian

* original publisher of Frederick Forsyth

FICTION/THRILLER   0 7472 3143 5   £3.99

Headline books are available at your bookshop or newsagent, or can be ordered from the following address:

Headline Book Publishing PLC
Cash Sales Department
PO Box 11
Falmouth
Cornwall
TR10 9EN
England

UK customers please send cheque or postal order (no currency), allowing 60p for postage and packing for the first book, plus 25p for the second book and 15p for each additional book ordered up to a maximum charge of £1.90 in UK.

BFPO customers please allow 60p for postage and packing for the first book, plus 25p for the second book and 15p per copy for the next seven books, thereafter 9p per book.

Overseas and Eire customers please allow £1.25 for postage and packing for the first book, plus 75p for the second book and 28p for each subsequent book.